MW01001720

The Unwanted

ALSO BY BORIS FISHMAN

Savage Feast

Don't Let My Baby Do Rodeo

A Replacement Life

The Unwanted

A Novel

BORIS FISHMAN

HARPER
An Imprint of HarperCollins*Publishers*

This is a work of fiction. Names, characters, places, and incidents are products of the author's imagination or are used fictitiously and are not to be construed as real. Any resemblance to actual events, locales, organizations, or persons, living or dead, is entirely coincidental.

HarperCollins books may be purchased for educational, business, or sales promotional use. For information, please email the Special Markets Department at SPsales@harpercollins.com.

FIRST EDITION

Art by Frenky362/Shutterstock, Inc.

Library of Congress Cataloging-in-Publication Data
Names: Fishman, Boris, author.
Title: The unwanted: a novel / Boris Fishman.
Identifiers: LCCN 2024035133 (print) | LCCN 2024035134 (ebook) | ISBN 9780063387447 (hardcover) | ISBN 9780063387454 (ebook)
Subjects: LCGFT: Novels.
Classification: LCC PS3606.I824 U59 2025 (print) | LCC PS3606.I824 (ebook) | DDC 813/.6—dc23/eng/20240802
LC record available at https://lccn.loc.gov/2024035133
LC ebook record available at https://lccn.loc.gov/2024035134

25 26 27 28 29 LBC 5 4 3 2 1

For Agnes and Montgomery

May you know all this only from stories.

I

Escape

On the day Dina heard the news, she had returned from school to find her father, George, playing the truant once again. He was at the kitchen table, in slippers, instead of at the university where he belonged. It had been happening all week. But Dina's family was not on holiday. No one explained anything to Dina, who stood at the kitchen threshold, apparently invisible.

George was staring at the old refrigerator and soothing his moustache with a knuckle. The moustache, which hung out past George's nose, was nearly its own person. "George's moustache comes into the room, and then we wait for George to come, too," the neighbor Mr. Hak had said once to Dina's mother, Susanna, while Dina milled at her side. Susanna tried to satisfy Hak with a smile, but Dina could tell her mother was doing it only because they were minority-sect and Hak was dominant-sect, and Susanna had told Dina that they should try to make dominant-sect people extra happy for a little while.

Susanna sat next to her truant husband in the kitchen. She was staring out the window, her palms flat on the kitchen table, as if she feared letting go. Motorbikes whined outside. Dina dropped her satchel to the floor, intending to make noise. No one noticed.

"Eat shit . . ." Dina said. "Who died?"

Susanna looked over. "Died . . ." she repeated, briefly persuaded. "Also, you say 'eat shit,' do you?"

"No one died?" Dina said, disappointed. Dina did not want anyone to die, especially now, when people died all the time. But she liked emergencies.

"No one died," Susanna said, looking at George as if to confirm. Now, George was looking at the window. Usually, this kind of mental absence meant that he was elaborating a lesson for class or his retort to a colleague with whom delicacy was required because of the sect issue. As of three days before—as of the morning George did not switch out his slippers—George was done with such enviably minor problems. But as the proverb said, the man about to be hanged still washes his face.

Susanna felt a familiar irritation—again it would be her duty to explain difficult things to their daughter. It was Susanna who had to explain why people were fighting, why Dina's school was moving to an underground shelter, why they wouldn't be going to the seaside for a little while. Until when, Dina wanted to know. A little while, Susanna said, which was a compromise between "nothing will ever be the same" and "everything is fine." This "a little while" became Dina's measure of time: She wanted to know if she could play in the yard "a little while" (no); whether her friend Harry would return to school in "a little while" (of course, though this was a lie, because Harry was dead), whether dinner would be ready in "a little while" (Susanna was relieved to offer an unhesitant yes, to have something whose duration she could control).

"We have some little news for you, my heart," Susanna now said to Dina.

So maybe it was an emergency, after all. Dina slid onto her stool and rested her hands in the folded position required at school, which meant she was listening closely—she wanted everything to be in order as she received the news. She wasn't even shifting around in her uniform, which by virtue of Susanna's constant starching was a great enemy.

"I'm ready," she announced.

Susanna extended her hands. Dina placed her palms inside her mother's.

"Who combed out your hair so nice for you?" Susanna said.

"There is a new teacher," Dina said. "She's young. She's nice. She says my hair is like a wood."

"What's her name?" Susanna said.

"I don't remember."

"Your hair is like a wood / like the strings of Father's oud," George said, coming alive. "Is she minority or dominant?"

"Who?" Dina said.

"The new teacher."

"I don't know."

George made a noise of bewilderment—how could you fail to know such a thing about a person? As a piece of information, you could hardly avoid it. His daughter lived in the clouds.

Susanna rose, letting go of Dina. But she had stood for no reason. She sat back down. She needed a new place to put her hands. She rose again, stood behind Dina, raked Dina's long curtain of hair. Susanna had admonished herself not to take advantage of the tranquilizing qualities of this activity—Dina was not a toy. But Susanna could not resist now.

"What I am about to say to you, no one is to know," Susanna said, bending close to Dina's ear. Susanna's palms ran with sweat. "Do you understand? If Grandma calls, you must be just as bored and sullen as always. Okay? No one is to know. Promise."

"Promise, okay," Dina said.

"We will be leaving, my heart," Susanna said.

Dina continued to await information, but none came. "The apartment?" she said with new disappointment. A new apartment could be exciting, but she had wanted something riskier. A trip to the seaside. A move to the seaside.

"No," Susanna said, starting a braid.

"Are we moving to the seaside?" There was no way that's what it would be, now that Dina had said it, but she couldn't help herself.

Susanna stared at George, but he remained silent. "Farther," Susanna said. "But there will be sea, yes." The braid finished, Susanna made herself let go of the hair and returned to her seat so she could look at Dina. She folded the hands in her lap, then unfolded.

"Far away like what," Dina said with suspicion.

"Like another country," Susanna said. "But we can't speak about it, okay? It's for us, here, only."

Another *country* . . . It was more of an emergency than Dina had wanted. She felt the dropping thing in her chest—some shelf that usually kept her together now falling away, and leaving a weightless dread in its place. She liked to be organized, ready for the excitement when it arrived. The one bad thing about surprises was that you couldn't control them.

"Okay . . ." Dina said experimentally. She awaited new information, but again, her parents had drifted off onto planes of distraction that seemed not to include their daughter. "I would like to be excused," Dina said resentfully, reminding them of her existence. No one replied.

Dina sprang from her seat. But it was only when Susanna smelled the dusty unpainted cement of the stairwell that she realized her daughter had left the apartment. To confirm, the heavy upholstered door of the apartment lumbered back into place. Through the thin walls, Dina's feet pounded the stairs. Susanna looked wearily at George and went after her daughter. She found Dina in the yard, in Madame N.'s semi-covered garden, eating a tomato while the old woman worked the knobs of her ancient knuckles through the stakes.

"Dina-bird," Susanna said, watching Madame's back. Madame had allowed Dina to pluck a tomato, which meant she was feeling favorably disposed. And Madame's ears, having strained to catch reportable talk for nearly a century, were no longer the fine-tuned weapons they once were. But the old woman had ears everywhere on her body. And a mouth that knew whom to whisper to: Madame N. was someone who could get polycarbonate during a war—enough only for two sides of her garden, but still. Susanna had to speak carefully. Her heart was turning like a motor. She tried to think of the washing, of George's socks.

Susanna glanced down the poplar-lined path that went out to Engineers Street. In recent days, their building had acquired a yard sweeper in the faint-blue overalls of the service, though he also wore a jacket of imitation leather with pleated wrists, a combination that made him seem demented. Though a sorghum-bristle broom leaned against the dirty yellow brick of the building, Susanna had never seen him use it. He was there now, eating plums from a purse.

Susanna made herself turn back to her daughter. "Are you going to run away every time you are asked to eat your father's spicy fish?" she said.

Madame N. tsked her mouth. Susanna had succeeded in diverting her attention from Dina's distress to Dina's misfortune in apparently having a mother so incompetent at a woman's business that Dina's father had to put in time at the stove.

But now Susanna would have to make the dish, because it had a powerful scent and the old woman would detect a suspicious absence of fumes in the stairwell. And Susanna would have to make it poorly, or it would not pass for a husband's endeavor. But they didn't have fish, and the fishmonger charged more, more than double, for porgy now, because the porgy had to circumvent the rebel areas, and the rebels liked porgy, too, so there was just less of it. Just now, Susanna would have preferred fish to rebels, even if the rebels said they were fighting for people like her. In peacetime, minority-sect people got by, tenuous but stable. Whereas now, anyone fleeing must be fleeing a sin—officially, the country was paradise for both sects. In four years, the government had not acknowledged the civil war, only "periodic disturbances."

If you stayed, you might be killed for staying, like Harry's family. If you left, you might be killed for leaving. If you looked at the sky, you were looking for a government plane. If you picked your nose, you were referencing the rebel commander who had sprayed his snot over the pavement in front of a television camera when he was asked about the Leader; you couldn't touch your nose at all. When they were out, Susanna had to stare at her daughter's fingers because Dina had an unfortunate habit of picking her nose in public.

When George had come home the previous Friday to say that the Registrar's secretary had taken him aside to whisper in his hairy ear that the safety of his family was no longer certain, Susanna was ashamed to feel not dread but stimulation. They had spent four years waiting for ordnance to fall. Now they could do something. The price for stimulation was they had to leave the country. And little charades like burned spicy fish.

Over Madame N.'s stooped back, Dina looked at her mother. Susanna made a complicated movement with her eyes to indicate that *this was a great opportunity to practice the discretion discussed upstairs*. A mission of female solidarity always had the desired effect on her daughter. Susanna resolved Dina's foul moods by placing Dina on the balcony with a shoebox of her creams and lotions and asking her daughter to organize all this "glue," as Dina referred to it.

"I only wanted to help with the fish, and you won't let me!" Dina said, playing the game.

"I was wrong, my heart," Susanna said. "Let's go upstairs."

Madame tsked again—Susanna was also such a pitiful parent that she submitted to her daughter's demands. But Susanna was wearily proud to have misled the great tattle of the building. She took Dina's hand and they walked upstairs. Dina skipped over the stairs, the despotism of her parents forgotten. Her daughter had the memory of a frog.

"So this is why you have been acting so strangely," Dina said when they reached their landing. They were breathing loudly—the elevator had not worked in months. Susanna put a finger to her mouth, nodding at the apartment across theirs. Three of the neighbor woman's four sons were dead from the war (the live one was a drug addict), and her husband had left to earn money in Europe, so she had three war-mother incomes and one from remittance (which dwarfed the three others together), but nothing to do other than sit at the eyehole of her apartment.

Dina had meant that for the past week, Susanna and George were forever carrying things from one room to another. And in the evenings, instead of her father disappearing to the sitting room, where he was eternally organizing his letters and poems, his poems and letters; instead of her mother reading on the living room divan, her feet tucked under her bum; the two of them conferred endlessly in her father's domain.

When they got inside, Susanna swallowed three tablets of valerian root. The fishmonger was closing in an hour, and the way there crossed an unsafe intersection. How often they had smacked their lips in longing for sea bream, especially gilthead, and the seaside; both had been lost to them for years now. So let the porgy be an overpriced farewell to the shop they had begun patronizing before Dina was born, when George had read that fish possessed proteins required by pregnant ladies. Susanna barricaded Dina in the kitchen with an assignment to dole out the required spices, and left without telling George. She made it safely and bit her lip as she watched the porgy carbonize in the pan. They slogged through ruined spicy fish, George exclaiming with disbelief at the shame of such a rare treat ruined. Susanna thought about explaining, but it would only stir up challenges and questions. Nerves, Susanna said. George shook his head.

Meanwhile, Dina revived. Once she thought about it, she could hardly say what she was leaving behind other than school, and what would she miss there? The bitter coffee on Teacher Mariam's breath? Kar, with the sputtering acne? Robert was nice—once in a while, he and Dina passed notes in which he explained that a meteor was God coughing. But he was only one boy.

And what about the city? There was nowhere to swim, except the neighborhood pool, but people peed in it. Otherwise, there were old buildings. The school had organized a trip to the historic section when it was safe. Dina saw endless blocks of faded white stone. A bird with a forked tail alighted and sprang off at once because the stone had crumbled under its feet. Teacher Yasmine had droned on about how important it all was.

Dina was so caught up in these thoughts that only as she was nodding off in bed, her finger wedged in a page of *Uncle Neem's Fairy Tales*, did she realize that she hadn't asked why. Why were they leaving *now*, when so many had already left. And where were they going? Only *when*: two days. She felt angry that she was expected to organize her life in two days. But before she could focus on the dark pleasure of having been wronged, she slipped away into sleep.

* * *

In the morning, Dina shuffled in her slippers across the linoleum, tried the bathroom taps—by this hour, they were long dry, but she enjoyed the inspection—and only then remembered it was not an ordinary day. No, the family had a very special secret. She called to her mother, and Susanna came with a pitcher of water from the pot she collected early in the morning. As an older person, Dina would often recall this simple daughterly power: She called, and her mother appeared. Dina would recall their faces in the mirror together, one oval inside another, the painted lashes shooting out of her mother's dark-brown eyes, her rouged sand-colored skin, the painted lips bobbing in the pink sand like a buoy. Her mother covered her face in the glue first thing every morning, and Dina asked with aggravating frequency how much time remained until she was allowed the same.

Susanna worked Dina's hair to make a braid and studied her daughter's face in the mirror. In a charity package from Germany, they had received a book about a female scientist who took evening walks through tall grass with her children. Susanna liked to imagine the hair falling through her fingers as the tall grass that swished around Maria Margaretha's skirts.

Dina understood that her mother was inspecting her face for signs of distress regarding yesterday's news, so through the toothpaste in her mouth, she yelled out a song from the radio: *I said stop, but you returned. You are the killer of this love. Surrender, criminal. You're both the knife and the wound.*

Susanna was both relieved and irritated that her daughter seemed to feel none of her unease. "You're missing about four verses," she said. "Keep your voice down, your father is sorting his papers."

Susanna looked toward the frosted glass oval of the sitting room door, behind which a gray shape shuttled in the weak light of morning. George also seemed suspiciously undisturbed. He had gone to the bank to withdraw the necessary sum, organized their passage with the raft people, and vanished to the sitting room, where five steel cabinets plumped in a corner like unwanted guests. And George had managed to sleep, blowing herbal air out of his mouth. (He chewed mint leaves before bed.) He had even attempted intimacy once.

Susanna was the one who couldn't close her eyes—one night, she took six tablets of valerian root. She was bracing for the arrival of the slow train that carried news from George's mind to his heart. He was the last minority-sect instructor at the university. He would never become full professor, but after twenty years, he had achieved everything minus. He taught the poetry of the dominant sect. Under their breath, minority-sect people said: "Good little dog. Look how fast he runs to the bowl." But the university administration, all dominant-sect, did not have this problem. His course was always oversubscribed, which George helped by semi-annual deliveries of Johnnie Walker Black to the concrete pillbox that housed Admissions and Registrar. Even during the spasms of violence to which their nation periodically submitted, like a haircut, George and his family were safe. For some reason, that reprieve had ended the previous Friday.

"Come on, let's brush," Susanna said to her daughter.

Dina stuck out her nose.

"Don't make a Jewish nose at me," Susanna said.

"Can I take *Uncle Neem* with me?" Dina said.

"Yes, of course," Susanna said, and poured more water into Dina's hands. Instead of moving her hands across her face, Dina moved her face across her hands.

"Whose uncle is Neem?" Dina said.

"What?"

"It's *Uncle Neem's Fairy Tales.*" Dina tried to make George's noise of exasperation.

"It's just the name of a book, love. There were a lot of Neems in your grandparents' generation. Uncles like to tell stories. That's all. Stay in one place."

"What will we eat?" Dina said.

"I will give you the semolina, but only if you brush your teeth for one minute, nonstop."

“No, I mean, what will we eat when we—you know.” Dina looked with great meaning at the wall, and all the people she was warned were listening on the other side of it.

“At home, you can say it out loud,” Susanna said. “We’ll buy food, just like here.”

To be safe, Dina saved a part of breakfast, anyway. She really wanted the semolina, but semolina was impractical if you were saving rations for a journey, so she requested bread with cheese instead, no vegetables. Vegetables could go soggy. You had to think ahead.

* * *

The problem of what to place in the suitcase was reduced by how much it was necessary to give up to get the things they might need. Perhaps they would end up in a place where the cold was not gentle, so a sapphire pendant George had given Susanna for their fifth anniversary turned into a snowsuit for Dina and a modestly worn cable-knit sweater for George. Susanna had to limit her barter to items that wouldn’t draw notice when she stepped outside, so jewelry was best, but she was down to her wedding ring.

Earlier in the week, in the name of consolidating their secrecy—but also to steal a glance at George’s papers after the uncomfortable discovery she had made earlier in the week—Susanna had tried to use the sitting room as her staging area also. George regarded her discreet, suitcase-shaped pile with resentment. When Susanna walked in with a feather-stuffed jacket for Dina, he asked if she couldn’t have found something with less volume, though he did not dare question items for their daughter directly. When Susanna walked in with her old engineering textbook, however, he pointed accusingly at all the poetry books that would remain behind on his bookshelf. When he was in the toilet, she removed the engineering textbook, though it was likely to be of more use than one of George’s poetry books—engineers, unlike poets, existed in a pre-Babel of silent harmony—and retransferred the packing pile back to their bedroom.

George appeared there periodically, waving a translucent sheet at Susanna: Listen to a letter his father had written his mother after he had seen snow for the first time during his judicial training in the USSR. Listen to a letter a student had written thanking him despite his poor grade. ("Sir, you have wakened me.") Listen to a letter George had written against the establishment of a minority-sect advocacy group at the university—he did not see the value of special dispensations, of setting the minority-sect people apart in this way. Or this one George had written to the cereal company pointing out a spelling error on the new boxes. But as the days leaked away and the piles in the sitting room only grew, he emerged less and less.

Susanna had encountered the correspondence when she had encountered George, thirteen years before, when she had been assigned to his poetry class, three times out of four the assigned arts elective for aspiring engineers such as Susanna. The Registrar sent George a letter for every enrolled student, as Susanna learned when she entered George's crowded apartment in the high-rises by the military hospital, for the first place George showed her was not the parlor, nor the kitchen, nor, God forbid, the bedroom, but the old sitting room with its cabinets of letters and poems. Some men pulled out their wallets, their record collections, their penises for God's sake, but in the sitting room, his moustache jumping in excitement, George pulled out the letter on which the Registrar had written:

Esteemed Instructor—

It is my honor to inform you that I have enrolled in Introduction to Poetry Susanna T______. She is the daughter of Paul T______ of Arid (12km from Dostat). The student is minority-sect. She is a first-year graduate student in engineering with average grades and no prior academic experience in the arts. Her political opinions are unknown. I wish you a productive exchange with this student.

Respectfully,
Registrar

Susanna understood that George was palming the letter as proxy for another kind of caress. But why? She was a girl with a long face and sprayed hair that lost its shape by lunchtime. Around her were women students whose hair never lost their haloes (because they slept in hairnets) and who wore business-suit jackets even in June, discreetly retouching the powder on their foreheads. And why did she want him, so round and ready for the lecture podium? Romantically, she ignored the practical answer that they were minority-sect, and that halved the options.

And for what was he saving all these papers? A biographer poring over his poems? A son eager to solve the mystery of his father? But Susanna had listened to her father tear down her mother for sloppiness because he would not accept that she was psychotic, so Susanna wished to accept. With time, she understood that the metastasizing correspondence, instead of finally being organized by George one of these days, thereby allowing the sitting room to reclaim its supposed purpose, would instead serve as the updated purpose. Usually, instead of intimacy, that is where George went after dinner. And by the time he returned to the bedroom, quite often aroused by his tasks of organization, she was snoring lightly, the bedside lamp still burning.

But George could tend the Annals of George if he remained as interesting to speak with as he had in their walks after class and then on the goose down mattress in his apartment, which George's elders had hauled from the north, where they had geese. He had flattered her, an engineering student who knew only a little more about engineering than anything else, with questions. He had wanted to know how bridges could span such amounts of water. A small one over a muddy yellow river had transformed George's ancestral village, making it easier to conduct trade, communications, and ethnic cleansing of his elders by people on the other side of the bridge. In a way, the bridge was why George's ancestors had fled and he now lived where he lived. Without the bridge, he and Susanna couldn't have met. What kept the bridge from falling into the water? (As George's elders surely wished it had.) She tried to explain about girders, cutwaters, piles—she herself was only beginning to piece it together.

"You have good teeth, so I know you visit the dentist," she said, finally. "He will brace a part of the mouth, so one part stays fixed while he works on another. Like that."

Several days later, as they neared the university gate, past which they couldn't keep walking with defensible reason, George gave her a sheet of paper. At the top, underlined, it said: "Metal Snake." She read:

Before knowledge, we walked on water like Him.
He is magnificent. He has forgiven,
And given
Us metal to do what our legs no longer could.
This new snake is good, but
Knowledge means it always makes us think of the old.

When she looked up, she said: "Bridges are made from concrete. And stone." And was relieved when he laughed.

Though half his face was concealed by the moustache, he was a gracious, attentive, and forgiving lover. You would not assume it from his appearance, but once the vest and loafers came off, here was a man of amiable girth, agreeably spread, so unlike the bony graduate students who were her usual fate. Initially, George struggled to accept that intercourse could not give her orgasm. But he, too, wished to accept. And he insisted, most times, that she go first, though there were also times when he couldn't help his yearning. She liked both of those things.

And as she miscarried year after year, before their Dina finally appeared as if made from what remained of the fog of their hopes (and fish proteins), he did not make the turn that so many men would have made, even as he heard the neighbors, whose pity at her barrenness gradually turned into suspicion of an evil mark on the family. After two years, George's parents also gave up, and Susanna began excusing herself from the family table so they could urge George to divorce. A good woman, but so good he was ready for the family name to come to an end? George listened until he could listen no more. Even Dina's arrival had not really allayed the unease, the neighborhood mothers rushing to pull their children away when they got too close to the child who had taken too long to show up. No one who required this much persuasion could count on a clean destiny.

When the fighting started, Susanna's erstwhile infertility became one with the new scarcity all around, and the doubt that surrounded the family increased as people remembered that these people were minority-sect, what was one to expect. Now, even Johnnie Walker Black wouldn't suffice, though the Registrar took the bottle, baring the brown-yellow teeth that disfigured his square, handsome face, and even bowed. The greatest insult, as George told Susanna the story in a quietly furious tone, was that the Registrar left his secretary to inform George that he was being released from his duties at the university so he could "look after his family." This was the soft language people like that used to indicate to favored minority-sect people that someone had decided they were in the way. It seemed to Susanna that the greater insult was the threat to their lives, but she didn't speak up.

* * *

In class, as Teacher Mariam did the bomb-shelter protocol, Dina was ready to burst. She stared at the back of Robert's neck, but he was looking dutifully at the blackboard, as if they did not get the protocol every day, as if they would actually have time to get down there before the bomb arrived. Robert was such a nerd sometimes. But Dina's choices were limited—Manut had gone away, and Harry, and Aden. She knew Harry did not go away. She had heard Susanna and George whispering about it in the kitchen. But Dina did not like to think about all that. In the newspapers George brought home, she only looked at the pictures, and there were never pictures of Harry, which meant he was probably fine, his family just had to go away for some reason.

Dina tore a square of paper from her notebook and pulled Robert's sleeve. He lowered a cupped hand.

He bent his head over the note for some time. She savored her command over his attention. Finally, he answered. His note said, "My mother says that the only good news is when there is no news, therefore this news is bad news is my guess."

"Forever?" he said later, after she told him, as he ate his everyday snack of fried dough with honey and they dangled their legs off what had used to be the pommel horse for what had used to be the gymnastics class. The pommels were between them.

"Not forever," she said, whipping her braid back and forth. "A little while. But everything will be different."

He contemplated this. "Will you miss it here?" he said.

"No," she said, trying it out. "I mean yes," she caught herself. "I will miss the sea."

"But you don't remember the sea."

"How do you know?" she said.

"You told me. You went to the sea once with your parents. But you don't remember it."

"Well, that is why I will miss it."

He thought about this, and bit off another piece of dough. His mother had made it too crusty, and a spray of crumbs settled on his shirt. Dina couldn't stand the mess and reached over to clear it. He submitted nervously.

"Look," she said. "Do you want to kiss?"

A terrified expression came over Robert's face. It began to fill with color. He had freckles on only one side, and they vanished under the splotches, as if it were blotting paper. He managed to say: "Kissing is for ladies and gentlemen only." He added, gaining confidence: "They must be married, also." And concluded, for authority: "My father says."

"You're not being fun about this," Dina said, and slipped off the bar.

"Will you miss me?" he said, quietly enough to deny he had said it.

"Missing is for ladies and gentlemen only," Dina said nastily. She eased up: "You can't tell anyone, okay? Can't tell your father."

"My father has a new job," he said.

"Who has a new job now?" Dina said. "Maybe he says he has a new job, but he goes to an ice cream shop, and eats ice cream all day. That would be an important job."

Robert hesitated. "He is helping to rebuild the city."

"Well, that's stupid," she said. "Because the city will keep falling down."

"It's not stupid!" Robert said. "It's an important government job. Because of him, there will be buildings again! He is very powerful!" He slipped off the bar and ran off, leaving a trail of crumbs—here was someone you did not want on your team for hide-and-find. Dina felt the dropping thing in her chest, this time with flavors: guilt, fright. She had made a mistake. A person with a government job should definitely not know they were leaving. She ran after Robert, but he had already rejoined the file of children returning to class. In the next period, she pulled his sleeve again, but he didn't respond. She asked for the bathroom, and when she was passing his desk, threw a square on it that said, "Of course, I will miss you!" As if he understood that Dina didn't mean it, he didn't reply.

Later, Dina woke in the night, convinced that Robert had told one of the teachers. She was sweaty and listless at breakfast, and forgot to pocket a part of it, which added to her self-criticism later. Susanna checked Dina's forehead, and George dug out the ancient thermometer. Its mercury was usually stuck at 39, as if everyone always had the same fever. But sometimes it responded. However, there seemed to be no fever, and there was a ready explanation for Dina's nervousness, and it was best to keep things regular, so Dina was sent to school.

On the way to school, Dina realized there was an easy solution—she would tell Robert their plans had changed. They weren't leaving. When she reached school, the punishment she expected from Teacher Mona at the door didn't materialize. She thought maybe the teachers would wait to punish her until they had her out of sight of other children, but there was none of that either, only the slight skepticism with which they habitually regarded her. (It was really unfair, for Dina's grades were perfect, so what else did they want?)

However, Robert had nothing to say to her at snack, though he didn't move his tray to a different table, so they sat in silence until the Diab sisters showed up and demanded that Dina sing "Solitude for a Lifetime" with them, which Robert used for an excuse to slip away. In fifth period, he passed her a note. It said only: "When do you leave?" Relieved, Dina wrote, "Tomorrow night. My mom says. I don't know. There are important arrangements." Then she realized she had just done the opposite of what she'd resolved that morning. She hated herself. She wrote another note: "By the way, this is our secret, okay?" But Robert didn't write back, and Dina began to feel even worse. Everything suddenly felt hopeless and wrong, and she resented Robert for spoiling her excitement.

In seventh period, Robert turned around and deposited a note on Dina's desk: "When school ends, meet me on the street end of the gym."

She wrote: "I can't, my mother will be waiting for me."

But then her curiosity began to bother her. She passed another note: "Why?"

"Why what?"

"For God's sake, why do you want me to meet you?"

"I want to show you something."

"At the gym?"

"No, in our apartment."

"What is it?"

"A surprise."

She struggled. "How far do you live?"

"Ten minutes to walk if we don't stop for candy. Sometimes I stop."

"What is your favorite candy?"

"I'm not sure."

"How can you not be sure?"

"I don't buy it. I only look at it."

She felt foolish.

"What do you have for last period?" she wrote.

"Library."

"Okay—you leave ten minutes early. She won't notice, she's blind, anyway. I will meet you. We'll go very quickly, okay?"

* * *

After eavesdropping out of view for a moment, Susanna felt guilt and knocked on the glass of the sitting room. The form inside stilled.

"I am heading out," she called softly.

"With—" the muffled speech came.

"The cups," she said.

"The cups? That was our—"

"Wedding gift," she finished. "Your parents should have given us thimbles instead of silver chalices, they would have fit more easily." She imagined George's rueful shaking head on the other side of the door.

"Those cups—" he called through the glass.

"Came on the wagon from the north."

"The first drink I took—"

"Your father took, your grandfather took . . ."

She must have expressed enough solidarity because he said nothing further.

"What about some help in there?" she said through the door. "A woman's hand makes the task go faster."

"I'll manage," he said. "I'll manage."

She remained in place, looking at the apartment around her. Even Susanna's stealthy replacement of George's doilies with runners and of cushions with upholstery, and the experimental dove-gray she had given to several walls unclaimed by wallpaper, was powerless against what had preceded her and was, at first, too expensive to replace, and then too scarce: the Bulgarian pink-leather sectional with cherrywood armrests; the mirrored glass case with lacquered drawers, painted with black swirls on an emerald background, where George displayed the gifts he received at university; that wallpaper, in a pattern of subtle gold crosses; the gilt oval frame in which Susanna and George gazed at each other on their wedding day; the hanging Persian carpet; the cracked wall tile in the bathroom. She slept in George's bed, and washed in the same bathroom, and grew tarragon on the balcony once, before poison appeared in the air, but her primary commute was between three places: Dina's bedroom; the living room divan where she read; and the kitchen, with its second-floor view of a narrow upright rectangle of sky.

Sometimes, in the early years, over spicy fish made the right way, or bread rings and zucchini with rice, dusk swallowing the dust of the city outside the balcony door, after much encouragement from Susanna George would shyly submit, disappear to the sitting room, return with cheeks aflame from nervousness, and recite a new poem.

Like seedlings, words want to be roots.
But first they have to give up their wings.
But first they have to use their wings
To fly from my tongue to your ear,
And down the cat's paw of your neck,
Away from the soft fine hair of those arms that I've held,
Into the breast,
Down through the chest,
Into the belly
That waits for God to confess.

But then, after four years without, God finally blessed Susanna's belly, and in the joyous tyranny of early parenthood, the orations fell away. Then the war. Susanna had only recently remembered the poems and felt embarrassed for having stopped asking. One day when George was at university, she went to the cabinets. Unsurprisingly, he had a neatly marked folder marked *Poems*, each one dated and concluded by George's florid signature. She picked one off the top, written only the previous week.

The peacock with its mantle
Struts toward the market.
It has learned to read,
But only reads in darkness.

His style had changed—the poem was more cryptic, and the emotion had vanished. It was unsettling, like seeing someone you love do something unknown in private. With shame, Susanna had wondered if her disinterest was the cause. However, despite the war, George had become no less effusive with her, so perhaps she was merely misunderstanding the ways in which a poet evolved. The new verse read like a child's story, so maybe what she was seeing was a man, forced to care for a family across difficult years, retreat to simpler moments in his private time. Perhaps he was writing poems for his daughter. The next day, while she was consumed by these thoughts, a decorative crystal egg she was polishing slipped out of her fingers. George came out of the sitting room. Seeing the splintered glass on the floor, he said, "It's just as well." She didn't understand what he meant. It wasn't until George's termination that his comment made sense. But he had made it a week before he was terminated.

Later in the day she had broken the crystal, she had asked if he would recite her some poetry. The failed pregnancies, Dina's belated arrival, the war—these had overtaken her attention, but this was no excuse, she said, though she was aware that only a guilty party justified itself with such effort. So she was prepared to be called out for this, but not what George said: He had stopped writing poetry shortly after they'd met.

That night, after she was certain he was asleep, she climbed out of bed and walked to the sitting room. There, she found the cabinets locked.

* * *

Robert was waiting for Dina, as she had instructed. They walked down Avenue of the Faithful, unsure what to say now that they had to do it without paper. At one point, she remarked that the heat would never let up, then shook her head at her banality. Ten minutes passed. Their journey was interrupted by the appearance of a street-cleaning truck, which blocked their path through two changes of the light. She asked how much longer.

"I'm not sure," he said. "Because I often stop at the candy shop."

"And your parents don't care when you come home?" she demanded.

He didn't answer, and she felt guilty again: his parents arrived home from work long after Robert. She imagined that he had to look after his siblings until the real parents arrived.

Five minutes later, they had crossed into a different neighborhood, a mixed district of low means. Here, there was washing on open window latches, and all the things that were sold in stores in Dina's neighborhood were here sold on the street. They passed the man who sold flatbreads from an old carpenter's workbench, then the man with the honey, then the one with watermelons in a wheelbarrow, the corded veins of his arms like electricity cables plugged into his armpits. The sweat was pouring down Dina's face. She stopped. The dropping thing was happening in her chest. "What surprise is it?" she demanded.

"It's on our balcony," he said.

She knew she should turn around. But by now, she didn't know how to get back.

"I want to turn around," she said.

"It's just around the corner over there," he said, pointing vaguely. He looked at the ground. His ears had little points, she noticed—he was outlined by the light of the sun. He had the spray of freckles on one cheek, but the other wasn't empty—there was a single freckle, just under the eye. And the eyes were blue—in the reduced light of the classroom, she had always thought they were gray. Framed by the sun, he appeared to be somebody else.

It was hard for her to think clearly in the heat. Her braid felt like a lead arm coming out of her head. She didn't have a watch but she knew too much time had gone by. What she had done now struck her in its full stupidity.

"You will walk me back, right?" she said.

"Of course."

"Okay, let's run."

They ran, and it really was around the corner, and soon they were in the elevator of Robert's building, which smelled of urine and boiled fava beans. All because she couldn't resist surprises! She told herself to press the Stop button, get out, run down the stairs, but she only watched the numbers climb on the panel that lit up with the floors, Robert in the corner, staring down at the stained needlecord of the carpet.

* * *

On the last day of their lives in their city, without telling her husband, Susanna packed for barter the bottles of perfume George had purchased for her every year on Dina's birthday until the war started. There were four bottles; one was nearly full. She buried George's silver cups, a Longchamp handbag, and the perfumes under glass bottles for the recycler and a knife case that said here was a housewife out for nothing more than her monthly visit to the sharpener.

Outside, the yard sweeper was hiding from the sun in the poplars, though he still wore his jacket, wrong by two sizes at least. He was chewing again—sunflower seeds today. He was short, but the beard was neatly groomed, and though the eyes were tired, an alertness there made her, and the contents of her bag, feel scanned. One of the eyes fluttered several times, then stilled, like a cinema screen trying to resolve. The tic gave the man's resting sneer a hint of youthful uncertainty. The broom stood in its place. Susanna looked away quickly and strode forward, the glass clanking at her side.

He called out to her. Her chest wobbled. She stood in place, her back to him. He did not call again, and she did not move. Finally, she turned around.

"Good day to you," she said. She tried to seem calm, then realized a housewife on errands would feel impatience, then realized the wife of a university professor would feel irritation at being addressed by a working-class man. By the time she had worked it all out, she had already twisted her face into a gesture of conciliation.

"The sharpener is sick today," the man said from the pocked shade of the poplar. He wedged a shell between his teeth.

"Thank you," she said. "You have saved me an errand."

"I will sharpen the knives for you."

"I couldn't ask it of your time."

"Give them here, please."

They faced off in the buzzing heat of the morning.

"You look like the crooner in that music video," she tried. "When he's walking in the tree grove, do you know that one?" He continued squinting at her through the light. "You haven't seen it," she said.

"Knives, please," he said.

"But what will I cook with today?"

"You didn't leave yourself even one?" he said. "Tsk, madame." He crunched two seeds at once. "I will finish before you return." He stepped out of the shade, and came so near that she took a step back. She smelled the salt from the sunflower seeds, trapped like silver dust in his beard. He lifted the case of knives from the bag in her hands. His eyes hovered over the glass, and underneath it, the goods that said here was a woman selling her possessions because her family was fleeing the country. But he didn't notice, or react.

"Mothers hold up the sky," he said, and returned to his place by the curb. He tapped it, as if to test the cut of his sandstone. "Go."

She went, clanking, thinking about how to feed Dina and George without knives. Also whether the knives were dull enough to seem believably in need of sharpening. She berated herself for submitting so readily. It was because of the secret of their departure. Because of the unwantedness with which she walked the streets of the city. She, George, Dina—they were an imposition. It was a lingering generosity that they were alive. The fear she felt when she stepped outside these days made her queasy.

She walked, trying to keep clear of the wrong streets but occasionally straying. If she were pregnant with Dina now, she would have to hope for a midwife. Sometimes, women delivered at checkpoints. There was one, the word had gone around, near what used to be the football stadium, where one of the soldiers had been a resident in obstetrics. So women in labor from certain neighborhoods went there. But then he was sent somewhere else. Or killed.

Every day, Susanna visited a different bank branch to withdraw what was left of their money. The largest, near the Italian furniture store, had been bombed along with the store, of which remained only a four-poster bed surrounded by rubble, its frilly perimeter perforated by shrapnel and soiled by debris. It stood there, uncleared, until the sun had turned what white spots remained the color of urine.

Many bank branches had shuttered, so each day she had to go farther. The tellers she approached if the ATMs were out of service surely wondered why this minority-sect woman was so far from her neighborhood, but so far none had caused a problem, and one even slipped her an envelope with twice the daily limit, though she did not meet Susanna's eyes as she did so.

Now, Susanna went up the Avenue of the Conquerors, down a side artery, and into an alley of glassblowers where a man took in goods for the things that people like her needed. Eventually, she managed to barter for three pillows that rolled up into nothing, three Mylar blankets, pain medicine, iodine tablets, a compact desalination kit, sunscreen, three pairs of warm socks, and two plastic ponchos (one of which she would cut up to fit herself and Dina). Life jackets they were supposed to receive on the raft. At a market, she bought enough nuts and fruit to cover it all and make it seem like she had bought only groceries. The recycling bottles, an alibi in any neighborhood, she decided to hold on to a little longer. She felt the satisfaction of something achieved. She wanted a little celebration. Even a hard pastry with raisins was celebration. Then she realized she was two turns from the university. She would not go inside the gates. She would just look through the iron bars at the place where her life made its turn.

* * *

At the apartment door, Robert pulled out a strangely large key, and fiddled to get the right angle. Behind him, Dina was so tense that she nearly tore the key out of his hand. Finally, he managed.

The apartment was so small that the kitchen and sitting room were part of one room. Soft-focus portraits of the Leader hung on two of the four walls, one civilian dress, one military. Dina could see only one bedroom—they must all sleep together, she realized through her cooling sweat. On the kitchen windowsill, various dairies were in the process of curdling. The kitchen was also the workshop—there was a sewing machine, an old pressing iron. They used the kitchen table for the board. An old cassette player sat on top of the rumbling refrigerator, half the size of the one owned by her parents, the cassettes organized in neat piles. It was dark, silent, and cool. There were no siblings.

Dina was so busy taking in this chastened life, and failing to keep the expression on her face neutral, that she also failed to notice that Robert had vanished. She found him on the other side of the balcony glass. He waved to her, a hesitant smile on his face. As she walked toward the door, the telephone rang. It startled her in the silence. She looked through the glass at Robert, but he didn't seem to hear it. She opened the door and stepped out.

The balcony was small, but because of the high floor, it looked out on the smog-shrouded breadth of what was virtually the entirety of their city. Partly, it was a sad view, because you could really see how much had collapsed, but views like that could not be entirely sad. The air was clearer up here, and a little cooler; Dina's sweat finished drying. This was a place to sleep outside in the hot months, unlike her parents' apartment, close enough to the ground to hear the belch of every motorbike that passed in the night.

She noticed it last, though Robert was standing by it like a benighted salesman. Even in the heart of his domain, she did not notice him.

"What—what is that?" she said.

It was a pool. A child's pool, slightly deflated—or almost inflated—with a little water covering the bottom. Behind it, wavering in the slight breeze, were cutouts from large panels of construction paper. Serrated edges cut across a black sheet. An orange sphere had been attached to the back of the black. And there were lots of blue squiggly lines all around.

"You said you didn't remember the sea," he said.

She whipped around to look off the balcony once more, as if she had initially missed a smudge of water on the horizon. But the sea was hours away and that's not what he meant.

"This is what it looks like," he said.

"What does?" she said.

"The sea," he said, with some uncertainty.

"You've seen it?" she said.

"My mother is from there," he said. "She has a picture. It has mountains behind it, and the sun is very orange."

"And the blue squigglies are the water," she said.

He shrugged.

"And the pool is . . . The pool is more water."

He nodded.

She began to laugh. "This is why you—" She laughed harder. The dropping thing was gone, and she felt anger instead. "I'm sweating like an aerobics video!" she yelled. Robert was blinking rapidly.

She caught herself. "No," she said. "I'm sorry, it's very pretty. I was afraid, you see . . ."—but telling him why she had been afraid to come here was going to hurt him even more. So they just stood there in silence, Dina trying to keep her belly from jumping in laughter. A pool!

"Where—where did you get it?" she tried.

He sat down heavily on a foldout plastic chair, and wiped at his face with a sleeve. A web of the chair popped under him, one more indignity. "My father is not an engineer," he said. "He works in the pool store. He *was* an engineer. Now, he works in the pool store."

Dina understood that at this moment, it was important not to gloat. Carefully, she moved her braid over her shoulder and ran her hands up and down the hair. Her mother had pleaded with her not to do that. Each sweep loosened more hair, so that the clean cord of the braid came to seem like a whisk broom haloed by dust. "My mother is an engineer," she tried. "*Was* an engineer. Was an engineering *student*."

"What do engineers do?" he said.

"I don't know exactly," she said. "Buildings, like you said."

"My parents will be home soon," he said.

"Thank you for this," she tried.

"It's okay," he said. "Goodbye. I wish you health."

"You know," she said, "I just remembered something about the sea."

He looked up and dangled his legs.

"Yes," she said. "Just now," she emphasized.

He kept dangling.

"I was so excited the night before our trip to the coast that I couldn't sleep," she said. "And then at breakfast, I was so tired, I dropped tea over myself. My mother changed my dress. And then I dropped tea over myself a second time. And this time, I broke the cup. I was little, so I started crying." She looked up, hoping that her double admission of clumsiness, garnished by tears, would make him feel accompanied in his defeat.

Robert was squinting into the sun, so his expression was hard to make out, and she barreled on. "My father left the room. He was silent the entire time we drove. I slept the whole way. Can you believe it? I did not see the sea when we arrived. I saw it only from the window of the hotel room after I woke up. My father was gone. I think he was angry. There was one pomegranate on the table. I felt very thirsty. I wanted the pomegranate juice very badly! I asked my mother for it. I think she really wanted to do something nice for me. We had brought a knife, and she cut it into quarters. But I didn't want to suck the seeds. I wanted the juice. I started to whine. I know it makes my mother unhappy, but she can't scream at me. My father can leave the room, but she has to fix it. So I do it only with her. Anyway, you won't believe it. She went behind a closet door and started taking off her clothes!"

Dina stopped herself—she assumed the intimate detail would make Robert uncomfortable. However, his face remained fixed in the same expression and his eyes didn't leave her. Dina's hands went up and down the braid.

"Finally, my mother was standing without clothes. She was holding her underwear."

When she said that, Robert looked away, and Dina understood she needed to finish.

"She put the pomegranate quarters in the underwear and squeezed. And the juice came out. It was like a cheesecloth, you understand? She couldn't use the hotel's towels, or she would spoil them with color. While she did it, my father returned. He was still angry—his moustache jumps around—but when he saw her, without clothes, he just stopped in the doorway. My mother put me on the balcony with the juice. A balcony just like this one. And I sat there drinking juice and looking at the sea. A balcony just like this one," she emphasized again. "I don't remember what happened after that. Isn't that funny? I just thought of that. So thank you." She waited for acknowledgment and then impatiently added: "Yes, this beautiful idea of yours made me think of that for the first time."

He nodded at her again.

"I should go now," she said.

"Can I touch your hair?" he said.

"Okay," she said hesitantly. Robert was extracting his price in a different currency. She held what remained of the braid out to him, over the shoulder, in both hands, like a trumpet. He slipped from his chair, his legs making the sound of a present being opened as they separated from the webbing. Avoiding her eyes, he extended his hand to the top of her head, where the hair separated for its forked passage down her temples. He patted her slightly there, as if she were a wise animal. His eyes scrutinized the top of her forehead, where, she was certain, more sweat was now forming. Robert nodded and retreated to his chair, wedging his hands under his thighs. The breeze lifted the front strands of his hair.

"I wish you health," he said again, squinting out at the city he'd never leave.

So be it then! she thought. She had laid out for him a tale worthy of Uncle Neem, and he would act the stranger? She had said those things—the naked woman, the word *underwear* with its erotic charge—because she had been insulted when he had declined to kiss, and wanted to demonstrate to herself that her power of solicitation was greater than his modesty. And he had responded to the summons. He had asked to touch her. But for some reason, she was unsatisfied.

She stepped toward the balcony door, willing him to call to her, and he did. He said, "You already told me that story once. You were upset because you remembered the pomegranate, but you didn't remember the sea."

She turned away her mortified eyes, and stepped into the living room. She didn't open them until she was at the door. As she emerged from the building's cool gloom into the sweltering street, her head buzzed with something more wicked than shame. Eventually, she heard blaring horns, shouting. By a repairman's store across the street, next to a wig shop, a motorbike had punctured its tire on a nail in the dirt. The motorbike driver yelled at the store owner. "You must fix the tire! You must take responsibility!" He kept saying the word—*responsibility*, *responsibility*—as he poked the man's chest. The store owner swept away the fingers and shouted back. Someone in the wig shop slammed the front door.

Dina swiveled around, trying to recognize something about the way they had come. She could not be a girl alone on the street—the altercation drew people's attention, but it was also drawing more people. She positioned herself behind a woman who was observing the argument with a dull expression so the woman wouldn't see her but others would assume she was merely a respectful daughter standing at a distance. Earlier, Dina had secretly enjoyed her terror, the emergency. But now she was really afraid. The fake mother in front of her said, "They are so loud," and shuffled off, shaking her head, leaving Dina with no cover. The gazes of the adults in the street fell on her in questioning ways.

Stupid girl, she berated herself. She couldn't wait for her family's disappearance, so she had to engineer her own. Once, her grandmother, her father's mother—she didn't know a grandmother on her mother's side—tired of chasing Dina around their apartment, breathed the sour smell of an old woman's mouth at Dina and said: "You took forever to come out, and now you won't be still." Dina had giggled, thinking that her grandmother was marveling. But then the old woman said: "Life will stop you." Dina stopped laughing. And her grandmother proved her point—she had a stroke and Dina quit running around. Now, she had to sit on her grandmother's knee while the old woman pressed the sides of Dina's nose because she didn't want Dina to have a nose like a Jew. It annoyed Dina and one day, she stuck her fingers inside her grandmother's stroke-splayed mouth and tried to straighten it. The woman dropped her and ran into her bedroom. But she didn't touch Dina's nose again.

Of course, Dina no longer had the square of paper on which Susanna had written her mobile number. She had been very careful with it, partly because Susanna demanded regularly to check it, but it was Susanna herself who had destroyed it by washing Dina's uniform with the scrap still in its pocket. Well, it was Dina's fault for leaving it there, and Susanna's fault for not checking, and whose fault was it that Susanna had stopped asking and Dina forgot to ask Susanna to write it again? Dina really wished she had the number just now. Her eyes on the ground, Dina asked two passing women if they knew the way to Revolution Street, but they didn't, and one stopped long enough to eye her with suspicion.

Dina wheeled around, looking for a solution. She didn't know any prayers, but she tried one—*Omnipotent God I am sorry I made fun of Robert please help me find our house*—though she understood she did not deserve to have it heard. She waited for another moment, anyway.

The second woman who had stopped, the suspicious one, was pointing at Dina. The woman to whom she was speaking moved her head: No, she didn't know what family. Things were dropping and dropping, now in Dina's forehead, her shoulders, all the way down in her feet. Her toes felt filled with fear, like little balloons. Her fingers worked through the braid. She looked in the tinted glass of the wig shop—enough hair had splayed out for the braid to resemble that gauzy mantle that trailed bride ladies when they married. That's probably what made people stop—she looked like a crazy homeless girl.

In the glass, she tried to pat her hair down into something like order. That was when she thought of it. She turned around, as if she expected a jury to jeer at her presumption or marvel at her ingenuity. The owner of the repair shop, who was older, pushed the owner of the motorbike, but gently, in the soft part of the shoulder, with his fingers curved in, scooping the flesh as if it were ice cream. Responsibility, responsibility.

* * *

Susanna had not returned to the university since shortly after she had walked out with George. She had abandoned her schooling and ceded the territory to him. There was no way for her to return there without drawing attention as the student who had seduced the professor. George was not regarded as the teacher who had seduced one of his students. George was spoken to as if he had married another person entirely. It no longer mattered. But the man about to be hanged . . . The proverb had many applications.

The university was the last place she had been someone who was not yet wife to one person and mother to one more. It was a lonely time, but it was impossible to regard it with anything but longing. The university was her sanctuary after Arid (it was her father who insisted she study); the place where she experienced love for the first time (not George); where she had determined she would become a person with skills that made her independent (could she really blame the war for failing at that?). These recollections came upon her with an unwelcome force, and she realized, shamefully, that she had stayed away from the university not because of George but because she was ashamed of how readily she gave it all up.

On the morning Susanna had taken the bus to Dostat and then onward, her mother had regarded her from a corner of the soaring darkened central room of their home like a sedated jackal. Her father had sedated her. With time, it occurred to Susanna that her father had sent Susanna away not because he believed in education but because he wished to save Susanna from the madness that would claim her life as it had his, as Susanna did not have the severity to abandon her mother. So he used the authority he had over Susanna as a man and a father to free her by force. She was forbidden to return because he, not she, was cruel. It was a great gift, but she didn't understand it in time. Here in the city Susanna had simply found other people to whom she was obliged, like a released animal that does not know how to do without the restraints. She pursued the romance with George with an intensity she could hardly understand now, other than its resemblance to the obsession with which she also pursued her unborn daughter. For four years, Dina, that slippery fish, had eluded her, but eventually, even stubborn Dina had to give in to Susanna's resolve to drag her daughter into the world.

There was no history of insanity on her mother's side—her mother was the inauguration of new genetic spoilage—but it was hard to go back to Arid also because Susanna felt that in becoming a mother, she had become eligible to join a mental relay with only one direction to go: Dina. In other words, Susanna was now a person with things to lose. When the child didn't come year after year, Susanna was certain that her mother's genes were the reason, but the problem also contained the relief—without a child, the seed of madness remained unfertilized. Susanna spent the nine months of pregnancy in a kind of shock that was easy for others to ascribe to the nervousness of a first-time mother. It didn't end with the birth of a seemingly healthy child. (Susanna never said, out loud or in her thoughts, that Dina was healthy, only that she *seemed* healthy, so as not to state it categorically and challenge fate.) Every day that Dina came through her bedroom door, singing songs; every day that Dina came home, twirling the braid that eventually reached past her waist; was like a crane carrying somewhere else, for one more day, the stone of misfortune. Here was a bitter thing for which you could thank the war—as the more immediate calamity, it had overtaken these fears.

Through the iron slats of the fence, the university grounds were still handsome, with their parallel row of palms and a small grove of apricot trees. There were very few students now, but the ones whom she saw on the lawn, baking in the savage heat, had their textbooks open, and some threw a Frisbee. Somewhere in the distance, there was a report of artillery, followed by a plume of smoke, the pop and crackle of small-arms fire, and then silence, like the flare-up of an old family spat that was too familiar to occur in new form. How tempting it must have been for the students to take shade under the vast stone portico of the main hall, but it had been bombed and seemed ready to topple. What classes continued took place outside.

George would be angry to learn she had come here, after the warning they'd gotten. But she didn't want to return to the apartment building. She didn't understand the affiliation of the yard sweeper, but she was certain that it was malevolent in some way. Regardless, where else could she go? She said farewell and dragged her feet away from the entrance.

The sound of her name reached her slowly. Her husband's surname, for all to hear. She turned around to find a man with a handsome face the color of old pottery in a faded, double-breasted gray suit with gold buttons. The face was scoured by so many lines that it looked like a folded mask with incisions. He was holding folders and, for some reason, a chipped kettle.

"Am I right?" he said, showing her teeth the color of spoiled pears. "Are you not George's . . . ? One remembers such a face."

She colored and instinctively moved her hands to gather her hair, which had unraveled in the heat. She could feel the sweat on her neck. *The cat's paw of your neck* . . .

"Greetings to you," she said nervously. "Yes. Susanna—"

"I never forget," the man said, tapping his forehead. His expression faded. "I am the Registrar here. I am nervous to inquire after George."

Susanna looked at the Registrar quizzically.

"When he stopped coming, I assumed something had . . ." He didn't finish.

"Stopped coming?" she said.

"To work with us here. He was an ally, madame—it doesn't matter what his identity card says. Just you find a man in this city who knew more about our poetry—and himself not one of us." He scrutinized her. "You seem unwell."

Her mouth was dry. "No, you are right," she managed. Her heart felt leaden. She was not light-headed yet, but she could feel its approach. She tried to think quickly. "George is no longer with us. I'm sorry for my confusion. I'm grieving."

The Registrar's hand moved to his breast. "I'm sorry. He was of great assistance to us."

"I will go now," she said.

"I have upset you. I have added to your grief."

"No—"

"I can walk with you," he said.

"I don't wish to inconvenience you."

His eyes lingered on her. "George is no longer with us," he repeated, but now it sounded like a question instead of a statement.

"George is alive in the Kingdom of Heaven," she managed. "George's memory is alive. That is why I came here—to remember him. Perhaps we can meet for tea one day, sir—when the mourning period has ended."

"Always welcome," he said, reassured by the invitation. "The door is open for you, madame." He considered the collapsed stone around them. "There is no door, madame. Sometimes, we don't have doors." He shook his head.

"I will go now, please," she said.

"Of course," he said, and bowed slightly. He turned away and walked up the path to the portico, as if he knew when the shells would and wouldn't arrive. She stared at his back until he turned to look at her. She couldn't look away in time, and they stood looking at each other until he nodded and disappeared in the shadows.

Susanna was sweating. She didn't feel the strength to keep walking. Outside the gate, she held up a hand for a taxi. When she gave the address, the driver gave her an inscrutable glance in the mirror and pulled down the privacy screen. So George had not been dismissed? She didn't understand. The radio wailed "Tell Me, Tell Me, Tell Me," but the driver, perhaps wishing to be considered a serious person, switched to the news station. They listened to their Leader declaiming about all the buildings that the country's patriotic engineers would be restoring as part of the bright future that awaited them all.

* * *

Susanna saw him before he saw her. Did the sweeper not take a break? At least he left for the nights; he was gone when she had walked out the evening before. Her knees felt as if the kneecaps were about to slough off. She forced herself to stride forward with what she hoped seemed like lack of fear. The man was steaming in his large jacket.

"Greetings to you," she called out.

His eye flutter-fluttered, briefly replacing the judgment in his face with an expression of startled innocence. He waited until it was over.

"And the recycling plant was closed also, I see," he said, nodding at her hands.

With horror, she realized she was still holding the bag of bottles. She had entered and left the taxi with it. She felt wobbly and lost her step, her bags splaying around her. The concrete, which had been roasting all day, burned her through her jeans. She felt its divots in her knees. Two bottles went skittering down the pavement. The sweeper retrieved them and crouched beside her, the scent of sunflower seeds mixing with sweat.

"I have been unwell today," she said. "It's the heat. Will you kindly dispose of the glass for a lady?"

She allowed him to take her elbow. Taking advantage of the vague sympathy she had earned, she proceeded toward the building entrance without further self-justification. She felt his eyes on her back.

She was by her apartment door, raising her hand for the knob, when she realized that the hand was empty. She had also left downstairs the bag with everything she had bought for the trip. She clamped her hand over her mouth, and made a strangled sound. The door across from theirs creaked open, as she knew it would. The neighbor woman's unpainted face emerged and scanned the stairwell with suspicion.

"It's a woman's time, Mother," Susanna tried to explain. "And the heat. Together, it's too much." Susanna could have been telling the truth. Her menstrual cycles appeared at the most inconvenient times.

"Put buckwheat groats in a sock," the woman said in a loud whisper, still checking the stairwell. "When they turn on the gas, put the sock in the oven five minutes, then apply on the lower part of the belly."

Susanna made a noise of acknowledgment.

"Your knives are on your doorstep," the woman said.

Susanna turned back and looked down. Indeed, they were.

"I asked George to leave them out for me, so I remember to take them to the sharpener," she tried.

"The sharpener is sick today," the neighbor said.

"I didn't know," Susanna said.

"Couldn't you see that his windows are draped?"

So the man downstairs was telling the truth. And he had returned the knives. Was she imagining his ill motive? But he knew which apartment was theirs, she realized with a chill.

"George is not at the university?" the woman said.

Susanna hated her in that moment. Since his termination, George had been invisible inside the apartment, but from her eyehole this fishwife knew, anyway. She could smell it. But she was asking it like a question.

"He took ill," Susanna said. "There was damage from a shell at the water-treatment plant, didn't you hear?" She said it in spite, so the woman would see she didn't know everything. But the lie was stupid—George was ill from bad water, but everyone else in the building was not?

"Buckwheat groats," the woman repeated in a tremulous voice. She knew she was in the presence of something with which she did not wish to be associated. "Or ingest fennel extract," she added. And the door slammed shut.

Susanna opened the case of knives, not wanting to see what she'd find there. None had been sharpened, but one was missing, the one with the elaborate handle, inlaid with stones, which had been in George's family for a long time. He used it only during the holidays, and it had gone dull from disuse instead of the opposite. It would get lots of use now, she thought. But she was confused all over again.

George was standing in the kitchen, absentmindedly wiping the last of the eggplant with a half-eaten meat pie.

"I saw your Registrar," she said to his back in a clogged voice.

The meat pie stopped moving. "What do you mean?" he said, turning around. "Why are you crying?"

"I was near the university. He saw me."

George's face darkened—but the effect was ruined by the meat pie distending his mouth. Quickly, he finished chewing. "You know not to go there."

"He couldn't have fired a dead man, let me tell you. For that is what he thinks you are."

"Lower your voice, please."

She walked to the window and closed it. "What have you not told me? If this whole life wasn't cursed, I would think it was a woman—but I don't think it's a woman."

George dropped the remainder of the meat pie into the plastic container. A fleck of eggplant clung to his moustache. He lowered himself heavily into a kitchen chair. One of the legs had gone loose again, and he nearly tumbled. Groaning, he pulled out the drawer with the screwdrivers, and began rooting through the sandpaper and spackle. He stopped and shut the drawer. "It makes no difference."

"Your deceit?"

"The leg, the leg of the chair. We are finished here."

They stood in silence. An ambulance wailed somewhere beyond the window. With it closed, it was even hotter. They couldn't run the air conditioner—the circuit breakers couldn't handle it, and they had no hope of finding someone to replace those.

George slid back into the chair and put his head in his fingers. She perceived a falsely dramatic gesture meant to elicit her sympathy. "I had a student," he said, removing his hands and knuckling his moustache, still missing the eggplant. "Kamil. I knew, vaguely, he had joined the rebels. Or maybe I didn't know, but when he walked into my office and told me—I wasn't surprised." As he spoke, George's hands were opening and closing, opening and closing, and she knew these were his gestures when he lectured.

"Kamil was always principled to the point of harm," George said. "He gave away some blind students who were cheating once. He's dominant-sect, you know. He joined the rebels from principle. Anyway, he came to ask me for money. They think emptying the account of a university professor will make a difference. But I guess if you ask enough professors." He paused and looked away.

"So our hopes are with a bunch of barefoot children who have to shake down professors for money?" she said.

He called her name harshly. "Not *our* hopes. They don't speak for us. Because of what they started, how many people have died?"

"You prefer the regime, then," she said. "They are polite enough to inform you in advance that your family will be killed."

"I command you and I beg you to lower your voice."

"I command you to tell me the truth."

George shook his bewildered head.

"Well?" she prodded him.

"I said to Kamil what you said to me. '*What can a professor offer you?*' And Kamil said, 'On what you will give us, we will march ten times as far as the army.' He's right, you know. Those barefoot children nearly took the capital before the army woke up. Their principle is their power. And it's their damnation. We are surrounded by countries who would arm the rebels up to their eyes. But the rebels are idealists. They won't sell out for patronage. They—"

She cut him off, and said in a quietly disturbed voice, "What did you do, George?"

"I offered to take a collection. Several people. Minority-sect, but some dominant-sect also, sympathizers. You have to throw something like that in to make the story seem believable."

She realized, with disbelief, that he was congratulating himself for his cleverness.

"In exchange, I told Kamil I wanted a meeting with his commander," George said. "I was putting myself in a position of danger, collecting money for rebels, and I wanted assurances. Kamil said he was authorized to give all the assurances—if we ever found ourselves in a position of trouble, they would find a way to help. I said that I meant no disrespect, but it would have to be his commander. Kamil waved his knife about, but this is where the authority of a professor, perhaps only residual, but it means something. He agreed."

"Without my knowledge, you are making deals with rebels?" she said. "I do not know my husband."

"And you?" he said, his voice rising, though he lowered it quickly. "Have you wondered why we haven't been touched? By either side? Because on one side, your husband debases himself every day licking the soles . . ." He couldn't finish the sentence. "And the rebels? Half of them were our students."

She was silent. That was the first time she had ever heard him refer to his role at the university that way. She didn't know he knew that it was a debasement. "That won't make a difference," she said. "Your students murder just like the others. If you didn't think so, we wouldn't be running right now."

"You're right—but it hasn't come down to it, not yet. We will be last. Last."

"What did you do, George?" she said again.

"I informed the authorities. I went to the police." He paused, and then said, "I informed the authorities," as if it would mean something different this time.

"You don't even know where the police precinct is!"

"I was thinking quickly. It's what came to mind."

"And then?"

"I was supposed to meet this commander near the university. I told Kamil I had one hundred thousand, collected from seven people. Again, you have to be specific like that. And before the commander got to the meeting point . . . the authorities . . . intercepted him."

"You sent a man to his torture and death."

"To keep for my wife and daughter their lives."

"You are certain you picked the right side?"

"Lower your voice, *please*," he said. "After putting up with spicy fish like gravel, it would be a shame to be found out this way."

She distended her mouth in a joyless copy of a smile. Life in her homeland had given her practice. "I don't understand," she said. "Why did you quit the university? That is the side that you helped."

"I didn't quit. Kamil was waiting for me in the office the next day. I thought he was there to finish me. Amazingly, he didn't suspect me. That is the thing, you see—too much principle blocks intelligence. Anyway, he said *he* would now take the money. I told him I had left it at home. And I never returned."

"You fool! What did you think would happen? You are not so stupid to think that Kamil's people don't know where you live?"

George was silent.

"That's why you haven't gone outside," she went on. "But you have allowed your wife and daughter to go."

"They will not harm a woman and child," he said, studying the floor's pattern of tiles.

"So . . . who is the man outside?" she said.

"What man?" he said, raising his eyes.

"There is a man outside. A sweeper."

"So?"

"I don't think he is a sweeper. I don't know. I don't know what to think."

"Your nerves are jumping, Susanna. Your makeup is streaked on your face. Why don't you take some time in the bath? We are leaving tonight. It's over."

"Why would we get a sweeper now when they don't take the garbage for weeks? He hasn't touched his broom, let me tell you."

George didn't answer.

"You fool," she said finally. "You fool. How do you think the people in Europe will react when they learn you are a shill for the butcher in charge?"

"Lower your voice! They don't have to learn it."

"What were you thinking . . ." she said. She lowered herself to the tile.

"Consider the opposite," he said. "Say I gave the rebels money. Do you think that would remain a secret for long? They would come back for more. And then we wouldn't have money to leave." He paused. "It's time, Susanna. From both sides, there is no room. I did something I thought might give us a little bit more, for a little bit longer. But I'm glad it didn't work. For four years, we've been waiting to round the corner. But there's no end to it. No end. This is the only life Dina knows. We must go."

Susanna looked up with alarm. "What is the time?"

"The time is to leave, I'm saying."

"No, the time, the clock," she said. "I should have picked Dina up twenty minutes ago." Susanna ran out the door, damn the neighbor woman. Now, the man outside wasn't there—he was in some cellar evaluating her Mylar blankets. She had submitted enough of a sacrifice to disappear him for a moment. When she reached the school, her daughter was gone, too.

* * *

Dina expected to feel very guilty, but she felt daring, ingenious, resourceful. She spun and ran toward the end of the street, where it intersected with a larger one, then made herself stop running and skip—normal, everything normal. She put her hand up for a taxi. Three went by, their lights on, before one stopped, trailing fumes of diesel. The man at the wheel regarded her with slow eyes swimming in fat. She knew that meant he was chewing, but she couldn't be choosy. Before he could open his mouth to reject her on account of her age, she said, "How much to Revolution Street, thirty-seven."

He studied her slowly. "One thousand," he said.

"To Revolution?" she said, trying to sound exasperated. "I could walk there in fifteen minutes."

"So walk there."

"I will give you five hundred extra if you wait here five minutes," she said. "And put on your seat belt."

He looked down at his belly, as if surprised to find himself attached to something so large. "So be it," he said. Good that he was chewing, she decided; he was docile.

At the wig store, the radio was set to a political address—all the broken buildings would rise once again, their Leader promised. Behind a gray counter, framed by two artificial potted fiddle-leaf figs—in a nicer neighborhood, it would have been a dry cleaner's—wigs hung like skinned badgers. Before Dina could study them, a thin figure emerged from the back. A crumb of cake still clung to the wrinkles by the woman's lip. She had to ask Dina twice to understand what she wanted. But she shook her head—they did not do the cutting here. It was a wig shop, not a hairdresser's. And they did not deal with children at all.

But then she really saw Dina's hair in the light, after Dina undid her braid. It was like silk, even with the mess she had made of it. The woman ran her fingers through it. Dina tried not to recoil; it was like being touched somewhere you shouldn't be touched. The woman reconsidered—in special circumstances, the shop could be flexible regarding the child policy. But the child had to cut—the responsibility had to be Dina's. Dina demanded scissors. She turned toward the oblong mirror, its gilt frame smudged with black spots, as if it had been hung by hands covered in paint. Dina put her finger two inches from the rim of her hair.

"One thousand," the woman said.

Three inches.

"Two thousand."

Five inches. "Five thousand," Dina said herself.

The woman's cheekbones rose. "There is a bright future or a dark future waiting for you, God will decide."

Dina cut.

Outside, Dina was gratified to see that an adult—slow-minded from chew, but still—had obeyed her and the taxi was waiting. There was a cap of badly cut hair swinging around Dina's ears—she looked like a mushroom. The taxi driver's eyes got smaller as she approached—even in his dullness, he could tell something substantial had changed. Dina felt the weak afternoon breeze graze her head in unfamiliar ways. She was about to reach for the back door of the taxi when another weaved abruptly out of the roadway, setting off a fury of horns, and swerved to a stop behind them. Dina knew her mother would emerge; she willed it. Dina smiled. The dropping thing stopped. Not because she was found—she wanted Susanna to see her brilliant solution.

* * *

When she reached her daughter, Susanna, her face coursing with rage no longer arrested by worry, did something she had never done before. She slapped Dina's cheek. Then covered her mouth in horror. Dina's smile disappeared, but she felt a strange satisfaction as her cheek stung with color. People stared. Susanna pulled her daughter close, and mouthed "No, no." She pulled away. "What have you done?" she said, the second time she had to ask a family member the question that day. Dina would forever remember her mother's expression, terror watered by helplessness.

Dina's driver leaned toward the passenger window. "Madame, I don't need tickets to a theater. Taxi or not?" They had to choose between Dina's taxi and Susanna's taxi. No taxis for years for this family, and now two in one day. They sent Dina's on its way. Dina's driver threw up his hands, and what he wished to say the tailpipe said instead, with a giant diesel-choked pop.

On the ride home, Susanna clutched Dina and sobbed. Her daughter looked impassively past her mother's head, the sun-singed smell of Susanna's hair filling her nose. Susanna had one long hair the color of bone. Dina wanted such a silver thread for herself. Also, Dina was thinking that even the thin skin of water in Robert's pool must have taken days of early rising and collecting, and Robert's family's doing without an equal amount. And Robert's family lived in a neighborhood that got less water than theirs—even Dina was old enough to know that.

"How did you find me?" Dina said, guilty and excited at having had to be found.

Susanna had given money to Teacher Mona in exchange for the phone numbers and addresses of the only two schoolmates known to Susanna. (You just knew you could do that with Teacher Mona, as you could not with Teacher Mariam; Mona's eyes said she was willing. But Susanna had, until today, never tested this impression.) At Kar's home, Susanna's pounding was answered by a hunched woman whose terrified eyes made clear Dina wasn't inside. No one answered the telephone at Robert's, so she went on to his address.

Dina was suitably impressed. Her mother had, in her own way, been resourceful and ingenious also.

When they walked in, George rushed to his daughter, and Susanna began crying again. Now, Dina was crying as well. Susanna and Dina cried as George watched, not knowing how to fit into the scene.

Until that evening, Susanna had been less fearful than she expected. Leaving was so inconceivable that she didn't know what to be afraid of, unlike the slow mental attrition of the preceding four years. The chores of departure felt suspiciously like the chores of any time, too many and varied. Their lives here had ended long before George came home to tell her he had been removed from his post. They ended when it became necessary to cross a checkpoint to visit Dina's grandparents. When Remy, Juliana, Youstina, and Harry Soudane were murdered.

Confusingly, some things continued to work the same way as always. The pool was still open; Dina's school was still open, though they merged grades to compensate for the students who had vanished; the store that sold party supplies; the banquet hall. People still married, still delivered, if at checkpoints. Certain things became more precious—a taxi ride, fish. And throughout, there was still one door with an exit sign: an office, payment for spots on a raft, instructions to wait. Susanna had moved through the departure preparations with a cold competence that surprised her—unless it was numbness.

But then she chose to walk toward the university gates instead of satisfying herself with a pastry, and then her daughter had vanished, and suddenly it seemed very undeniable that things were not required to go neatly. Suddenly it seemed very possible that the fate of the Soudanes could be theirs, right here in George's tacky apartment—or in the yard, for all to see. If that was not the purpose of the sweeper downstairs, what was?

Susanna ran her hands through her daughter's hair over and over. Now she didn't stop herself.

Susanna sat with Dina all evening, without limit on Disney videocassettes. She gave her tea, cocoa, the ice cream Susanna had been making herself since the grocer's freezer had perished, though their freezer hardly worked and the ice cream had to be consumed right away. Dina didn't mind.

None felt hunger. Only Dina nodded off—even George couldn't sleep. He remained in the sitting room, reading his letters. Susanna kept a shoebox-sized space empty for them in the suitcase, but when he finally emerged, at 1 A.M., eyeing with wariness the strange-looking child on the divan, he was holding a plastic grocery bag twice that size. From his expression, Susanna understood that he couldn't choose further; the bag of letters would have to come separately. After having made peace with what she had to leave behind to make space for the letters, Susanna was confronted by the luxury of an unanticipated rectangle of space in a suitcase that otherwise didn't have room for a hair. (In the end, wasn't this marriage? He transferred his impossible situations to her.)

She packed a heating element, more menstrual pads, and a small hand-carved olivewood chess set made in Dostat. When she came across something made there, she bought it: a spindle, a clock. She had never found an item stamped Arid—it was too small. She missed the yogurt. Her father spooned honey into it, and then that into her mother's dumb, waiting mouth, but Susanna liked the way it bit her tongue without the honey. George had used to joke that they would take a vacation to Arid, purchase a tub of yogurt for each day of their stay, and never leave the hotel. The idea made her hopelessly sad, though for different reasons then and now—then because she had abandoned her mother, now because she and George would never get to do something like that. There weren't any hotels in Arid, in any case. It was tiny, and nobody went there. In the rush, Susanna forgot about the engineering textbook.

On the divan, George dozed over the arms crossed on his chest. Dina was curled up next to him. Susanna fought sleep. She didn't want to risk the alarm, which was audible in other apartments—she had been apprised of this by the neighbor woman—so she opened a window that rattled from the wind; that kept her from slipping too deeply. They sat in their raft of dreams and waited.

* * *

Several minutes before three, they crept out, Dina clutching a drawing pencil, Susanna clutching Dina's sleeping body, George clutching the suitcase and his bag of letters, each of them wearing several coats. Before the door closed, George took a finger to his lips and placed it against a thin crack on the wall from something that exploded somewhere nearby at some point.

From custom, Susanna felt the neighbor's eyes across the hall, but the old woman wasn't there—her snoring made no less noise than Susanna's alarm clock. The building warden had put out the stairwell light, and they took stair by stair in the light of the partial moon through the lattice windows. Susanna prayed the man outside was gone.

Between the third and second floor, Dina's pencil fell from her fingers and went skittering down the stairs. It took every step before coming to rest on the mat outside 202. They stopped, listening to their hearts. But there was no sound, no line of light under the door. None of them had the hands to retrieve the pencil, and they didn't want to risk making more noise by setting down their things, so it stayed in its place, the words DINA—DON'T TOUCH scratched into one of its sides. When they reached the ground floor, Susanna put the letter to George's parents into the mail slot. Dear Grandmother and Grandfather, it began, as if in her news, Susanna was hiding behind her daughter. If so, George was hiding behind his wife.

Outside, George rubbed Dina's back to wake her up so they could move more quickly, but Susanna caught his hand; she moved more quickly with Dina immobilized on her shoulder. Or as quickly as she could wearing a quilted jacket over an overcoat over a belted mackintosh—she was sweating in her neck and armpits, and between her legs. The sweeper was gone—she felt relief moving through her. They walked toward Engineers Street. When the war began, the buildings had started to fall down instead of go up, and Susanna had started calling it Not-Engineers Street. But now it was supposed to be their road to salvation.

Incredibly, the old yellow Peugeot they were told to expect at 3 A.M. did in fact appear several minutes later, stopping under the single streetlight that still worked on their side of the street. The light was a fluorescent shear across the faded yellow of the hood. The door opened with a squeal, and the driver stepped out. He fastened a wrapping across the lower half of his face and opened his palms to the sky. George stopped and exhaled in disbelief, as if his body was finally freeing itself of some stubborn gas.

From their place ten meters away, they watched another body separate itself from the poplars by the streetlight—the yard sweeper. Lunging for the driver, he cut the air with something metallic. The driver cried out and crumpled. But then the body came to life and reached for the sweeper, who now fell with a cry of his own. The men struggled, cursing and groaning, until a hand freed itself, a glimmering point at its edge, and plunged back in. There was a slow, sad, surprised sigh, and the bodies were still. A light went on in one of the windows.

One of the bodies unsealed itself and turned toward them. George dropped the suitcase and letters and grabbed Susanna's arm. Approaching them, the sweeper said, "Your knives are duller than your brains." George's hand pulled Susanna away from him, but Susanna resisted, rooted by her need to understand. By now, lights were on in several windows, giving away those who had private sources of power. "Well?" the sweeper said. "This is yours." He held out George's holiday knife, from which a trail of blood ran to the edge and down to the pavement. "Poor manners," he reproached himself. He wiped the knife on his service trouser, and extended it again. But George and Susanna just stood there. The sweeper shook his head, pocketed the knife, and turned toward the body. He still wore the demented jacket.

"Wait," Susanna said to the sweeper, trying to give it the tone of command she had failed to muster earlier. The body on the ground was moaning weakly as its owner expired. A bloody mucus slowly soaked the face wrapping. The sweeper unwound the cloth, releasing the head, which slammed to the ground. Then he pulled the bloody pulp by the hair so George could see it was Kamil. "Now okay?" the man said. George looked at him blankly. The sweeper had thought Susanna had called his work into question. Like a butcher, he was holding up the cut to show the customer there were no grounds for complaint.

Dina, who had awoken when George had reached for her, tried to make sense of what was happening behind her from her position in Susanna's arms, facing the murderless part of the street. She had heard men moaning and grappling, but it was no time for a wrestling match. She thought it would give her credibility to tremble sleepily once in her mother's arms, and she did.

Windows lit up because the tenants wanted to understand the commotion, then went dark when they understood this was not a situation they wished to be asked about by the police, though surely they continued watching in the dark. The bricks in this building were mortared by envy and fear.

The sweeper began to drag Kamil's body toward the trunk of the Peugeot. Susanna ran to the car with her daughter.

"Do you want an ear?" the man said. "Like a receipt."

"This was our driver," Susanna said.

"This was your murderer. Your husband did not teach him well." The sweeper giggled.

"So you have to take us," she said.

The sweeper laughed, the eye twitching again. For the duration of the flutter, he looked like a boy enduring reprimand by a parent. Finally, it was over.

"We will pay," she said, shifting Dina and looking at George, who was still standing where she left him, trying to understand. The sweeper hesitated, then continued dragging the body toward the trunk. "You take yourself," he said. "It's free."

"You want us to drive through the checkpoints between here and the sea, like we are on holiday? You are not a stupid man. And you could use a new jacket."

The sweeper heaved the body into the trunk and said, "Fifty thousand." She could see that for him, it was such a fantastic amount that he expected them to send him home. Until their circumstances had reduced drastically in the previous week, it had not been a fantastic amount at all. But now it was a fantastic amount for all of them.

George raised his hand to object, but before he could, she said, "Yes." And before the man could reconsider, she got in with Dina, and said, again with command: "Let's go. They are looking at us from the windows." Both men obeyed. George and Susanna crushed together in the back, wishing to be away from both the driver in front and the body behind. Now Dina was facing the sweaty torn leather of the backseat. She tried to shift on Susanna's shoulder so she could have at least one secret eye on the front, but her mother shifted her back and Dina's nose was again in the foam liner bursting out of the tear.

Their suitcase took the front seat, which in a vehicle on its way to the coast meant only one thing. Every day, there were hundreds of such vehicles, converging on the exit like flushed vermin. Those were the words their Leader had used—the conflict (he never called it a "war") had flushed the vermin from their hiding places. Through the flight of the vermin, the Leader was purifying the nation. And yet, no raft conductor on the coast could operate without the approval of—without levies to—the palace.

"Really," the man said, counting the bills George had been made to withdraw from the mesh pouch in his underwear. "I can't believe you kept such a dull knife."

Dina decided that she should try stirring. "Maman, is everything all right?" she said with fake sleepiness.

"Nothing, nothing," Susanna said. "I wonder only who sleeps harder, you or the lady across the hall."

"She has breath like farts," Dina said, and resettled herself gloomily on Susanna's shoulder.

* * *

The rebels controlled the roads between the city and the coast, three hours away, so the sweeper would have to drive a hundred kilometers out of the way. Shortly after they turned from Engineers onto the wide thoroughfare out of the city, he wove toward a curb. Off to the right, forklifts maneuvered under the floodlights of a concrete plant. Through the back window, Dina watched the driver come around, but then, frustratingly, he was obscured by the lid of the trunk. She heard something thump the concrete. Then the sweeper moved their suitcase to the now-empty trunk. As they pulled away, the rear window cleared enough distance for Dina to see a body discarded on the lip of the curb, so carelessly that it rolled into the street. Her mother's head, turned to the forklifts, was pressing against hers.

"Relax, madame," the driver said. "We don't have to hide bodies in concrete these days."

George interrupted them with a cry. Where were the letters? George had had the bag in his hands. He had dropped it along with the suitcase when he thought they would run, but retrieved only the suitcase. That cursed yard, Susanna thought—it existed to usurp their belongings. George tried to explain, but the man cut him off. "You are stupid. The police will be there any moment. You want me to drive in daylight?"

"They are your police," George said. "*Our* police," he rushed to correct himself.

"Different departments," the man said.

George looked at Susanna. Defeated, she nodded. George unbuckled his pants, reached into the zippered mesh, and extended five thousand to the front seat. The hand there opened and closed, summoning more. George added five thousand. The car squealed as it made a 180-degree turn in the silent lanes of the road.

They stopped a block away from the apartment building. Already it felt like somebody else's home. Susanna whispered the charm against returning immediately to a departed place. It was a private superstition, maintained since her mother had left for a "rest home" when Susanna was four and returned three months later much worse, almost feral. (A quarter of a century later, Susanna was eating soup on the divan, watching a program about mental asylums in India, when she understood her mother had had a portion of her cranium scraped. Dina walked in on Susanna so transfixed by the television that the soup, midway to Susanna's mouth, was dripping from the spoon onto the divan.) Susanna's child mind made of the correlation a cause. Several months before their departure, Susanna was already on Engineers when she realized that she had left the gas lit under a pot on the stove. Her choice was bad luck or an exploded pot. Gloomily, she returned to the apartment. But since she'd left, the gas had been cut off. There was no flame under the pot. She sat down and wept.

The sweeper had stopped next to a bakery; though it was still shuttered, they could smell the bread baking inside. A solitary police car already idled by the front walk of their apartment building, next to a crowd of tenants. Now, the residents were eager to mass around the police, professing their ignorance of what had transpired.

"Stupid man," the sweeper said, shaking his head, and opened his door. Through the window, Susanna watched as the driver slipped off his enormous jacket and pushed it on George. Susanna rolled down the window.

"On my head—what are you doing?" she said to the sweeper. "*You're* going. That's what we paid for."

"Me going is another fifty thousand," the man said.

"George, if I didn't have my daughter sleeping on my shoulder . . . please don't go. They are letters. We will write new letters, George!"

But George didn't respond. In the tenseness of the moment, Susanna failed to reflect on the strangeness of this—her husband dodged responsibility for certain family tasks, but he never ignored a direct entreaty. From the corner of her eye, Dina watched her father fumbling into the driver's jacket. How this fit into the rest of the evening's events, she couldn't say.

George was broader, so the man's jacket sat on him more or less correctly, though George had never worn an imitation-leather jacket with pleated wrists. But that was the point. The sweeper touched a finger to the area under George's nose and flicked it away, like excess salt. George didn't understand, but Susanna did. Weakly, she mouthed "No." Only Dina heard.

George banged on the window with his knuckles, his wedding ring clinking the glass.

"The scissors, please," he said hoarsely.

"They're deep in the suitcase," Susanna lied.

George pointed at the driver's pocket. The driver brought out the knife, Kamil's blood still pocking the blade. Susanna understood that she should give them the scissors, which were in her purse for protection, but, hating George, she did not. The man began scraping down George's moustache. It was agonizing to watch. Now, the blade was sharp enough for surgery and the surgeon was skilled, too. The driver managed to hack off most of the moustache without drawing more than a spot of blood here and there. George touched the area gingerly with his fingertips. He opened the door and squatted before Susanna. "Half the previous age, I'm sure," he tried.

She wouldn't look at him. He rose, his knees cracking, and receded. She spun around to look at him through the back window, briefly giving Dina a view of the front seat though not the action, which had moved to the back. George disappeared around the corner. Susanna pulled Dina's hair so it would become longer. Dina had to grit her teeth not to cry out.

"Letters!" the driver exclaimed when he returned to his seat. He shook his head and giggled again.

They sat in silence. The bakery was on to sweet fritters. The letter they'd mailed to George's parents included the deed to the apartment, which they'd managed to transfer because there was a notary one neighborhood over who was willing to do it for people like them, and for only three times the usual cost. (It was the neighborhood where Dina had become lost; the day before, while Dina was at school, Susanna had stood in a poorly ventilated office two blocks from Robert's apartment building.) Everyone understood the notarized paper was powerless next to the government official who decided its worth, but if you could do it, you did it.

The driver was fiddling with his watch. He brought it to his ear and tapped the screen with a fingernail.

"I will wait until four," he said.

"And then?" she said.

"I take you to the coast or you go back to join your husband. The second is much faster for me." He held the watch to his ear again. "That bastard broke my watch," he said.

"Who was that man?" she said.

"My wife bought me this watch. How do you expect her to react to this?" He tsked. "It's my fault. The butcher doesn't cut meat in his wedding suit. But if I don't wear it, she will ask what's the issue, is it broken? How to solve this problem?"

Susanna could not imagine responding to this. "Please tell me," she said, trying to put impatience into her voice. The man responded to command more than to plea. "Please explain."

"Your husband can explain."

"My husband is not himself."

The man turned on the radio, as if he wanted a soundtrack for his tale, but Susanna hissed at him—the child was sleeping. He looked at her and giggled again: The child could sleep through murder, but not a duet? Susanna did not stoop to persuading. Her only chance with this man was through insult.

He switched off the radio. "With time," he said, "Kamil and his people had to understand that your husband gave away his commander. And if Kamil wasn't sure, his mole in the conductor's office saw your names on the raft register—if you're running, you're running from something. Of course, it would be Kamil who came for you. It's a matter of honor—your husband made a fool of him. And for us, Kamil is a nice little fish to fry on the fire. He had forty men under him."

So they had been saved by the government side. Of the things that had trickled back from those who had made it to Europe, the most important was: Do not disclose government affiliation. Not even a janitor at the civil-construction bureau. Merchant, tailor, bottle caps, bakery, warehouse, violinist, clergy, inter-sect outreach—what you like, only not government affiliation. (Europeans particularly approved of inter-sect outreach.) Susanna stared numbly. She had thought their biggest problem was that George had worked at a state university.

"Why did you take the knife," she said weakly.

In the darkness, the pistol he withdrew looked like a snub-nosed ferret. "Guns are loud," he said. "You gave me an idea. You were making a little lie of your own, weren't you, madame, going to the sharpener."

"How many people have you killed?" she said.

"When, today?" He laughed, his eye going wild—tic-tic-tic. She smelled the cigarettes on his breath. He scratched at his thin black beard.

"You are lucky you got me," he said. "I believe what we are doing. I believe what He is doing." He tapped the radio, by which he meant the Leader. "We have people who do it only because they're afraid to disobey. And that means if Kamil had come with money, the person in my seat is buying his wife a new washing machine, and Kamil is the one in this seat. Understand? And the three of you are the bodies back on that curb."

"So you are a person of principle," she said. "Kamil was, too." She looked through the back window, but it showed only the night. What was she supposed to do if George didn't return? She was too tired to consider the consequences. The delay caused by his disappearance made her angrier than even his earlier deceit. Well, she had sanctioned the disappearance, hadn't she? She always sanctioned. If he returned, she would force him to be responsible.

"Why did you do that to his moustache?" she said.

"He had to become another man," the driver said. "Or you would be asking for one less ticket on the raft." He busied himself again with the watch.

Susanna moved her hands through Dina's severed hair, trying not to pull, Dina trying to be a dead weight in her arms as she tried to understand the difficult-to-understand things the driver was saying. The hair felt like a saw-toothed curtain. They had never cut Dina's hair. For the first four years, it grew very slowly. Dina came to think of this as a defect, and ran to the mirror every morning to check if it had grown in the night. They decided they would take her to Fares, the barber who had for many years adjusted George's moustache. The barber's snipping would renew the hair and make it grow faster. The war had hardly begun then—it seemed, at times, like it might be averted. George set off for Fares's shop with the pride of a man about to introduce his daughter to a person with a small but meaningful role in his life. But Fares, George reported with a vacant expression, had closed his business.

The nearest minority-sect barber was in an unsafe neighborhood—they tried once and saw people running as small-arms fire went off somewhere behind them. Around this time, as if in retaliation, Dina's hair began to grow at almost abnormal speed, a glorious insult to everything their lives had become. Susanna dreamed once that Dina had cut it, and Susanna was on the floor frantically collecting it so she could reattach it. The floor was dirty, the hair was mixed up with dust and debris, and Susanna's hands were gray with it.

Susanna turned around again to check the back window—abruptly enough to discover on her shoulder a wide-eyed daughter.

"How long have you been awake?"

"Stop turning and I'll go back to sleep," Dina said.

"I'm sorry."

"Good night," Dina said demonstratively.

The car radio said 3:57.

The driver stepped out and spat. He fiddled in the trunk and returned to the car holding the bag of raft supplies Susanna had left in the yard that afternoon, crumpled and torn.

"I don't need most of it," he said. Tic-tic-tic.

Susanna laughed through the gravel in her throat.

"What's funny?" he said.

"I'll tell you," she said. "I was saving room in the suitcase for a small part of the letters. Then he came out and said we would need to take more letters than he thought. So I filled the suitcase with other things I had already said goodbye to. Now I have to say goodbye to them again because you have returned to me other things whose disappearance I had already accepted. In the middle of all this, he has lost his letters. It's a comedy, don't you think?"

"*I came to find you / But already you left to go searching for me*," the driver sang out, not badly.

"*I am always where you used to be*," Dina mumbled the next line from her false sleep.

"*Is it still love—*" he started, but saw Susanna's admonishing eyes in the rearview and quit. Dina shifted hotly on Susanna's neck.

"Why does your face do that?" Susanna said.

"You want to know about me, do you?" the man said.

"I am trying to distract you from the clock."

"This eye is tired," the driver said, pointing to it. "This eye sees too much. He has to rest."

Susanna didn't know what to say to this kind of village talk.

"My mother says this from the time I am small," he said. "'*My heart, this magic eye must rest!*' When I was a boy, my father and I were walking on the edge of the village—for firewood, we were having to go farther and farther, because they had clear-cut the forest in the Balsam District, do you know it? It doesn't matter." He hadn't uttered this many words to her at once, but once he got going, he spoke in a rush. "I was behind my father, because I had the wagon—he would take the small sticks and leave the big ones for me. I hadn't said anything to upset him. Nothing, it was silent. He picked up a large stick. I thought it was another one for the bundle. And he turned around with this look in his eyes. The stick was up in his hand, like an axe—"

Susanna yelped as the door opened and George tumbled into the seat, bringing a new gust from the bakery. His breath fell out of him in hot waves, and sweat ran down his face. He clutched the bag of letters. His eyes were aflame with a primitive light at having carried it off.

"I know I am dreaming," Dina said to him, "because what is going on with your face?"

"You are dreaming, little bird," he said. "We are all dreaming."

"You see," the driver said to Susanna, the eye going click-click. "You insult the jacket, but it's useful." He giggled. "If you hadn't insulted the jacket, I would have said thirty-five."

* * *

They slept in the back seat, even as they bounced over the washouts and rutted roads between the three villages that allowed them to bypass rebel checkpoints. The villages knew their purpose. The driver reached back to shake George, George passed on another bill and slipped back into sleep.

They were on the coast by morning, the sun tempered by the wind whipping off the water. Dina, groggy from shredded sleep, walked past the man lugging their suitcase out of the trunk, thinking he was a porter. But it was her father, unrecognizable without his facial armature. Her head retracted. *Eat shit* . . . She'd never seen that part of his face. It didn't make him seem youthful or undefended or even forlorn. (In short, she wanted him to resemble a pop star.) He just looked like somebody else.

The engine still going, the driver considered them in the frame of his window. They were already covered in yellow dust despite the truck that went around spraying water. They looked like a photograph, the patriarch in his coats next to the mother in hers next to the child in pajamas under corduroy pants, hands on a valise, a shoulder, a hand. The valise was spotted with Kamil's blood. Under his pleated trousers, George wore sneakers. They, too, were already covered by a vomit-colored paste of watery dust.

The driver's eye went tic-tic-tic as he regarded them over his flattened nose. "Walk toward the river, not the sea," he said. "The conductors are down there."

George shifted in place. If a mole in the raft conductor's office had tipped off Kamil that his prey was about to flee the country, Kamil had murdered their originally assigned driver to usurp the role. But when? If it had only happened the previous evening, the conductor might not know that he had lost a man because of George and his family, and they might be able to slip through. But if the conductor already knew . . . More money would solve it, but it would take all they had left, if not more. They could also join the back of the line with the other conductor who operated from here, but people without a reservation sometimes waited for weeks, and they'd have to pay the fee for three raft spots all over again. Like children being dropped off at an angry relative's house, they were reluctant to part with the driver.

"You think the conductor hasn't been called?" George said, fishing. "Kamil . . . eliminated their driver."

"Look at this James Bond," the driver said. "What if the conductor himself called Kamil? What if the conductor is the mole?"

"The conductor is unaffiliated," George said. "That much I am sure of. It's bad for business to take sides."

"So you shouldn't have a problem."

"The conductor is going to want to know what happened," Susanna said.

"You think this is a company with secretaries?" the driver said. "Play dumb. It shouldn't be hard for you."

"You, a person with a gun and a knife and the government behind you, you judge us," she said. "I want to know what you would have done in his place." She meant George.

"I would have left this country a long time ago," the driver said. "Only very cruel persons can play the games that are left."

Dina took a step toward the driver and reached into a pocket of her corduroy pants. Susanna had struggled to choose a pair that made them seem neither wealthy nor destitute. It didn't matter, as the dust instantly turned any clothes the same condition and color. To abandon one's known life was to begin to aim more incorrectly with one's worry. A new gust of wind pricked the side of the Peugeot with debris. In any case, they had been neither wealthy nor destitute—almost any pair told the truth.

Dina's hand emerged holding the bread with cheese she had put away earlier in the week. Despite her plan, she had failed to collect anything else. The three adults eyed the food jealously. The bread was so hard Dina's teeth squeaked against it. Through a full mouth, morsels of bread flying at the driver's face, she said: "If you hadn't insulted my parents, I would have given it to you." She turned and skipped away through the sand. The driver giggled and wagged a finger. The finger said, "You watch for that one." He rolled off, the tires softly pressing the sand.

They never learned his name.

* * *

Robert had tried so hard to achieve so little, and here it was, without effort, an undulating blue animal spotted with turquoise and teal. It was like the billiard table at the Sunrise Café, except the felt moved, renewing itself gently at the shoreline wave by wave. Dina held on to the sash of Susanna's quilted jacket. They stood on a small promontory, wind smacking their hair, salt and muck in their noses. The sun here was colder. There was trash all around the shoreline, below a crag of rocks, but it wasn't there if you kept your eyes on the horizon. It was a clear day, but not clear enough to see the other side. The journey was supposed to take three or four hours.

People held on to numbers like these as closely as the little papers listing the family's blood types that everyone carried around in case, today, the shells fell on them. The numbers circumscribed the boundaries of an anxious hope—one hundred kilometers from their city to the coast; four hours by raft to the other side of the war; forty people a raft. George did not participate in the endless incanting of the numbers. It was a point of pride for him, Susanna knew—a mark of his distinction and powers—not to require this information.

They had not seen the sea in five years. They had valued that last holiday so meagerly in view of what was to come. Dina was three. The change in scenery had interfered with her appetite, and Susanna had quarreled with her after Dina pushed away a bowl of pomegranate seeds. Susanna left the hotel room, and groaned as she felt a slick of blood between her legs—had one of her menstrual cycles ever arrived at a convenient moment? Reluctantly, she went back. Walking in, she saw that George had stripped off his white undershirt, dumped the pomegranate seeds in, and was crushing this makeshift cheesecloth between his hairy knuckles, juice trickling through—he didn't want to stain the hotel towels. Dina watched, as transfixed as a child is transfixed. Susanna went into the bathroom and crushed her own stained underclothes in the water. (Those days when the water ran freely!) When she emerged, Dina was gulping juice from a small glass. George's face shone with perspiration and pride.

The intake tents used by the conductors stood on a flat part of the slope down to the river. Behind these were rows of tarpaulins pinned over stakes. If the conductors managed successfully to ferry their cargo across the infernal water, different bodies inhabited these every night. Behind them were the bathroom tents—a series of holes in the ground covered by tarps of their own.

This village, and another like it, was the closest you got to free territory in their country. The rebels and the government had decided that, while they were busy elsewhere, it was more profitable to share levies from these places instead of destroying them to control them outright. Because of this, they were accidental models of shared governance. The conductors' intake tents were surplus vaccine tents the Ministry of Health put up every year by the military airfield in their city, the ones with the radiating red and white stripes that made them look like a circus. Agents for each side wandered the dusty paths, but these generally deferred to the conductors, and stirred from their positions at what passed for the village coffee shop—they had no choice but to use the same one, that being all there was—only to collect said levies or investigate the appearance of a Person of Interest.

In Europe, they had begun talking about closing their water and paying everyone here *not* to send anyone across, in which case the government and the rebels would begin paying the conductors (not to take people) instead of the conductors paying the government and the rebels (for not interfering with them as they took them). It wasn't hard to guess that Europe's patience would run out before the war did. In fact, if Europe was willing to pay the Great Leader to stop people from going across, that ensured the war—which made people want to try, and required the Leader to stop them—would go on for a very long time. George was right. There was no life here for them any longer, only flavors of death with open eyes. Susanna wondered if George had made the mess with Kamil to make the decision no longer avoidable, so they could slip through before the gates closed.

George, Susanna, and Dina stood fixed at the edge of the decline from the promontory to the tents—the parents because they didn't know what to do, the child because her hunger had been sharpened by the cheese sandwich and there was a vendor with chickpeas in lamb broth a hundred meters down the slope. You could see steam coiling out of his pots; the wind brought the scent of lemon and lamb. And he had tea. Sugary tea. With condensed milk. And flatbread. Dina tingled with hunger and looked expectantly at her father's strange face. He nodded yes, grateful to avoid having to choose an intake line a little bit longer.

Their country's unwanted people had reconstituted by social strata in the beaten, wide clearing next to the vendor. The people with money got in line for the food. The people without money organized themselves in small patches in the clearing and began to withdraw from their roped duffels and oilcloth bags what they'd brought to eat from home. Each family had multiple children, though one young man sat by himself, lowering the tip of a long, serrated knife into a glass jar of preserves and clearing it with his tongue. A little shock of hair swept down his forehead. He was alone, and Dina thought shamefacedly of Robert.

In line, the woman behind them attempted to shield three heads from the dust while her husband called unhappy instructions about an order of medical uniforms into his cell phone. Only government doctors wore uniforms now, and even though this man was a refugee—someone who had violated some contract that required him to be burdenless and invisible—the threat of his state affiliation radiated from him like an odor. Little by little the people near him increased their distance, so that there were two lines, with the marked family in an abandoned middle. George and Susanna inched closer to the man ahead of them. He wore a plaid wide-lapeled lounge jacket and the dusty olive trousers of an old police uniform.

He was picking his nose and wiping his fingernail surreptitiously on the lapel.

George felt Susanna's gaze. He looked at her, and she looked away toward the sea.

"Because I made one phone call, Susanna?" he whispered. "Because I gave one bad man to other bad men? When will this end?"

"What a power, by the way," she said. She found the bottle of valerian pills in her purse and snuck two small white dots under her tongue. "But I was thinking about your face."

His hand went to his mouth. "Yes, it feels strange," he said with conciliation.

His acknowledgment disabled her desire to argue. Remarkably, she reflected, the murder she had witnessed earlier that day was her first. In four years, she had heard about many, and imagined many more. She lived in a land of death. But that was the first she had witnessed. Somehow, she felt, it should have degraded her more. Even the sea before her was becoming ordinary. At first, the war had sharpened their longing for things, but after flickering harder, the candle sputtered and went dead. Now, nothing felt like anything.

"How did he know the blind students were cheating?" she said. "You said he turned in blind students."

"Who?" George said distractedly. His face showed distaste. It was the expression—the lips puckered, almost embarrassed—he wore when he was confronted by a job poorly done. The driver's? Someone else's? But it was himself George was rebuking, for not obtaining false identifications for all of them. George had relished his distinction in not having to prepare. Well, he didn't prepare. He had been complacent.

"Kamil, Kamil," she said. "The blind students. You said."

"Oh," he said. George didn't think the conductor could order the harm of a woman or child. As for himself, he imagined being summoned from their tent that evening, his throat cut behind the latrines while the camp shat out lamb broth and chickpeas, his body lowered into a special pit everyone knew not to go near.

"Kamil's brother is blind," George said. "He was the one in charge of the cheating."

"He turned in his own brother?"

They had sixty-five thousand left after the sixty they had given the driver, and all the tolls on the way. Each raft spot cost twenty thousand, so if they went with the other conductor, that would leave them with five thousand. Not even enough to persuade a man to turn his car around so you could go get your letters. George looked to see that the plastic bag was where he left it, by the valise in the sand.

"He knew it by the color of the printer paper," George said to Susanna. "The family is well-off. They had a braille printer at home. The paper was different from the cheap stock at the university. Kamil must have been suspicious—he came to the blind classroom during the exam because he said his brother had forgotten a medicine. And every one of them was holding paper like what their printer used at home, the correct answers already punched in. I don't know how they got the questions ahead of time."

Numbly, she evaluated this. "They always lie to get their truth."

"What truth? Blind teenagers—they just wanted to make the grade."

"I mean Kamil. Spying on his brother, the ruse with the medicine. The deception is always innocent if it's theirs."

George nodded absentmindedly. These people—conductors, rebels, administrators, government men, Fares the barber, they were all the same man, the man with the power—had made misery of their lives for four years. As if life had been a candy before that. And the ordinary people, like dogs who remember the beating, knew what to do once someone got it in mind to start shooting again. They began the great proud ritual of doing with less, then less, then virtually nothing. History had given them regular practice. George's mistake had been to think that he was exempt from this formula.

First, they gave up the seaside; then fish; then, temporarily, school for the children. It was all right, perfectly all right—a man two buildings over knew some algebra, and his sister had studied French for two years. In times of duress, the intellectuals were especially useful. Then, after the street of tailors was destroyed in a bombing, the shirts got mended with fine-grained sandpaper. Then it was on to the men whose cars no longer started, even after the shoe vendor's savant son had looked at them. Because even though the original French part was copied in China, the Chinese cargo ships could not get through because the French had installed a blockade. The French would not remove the Great Leader because you couldn't do that to sovereign countries, but their great historic conscience would not let them do nothing, so they inflicted maximal damage for minimal use by blockading the things that ordinary people needed. You could be sure the Great Leader was not bicycling to the places he needed to go.

And then you had to give them your moustache.

George was tired. He had slept two hours sitting upright on a divan with his arms across his chest, and then a little bit in the car. His head was ringing with pain. If he got a blade to the throat in the evening, he would offer them the last of the money. But he wasn't giving it up just in case. They had taken enough. They would go to the conductor they'd signed with already.

Two men in the clearing had started an argument—a child of the first had been playing carelessly, kicking sand at the other family's meal. They shouted at each other with the weary obligation of insulted pride while the families ate in silent embarrassment. These village people were primitive. And now George was among them.

"George, we have to decide," Susanna said. "We have cost them a life. We are safer with the other conductor."

"The other conductor will take the rest of our money," George said.

"Damn the money. Once you make it to the other side, they take care of you. They give you a stipend. I can make a lot from a little."

"You know all these details?"

"I do. People talk."

"With the other conductor, we start from the end of the line. How long do we wait here until we get a spot?"

"You aren't worried to go to a man whose employee was killed because of us?"

"So, what, they will kill us in return?" he said. "We had nothing to do with it—they have to understand that. They want to reject us, anyway? So be it, then we can go to the other conductor. There is always time to give another man sixty thousand."

Susanna willed herself to disagree, but couldn't bring forth whatever it took. Placing an envelope with cash in her hands as she boarded the bus to Dostat, her father had said: "If you can solve a problem with money, it isn't a problem." He took her cheeks in his hands—she was stunned, for he had rarely touched her. He seemed to be framing her for a mental photograph. He rubbed her skin with a knuckle, then placed his palm on the top of her head, where her hair parted before it became a braid at the nape of her neck. In this way measured for his memory, she was released to ascend the steps of her new life.

"What are you talking about?" Dina said from a patch of sand. She drew in it with a stick.

"Nothing, my heart," George said. He tried to touch Dina's hair, but she squirmed away. He thought she was embarrassed by her own haircutting folly, but she was embarrassed by his. She went back to beating the sand. The man on the phone behind them said, "If you don't do as I say, then, God help me, I will make sure you are in a condition to require someone in those uniforms to minister to you."

"Your father was not always a scholar in loafers, you know," George said, trying to distract Dina. He tapped together the toes of his mustard-colored sneakers. "When your father was in school, he supported himself as a laborer. He could put a roof on a building in one week. Sometimes we had lunch from a cart just like this. I used to slurp just like this, standing."

"So you are back where you started," Dina said matter-of-factly.

The man ahead of them laughed, concealing his nose-picking finger as he turned to face them. "You do not need spice in the lamb, sir," he said. "Here is natural spice," meaning Dina. He bowed slightly, considering the family. "You have beautiful daughters."

George's weak smile went away. Understanding his mistake, the man covered his heart in embarrassment. "A blind man's missile," he said.

"That is what my wife says. I fire, and always the wrong place. Please forgive me. I didn't understand."

George forced open the corners of his mouth in another half smile. That this had happened so rarely despite the visible difference in ages between him and Susanna was a signal of how circumscribed their lives had become. Anyone they could encounter already knew.

"Your meal will be my gift," the man said, pointing to the vendor.

"That's not necessary," George said.

"Please allow me."

"It's all right," George said. "It's all right."

"God will look after you on your journey," the man said. "Tell me, does anyone in your family speak English?"

George hesitated, then indicated Susanna. When George was in college, it was still French. Dina spoke some English, too, another private world between her and Susanna.

"Your wife must volunteer to become an interpreter," the man said. "They need the interpreters over there."

"May we have the problem of choosing what job to apply for because we are already there," George said.

"Yes, you waited too long. It used to be like taking the *Titanic* ship to London—they awaited us with flowers. Their boats waited at the edge of their waters. But it's like that fairy tale about the tall man who decides he doesn't want to be tall anymore. One day, they realized they weren't as generous as they thought. They felt very bad about it! What is your skill, please?"

"Professor," George said with dignity.

"No value," the man said. Seeing George's face fall, he rushed to add, "Only because without English." George was embarrassed to have been caught feeling embarrassed—his emotions were transparent without a moustache to cover them. For some reason, he thought of the billboard advertisement that collected stray fire outside their apartment building. For four years, it had advertised the same face cream.

"I am an engineer," Susanna said.

"She was an engineering student for one year," George corrected her.

"That's it," the man said to Susanna, ignoring George. "Begin as interpreter. Get the trust. Then inform them of this skill. They will put you in a training program."

"You have never worked as an engineer," George insisted.

"So? There's a training program," Susanna said.

"And this one will be an artist?" the man said, indicating Dina. She had drawn mountains, and squiggly waves, and a sun. An apartment building stood in the water.

The man collected a flatbread smeared with honey and a cup of dried figs, and took out a crumpled wad of bills from his trouser pocket. George winced, and Susanna winced knowing George would—for her husband, to touch food with a hand that had touched money was a defilement. George was shored up by the vendor's long glance at the same—the vendor wore a plastic glove on his left hand, for the bills and coins he received.

After a blessing over the food, the old man leaned down to the artist, and extended a fig. "This is for you, small one," he said. "You have to keep strong." Dina screwed up her face—his fingers were yellow and cracked, and the joints were not healthy. "Dina," Susanna admonished her. The man waved his hand to say it was all right and straightened himself with strain. He was like a bent derrick that had found no oil. "I will wait until you have your food," he said to George. "And then I will tell you something."

George looked at him doubtfully, but after he had settled Dina and Susanna on the valise with their broths, he stepped over to the old man. They watched the men in the circle, who had run out of insults but felt obliged to continue, saying the same things over and over.

"God willing, you will reach your destination," the old man said, rolling the dried fig between his weak teeth. "But when you get near their water, a little powerboat will appear. The conductor will leave you."

"What do you mean leave us?" George said. "How are we to get to shore?"

"The Europeans are becoming unhappy. They're still taking people in, but they are looking for ways to make people here think again. The person driving your boat, they arrest him. It happened for the first time only last week. Maybe it's temporary, but I doubt it."

"I still don't understand."

"Do you know how to pilot a raft?"

"Of course not."

"Good. Don't touch those controls. Because the Europeans will charge you as the driver."

"And what happens to everyone in the raft after the conductor has gone?"

"If you float toward shore, you are accepted. If you float backward . . . You have a beautiful family, I do not wish to concern you."

"Just say it, please."

"Last week, one boat didn't return. The conductor even went out again to look for them, but no one knows where they've drifted."

"Why are you telling me this?"

"Nothing. I insulted your family, I have a debt. Trust me, usually, I keep silent. This is an unhappy place. It's best to keep silent. Keep your family close, and keep silent."

"How do you know all this?" George said.

"I patch the boats," the man said. "Myself and it was one other, but his mother is ill, so now it's only myself. It's good work. Rafts are easy." He thought about it. "I'm an old man. Old men see everything, but no one sees them."

"What did he say?" Susanna said when George returned.

George descended heavily onto the valise, raising a plume of dust. Dina had choked down some broth and already vacated her spot. The broth was lean but flavorful, the lamb not too fatty and the chickpeas crisp despite their time in the broth. George swiped liquid from his lip with the back of his hand—what the moustache had used to do.

George was deciding whether to answer his wife truthfully when the young man with the long serrated knife cast away his cigarette and shouted that his eardrums were on the verge of rupture from the bickering men. He cursed them both, and, stepping between them, said, "When both men are right, there is only one way to settle the conflict. The food of the wives." The down-swept shell of his hair bounced a little as he kneeled before one of the spouses and lifted a flatbread smeared with eggplant and stewed tomatoes. From the other he took a piece of chicken fried in a crust. They did not resist, perhaps owing to his confidence. Some people permitted themselves to laugh. He turned back to the men: "Now each of you eat from the other kitchen."

And like that, it was over. A man would insult another man, but not his wife, and certainly not her kitchen. But the men also could not permit themselves to participate. Gratefully, they grumbled away to their places. Which left the young man holding a varied and appetizing meal. Which surely suited him after a lunch of nothing more than preserves. He was clever.

But then, one of the men changed his mind and began to yell at the young man with the knife. Unwilling to be outdone, the second man joined him. The young man had succeeded in restoring their amity but at the cost of a new shared target. But it was altogether unbearable to listen to more of the discord. George was startled by his wife's voice: "Savages! My head will break if you speak for one minute more. Young man, leave them immediately. Come here. You will eat with us." George looked skeptically at Susanna, but she ignored him. And now the argument really was over. The men would not argue with a city woman. All this caused even Dina to return her attention from her paysage in the sand.

When he came closer and introduced himself—Yacoub—Susanna and George understood the real reason why no one had resisted his initial confiscation of food—he was dominant-sect. If so, what was his place here? He had a gaunt face with weary eyes, a romantic effect undone by a hesitant moustache, which he seemed to encourage with great concern and moderate success. His skin was so dark from the sun it was gray. Under a faded sweatshirt, he wore only a T-shirt with a frayed neck and some kind of charm on a leather thong. The jar of jam distended the back pocket of his jeans.

Susanna couldn't insult him by offering to purchase him food, so she opened the valise and withdrew cucumbers, radishes, and dough pastries with beef she was saving for points in the journey where there wasn't a lamb vendor. Susanna and George had eaten, but they couldn't insult the young man by making it obvious that only he was hungry. They would pretend to be hungry, too. Two meals gone for no reason, George thought, but he kept his tongue.

"God bless your hands," Yacoub said as he took the entire pastry in his mouth, remembered his manners, and withdrew enough to make it seem like he'd only wanted a corner.

"The blessed hands must be your mother's," Susanna ventured, "if you took only her preserves on your trip." Susanna bowed her head, meaning to offer vague deference to a dominant-sect person. She was out of practice communicating with anyone to whom she wasn't related. "May you have an easy journey," she said.

"Oh, to kiss my mother's hand now," he said.

Susanna apologized, thinking that she had invoked a deceased person.

"No, no, it's not that," he said.

"Let's eat then, and cast aside our worries for the duration of the meal, at least," Susanna said, speaking again with formality.

"I had to leave quickly," Yacoub said through a full mouth. "I had bread, too. I ate it."

When he was nearly finished, he asked Dina for her drawing stick. Dina's seascape acquired dolphins, whales, and stingrays—things Dina had never seen but understood to be fish.

"Tell me, how does a whale scratch his itch, do you know?" Yacoub said, crunching a radish. Dina shook her head. He extended his knife to George, so George would have no doubts as he played with his daughter. Then he leaped backward as if the sand beneath him were water, raising a giant fog of dust and a chorus of objection from Susanna and George, though Dina laughed loudly. It was startling to hear.

The young man itched himself all over, causing Dina to laugh again. Before long, the whale had transformed into a shark, which was after the young girl with the stick.

"Their bodies are made of rubber," George remarked.

"I've forgotten what other people are like," Susanna said. "You had the university, at least."

"Yes, boys like him . . ." George started. He stopped because his eyes fell on Susanna's hand. Susanna snatched it away.

"Let me see it," he demanded.

"Sorry," she said, revealing her hand. She pulled the hex nut from her finger.

"Where is your wedding ring?"

"I traded it."

"You gave away your wedding ring?"

"I tried to use the handbag your parents gave me. He was going to take it, but then he saw my ring. He wanted that instead."

"And what did you get for it?"

"Things for us," she said.

"What things?"

"They're in the suitcase," she said. Since the driver had given them back, she was telling the truth, though she knew she would have lied if he hadn't. As she distributed the returned items into the suitcase, she had smelled the sunflower-seed dust that covered his fingertips while he went through the contents.

George turned away and shook his head. "Your wedding ring . . ."

"I'm sorry," she said. "It was unplanned, or I would have asked you."

"But why not tell me? Instead of this deceit. I am not a child."

"Shall I say the same to you?"

"I see," he said.

* * *

They stood in line for the conductor they'd paid, practicing unpracticed-seeming oblivion. The line moved through open terrain battered by wind off the water, so sometimes they shivered in the heat, a relief as they stood for hours. With the exception of a military airplane that, at one point, strafed the air at an uncomfortably low altitude, the line seemed like a line anywhere, including the search for weapons at the entrance. Men were searched openly, by a bald, heavyset man in house slippers, and women were brought to a tent off to the side, operated by a sweating woman in a dirty apron who loudly yelled for the women to come forth even though they stood directly before her. To the right of the women's inspection tent, another woman, old and stooped, bent over a raised garden bed, from which herbs and flowers tried to struggle forth. It was a family, Susanna realized—the old woman was the man's mother. The conductor had collected them from some nearby village, and given them decision-making power they now rushed to abuse before it was taken away. The dome-headed husband spun the men under his inspection like tops, and his wife waved her hand impatiently at the women as if they were deaf children who had ignored earlier commands. Only the old woman seemed uninterested, swatting the plants with stiff hands like mitts.

In the waiting line, the supplicants argued about the promises the fishing website had made about water conditions tomorrow; some men insisted on the worst while others the best. The women talked about prices, staples that had disappeared, and the substitutions they had contrived, though they avoided discussing the cause. The children shrieked, collapsing in the dust. You could tell the city children, relieved or alarmed to be away from city congestion and shelling, because they were overly hesitant or overly eager.

The landscape was settling into an afternoon's doze. The women whose families had already received their confirmations floated toward the river with washing, even though the water was soiled by feces. The women already there bent over the water and straightened like crows dipping their beaks. There were people who stayed here for days, even weeks—Susanna felt she was watching a city arise from the dust. She tried to resist another infusion of valerian root and blessed Yacoub for taking Dina for a walk by the water. The two of them had left in a happy bubble of noise. They already had some private language together.

Susanna tried to imagine the intake proceeding without problems. But she felt only bitterness—even the sight of that old woman's pathetically mangled flowers brought only grief. Before Susanna's birthday two years earlier—perhaps it was three—George had found flowers, a convoluted undertaking involving someone's relative, more than a week of waiting, and a cost George refused to divulge. Having concealed the flowers in a small rug he had purchased for the purpose—it wouldn't do for him to be seen with something so hard to procure, though how typical of George to conceal them in an even richer luxury—George was about to head home, excitement tearing at his chest, when he was pulled aside by Azze, the old mathematician, favorably disposed to minority-sect people despite, or perhaps because of, the fact that his brother was an interrogator in the Interior Ministry. Azze wheezed into George's ear that the Soudanes had been murdered in their apartment. George's face was sweaty and gray when Susanna answered the door. He set the rug on the hallway table, where it unfurled as they whispered in the living room. The flowers did not get a vase till the next morning, by when most had died in the heat.

* * *

The village tapered to a narrow bay between two promontories, the pebbly beach already in shadow. Yacoub was showing Dina how to flick pebbles so that they skipped across the water, but the rocks only fell from her fingers. Instead of being irritated, she laughed.

"But listen," she said, growing serious. "I have an important question. You must tell me the truth."

Yacoub straightened, his twist of hair bouncing like a spring, wanting to be serious for her. "I am ready," he said.

She considered the bluish-gray mass behind him, its periodic shush and swell. It made her think of Susanna rocking her when Dina's forehead was hot. "Do you have to get married?" Dina said finally.

Yacoub laughed, then stopped because he wanted to respect her question. He crouched so their eyes were at the same level.

"Yes," he said. "Only unhappy people don't have a family." He flicked a stone at the water.

"There are so many people, however," she said. "How do you know you have chosen correctly?"

"Anyone who asks this question will choose incorrectly. You must not think about it. And then you will know. Not for a while, of course."

"That makes no sense," she said.

"Exactly," he said, nodding. "It's like believing in God. It's the opposite of one plus one."

She considered this. It made no more sense than his previous explanation, but she decided not to press. "All right. One more question."

"But it's my turn," he said teasingly.

"Fine, quickly."

"I was teasing you, I don't have a question."

She looked disappointed.

He corrected himself: "Okay. Why are you thinking about husbands?"

"I want to be prepared. What if I have met him already, but I wasn't paying attention?"

"You are doing one plus one."

"Fine. It's my turn. People who are married, but they are angry. How do you fix it?"

He didn't laugh this time. He poked a stick between several pebbles. His head was resting on his knee.

"I will give you a good solution," he said. "My parents quarreled very badly once. It had to do with my brother. He was in the army. One of them thought he must do his duty and serve, and the other thought he should run away, hide. It went on for several days. My mother made no meals. My father did not work. They sat in the kitchen and smoked in different directions. They had no choice but to sit at the same table because we had only one table. They shared a lighter and the cigarettes. They even poured each other coffee. But when they left this trance, they remembered they were angry with each other. I couldn't put up with it anymore. I was hungry! Cheese with bread three times a day is not fun for a boy. So I sat down between them. I took my father's hand with one hand, and my mother's hand with the other. Like this." He extended his hands, as if he planned to take flight.

"We sat like that for a long time. Then my mother switched hands so that she was holding me with the far hand instead of the near. My father did the same. And their hands that were free went around my back and joined. And then each of them put a head on my shoulder. Different head, different shoulder. Nothing changed, you know. One of them had to win. And the other one got to be right. My brother left and . . . didn't come back." He wiggled stones with his stick. "So I don't know. Why are you asking about this?"

"I'm not sure," she said. "There was this wrestling match earlier that . . . I think someone got hurt. And I cut my hair, but only because—"

They heard their names from the promontory above the shoreline. George was waving them back.

"I don't think I understand," Yacoub said.

"But something is making them mad at each other, so."

They heard their names again.

"We should go, curious Dina," Yacoub said. "It's okay not to understand. That is a life condition for me." That got a laugh out of her, which pleased him.

As they walked back, Dina wove a hand inside Yacoub's, perhaps to practice. Yacoub checked George's expression to make sure this didn't disturb him, but George's mind was elsewhere. When they caught up to him, Yacoub flipped Dina onto his shoulders. From Susanna, they received a distracted smile. Her eyes were fixed on the line. Pretending to look for a handkerchief, Susanna withdrew a pill of valerian root and was about to lay it under her tongue when Dina yanked her sleeve, causing her to drop it in the sand.

"Dina!" she yelled, and Dina shrank away. Yacoub smiled with embarrassment at having witnessed Susanna's impatience.

"I only wanted to know how much longer," Dina said, crashing to a seat in the dirt. People around them began to look.

"Let me, madame," Yacoub said. "I can distract this one."

"I want to go to the bathroom," Dina said. Susanna didn't believe her, thinking that Dina was saying so only to inconvenience her mother.

"I'm sorry," Susanna made herself say. "I'll be glad to step away from this line." How many times had she apologized since the previous night? Her eyes searched for the white pill in the sand. It wasn't the last, but the supply wasn't infinite, not at the rate of consumption.

After the women left, George and Yacoub, unprepared to be alone, stood awkwardly, each looking for something to say. Yacoub rubbed the leather necklace around his neck.

"Do you know about whales, then?" George finally said.

Yacoub bounced his curls eagerly, grateful for the overture. "Only on YouTube, sir. For four years, I have worked right next to the water—but I have never been on the water."

"What was your profession?"

"The shipyard on the coast. A welder."

"Why would you run from something like that?" George said. "That's good work. The area's safe. You're—"

Yacoub nodded. "Dominant, yes."

"But you're with the rebels?" George said skeptically. "No, not you. A brother?"

"Nothing like that . . ." Yacoub said. They had come to a crossing place. One feared to ask another's story, both because one might not have enough room in one's heart for the weight of the story—so all one might do is nod numbly in a way that only caused insult—and because it was better to not be involved. Respectfully, Yacoub waited for the signal from George. In just several sentences, they had arrived here, but one was never more than several sentences away.

"Tell me, tell me," George said.

"It's a stupid story," Yacoub said with relief.

George waited.

"The director of my department has a daughter, God curse her,"

Yacoub said. "She came to visit him once. She saw me. She asked for my phone number. I didn't know what to do."

"She asked you?" George said. "You would respond to someone like that?"

"It's different than it was in your time," the young man said. "I don't mean insult."

"My time was better," George said.

"It's only because she went to school in Holland," Yacoub said. "Or Belgium, maybe. However, if I give her the mobile number—"

"You will have problems if the father finds out," George said, "because you are only a welder."

"If I don't give it—"

"It will be an insult, and she will tell her father—"

"That I stared at her, or made a bad comment, exactly."

"So what happened?"

"On my head, both things happened. I gave the number, and he found out. He gave me a warning. I wrote her and said we have to stop writing messages. But she wouldn't stop. She kept writing me. 'Guess what I am doing now,' or 'I am in the park, and I see a boy and girl holding hands,' things like that. So I stopped answering. She became angry. She said, 'If you don't answer, I will tell my father you tried to kiss me.' Now what do I do? A day went by, maybe two days. Finally, I wrote her. 'Please, miss, why would such a nice girl do that?'

"That night, my phone buzzed. I always turn off the buzzer because my mother has breathing problems, so she sleeps poorly. We are all in one room, so. But this night, I forgot to make it silent. One night in a hundred. It's proof there is a God. The phone buzzed. It only said: 'Too late. You have one hour.' So I kissed my mother and father—my father was so confused when he woke, he thought my mother had an attack—and I took the bread that was on the table, and the knife that was in the bread, and my father ran after me with the—the . . ." He stopped and joined his thumbs at the sides of his nose. Courteously, George looked away. "With the jam,"

Yacoub went on. "He had tears in his eyes, but in the house, he had been very serious, very prepared. 'Take your sweatshirt, running shoes will be better, take the alley that flooded, they are less likely to go that way . . .' He was prepared in his head."

"And your parents . . ." George started and trailed off. He didn't know how to ask it.

"They are elderly people. They had two children early and thought they were finished. And then twenty years later, I appeared. My sister died as a little child, and my brother was killed in army service. Now I am older than even he was when he died. I told my parents, when the director's men came, to tell the truth—I had gone to the raft. I am not that important. He wanted me gone from her life, and now I am farther gone even than that. Between that and my parents' age, I think they will leave them alone."

In the distance, they watched Susanna and Dina, hand in hand, pause near the old woman by the soil beds. The woman tore something from a clump and held it to Dina's nose. Dina sniffed earnestly.

"Don't tell them this story," George said.

"Of course, sir," he said.

And then George laid a hand on Yacoub's shoulder in what he hoped felt like a fatherly gesture—because the idea was already forming in his head.

* * *

Dina was sniffing rosemary.

"I don't smell anything," she declared.

"Dina," Susanna chided. Her daughter still hadn't learned how to say the things other people wanted to hear.

The old woman coughed and said something they couldn't decipher. There was something wrong with her voice. She had a sun-beaten face. Wrinkles webbed out from the little chips of gray ice through which she studied Susanna and Dina.

"What's wrong with your voice?" Dina said.

"Dina!" Susanna said, yanking Dina away. "Forgive us, madame. My daughter has no manners today."

The woman coughed again, and they could nearly see the phlegm rising inside her. She spat—not exactly at them, but not away from them, either. "There is vermin throughout the soil," she said in the garbled voice. The word had lost its original meaning because their Leader used it so often now. "You have to flush the vermin," she said, just like he did.

Susanna stiffened. She was about to move toward the bathrooms when the woman turned to Dina. "There is a checkpoint here," she gargled, pointing at her throat. "There is a creature with wings at the checkpoint, always silent—he won't allow noise. And when the wrong people arrive, he screams at them. They run, and everything is mayhem. That's the noise that you hear." Out of that depleted face, the words came like the crackle of a faulty radio.

For once, Dina didn't know what to say. Susanna remained awkwardly in place. She didn't wish to disrespect the woman by walking away, but she didn't need her daughter to listen to these dark village imaginings. Helped by Yacoub's appearance, their departure had spurred in Dina mostly excitement. Susanna wanted Dina to stay that way. She would keep feeling the worry if Dina got to keep thinking of it as an adventure.

"My mother grew herbs on the balcony," Dina tried. "But then the gas came. They died."

"That wasn't gas," the woman said. "God must have had a poor meal."

Dina thought of Robert, who explained everything this way: Rain was God weeping. His parents argued because some item was mislaid by one of God's agents. When these agents failed at their tasks, the grit of God's anger got in the oil that made things work properly: machines, plants, parents.

The woman pointed to a patch of pink five-petaled flowers. "This flower is stronger than all of us," she said. "It doesn't need water." Susanna thought of the woman who came to clean after her mother once a week. She always put flowers in a chipped vase, until her mother smashed the vase and tried to cut her neck with one of the pieces. "Smell it," the woman graveled at Dina, but Dina stepped behind a flap of Susanna's jacket. Susanna pushed Dina forward. Reluctantly, Dina stuck her nose in the petals.

"I don't smell anything," Dina said.

"Smell harder," the woman said. "Then you will poison yourself. The flower is pure poison."

Dina recoiled toward Susanna, who stared at the woman hatefully. The wind whistled between them. Susanna dragged Dina away as the woman followed them with her eyes.

"The little dog is correct," she called after them. "The flowers have no scent this year."

* * *

As their turn approached, Susanna wanted to tell George about the old woman—Susanna had told herself she was harmless, but she didn't know whether to trust her judgment. But he would take her shoulders and tell her it was nerves, to hold on—they were almost through. Susanna stood and trembled, tears like grapes at the edges of her eyes, her smiles less persuasive each time that she tried.

When their turn came, Susanna's heart fell though, somewhere, she had known this was going to happen. The man who inspected men batted the air with his fat fingers and George stepped forward. Clutching Dina's hand, Susanna did the same, hoping to preempt the impatient summons of his wife. But then the old woman turned from her place by the plants and barked at the wife. The wife, confronted by a displeasure greater than her own, lowered her head and stepped out of the way. Looking at Susanna, the old woman pointed at the sand under her feet. Susanna tried to look at her with a collaborative expression, then a pleading one, then gave up and moved forward.

Dina pulled Susanna's hand. "I don't want to go," she said. "Let's not go."

Susanna crouched before Dina. "Now, my heart," she said, trying to control her voice. "She's a strange one, isn't she. Like a dragon in a fairy tale. But we have to be strong. It will be over quickly. I will not let harm come to you. In and out, okay?" Dina kept squeezing her mother's hand in a misplaced variation on the remedy proposed by Yacoub; perhaps you had to have more than one person's hand. At last, resentfully, Dina nodded. The old woman raised the tarp covering the inspection alcove, and they stepped inside. It was an empty patch of dirt with a low table and two stakes that held up the tarp.

"Now, Dina, my love," Susanna said loudly once they were inside. "Let's let this kind woman do what she must." Dina shrugged and stuck out her hands like a suspect. The woman let the tent flap fall and moved heavily toward them. In the semi-enclosed space, they could smell her as they could not outside: Something sour, like lentils left out too long. She crouched with a startling agility, like a woman who planned to give birth, and put her dry, cracked hands over Dina's ankles. Two fingers slipped inside the hem of the socks.

"Ow," Dina yelped.

"Dina, love," Susanna said and put a finger to her lips.

"Her hands are cold," Dina said.

"So, you can say it to her. 'I'm sorry, madame, your hands are cold.'"

Dina stared at her mother and refused to say it. Susanna stared at Dina. "Cold," was all Dina would concede. The woman didn't respond, only wheezed from somewhere deep in her throat. They smelled the rot of her mouth. The joints stuck out like ball bearings and the hands were as abrasive as the grit they put in your mouth at the dentist, so Susanna noticed only now that the fingers didn't have nails. Every nail was gone. Susanna squeezed her teeth and hoped Dina wouldn't notice.

The fingers moved under the hem of Dina's corduroys. Dina studied the ceiling of the tarp. Finished, one of the old hands reached for the button. "Hey," Dina pushed it away. The hand returned and twisted Dina's ear.

"Ow!" Dina yelled.

"Madame," Susanna begged.

"Inspection," the woman said wetly.

As one hand held the ear, the other unbuttoned the corduroys, and lowered the zipper. The pant flaps fell away. The fingers of the free hand passed around the waist. Then a single bony finger lodged inside the underwear and ran around the band.

"Mama!" Dina shrieked.

"It's not necessary, she's only a girl, please," Susanna said through the film in her eyes.

The woman kept on. Finally, the band of the underwear snapped back in place and the finger emerged. Dina stared at her mother, unable to understand why her mother was not coming to her rescue. The hands moved into Dina's hair. Dina's shoulders jumped and she nearly knocked the woman to the ground.

"Who cut this hair?" the woman said, holding it in her fist until Dina whimpered.

Susanna thought her bowels would abandon her. How powerful the sudden wish to be reunited with a husband she had disdained all day. Finally, the woman let go of Dina. Susanna breathed out and closed her eyes.

A moment later, she felt a rough wooden node at her ankle. The woman was now holding a stick. The node scored the skin between the hem of Susanna's jeans and her sneakers.

"I assure you, madame," Susanna said, struggling to keep her voice even. "You won't find any weapons. Why would we endanger our chances that way? You have our names and our savings."

The end of the stick banged painfully up the leg of the jeans until it arrived at the waist. Dina was sitting in the sand, staring at her shoes. She untied her shoelaces, then tied them.

"Madame," Susanna whispered. "Not in front of my daughter. Please."

"Open the button. The button and the zipper."

"Mada—" Before she could finish, the stick whipped the soft meat of the thigh. Susanna tried to lick back her tears. She opened the button and lowered the zipper.

The serrated mouth of the stick hunted around Susanna's waist, first over the band of the underwear, then against bare skin, scoring the skin.

When that was over, the stick poked roughly, through the underwear, at the vagina. Susanna yelped. She closed her eyes and held her lips together. A tear plumped down her face. Blocked by the woman, she was half-visible to Dina. She wanted her daughter to keep looking down.

The woman kept poking the stick against the vagina. When Susanna unsealed her eyes, she saw her daughter looking up at her with dismay. Finally, it stopped. "Get dressed before your husband sees," the woman sputtered. She moved toward the flap and flung it open so the undressed woman inside was visible to anyone who looked. She kept the flap open as Susanna buttoned herself and dried her eyes. As she was stepping out, Susanna made herself come close to the woman's rotten face, and, through the mucus in her throat, said, "I have a pad in my underwear. It's that time. I felt nothing."

Outside, George ran toward them. What had taken so long? Susanna had held up the line; the entire operation had stalled. Susanna was grateful George didn't notice her expression. But when Yacoub's eyes crossed hers, his face, otherwise so ready for merriment, faltered with dark recognition of a person at the mercy of others.

* * *

When they entered the conductor's tent, George holding the valise and Susanna holding Dina, they became enshrouded in clove cigarette smoke so thick it wove through the air like a separate being. In the middle of the tent, a man at a desk ashed his cigarette over the ground though there was a glass ashtray under his wrist. By the other hand was a glass of tea, a small dish of dried fruit, and the rudiments of his task, which was as administrative today as it would not be tomorrow: a computer, a cashbox, cables, and wires. Over his head, a single lightbulb reached down like a finger. In the corner, an errand boy sat in the sand picking his feet.

George had prayed it wouldn't be a young man, a man of impulse, and in this he was gratified. The man at the desk was in his middle forties, as lean as George was not, with tea-colored skin and an aura of dark hair around a bearded face. Around his neck was a necklace strung with what looked like soda-can tabs. Otherwise he wore no jewelry, had no markings.

The man took a sip of his tea, sighed, and placed his forehead against his gathered thumbs as the smoke climbed through his hair. As you drew closer, the scent grew more concentrated, as if his skin and clothing were bleached in it.

"This is the job of cold tea," he said finally. "Your tea gets cold, you send the boy out for fresh, and by the time you raise it to your lips, hours have passed, and it is cold once more. Is it four o'clock?" He snapped his fingers at the boy. "How many teas have you brought?"

The boy looked down. "At your command, sir," he said.

"Bring me a fresh one." The man sprayed the tea across the dirt-packed floor. The boy ran out.

"What troubles you, young lady?" he said, looking at Susanna.

"This is my wife," George rushed to say, to forestall the clumsiness of what had happened earlier.

"Madame," the man clarified.

"Nothing, sir," Susanna said, keeping her gaze on the ground.

"It's a shame for a beautiful woman to feel such worry," he said. "You should not worry. We are here to help." His eyes came back to George. "Name?"

George breathed out and said it.

The index finger went down the handwritten pages. "George, Susanna, and Rina."

George nodded. In the silence, the smoke curled toward the lightbulb.

"Dina," Dina said. "Dina, not Rina."

"I was testing," the man said. "You are awake and your parents are sleeping."

"If you just speak up, sir," Susanna started, and the man's gaze settled on her once more. Standing this close to the man was like filling one's mouth with an ashtray.

"You're right, madame," he said. "My mother always said I had a tender voice. A tender voice for a tender boy."

He turned back to George. "I have been waiting all day to speak with you, sir. What did you do to become so interesting to so many people?"

George's forehead blossomed with sweat.

"Or perhaps it was you, madame," he said, turning to Susanna. "Perhaps you were the person of interest."

"We don't know what you mean, sir," Susanna said. The stale heat of the tent, the cigarette smoke, her sleeplessness, the three overcoats, the weight of Dina's head against her leg, the cursed old woman—Susanna felt near suffocation.

"Don't you?" he said. "Were you driven by the man whom you paid? No, that man's mother has to bury her son."

"We did not pay the driver, sir," she said. "We paid your . . . associate. The man who drove us said he was a replacement. It's not for us to question." Susanna felt George stiffen in his shoes. She was weaving a tale without consulting him.

"The man who drove you," the conductor said. "What did he look like?"

"Like anyone," she said. "Dark hair, beard. We slept most of the way."

"Did he have a stutter?"

"No."

"Did he have a trembling hand?"

"No." Then she added, trying to sweep sand over the tracks: "Maybe?" She owed nothing to the driver, but an accurate description would identify him as a government man.

"Maybe I should leave you here a couple of days until we get to the bottom of it," the conductor said.

"You must do as you see fit," Susanna said. Then, she said: "God will tell you what you need to know. God doesn't lie."

"But people lie," the man said. "In my experience, it's the lying man who rushes to talk about God."

"Sir, we are at your mercy," she said. "But I ask you to release us now. I suffer from headaches, and the cigarette is making me dizzy. That is the discomfort you saw on my face."

The conductor clicked his mouth. "I'm sorry, madame," he said and threw his cigarette behind his shoulder, though it continued to smoke in the sand. He withdrew a yellow walkie-talkie, which crackled to life under his fingers. The nails were long but clean. Without greeting, he spoke instructions into the device.

"The ladies will be shown to their tent," he said. "And the men will finish this business."

"I would like to stay here with my husband, please," Susanna said.

"Susanna, go," George said. "Go to the tent."

With her eyes, she made pleas he didn't understand. "We should stay together," she tried.

"I am not asking, madame," the conductor said. "But you must not worry about what happens here. We will finish the details. You are on the raft tomorrow."

She felt a swell of relief. She heard the tent flap open, and the sound of feet behind her.

"A quiet tent to the back," the conductor called out. "Away from the latrines." He turned back to Susanna. "With my compliments, madame."

Her daughter's head was wobbling toward sleep at her leg. Susanna hoisted Dina into her arms, for her own armor as much as the girl's comfort.

When she turned around, she saw the familiar old wretched face. The old woman swung another flap for Susanna to pass through.

They had been in the conductor's tent for no more than ten minutes, but outside, the encampment felt altered. The bath of cloved nicotine yielded to the scrubby, astringent air of the shore, and the promise of dusk was insinuating itself into the thready, curdled-milk clouds that had been whiting the sky all afternoon. Mostly, however, it was that the settlement—the people who remained in the line; the vendor, who was packing his pots onto a cart attached to a bicycle; Yacoub, who awaited them by the cursed flowers—felt like, indeed, a settlement, a place that she already recognized and had laid its claim to her in some way. Gradually, she realized the old woman was speaking. Susanna tried to listen. She had to ask the old woman to repeat herself, and she forced herself to do it without apology. As they turned toward the tents, Yacoub began to walk toward them.

The wind had picked up and whistled through the old woman's words, but the message was unmistakable, and it descended on Susanna with the cold weight of something impossible slowly revealing itself as her fate. "Tonight . . . ," the ancient woman screeched in her repellent voice. "A visit . . . private . . . tell no one . . . if you wish . . . journey . . . condition." Susanna stopped, setting down Dina, though the old woman continued walking. Her face drained of color. Yacoub caught up.

"Like rubbing yourself with ash from an ashtray," he whispered, and nodded toward the tent. "But they gave me my knife back." He finally noticed Susanna's blank, astounded face. "What happened, madame?" he said. "Look at that little one—she can sleep standing, I bet." Susanna looked down, surprised to find her daughter attached to her leg. She tried to make words come in order to throw Yacoub off. Fortunately, he said, "I'll go get your valise—unless Mr. George will." He waited, but no answer came. She made herself nod, and he ran off.

Susanna tried to move forward toward the wasted crow who stood ten yards ahead. But then she could walk no farther, and stumbled in the sand. There, she began to retch, the bile steaming out of her alongside the broth and the chickpeas and the valerian root and the clove smoke and everything else. It flecked Dina's ugly hair, as Dina grogged awake.

Susanna tried to apologize, but it caused another wave of heaving. Susanna stayed bent over the sticky, wet sand to try to gather herself. The arm she used to support herself shook. If it gave, she would fall into the muck. Dina, awaking slowly to the scene around her, scrambled to her feet and, instead of helping her mother, ran toward the old woman.

"What did you do to her?" she demanded.

The old woman withdrew a pile of little stones from her pocket. "Here," she said. "You can play with these." They were fruit pits, chewed over and freed of most of the meat.

Dina screwed up her face in disgust.

Susanna screamed for Dina to return. Yacoub was rushing back. The people who remained in the line also noticed, but did not step out to help. It was better not to interfere.

"What do you want with my mother?" Dina yelled.

"Your mother will give us the only thing she is good for," the old woman said.

"What are you talking about?"

"It's not your business."

Dina dug into the pocket of her corduroys and drew out her own pile, untouched since the previous afternoon, which felt many afternoons ago. "I will give you five thousand if you leave her alone." As soon as she said it, Dina berated herself for not starting with three.

The laugh came out of the old woman like a saw on stone. "Like a whore in a bazaar, you bargain," she said. "You people are worse than gypsies and Jews."

"Your voice is not because of that silent dragon at the checkpoint," Dina said. "It's God's displeasure. You are damned. He damned you."

A young body moves more quickly than an old hand, and the slap got only air.

"If poison gas is God farting, your mouth is God's toilet," Dina screamed, backing away. "Your voice is the sound of God shitting."

"Dina!" Her mother's voice came, weak and wet. "What are you saying, Dina, for God's sake."

"Why are you throwing up?" she yelled at her mother. "What did they do to you?"

"It's the sand. Hard to—to breathe." Susanna tried to wipe her mouth. She felt Yacoub's hands under her arms. As they hobbled to the tent, the old wraith advancing ahead of them in the twilight, Susanna told Yacoub that she had woman's troubles, and together with the smoke, it had caused her to become light-headed, and could Yacoub stay until George came, and if Dina became restless, he could give her *Uncle Neem's Fairy Tales*. Without waiting for an answer, Susanna put six white pills under her tongue, fell onto a cot in their tent, and turned toward the blue aid-agency tarp that constituted the new boundary of her world.

* * *

"May God bless you," George said to the old woman as she showed him his tent. "Three cots is a luxury, we understand that." They were down thirty thousand in exchange for the life they had indirectly claimed, but George felt proud for having negotiated it down from forty thousand and it was still better than what they would have had to pay the other conductor. His gamble had paid off. He was eager to report this to Susanna, also that the soda-can tabs on the man's necklace corresponded to the successful crossings he'd made—seventy-four in one year.

Outside the tent, Yacoub was stoking a small fire in a ring of chipped, uneven stones. Dina was inside, resentfully reading *Uncle Neem*. Yacoub had pressed it into her hands in a pleading way—if she refused, the failure was his.

"I don't know if I am light-headed from those cigarettes or my relief that we're through," George said.

"It was like rubbing your face in the ash of a thousand cigarettes," Yacoub said. He coughed. "Madame isn't feeling well."

"What is it?" George said.

Yacoub looked down and worried the charm around his neck. It looked like a miniature encasement, probably with a photo inside.

"I understand," George said. "Don't be embarrassed. Once a month, it's as if a death has found our home. God forbid. It's all right, let's let her rest. I wanted to speak to you about something, in any case. We'll set up the food. You have convinced the fire, I see."

When they sat down, George poured small thimbles from a tiny bottle of brandy he had stashed in the luggage. He tried to think of a way to begin. Yacoub poked the fire to no purpose.

"You're thinking of your family," George said.

"I think I have made a mistake," Yacoub said.

"Allow me to listen."

The young man nudged the fire with his stick. "I took all the money my parents ever collected. Everything they ever saved, sixty years—I took it.

We don't have family anywhere—we had one cousin, and he took a boat like this one. I already gave the conductor the money, of course. But they will give half of it back if you change your mind."

"So you will stay here? Where will you go?"

"The other side of the country. The Triangle. It's far enough. Just until things die down. Or maybe the conductor will let me work to get back the first half of the money. I can fix boats. If so, I'll stay here awhile."

"My wife's family is from the Triangle," George said. "You don't want to go there. And you don't want to wait for this war to die down, or you will wait a long time. If you make it across, you might be able to bring your parents there. Isn't that better?"

"Why would they want two elderly people?"

"It's called family reunification," George lied. "It's a big principle in their human rights. Once one person makes it over and receives asylum, the rest of the family is just a technicality. Immediate family only, of course. It's like—I am sure you've heard that if you have a child on their soil, that child is their citizen."

"No, I didn't know that," Yacoub said.

"At the university, it's spoken of all the time," George said, hoping that added authority. He beat at his clothes with his palms. "It's as if I am still standing next to him and his cigarettes."

Yacoub shook his head. "It's a good advertisement against smoking. They should bring schoolchildren there."

George, whose smiles used to dissipate bushily in the fur under his nose, now felt only the start of an evening chill on his lip. "It's suddenly cold here, isn't it?" he said and put his palms toward the fire. He looked up to check whether it was safe to turn the conversation back to the crossing. "Young man, it's better to be over there with zero thousand than here with ten, twenty, or thirty. There, you can make it back in one month."

Yacoub considered this.

"Besides," George said, "how could we get on without you?"

Yacoub smiled shyly.

George waited for what felt like a sufficient amount of time.

"You said you worked at the shipyard," he said. "Do you know something about these rafts?"

"I assume they're Seahawks. Or the German kind. I can't pronounce the name."

They sat, sipping. George looked inside the tent—Susanna was motionless on the cot.

"Listen," he said, lowering his voice. "Tomorrow, the driver will abandon the boat."

"How can that be?" Yacoub said. "Where?"

"They drive you up to European waters, and then a smaller raft shows up with his friend. And they disappear. I don't know why, but that is what they've started to do. No one on the raft knows. Except you." George checked whether this flattery had achieved its purpose. "The people will panic," he went on. "People are desperate in this kind of moment. It can cause serious problems. So I will begin speaking to everyone—to reassure them, to say there is a plan. And you—you go to the controls. And keep driving it."

"But in what direction?"

"By then, we should see land."

Yacoub thought as the flames of the fire sashed around in his eyes. "The bags people have here look like there is a whole house inside," he said. "I'm sure someone has a compass."

"Don't ask for it now," George said. "Just find out who has one."

Yacoub nodded. He patted the amulet on his chest the way a man pats his back pocket to check for his wallet.

"What do you have there?" George said, trying to build the intimacy. "If it isn't a secret."

"No secret," Yacoub said.

"A photo?" George proposed.

"Not exactly," Yacoub said. He looked up to perform the customary check as to whether intimate disclosure was welcome, but no checking was necessary—George, eager to hasten the connection between them, gazed at the young man with almost a hunger. "When my brother was killed,"

Yacoub said, "he had just written my parents a letter. It was in his pocket, covered in his blood. A man in his unit held on to it—a long time because he couldn't decide if it was something the family wanted. But he brought it finally—a year later. My mother still has it. I cut a very small piece from it. His blood is right next to my blood."

"But you never really knew him," George said.

"Yes, it's foolish of me," Yacoub conceded.

"No, it is twice the devotion then," George said, rushing to correct his infelicity. "Twice the devotion."

Yacoub nodded.

"Without you, we'd be lost," George said, closing one of Yacoub's hands in his own. Yacoub nearly blushed in relief, and George saw that he had succeeded.

* * *

In the tent, a miniature solar panel supplied enough power for a sickly blue light and two phone chargers. George sat heavily on the edge of his cot, thumbing letters. Dina sat against one of his legs, *Uncle Neem* open on her knees. She was thinking about all the people who had used the blanket separating her bum from the ground. Even at distance, she could smell the skin oil and sweat. Susanna's eyes were open. She was lying on her back and sweating.

"Water, my love," George said, unable to tolerate the silence. "I'll get you some water."

Susanna thanked him in the hope of preventing further ministrations.

"If you only remembered to take the headache medicine before the attack sets in . . ." George began.

"Yes, I'll have to remember," Susanna said. Her body felt soiled. She was still wearing the three coats, and she felt the fabric of each on her skin.

"Some people are trying to read," Dina said.

"What's with you, daughter?" George said. "From the moment I came back, you've been strange."

"I also don't feel well," Dina announced. "I want Mama to take care of me. Where's Yacoub?"

"He's out looking for something," George said. Deciding that his daughter wasn't serious, George eased her off his leg and walked out for water. Dina and Susanna remained in silence. Dina paged through the familiar book and saw only the animals and the shapes of the words. George returned from the communal spigot. Susanna had brought cutlery, but not a cup. George said nothing. Plenty of empty bottles littered the ground by the spigot.

"We should try to sleep," George said. "It's just a couple of hours." He looked at Dina. "Dina-heart, your mother doesn't feel well. You can sleep with your papa."

"I want Mama," Dina declared.

Susanna exhaled hoarsely in protest, but Dina insisted.

"All right," Susanna gave in. "I have to sleep on the outside."

"No, I will," Dina said. She climbed in, wrapped her arms around Susanna, and squeezed hard enough for her mother to whimper. A moment later, Dina rose, took the valise, and dragged it toward their cot, turning it into a barricade.

"What's going on?" George said.

"It will make us warmer," Dina said. "Can you put your cot against us here on the free side?" The tarp would block egress on the remaining two sides.

"No," Susanna said. "Dina, no."

"Are you cold, my heart?" George said. "Yes, I can do that. If I snore, you won't have to get up to kick me." His levity succeeded with no one.

They waited for Susanna to give the final authorization. Susanna swallowed painfully. "As you wish," she said. "But to sleep now."

George shuffled paper and plastic for a little while longer, but eventually he quit and the women heard the cot creak under his body. For the second night in a row, Susanna fought sleep as her daughter and husband slept. She could stay in the cot, and take what chances would be theirs in the morning. But the option of the other conductor was out, as George had given away half their money. This was simpler. It would be over quickly. How many men had concluded themselves with her, when she was a graduate student, while she looked on from somewhere above like fowl fleeing the cold? She shuddered, and bit her lip to keep the tears from coming.

She checked her mobile. 12:17. 12:43. 1:01. Plenty of time. Plenty of time. She dozed off and woke with a start, feeling both tormented and fortunate to have missed the hour, but it was only 1:27, and the nap meant she was wide awake for two o'clock. Experimentally, she turned in her place, the cot springs creaking and straining, but no one woke. She waited a moment and sat up. Her hands were shaking. She pressed them against her chest, trying to keep the distress in her chest from becoming a sound. She rose in place on the cot. Nothing, other than a brief honking snore from George. No mint leaves here—she smelled a sour stream of digested lamb. She stood, her head smacking the top of the tent. The structure quaked a little.

The sweat and dust was all over her body. She tasted it under her tongue. Again, she felt as if her bowels would go. In her ears, her breaths sounded crashingly loud. It wasn't humiliation she felt, exactly, not yet. Rather, a nervousness, like what one felt before a significant exam—and shame for honoring the impending encounter with such feeling. But in truth, the feeling had started when they rose from the divan. No, sooner—when she looked at the clock and realized she had forgotten to get Dina. No, sooner—when she was spoken to by the Registrar. No, sooner—when she was spoken to by the sweeper. No, sooner—as she listened to Dina take the last stairs home while she and George awaited her in the kitchen to deliver the news.

Recently, during a hair-smoothing session on the divan, Dina had confided to Susanna that sometimes she felt things "dropping" in her chest, and . . . what did it mean? Susanna, who had come to worry less about the malady coded into their genes, felt her own dropping. Alarmed by Susanna's alarm, Dina's eyebrows slid toward each other like little mountains pushed up by convulsions in the earth. With her thumbs, Susanna smoothed the eyebrows away from each other, undid the earthquake.

"Some people, like your father," Susanna said, "are calm inside. Even when they shouldn't be." Dina's eyebrows were trying to come back together, but Susanna smoothed, and Dina let her. "But me and you—we are loud inside." Susanna touched the soft skin between the eyebrows. "Even when we shouldn't be."

But Dina had something fundamental of George in her as well. Like George, Dina sometimes noticed less. Susanna was grateful for it. This oblivion made her less vulnerable.

Susanna took a breath, closed her eyes, and stepped over her daughter, her foot hitting the earth awkwardly. A crackling pain went into her ankle. She felt a hot tear at the edge of one eye, which she wedged shut to keep herself from crying out.

"Don't go," the whisper came in the darkness.

Susanna froze. Her teeth were beating out a code, her lips were trembling. "It's just a little shot, my heart," she said. "It's just a little vitamin. They give it to you in the night. Only ladies. You're too young. Please don't wake Papa."

She heard Dina turn away from her in the dark.

When Susanna closed the flap, she saw the old woman waiting, indistinguishable from the night. The woman turned and began to walk toward a cluster of tents behind the interview tent. Under her clothing, she seemed to glide on the earth.

The settlement rang with the antic din of people too tired and full of anticipation to sleep. The fire rings burned, younger boys arriving with what wood they could scavenge. The prepared families arrived here with old telephone books, newspapers, all the forms they had held on to as minority people, now useless for anything but the health of a fire. Susanna thought about the driver, and the story he didn't finish. She could guess the ending. The ending was often the same.

Susanna had a bitter wish to return to their tent, seize the letters under George's cot, make a contribution to one of the fires. If the papers constituted his family's history, was she resentful because he had held on to his, as she had not hers? She had not, until recently, bothered to notice that both their families had been destroyed, notwithstanding the fact that her parents continued to live (as far as she knew). Maybe, invisibly, it was this orphanhood that drew them together on those university walks. They never spoke of it. Had George thought of this, too?

The old woman stopped at a solitary tent, this one canvas and sturdy, zippered. She waited until Susanna drew close, nearly invisible in the wavering light of the moon behind its passing ambivalent armor of clouds.

"He is waiting for you," the woman said in her battered voice. From the folds of her garb, she withdrew a small flat pack the size of a man's wallet. Susanna's eyes were on the ground. She loathed her quiescence. She could have said she had a venereal disease. But it wouldn't have mattered—there were other things a woman could be made to do. At least it couldn't last long—that day's sailing was scheduled for 3:15. Susanna looked up, and saw the little pack of freshening wipes. She stared at the old woman hatefully and took it.

"I know you have no pad there," the old woman said. "Your face tells the truth even when your mouth lies. He wouldn't touch you otherwise." She turned open the flap. The dental scent of clove struck Susanna's nose. For some reason, she thought of her mother, lost to herself and the world. She tried to keep thinking about her mother.

* * *

Every country has its Triangle, the place where the unwanted go. The government had built a state asylum in Dostat. It consisted of three wings made of endless halls and columns and gave out onto a pond crossed by swans. It was copied from a royal residence in Europe. Though the grounds had been laid with artificial turf, the wind found the dust and swept it into the pond, where it drew together in patches like scabs. The swans moved between them.

In the high-ceilinged room where the head physician received them, the circumference of her mother's head was measured and her knees were tapped, which the sick woman observed with a distant amusement. She laughed several times at inopportune moments, which seemed to confirm her mental infirmity (against her husband's last hope that the physician would reveal something different), but also indicated her comfort. Perhaps the high ceiling, which was domed, reminded her of the kitchen at home, the measuring and tapping of the way her head and knees were held by the woman who came weekly to wash her.

The family was released to walk the grounds before Susanna's mother stayed behind. They sat on a bench looking at swans. The bench was small for three, and the family crowded, an unfamiliar sensation. The swans were cleaning themselves, their necks slithering about their bodies like snakes. Then suddenly they stopped, beat their angel wings, and launched away until the webbed feet patted the water and the bodies again came to rest. An asylum inmate shuffled past. "They're mute swans," he said. He stuck out his tongue and ran his finger across it. "A gift from the Queen of England. They gave us the refuse."

On the bench, Susanna's mother moved her nails down her neck, raising welts. Susanna watched her, transfixed by the self-abuse, which usually occurred out of view or from the sight of which Susanna was quickly removed. Her mother scraped silently—usually she wailed or moaned. The mute swans had made her mute as she scraped herself clean.

Susanna's father watched the dirty water. He noticed only when his wife's neck already burned with contrails. He cursed his wife and slung the metal binds over her wrists. Now, she wailed. He moved her into the waiting wheelchair and pushed her away. Susanna ran after. By the time she reached them, her mother had grown quieter and was knocking her head against her husband's hand like a metronome. At the edge of the path around the pond, a sign acknowledged the gift of swans from the monarch of England.

Instead of taking the path back to the palace, Susanna's father continued to wheel her mother toward the parking area, until they were at the scratched doors of their Paykan. Susanna didn't understand, but was afraid to ask. He folded the wheelchair against the twisted bark of a disheveled carob tree. It leafed so close to the ground it seemed to swallow the wheelchair. In the front seat, her mother scratched her hair. Now the scalp was filling with welts. Susanna wanted to touch the hands, to still them, but she thought that touching would give her the madness.

* * *

Susanna's head had just touched her cot when the alarm on George's mobile went off, filling the mid-blue of the darkness with the pop and hiss of "Strangers." Susanna lay there, feeling the bodies near her come alert. Her own body burned.

"It's time, my women," George said, heaving himself toward the free edge of his cot. "Did my Dina sleep? Was the castle protected?"

Dina stirred uneasily, continuing to sleep even though her body was moving.

"Susanna, my love," George said. "They will leave without us."

"My cramps are worse," Susanna whispered. "A lot of pain."

George groaned. "Our fortune," he said. He rose heavily, and worked his nose loudly. "That man's smoking is intolerable," he said. "I thought I had that smell out of my nose."

They hobbled down to the shoreline with Yacoub's help. Yacoub had slept in an open-air dormitory of a dozen bunks. Dina stared at Susanna with hatred, and at George she didn't look at all, as she didn't know what she was supposed to feel.

The conductor was at the controls. Susanna felt vomit in her mouth. George's silent eyes asked Yacoub about the raft. The young man smiled with embarrassment—it was only a rubber dinghy with an outboard motor, a child could operate it. George patted him on the shoulder. Susanna vomited heavily into the water. The men grabbed her shoulders, trying to hold her up. She had nothing, just bile. Dina said she needed the bathroom. Number two, not number one. George groaned again. It was not going the way he had hoped.

"I will try to find a towel to hide you," he said unhappily. There were no concealed spots around them because of the roaming flashlights and stumbling bodies. The departure bay was the size of a large garden, floored with pebbles.

"I will not go with all these people watching," Dina said.

"Let us go back up quickly, then," George said, relieved not to have to open the valise, search for a towel. . . . "Kind Yacoub will help your mother."

"I want Yacoub to take me," Dina said.

Relieved again, George looked at Yacoub. "Of course," the young man said. "Young lady, I'm your guide. We will be very fast. I know where we can get toilet paper. Come."

"Please hurry," George said. "At three thirty, he will leave. He will not wait. He said so."

Yacoub and Dina were halfway up the incline to the tents when Dina spoke. "It is up to you what you do," she said. "I ask you only not to get in my way."

Yacoub laughed, but then sobered because he didn't know what Dina meant. "What are you saying, little one?" he said.

"Look out, and help me if you want to," she said. "But please don't stop me. There is a reason. Trust me. Please don't stop me. I only hope there's no one to see it."

"See what?"

"You will see."

They heard the five-minute klaxon from the raft, five blasts: 3:25.

They drew near the interview tent, which felt abandoned without its line of supplicants. Dina began to jog, the dust rising around them. Soon, it came into view. There was no one nearby, as the tent sites didn't start for another hundred yards, and the benighted woman must have been sleeping. A patch of clouds hung in the right spot and added to the consuming dimness around them. Four blasts.

"Help me," Dina said. Yacoub took her by her sides, and hoisted her to the lip of the garden bed. Her little fingers went to the roots. Most of the herbs came out easily, but some patches were harder, and this is where he helped her, and so did his knife in one or two spots. Three blasts. The flowers fell away, the stems crunching and snapping helplessly, a brackishness in Dina's nose from their gland nectar, and the sense of what she was doing. Otherwise, she was calm, emotionless save the pleasure of vengeance. Her mind went distractedly to Robert. She chased it away. Two blasts.

Yacoub whispered at her. She ignored him. There was another bed and she would not finish till finished. Gently, apologetically, he began to pull on her body. She wriggled out of his hands and told him to help faster, if he wanted to finish, or to go on his own. One blast. Soon, they heard the departure horn—one, two, three.

Dina could hear her father's screaming even before she and Yacoub appeared above the rise that led down to the water. It sounded like hate. She noticed that he had not gone to look for them. Then she remembered it would have meant leaving their mother.

The conductor started the engine before Dina and Yacoub had climbed in, the abruptness toppling George and anyone who wasn't already prostrate. Yacoub swept up Dina and leaped through the water. In the commotion, his knife slipped out of his back pocket and into the sea. Hands reached out and pulled them in as the raft sped away.

Dina was slapped by a second parent. She knew it was coming, and she smiled into it. Yacoub looked away. Susanna whimpered from her spot, where she had been soaked by the commotion. They had taken six minutes past 3:30, each of which had cost George five thousand, thirty thousand total. They left their country with nothing.

II

The Waiting Palace

The letters arrived the same day. For three months, their mail bin had been empty. There were only three kinds of mail: the letter that said you were invited for your asylum interview; the one that said you were cleared for Europe, or America; and the one that said you were not. The last group was deported within twenty-four hours. For three months, Susanna and George had longed for, and dreaded, the first letter. But you only ever stood to get one.

Susanna was alone inside the tent, pushing food into her mouth. She held a rolled flatbread in one hand and a dried sausage in the other, like flags. As soon as George had ushered Dina outside—one hour separated Dina's arrival from school and Susanna's departure for her job in the camp kitchen, and even George understood it was best to keep mother and daughter apart—Susanna had dug out the food.

Susanna heard feet on the packed earth outside the tent, then tuneless humming, and her heart went flat. It was the old man who delivered the mail. After the sound retreated, she crawled out of the tent, the flatbread dry in her throat. Her heart was drubbing her chest. George was looking at her from the clearing where he was pitching a beach ball with Dina. He said something to Dina, who shrugged heavily and followed him back to the tent. Susanna watched her family approach as through a hospital window. She was the sick one.

They had spent three months in a refugee camp tent the size of George's sitting room, each wishing for, and hiding the wish for, solitude. The morning they'd come ashore, Susanna had walked back into the water, still wearing her multiple coats. She was desperate to wash. George, terrified that she would be seen as a mental case, ran after her. Emerging, Susanna realized with horror that she had washed away all her valerian root.

For the first week, Susanna didn't rise from her cot. Eventually, even George, who understood little about menstrual cycles, felt emboldened to say that perhaps something graver was the matter—there was a doctor; it was not a penal camp. Susanna waved him away and became ambulatory so he would leave her alone.

If at first Susanna couldn't rouse her body, now she wouldn't let it fall still. Their tent consisted of a concrete slab warmed by an old Persian rug, the cots clustered around a nightstand with a lamp that sent out a weak caramel light. So you could sweep the rug, and shake out the rug, and sweep the concrete, and dust the lamp shade, and the lamp, and the nightstand, and then remember that you should have run a mop over the concrete, so that you had to go to the supply depot and rent a mop and bucket, go to the spigot for water, remove the rug again, wash down the concrete . . . She and Dina were like charwomen, working in silent rhythm and rage. Dina waited for her mother to explain her vanishing the night of the crossing. Her mother did not. Dina didn't dare bring it up on her own, and, for this, hated both herself and her mother.

In the third week, a young man in heavy-framed glasses arrived to say that Dina should now come to school. If Susanna and Dina had resented their enforced proximity, they had perhaps also relished it, like a scab. But they seized this opportunity not to see each other. They woke, had their cafeteria breakfast of muesli and goat cheese on rye, and Dina went off to learn what felt to their hosts like the average of what the students' ages required. Multiplication, English, photosynthesis, meteors. It's God coughing, Dina said under her breath.

After Dina vanished, Susanna's industry dissolved. This left her alone with George. She went to the camp kitchen and asked for work. She did not need to be paid. There's nothing, the kindly woman said, touching her shoulder. The woman had gray hair inflamed by a single serpentine streak of white so bleached it looked like disfigurement. Susanna went to the garbage bin in the back of the kitchen and began sorting, flattening, and crushing, raising noise, dust, and questions. The woman, Theodosia, took the point, invited her inside, invented work.

Susanna said she had to come in the afternoons. Perhaps she was avoiding her daughter after school; perhaps this was the best time for dinner-prep scraps. Surely Theodosia saw all the food Susanna set aside, but she didn't interfere. Some things Susanna managed to save for the small cold box in the tent, some she stuffed directly into her mouth. Dina and George went to sleep and awoke to the sound of chewing. In the evenings, when they had no choice but to be together, Susanna rose every several minutes to swipe something from the pile of breads, cheeses, and dips. In a month, Susanna's clothes grew tight, but George said nothing from a combination of politeness and fear.

Having crawled outside the tent for the mail, Susanna remained on all fours, like an animal. Incredibly, the mail bin held two letters: one for the family, one for Dina. Dina had never received a letter, even at home.

The family envelope bore the American eagle clutching greenery in one claw and arrows in the other, as if to say: your choice. Susanna stuck a finger, scaly from dishwashing, under the flap. The letter said that their asylum interview with an American consular officer in the island's capital was scheduled for tomorrow. Tomorrow?

Enclosed were three return-trip vouchers for the bus that plodded the flattish circumference of the island, whose interior was too rocky to sustain large settlements. The camp guard would load them onto the bus, the letter explained, and forty-five minutes later the bus driver would see them off at the temporary consulate the Americans had rigged up, alongside a dozen other countries, to receive the war's outflow.

The island was an oval, with the diplomatic people in the north, the refugees in the south, and the local people between. The sudden diplomatic influx had turned the island's capital from a town that still had goat tracks into a small city whose restaurants had outdoor misters. The wealthy local people resented the diplomats, who increased traffic and clogged restaurant tables, and the poor local people resented the refugees, because when the wealthy people had shown up to buy second homes, at least they had increased the property values.

Susanna extended the letter to George, then took it back—only she could read English. "Tomorrow," she said.

George regarded his wife. She was sitting in the dust, one leg under her rear end, the other out in the heat. She looked like a mad dog, her long skirt covered in dust.

"It's because they wish to limit the time a family has to . . ." she started.

"Smooth out its story," he finished.

"Keep your voice down," she said. Their hosts had settled them next to another family from their country, so you had to watch your mouth, just like at home. "Dina, your father and I need to speak," Susanna said. "Wait here for us, please." Dina stared at them with dark-brown eyes, the beach ball in her hands like a head.

Inside the tent, the detritus of Susanna's eating was all around, like evidence of adultery. Its smell battled with the eucalyptus that covered the island and infiltrated the tent especially in the afternoons. Its scent was so forceful that it seemed like sound, like crinkling.

"These are not situations where you have to give written proof," George said. He was grateful that they were forced to speak. "We're minority-sect. Our people have been murdered. America feels guilty because, unlike Europe, for a long time it did nothing. That's why we applied there. Europe is closing its doors, America opens."

"You worked for a government university," Susanna said. She looked through the zippered plastic opening that served as their window. Dina had been mincing by the tent, but seeing her mother's face, turned away to kick the ball.

"Almost every university is a government university in our country," he said. "If you want to provide for your family, that's where you have to work. There's nothing on the record about my time there that would give us shame."

"On the record," she emphasized.

"No one has to know any of that."

She laughed in an ugly way, baring her teeth, a laugh he hadn't seen before. "Even if they don't know about Kamil, you spent twenty years there. The last several—in the middle of a civil war—as the only minority-sect person on the faculty. It's the second-largest university in the country—you think they don't know this? You served that state very well, George. You aren't a victim."

He glared. "Servant, you call me," he said. "This servant built a wall around you. All that time, safe in your walls, you didn't object. I did the work of three men while the other two collected their salaries, and I got half what they did."

"And I made it last three times as long as their wives had to," she said. "I know all this. I am speaking as the consulate. With them, you need to show threat to life."

"So what, you will invent?" he said.

"I will tell another truth."

"What truth?"

"I will think of something," she said.

It was silent, except for the ticking of the watch entombed in George's hairy wrist. The afternoons were a time of defeat. The idleness of the camp enfeebled its residents rather than the opposite. After the children were pushed off in the mornings, the adults collapsed in front of their mobiles, and did not rise again until the small faces peered through the flaps of the tents at 2:30. Even some of the families that had initially rejected the offer of education had begun sending their children to school. Back home, these people had scrambled to survive, their minds on constant alert. Now they were safe, but their minds resisted the new comfort of the bodies. Their minds only wanted to sleep. Like mothers calling after children who had drifted too far into the forest, the bodies could not call the minds back from where they had decided to go. But the bodies could no longer join them there, either.

"I can talk about the Soudanes," George said. "Harry was a classmate of Dina's. Who is to say we weren't next?"

"You don't speak English," she said. "Regardless, I must speak. They look down on silent women. It'll make them want to help us less. A woman who speaks is a woman like them."

"We can rehearse, my heart," he said. He looked up cautiously to see whether she had heard the endearment.

Susanna stood at the flap of the tent, her back to him. She had heard but couldn't respond.

"What has happened to us, my dove?" George said. He wanted to touch her arm but lost his resolve and ended up grazing it with his fingers. "I was wrong not to tell you about Kamil. I was trying to protect. Instead, I betrayed. I understand. I have begged your forgiveness for three months." He hesitated, not sure if he should reach for the sentiment. "I miss my wife."

He imagined he could see her choosing words from a crowded box. "We have made ourselves foreigners," she said finally. "By having to come here, we have made sure that we will always be divided inside ourselves. Our daughter, too. That was what you accomplished." She felt savage and cruel. What she said was true, but it wasn't the reason she forced him away. "Don't tell Dina about her letter, please," she said. "We'll open it together tonight." She unzipped the flap and stepped out, nearly knocking over Dina.

"Have you been listening to us?" Susanna demanded.

"No, my head hurts from the sun," Dina said.

"Every day, your hat waits for you in the tent."

Dina pushed her way inside.

George followed Susanna out and watched her vanish down the path to the kitchen. What did Susanna want from him? She had abdicated her duties as a mother, so he had become the mother. But nothing would turn his wife back from the vanishing point toward which she strained. She was like a wounded animal seeking its own death.

Every afternoon, sensing the strange discord between mother and daughter, George took Dina away. He took her to the water, where they dug for bright stones until a hard wave briefly took her under, reinforcing his sense that some misfortune lay in wait. He found a barber and paid him to make the girl's hair less of a laughingstock, half expecting the scissors to cut into her head while the man's seven children stood watching. He and Dina raised fortifications in the sand and dug a time capsule into the wall of a dune—a hard loaf of bread pilfered from Susanna's collection, a round stone to symbolize the beach ball, and a poem George read out to her as she squinted at the powdery gold of the sun behind his head.

It turned out that it wasn't difficult to be with his daughter—George only had to stop being afraid of her. And she seemed to like being with him; she made fun of him, which she had never bothered to do before. The letters, poems, and messages pulled at George like another child—in his previous life, he had tended to them more than to Dina. He had to perform an inventory, to understand his liabilities. But day after day, he ignored the plastic bag under his cot.

Back in the tent, Dina had forgotten about the sun hat, and was arranging her socks in the shape of a dragon on the bit of rug untaken by cots. "Dina-bird," he called her. She looked up, and the way she was at that moment—her dusty sneakers tucked under her bum, her still-funny hair swinging around like a skirt, her mind lost in the way socks become dragons—swung at his heart so hard he had to get his breath. "I must ask you something very important."

She gazed at him, unaccustomed to being addressed with such gravity. Her poor father eternally seemed to be working off debt. It came to her advantage—she had a playmate, a pack animal who ferried her around, a soft mark when she wanted something she wasn't supposed to have. But she also lived with the sense of something having taken an irretrievable turn. Perhaps they would finally speak of it. The idea made her both excited and anxious.

He lowered himself heavily to his knees. He had tried sincerely, had he not, to avoid dragging her in?

"Dina," he said. "Please tell me what's happened between you and your mama. She hasn't been herself since we got here. Something is wrong. Help me fix, Dina-bird." George felt he was being disingenuous by not acknowledging Susanna's resentment of him, but something had happened between Dina and Susanna as well, he was sure of it. He had learned that his daughter liked to be an ally, so he had taken care to phrase his question in the form of a mission.

Dina ran the edge of a nail along her teeth like a toothbrush. Since the crossing, the issue of what Dina actually wanted had not occurred to her—she was busy with anger. But if it had, she took for granted that the resolution would involve her mother; that is who had to account for herself. It did not occur to Dina that it was also something she could discuss with her father. Having witnessed the malevolence that she had, could she simply describe it to George? Could that also relieve the awful feeling that had lived in her stomach since that poisonous night? Could she simply tell her father that her mother was . . . a drug addict? That in the night, while he slept, she had crept out at the insistence of that wretched old woman—Dina had not overheard exactly what was said, but the illicit always communicated by signals—and joined her for "vitamins"? That she had continued to take drugs after they arrived in the camp, rising in the night during their first weeks to wander the poorly lit paths, returning only at dawn, groaning and sighing as her addled mind finally released her to sleep? How could he fail to notice it himself, considering all the white dots she put under her tongue? Or perhaps he was a drug addict himself? He was there during the wrestling match the night that they left. Maybe the wrestling was about the drugs, too; the night was for drugs.

She contemplated offering to trade the information for the letter she had received. But there was no way to do that without giving away that she was listening to them talk in the tent. The clandestine listening was a waste—she hardly understood anything they'd said, other than they didn't know how to explain their miserable lives. But she couldn't ask for the letter.

"It happened the night that we left," she said finally, experimentally.

"The night that we left? But you slept through that."

"*You* slept through it," she said.

"My heart," he said. "I was walking with your mother. You were on her shoulder, asleep." He was insistent. He couldn't manage the news that she had witnessed a murder.

"That is not the night I am talking about," she said.

"The next night?" he said with relief.

"Yes, when we all went to sleep . . ." she started.

His bristly, unkempt brows—whose bristliness and unkeep had used to enjoy the counterweight of the bristly though not unkempt moustache, which he hadn't grown back—slid toward each other and his mouth was open. He looked like an ungainly, struck bird, out of proportion with itself. He was bracing. He wanted to know and didn't.

"Mama wouldn't let me sleep on her cot," she said, stalling. She wasn't sure.

"But she did, eventually."

"Not on the outside, not at first."

"Yes, I remember."

She stared at him. Waited and thought.

"Well?"

She kept staring.

"Dina-heart."

"What has happened between *you* and Mama?" Dina said. If she were going to give up her knowledge, he should share his.

"Nothing," he said mechanically. "Your mother doesn't feel well often. This heat, these cots . . . It's hard for her, that's all."

She listened to his lie with humiliation.

"Now tell me," he said.

"I said it," she said coldly, changing her mind. "That's it."

"You and your mother have been angry with each other for three months because she wouldn't let you sleep on her cot?" George threw his hands in the air and cursed. Dina put her hands over her ears. At home, when her father became exasperated, he disappeared to one of the apartment's many other rooms. Here there were no other rooms. He covered his sweating face. He despised himself, his wife, this place, the old place, every place.

"I'm sorry," he said. "Your father doesn't understand anything." He ran his hands back and forth through the web of his hair, which on dignified days resembled a cloudlike halo and now a helmet with dents.

"Can we play some more now?" she said.

He stared out at the bruising light. He shook his head angrily. She thought he was going to punish her and say no. But instead he said: "You want to play?" His eyes were inflamed with something molten and raw. "You're not tired of the beach ball? Fake ball, fake home? Do you know how many times your father stood in line waiting to be fed by charity when he lived in his country?" He pointed in the direction of the cafeteria. "Zero, exactly." He plowed out of the tent.

Outside, she saw him gesturing at the thin man in sports slacks and slippers whose family lived next door. That was odd—they didn't speak to anyone else, and no one spoke to them. Her father looked like he was asking for a large watermelon. The man went away and returned with the watermelon: a soccer ball. The man knuckled it, and the dense, hollow sound carried to where Dina was standing.

George turned to Dina. "You are the goalie, and I'm the striker, okay?" He didn't wait for an answer. He was breathing heavily. He moved around, measuring distances and instructing Dina to retreat toward the flap of their tent. "I have to get it past you," he said. "Through the flap and into the tent."

"What if I stop it?" she said.

"Then you win."

"And if I don't stop it?"

"I guess I will knock down the tent."

She observed him quizzically. So did the man who had lent him the ball. The first shot sailed sideways of the tent. George clapped all the same. Dina watched him, unsure. A small, shrieking child emerged from behind the neighbor and ran for the ball.

"Again," George said and kicked. This one flew high. The little boy, who wore sneakers rimmed by flickering lights, ran, squealing. His father squatted in the sand outside their tent.

"Again," George said, winding up. He kicked hard, and it came so close to Dina that she dodged and it sailed right into the tent, where it slammed into the bedside table, wobbling the night lamp. With a child's indifference to boundaries, the boy disappeared inside their tent and emerged holding the ball like a trophy.

"One–zero for the fathers," George said. "Again." When George had kicked it, he had thought of the driver lifting Kamil's dying head and letting it slam back to the pavement. That sound was different because that watermelon was full.

It was a strange game, but Dina went along. It was better than turning into a ghost inside the tent. George's stomach was jiggling over his unbelted trousers, and he swatted at his sweating forehead with the back of his arm. Once Dina was paying attention, she knocked away one, two, three balls, though it hurt her palms; the ball was tight as concrete.

"One–three for the daughters," George said. Occasionally, the breath in his lungs seemed to stall there. He had never exercised, but something about the parameters of his life at home kept his body from restlessness. But restlessness was all he felt now, the sense of a man too large for the space that he had. He wanted to shatter. That blighted thought was replaced by a gust of hope for his stubborn daughter, her still-clumsy fence of clipped hair outlined by the sun like a flag, a flag he had planted. He had sweat in his eyes when he launched the next ball. As it sailed, it vanished momentarily in the glare of the sun. After it reemerged, near Dina's head, through a smear of sweat, he saw her collapse.

* * *

The camp kitchen was gloomy and cool. Walking in, Susanna had a flash of that night—the dry, stinking fingers bleached in clove nicotine, the sweat-stained T-shirt over her face like a dead woman's. These moments came on like seizures. Sleep was the greatest trial. She would wash dishes through the night if she could. She opened the faucet, which walled out her thoughts. She knew that by staying silent, she was contributing to her demise. But speaking to someone about what was done to her felt as unimaginable as being touched again by George. She was grateful for his misdeeds because they provided a cover. This made her felt heartless. But how could she be the heartless one after what had happened to her?

After three hours, there was nothing left to wash, dry, stack, or check. She took an end cut from a loaf of bread, and rinds of a cheese the kitchen was done with, and sat down on a bench in the storeroom. She was trying to decide what they would wear tomorrow in order, again, to seem needy but not impoverished. For two months, Susanna had worn only the long, crinkling skirt she wore now, obtained at a rummage shop attached to the credit store. She no longer fit into her clothes. The matter of dress was easy next to the question of what persecution they were supposed to claim. Even what she endured was not adequate; it had happened after they had fled, and it was not systematic. Being minority-sect in their country was systematic, the slow wearing away of their souls and their selves. But that wasn't enough.

She was startled by the sound of a softly chiding voice. She didn't know how much time had passed.

"Susanna," Theodosia said again. She was trying to be gentle.

"Just a quick break," Susanna said, coming out of her reverie. "I finished everything."

"No, I mean—water." Theodosia pointed at the sink. Susanna had left the water running. Had she turned the water back on? Had she turned it off, the silence was unbearable, and she had turned it back on?

"I'm sorry," Susanna said, clutching her hair.

"I'll have to order a special flow restrictor just for you," Theodosia said. Seeing Susanna's stricken face, she added: "That was a joke." She tried to change the subject: "I heard your good news."

Susanna flinched. "There are no secrets in this camp," she said. As at home, the people in charge here knew everything. She, George, Dina—

they were contingent people. They were given to, but had no say in what had been given.

Theodosia took off her kitchen gloves and wiped the sweat on her forehead. She always tucked her T-shirts into her jeans even though that meant a roll of flesh hung out past the belt line. She was . . . fifty? Theodosia—Theo—was from Wales, the daughter of a miner who had asphyxiated when an improperly supported wall of rock collapsed on him and another man, a luckless Hungarian who had escaped the 1956 invasion by stashing away in the "dogs' drawer" of a train to Austria only to end up in an even smaller alcove of rapidly vanishing oxygen underground. The two men were alive for at least several hours, though there was no hope of getting them out in time with the technology available then. Theo condensed the hours to one and wrote a play—*The Hour*, in real time. What did trapped men of casual acquaintance talk about after learning there was an hour to live? It was harder to write than she thought, though it received polite attention. Her favorite moment was when the Hungarian said, panting, "One of us should kill the other, we'll get more air that way," and her father said, "You had raw onion for lunch, I am already dead." She invented it, and yet it felt true. The men laughed weakly. (The audience, too.) They held hands as they faded. She knew that part hadn't happened, but she liked it regardless.

Theodosia was trying to pull strands. Her father had been born the next island over. Wales had needed miners and the father's father had been a gravedigger—mining was just going a little deeper. For two months, Theo had wandered that island, trying to weave the scraps she discovered into a tapestry that remained so meager you couldn't cover yourself with it no matter how small you became. The island had a small industry in entertaining genealogy searchers like herself; the poorer the island, the more people left, the more people now came back with questions, the more of their money the island gratefully siphoned off.

Theo was reluctantly preparing to return to Wales when she wondered why she could only stay for Martyn Kasper (whom her father, Milos Kaspos, became on breaching the shore at Holyhead). And, of course, it was staring at her from just an island away. There was not a lot of competition for jobs managing these refugee camps. And she was not a manager at first, merely a volunteer. But she took to it. She had the skills, the organization, the compassion, the forgiveness, and the longing to be saved. Or, failing that, to save somebody else.

Theodosia told Susanna all this one afternoon. Susanna had not asked to hear it, but felt she had to listen once it was offered.

Now, Theodosia kneeled before Susanna. She was nearly six feet. She was about to take Susanna by the shoulders, but decided it would be a mistake to touch someone who, it was clear, did not want to be touched.

"I'm sorry," the tall woman said. "We are always trying to balance the information we need with your privacy."

Susanna nodded. The irony with these people was that things went better when you went at them with complaint rather than gratitude. This was the right moment to strike. Theo's guilt would be forced to alchemize into generosity.

"I need your help," Susanna said.

"What is it?"

"In the last several months . . ." Susanna searched for the right words. "I've become bigger. I don't have clothes for the interview." She stared at Theo's rolling waistline.

"Oh," the woman said. The lines in her forehead sailed apart. "Really? Nothing?" Belatedly, she made the connection. "Oh, you want me to . . . Oh, Susanna, I would like to, but they won't let us do something like that. You know better than I do—the people here come from unequal places. We don't want to reinforce that by offering things to some but not others. Besides, I am a head taller than you. None of it would fit!"

The extreme fairness that led these people to take in refugees also did not allow them to address needs that weren't communal. They gave collectively, not individually—to an idea.

"You are not the manager?" Susanna tried.

"I am the manager of the kitchen. But that has nothing to do with it."

"It's my fault. I don't know why I put things in my mouth all the time."

Theodosia thought about the right way to respond. Finally, she said: "The interview is tomorrow?"

"Yes."

"I can take you. We'll go together."

"It's not necessary," Susanna said. They could not give you what you needed, so they forced you to accept something else.

"What I mean is—"

"No," Susanna cut her off. "We can go by ourselves. They allow it." She rose. "The guard must put us in the bus, and the driver must make sure we walk into the consulate. Because they think we will run away. But where will we run in this place? There is rock in the middle, and water outside, and between is a highway. Some cave, do you think?"

"There are ferries," Theodosia said. "Not everyone is responsible like you."

Susanna could not think of the words to reply. She had used to feel anger more skillfully. Now it took more out of her than submission. The Susanna who had dressed down the village men at the transfer camp was impossible to imagine. She willed Theodosia to disappear on some errand so Susanna could go back to her rectangle of bread. They had just received a large cylinder of a salty cheese that she liked. The morning shift had sliced it into friendly little wheels, and no one ever wanted the ends.

Theodosia went to the window curtain and pulled the flounces closed across the gathering dusk outside. "Will you help me bring something out to the car?" she said. "I have to get going."

It was an hour before their shifts ended, so Susanna experienced this as a punishment—if Theodosia left, Susanna had to as well. No storeroom, no bread. But Susanna preferred this to false intimacy. She wiped her hands and extended them to receive a stack of aluminum trays and cake molds that Theodosia could have easily carried herself—the banishment of false intimacy had become idle abuse of authority. But you could not humiliate Susanna.

Theodosia drove a boxy old Renault the color of snow-flecked fir, or so it looked due to all the spots where the pine-green paint had scratched off.

A trim that ran around the lower part of its body lit up when the car came on, like a jukebox.

Once they'd loaded the trays, Theodosia slammed the trunk and looked at Susanna. "Get in," she said. "If you can stand the mess of it."

Susanna stared with uncertainty.

"You have an hour before anyone will think you're gone," she said. "And you need clothes. You said." Susanna remained in place. "That's what I meant when I said I would take you. Not tomorrow. Tonight. If I'm with you, the guard won't give us a problem."

Susanna swung around to see to whom they were visible. The parking area was hidden behind the kitchen. The aluminum trays were a ruse. Theo would not give her clothes, but she would take Susanna to buy them? With what money? What shop was open at this hour? Susanna didn't understand. She opened the passenger door before Theo reconsidered.

* * *

George and the neighbor and the neighbor's boy all ran at once. Dina was on her back, unmoving. George shook her so violently the neighbor placed a hand on George's arm. George unshouldered the hand, shook her more. Finally, he put his hands under her body and lifted, but lost his step, and had to submit to help from the neighbor. George ran to the infirmary. The neighbor's little son was crying. People looked out of their tents.

At the infirmary, George found the dreadlocked woman. She had been there when they'd washed ashore, along with a woman who had a severe crop—the two of them added up to one normal person's hair. The schoolteacher with the thick-framed glasses called things out through a megaphone, and the women pantomimed for those who didn't speak English. The arrivals watched in numb silence.

When they called for interpreters, George looked at Susanna, but she was too feeble to reply, and George didn't know whether to raise his hand for her, and then the moment was over. Many in the group didn't speak English; others were hard of hearing, from age, shelling, or shock; still others regarded the megaphone as an instrument of incitement and hesitated to reply even if they understood. But the quickest among them grasped a key difference between this place and the former: Back home, when questions were asked, only fools raised their hands. Here, the wise men. George felt he had failed his first test as a new person.

The sight of the medusa coils slithering down the woman's back stopped George at the threshold to the infirmary, Dina in his arms. His sweat cooled in the medical chill. "This is my punishment," he said to no one.

He proceeded by gestures. The sun, the ball, the little girl. There was disfavor across the woman's gray, veined face. Toward Dina's prospects? His qualifications as a guardian? Had his indiscretion compromised their eligibility for asylum? But he would accept every judgment if only Dina would revive. He cursed himself for losing his temper. There was so much temper, held back over so long, that you couldn't control its release. Did this mean that, past a certain point, you could never release it? The woman was working with a stethoscope and a blood-pressure cuff. There was a barbell in one of her eyebrows. Her face was so pale you could see the skeins of blue lightning in her forehead. She said things, but he didn't understand. He thought about running to get Susanna—this would get her attention—but he couldn't leave Dina.

When the smelling salts came under her nose, Dina coughed and awoke. George shoved her head against his chest, and said her name over and over. The dreadlocked woman waited. George released Dina.

Everyone noticed at the same moment. The fingers on one of Dina's hands were as rigid as pencils. The woman pressed the tips gently, but they stayed where they were. The woman turned to George and mimed a key closing a lock—the fingers had locked. "No problem," she said. "Give it time." She banged her watch. The joints did that sometimes, when it was bad contact with a hard surface. Time was the thing. George closed his eyes. However they went at it—time was the thing. They had too little before and too much now.

Time properly matched to need—that was the true definition of comfort, safety, and power. It struck him as a luxuriously intellectual thought, the kind he used to have all the time. That way of thinking felt as distant to him as their apartment, now surely inhabited by someone unknown, as he did not believe his parents could do much with the notarized affidavit. Another man's garbage now fell into the little woven wastebasket by the toilet. Until Susanna came into his life, George had used to clip his toenails into an old cooking pot. He missed his wife.

He looked back at his daughter, who studied the shape of an animal biscuit the young woman had placed in her good hand, after George seemed too absent to say yes or no to the offer. Dina looked like a slightly drugged animal. Cautiously, George pointed a finger at her head. "The head is fine," the doctor said. She made complicated motions to indicate that the ball could not have very well smacked her fingers and head both. George made a gesture to indicate falling asleep and raised his hands to ask why. "She got scared," the woman explained. "She fainted." He didn't understand. The dreadlocked woman made her eyes big in fright, and pretended to swoon to the ground. Eventually George understood, bent his head to express gratitude. He did not have the gestures to ask whether all this would be marked in their file. "Thank you," he said in English several times, his daughter's good hand in his own. Dina kept trying to free it so she could eat the biscuit. "Nice lady," he said to the doctor. "Nice lady."

Outside the infirmary, the neighbor stood with his boy. Silently, the men shook hands. "I want to go home," Dina said. George took her back and laid her down in her cot, where she fell asleep. He had never heard Dina refer to the tent as their home. It was just a figure of speech. But they had been there too long. They were walking on the edge of something, waiting to fall.

* * *

The passenger seat was crowded with wrappers, forms in triplicate where Susanna glimpsed Theo's surname (Nest), a roll of paper towels, and a flannel shirt with a torn elbow. Theodosia leaned over and began tossing it all in the back. "Come, come," she said. "Don't make me feel any worse about it." Away from the kitchen, she was less terminally polite.

Susanna climbed in, the new fat around her belly rolling up in reply. Somehow, she knew Theo would be careless in private. Perhaps these people did not wish to admit you into anything personal because you couldn't consider them with the same deference thereafter.

In Susanna's mind, considering the severe injunction against leaving camp, the guard was a gargoyle with a semiautomatic weapon, like guards at the banks in their city. But it was not clear this one had even a pistol. He was younger than her. When Theo slowed down by the guard gate, he looked up from a book, a mug of coffee cloaking a part of his face in warm steam. He smiled at Theodosia, and the black spots in his teeth showed through the fog.

The road curved as they headed left out of camp, the tires rolling softly over the carpet of pine needles that dropped in the heat. To Susanna's regret, the island was vanishing in the dusk. The sea was to the left, and on the right, so close to her window that she felt she could touch it, was rock face. An oncoming vehicle swerved past them at what felt like too high a speed. She was startled to be reminded of people who lived lives of problems unrelated to theirs.

"I don't think I'll ever get used to that," Theodosia said. "You think they're going to take your side mirror with them." She waited. "I'll ask you to keep this little adventure between us."

"Of course," Susanna said, feeling an unfamiliar power to decide one way or the other. Perhaps that was Theo's intention. "Can I open the window?"

Susanna held back the rushing wind with her hand. She felt as if she had prostituted her resentment to the privilege of driving out of camp. She had been given a gift she didn't request, and become giddy, like a child. But it felt feverishly exciting to be out.

Theo was big at the wheel, and sat upright at it, so that she looked to be cradling a creature in need of protection. Susanna wanted to keep listening to the road, but she felt she should express gratitude in some way.

She didn't know how. She should ask for advice; it would flatter. But she couldn't mention the only issue with which she needed advice.

"What is a person to do if the consulate says no to the asylum application?" she tried. "They understand, don't they, that, yes, some people lie, or say their problem was bigger than the problem really was. But some people will be killed."

Theodosia nodded. "I know you're worried. I'll tell you everything I know. Let's just ride for a bit."

Susanna felt reprimanded, as if she'd said the wrong thing.

"Watch this," Theodosia said and pressed a button. An aperture opened above them, and they were staring at black sky and stars. "First model with a sunroof," she said. "Moonroof. Close your eyes. Tell me where you are right now, if not here."

Obediently, Susanna closed her eyes and tried to think of an answer that would please the woman. Her mind refused to move. "I don't know," she said. "I'm sorry."

"That's all right," Theodosia said. "Just a little game."

Susanna wanted to make up for her failure. "What about you?"

"Well, I can't close my eyes," Theodosia said and laughed. Susanna joined her accommodatingly.

Eventually, Theodosia said, "It's me and my pop. We're driving across the river in Swansea. Past the port, the hospital. It really opens up there. It took a good half hour—we lived far on the west side, almost out of town. When we finally got there, it was a regular old country home, up a long winding lane, no other house in sight. But there were lots of cars in the drive.

"On the main floor was a gambling parlor and then downstairs this inner sanctum that looked like a bookie's. These big lunks standing around in the outer office. There was so much smoke it was jungly. They said I'd have to wait for my father. Pop wanted me to stay with him. They said no because there wasn't a woman to check me for weapons. I don't remember how he persuaded them—*don't make me leave a girl alone in a room with all men*—but they relented, in time. You didn't go to a place like that with your fifteen-year-old daughter. Threw them off, I think.

"And so we went into this sanctum inside the sanctum. Lots of dark, heavy wood, and this man at the desk, suit, no tie, I remember it like he's in front of me now. My father brought out an envelope. And then he did the strangest thing. He got on his knees. Didn't look at me, just got on his knees. I was frozen, staring. The man without the tie counted the money and came around the table. He leaned down—and he spat in my father's eyes. Can you imagine? He said, 'Next time, Martyn, you olive nigger, I don't spit. Martyn, you goddamn wog.' He slapped my father with the envelope. Across the cheek, slapped him."

Theo was quiet as the road rumbled beneath them. The weather must have been merciful to the roads, but other than mercy, they were neglected.

"We didn't say a word to each other until we were back in the house," she said. "He never spoke about it, and neither did I, and he died three years later. I've never really told anyone about it, actually."

Susanna waited for more. "What does it mean?" she said.

"I think he wanted to be humiliated in front of his child," Theo said evenly. "So he would never do it again. He couldn't stop otherwise, probably. When I was young, he was always asking my mother for money. Union dues, new hard hats, new goggles; now they had them paying for their own drills. I hardly paid attention—to a child, those things don't matter. But they're there to remember, if you'd like to.

"But then I thought: No. He brought me so they would go easier on him. They wouldn't hurt a man with his daughter right there. That's why my father insisted I go inside with him." She sighed. "Maybe? I don't know. It goes both ways. I'll never know. That's the point, I guess."

"Did he stop?" Susanna said.

"One day, years after he's gone, I asked my mother about it. And she said, 'Oh, you mean the gambling, then.' Just like that, as if I was asking about the time he took her to Newport. 'It was the third in our lives,' she said. But that's all she said. I didn't press her. I should. You're making me think I should, while I can." The cars moving past them sounded like little planes taking off.

"I miss my pop, though," Theo went on. "He was my mush. I love my ma, but I got left with the wrong parent. I shouldn't say things like that. She's a lovely old lady, Mum is." She looked at Susanna. "Not much of a joyride, that story. What are you thinking about?"

Susanna felt she had to say what it was. "I am thinking about what my daughter is noticing now. Not noticing, but noticing, like you say."

"They notice everything, they just don't know it yet," Theo said. She laughed. "Look at me tell you how it is, and no child of my own. The strongest opinions in this life come from people who haven't been in trouble a day in their lives."

Up ahead, the headlights illuminated a trio of small white crosses garlanded by the usual clumps of plastic flowers. Theo turned off the main road onto a narrower track punctuated by white-stuccoed homes, the second floors of which sometimes hung out past the foundation nearly to the roadway, seemingly with no supports. Susanna had not studied this kind of engineering. Sometimes, she glimpsed the darkened outline of a swimming pool or an orchard, but even this apparent wealth was of a humbler kind than wealth in her nation. The roadway was unevenly bordered and poorly graded, and the pathways between the homes and their pools and verandas were dusty tracks whipped by the sun, sometimes with washing on lines. The air smelled of oleander. They slowed down to a crawl, turned into a side street, and rolled to a halt in the back driveway of a home with red balcony railings.

"Even Cinderella had only till midnight," Theo said. "Fifteen minutes, okay?"

* * *

Dina slept for hours. George sat at her side, holding the good hand, resisting the impulse to check the other to see if maybe the fingers could already bend. They spoked out of the palm like a hand shouting Stop. Eventually, he drew away, and, ascertaining that the sound did not disturb her, began to rifle through the letters under his cot, the tailings of his former life.

Dusk fell and the wind picked up outside. It felt as if they were crossing a dark channel in twilight.

"Is it going to be like this forever?" Dina's voice startled him in the dark.

"You're awake," he said. He came near her and took the good hand. "No, of course not." He added, as if to reassure himself, "You heard the doctor."

"How long?"

Instead of answering, he said, "How would you like to have a party?"

"I can't go to school," she said. Only now did he grasp this elemental fact—it was her writing hand. So he was to keep the women apart in the morning now, too? He wished desperately for the consular interview to change something. Anything.

"Why did Yacoub leave us on the raft?" Dina said suddenly.

"My heart, we've spoken of it," George said.

"I don't remember," she said. Of course she remembered, he noted with irritation, but he couldn't refuse her now.

"He decided to leave us," he said.

"But why?"

"He missed his parents, I guess. He changed his mind."

She thought on this, not believing it, but also not sure in her disbelief.

"Let's not think of that now," George said. "Did you hear me? A party. Mama will come home, but we won't be here. She'll have to find us. Like a game."

"Then why doesn't Yacoub call us?" Dina said. "Is he mad at me?"

George swallowed painfully. The sequence passed his eyes: The Coast Guard cutter appearing between them and the shore. Yacoub looking at George with gratitude for having urged him to make the crossing. The dazed immobility of the passengers as Yacoub was restrained. George forgetting to remonstrate with the Coast Guard ensigns, as he meant to. Yacoub now looking at George in a different way, as he slowly understood that George must have known Yacoub would be arrested, as the conductor, if he took the controls.

There was an exchange between Yacoub and the Coast Guard personnel, and then, to George's incredulity, the young man was released to move toward George. In a puddle in the back, George tried to assemble himself for a confrontation. His eyes blazing, Yacoub stopped near Dina, who was asleep, holding her mother's limp hand. Watching George hatefully, Yacoub removed the charm from his neck and pressed it into Dina's free hand. "Your wise father has given me a gift," he said, though she couldn't hear him, as he continued to stare at George. "I get to see my parents sooner than later." He turned and went back to the ensigns.

When Yacoub was off the raft, George retrieved the strap from Dina's hand and slipped it into the water. A moment later, another passenger's long, dirty fingernails pressed his shoulder. "You lost this in the water," he heard. He took it back, and eventually made the mistake of giving it, under the demanding eye of the man who had fished it out of the water, to his daughter, who now toted it with her all over the place, stopping short only of wearing it on her neck, which he refused to allow her to do. He had gently proposed she place it in the time capsule they built in the dune, but she looked at him as if he were asking her to cut off a finger.

"He gave up on us," George said to Dina now. "He wanted to go home."

Dina didn't respond. She knew her father was lying. But it felt like he was trying to protect her because she had done something wrong. When she was tearing out that witch's plants, she knew Yacoub wouldn't leave her, even if it meant he wouldn't get on the raft. Had she forgotten that her mission had a cost for another? Or had she simply allowed herself to decide that hers was more important? Was Yacoub angry with her for forcing him into that scheme? Or had the witch cursed her after she found what they did? Dina knew that no sea was wide enough to outrun that kind of curse. The only thing that waned from that kind of distance was the strength of people to keep going. Whatever it was, she had cost Yacoub his future. She didn't fully understand how, but of that part she was sure.

Using her good hand, she pulled out the leather necklace with its miniature silver encasement. Her father had told her that the fragment of paper inside had been painted red by Yacoub's mother, for a keepsake. It looked to Dina like blood.

* * *

Susanna had the impression that the woman who answered the door had not been smiling only a moment before. She was in her early fifties. The sun had been unkind to her skin, though it remained pale. She had long black hair framed by a mess of frayed ends that she had gathered at the back of her head with a clip they used to seal bags of chips in the kitchen. On the lined white face were bright red lips. She wore a long white muslin dress with flounces at the chest and the hem. Her short heels made a clicking sound on the tile.

"Who is this beautiful woman?" she said, kissing Theo's cheeks.

"Mikki, we have to do an express version tonight," Theo said.

Before Mikki could speak, a pair of teenage boys slid through the area where they stood, trailing bits of biscuit, their bare feet slapping the tile. One held a tablet and the other tried to get a look past his shoulder. They took in one leap the steps down to an open living room in which everything was white—the bookshelves, the divans, even the floor. Plant life poured like green paint down the half wall that looked over it from upstairs.

"Step in, step in," Mikki said, with no acknowledgment of the boys. "Theo, take her down. I'll make coffee."

They went down a tiled staircase. When Theo put on the lights, Susanna saw a side room with hundreds of hangers. Here were alternate lives for ladies with interviews, ladies running away, ladies wanting to feel like somebody else: pantsuits, georgette crepe, silk moiré, even a wedding gown.

Susanna looked at Theodosia.

"I will say two things," Theo said. "Only you know your body. And we have too little time to be polite. Pick something."

Susanna stood uncertainly. She hadn't stepped in a clothing store in more than four years. Behind her, feet padded the floor and cups tinkled on a tray.

"Mikki, we need help," Theodosia said.

"You should always choose two things," Mikki said. "Something practical and something impractical." Her hands worked saucers, cups, spoons, carafes, and a sugar bin, rings and bracelets clacking. The mission had brought something alive in her eyes. She freed a hanger draped with a pleated powder-blue pantsuit with a short-sleeved top a darker shade of blue, tied at the belly. "Too much?" she said. Susanna stared uneasily.

"It's for the consulate interview," Theodosia said. "It's tomorrow."

"Oh." Mikki's bracelets rattled. "You're going to the consulate, and I am sending you to a beach club. You show me." But Susanna stood as if bolted.

"It's okay," Theo said softly.

Susanna hesitantly neared a shirtwaist dress with a white collar and paisley cuffs.

"Conservative but striking," Mikki said. "The lady has taste. But." She paused, frowning, then tapped a finger discreetly at the waistline; the dress was fitted for a slimmer woman. Susanna colored.

Mikki knocked more hangers until she was holding a mauve shift dress with a scalloped hem and ruched sleeves, and an overcoat from the same material. "Ponte knit," Mikki said, "but it will be a little cooler tomorrow. You'll survive."

Susanna felt it between her fingers. The fabric felt heavy, but she preferred that. Her throat felt arid. It was only then that she remembered the most practical issue of all. She had no money—none here, and only a little more back at the tent.

"It's settled then," Mikki said. "Those embassy ladies—they are tunic people, if you know what I mean. They'll appreciate this." Susanna tried to open her mouth and looked at Theo. Theo understood and only shook her head—it would not cost.

They rushed upstairs in what would have, under other circumstances, been a giddy and conspiratorial train. More biscuit crumbs had fallen in the foyer, in addition to spilled soda. One of the boys was working the mess with a small towel.

"At least you try to clean it, unlike that one, and he lives here," Mikki said. "Even if you use my makeup cloth to do it." She extended her hand. The young man surrendered the towel and slumped away.

Susanna smiled in embarrassment at having witnessed this intimate eruption. When she lost her temper with Dina for knocking down her valerian root at the transfer camp, Yacoub did not turn away, as another person in her country would have, to offer her the pretense it had not happened. He smiled, mortified, but he did not look away. She was mortified also, but she was grateful for his presence. Briefly, it had altered the frequency on which she, George, and Dina were stuck, like a radio that had lost all other stations. Where had this boy vanished to? Why had he changed his mind and asked to go back, as George had said? Susanna had not thought of the valerian root in some weeks. Could she regard this as progress? Mikki was speaking to her.

"So good luck tomorrow. I have to hope I never see you again."

Susanna tried to smile. She hadn't spoken since stepping out of the car.

"You shouldn't worry," Theo said when they were back in the car. "She works with fabric. There's endless discard. She saves it for people who need it. They spend summers here, but she goes all around the world."

They rode quietly, the dress on its hanger riding the backseat like an extra witness.

"You understand," Theo said, "that by trying to not break the rules, I'm trying to respect the people in charge. I know they do it imperfectly. But it's generous of them nonetheless. They're not a wealthy country. The wealthy countries give them money. But those countries are just paying to make the problem someone else's. But this country has responded."

"We're grateful," Susanna said. "We're not sure about many things. But we're grateful."

"I understand," Theodosia said. "Of course I do." After a while, she added: "I just want to say one thing. If you ever want to talk to someone, I will find them for you. That's all."

"Thank you for that," Susanna said. She stared at the black road. "And for not asking."

They drove the rest of the way in silence. The preceding hour felt like sleep. This large Englishwoman had sprung Susanna from her threadbare castle and they had sailed on the ship of the night to a queen who had opened her vault . . . It was being among women. Susanna had never spent time among women, not really. Her mother lived behind a mental screen; the university women first pitied her village excess at the makeup mirror and then spat at mentions of that whore who had seduced the professor; and then she was a mother herself.

She would never speak to Theodosia, or anyone, about what had happened, but it had been a gift to be among women. Even the boy, the friend of Mikki's son, somehow felt like an extension of the female kingdom. Susanna thought of Dina. Her daughter was like a retreating vessel. Susanna wanted to call it back, to launch after it, but each day passed without her having done it. In truth, Susanna was the retreating vessel.

"Now," Theodosia said. "Darkness is our friend. Keep the dress in the cellophane. We'll put it in a garbage bag with branches. Make sure a couple stick out. People will think you went off to collect kindling."

Susanna wanted to say something—not everything, but something. But it was too late. They went past the guard, now reading under the emerald light of a chipped banker's lamp—again he showed them his teeth—and down the rutted path that led to the camp. "Thank you," Susanna said. "I won't forget it."

"That was a lovely dress, the shirtwaist," Theo said. "But this is even better." She patted Susanna's hand. Susanna twisted her face in a smile.

Susanna did as Theo said and walked down to the tents like a peasant stiff-armed with kindling. Again, she thought of the driver, his father bearing down on him with a long stick and a wild look for reasons the boy would never learn. She wished she could return to an empty tent, to have some time to return to her previous self, but it was too late in the evening for that. The bag struggled in her hands like a shifting animal. Below her, inside stone rings by the tents, ribbons of fire flailed and unraveled. In the assembling darkness, they were like flickers of resistance on an unsustaining planet.

That their hosts had given up beachfront to build the camp was always held up as an example of their magnanimity, but seeing the camp from here, Susanna understood that the angle of decline made it useless for tourism. This lip of land was like the untucked corner of a housewife's shirt, the one she used to wipe dirt. And the slope was the land saying to the people on it: *Roll off. Roll into the sea.* There were several camps of temporary laborers from even poorer European countries in the interior, but relocating the refugees there would have concealed them. Their hosts wanted the world to see what they provided. As she walked, Susanna said greetings to those fires that had only women around them. Unaccustomed to the interaction, the women's eyes sought the ground, but their daughters sometimes stared at Susanna.

Susanna got her wish: There was no one in the tent. She allowed herself not to wonder why, though it was late for one of George and Dina's excursions. Then she noticed that the food was gone. She rummaged through the fridge, the cubbies where she kept the pre-buttered rolls, crackers, the swirls of chocolate spread—empty. The anger made her dizzy. So George's solution to the problem was to throw it all out with no word while she was away. Never a word to her directly—the coward! Her eyes fell on the handwritten sign:

Those wishing to rest
Must first pass a test,
And find the guava grove,
Where you are awaited with love.

Susanna rushed out, ignoring the neighbors, who were arrayed by their fire with a loaf of bread and several jars spread across a fraying towel. When she reached the guava trees, which had been fenced after earlier residents picked them clean, there was enough light off the infirmary barn lamp to see a new note impaled on one of the spokes:

You've gotten this far,
You've walked the night without fear,

Now walk toward The Gate
Like that young engineer.

"The Gate" was a pair of eucalyptus trees whose crowns grew toward each other; no one could say why, as the sea wind usually blew in a third direction altogether. The phenomenon was outfitted with a myth—a wealthy girl and a pauper, in illicit and reprobate love, had been transformed into saplings doomed to stand near but forever apart by a secondary god whose misbehaviors had somehow landed him in the debt of mortals (the girl's parents, who disapproved). In their eternal separation, the trees grew toward each other.

"Like that young engineer"—George was trying to ease her anger by reminding her of better times, by writing poetry to her again. If so, it was a failure—it would take her no time to regather everything he had thrown away. But she would never forgive him. Now, never. She was grateful—now she never had to find her way back to him.

Beyond the arbor, a narrow path through dunes wound to the sea, which hissed over the sand. She saw them by the flashlight Dina was swinging, like a ship that didn't know from which direction to seek help. When one of the beams caught Susanna, Dina dropped the flashlight and ran toward her. Susanna stopped—she had forgotten this eagerness from her daughter. But it had nothing to do with her—Dina was clutching her letter, which she pressed into Susanna's hands without touching her. Susanna moved past her daughter.

She stopped moving once she saw it all in the moonlight. He had thought of everything—there were even four ballasts on the edges of the blanket that she recognized as the long pavers from the path between the laundry room and the showers. All her food was here, organized in paper baskets he had nicked from the cafeteria, separated by lavender he and Dina had picked, wavering in the wind. She saw fava beans mixed with onion; the salty cheese; a long-necked bottle of an almond syrup diluted by water. Susanna stood there, vibrating and ticking.

"What is it?" George said to her.

"Nothing," Susanna said. "I was excited for the surprise."

He rose in gratitude. Then she noticed Dina's hand. She grabbed her daughter's shoulder in alarm, and though it hurt, Dina kept silent because she needed her mother's assistance with the letter. After George explained, Susanna leaned down to run her fingers over the rigid hand—no, it wasn't numb, she just couldn't move it. Could she please read the letter now? Susanna held Dina in a strained hug.

Then, in the cylindrical beam of a flashlight, she obliged her daughter:

Hi—

I'm writing this letter because my parents said I have to. Father Nik made them do it, like a charity thing. My older sister has to write one, too. It's all so you feel less lonely.

I'm 12. All my friends are 12 or 13. My little sister is 8. She doesn't have to write a letter because she's too little.

I like Xbox, aliens, and calligraphy. My aunt showed me the calligraphy. What do you like? I'm including a picture of an alien that I drew. [However, no picture was enclosed.]

I don't know what else to write. If you wanted to come play here, that's fine. Your camp is 10 minutes from us. You are not alone. Father Nik said we should say that. Father Nik is young. People like him because he was in America, but they don't like it when he says he will never get married. I don't know why that's a problem.

My father is also named Nik, so it's funny. He works a lot. He's always on the computer. He always tells me to stop being on the computer. I said, You're *always on the computer. He said, You're not old enough to talk back to me yet. My sister said, Next time, just say you're always on the computer because you want to be like Papa. She's smart. I'll try it.*

Vasi

"Should I write him?" Dina said.

"Dina-dove," George said in a thin voice. "Tomorrow we may receive our permission to go on to America, like this Father Nik. So it may not happen for you to meet this boy."

Dina's brows rode together. She was formulating an objection, but it had to be a persuasive one, worthy of her adversary.

Susanna sensed it distantly, as through a wound dressing: George was no longer waiting for Susanna to address Dina's troubles. This is what Susanna had wanted, though she also hated herself for her abdication. She would make her way back to her daughter—she just needed to gather a little more strength. In the meantime, Dina had turned toward George. Susanna felt relief rather than envy. It was as if she was assuring herself that they could go on without her.

This time, Dina did not intend to listen to George. Life had given her a new Harry, a new Robert, a new Yacoub. She had ruined matters with all, and Dina wondered whether by writing this boy Vasi, she was subjecting him to danger as well. But she did not have the discipline to refrain. Her score was zero–three, as her father would have said about soccer. She had to try once more. And if things went wrong with this boy as well, she would swear off them forever.

Dina asked to go to the tent and start writing—and if they were waved on through to America, she promised they could trash it. George didn't know what to say—he wanted Dina there as a softening agent between himself and Susanna, but he also wanted to be alone with his wife. Before he could decide, Susanna told Dina to go. The girl ran up the path, her sneakers filling with sand. George and Susanna sat silently on the blanket and listened to the waves.

"I'm sorry," Susanna said. "It's lovely. But I don't feel hunger."

George reached for her hand, withdrew, reached again. She allowed it to be held.

"For months," George said carefully, "we have listened as you have filled yourself with these things. I say to myself, *Let it be, the ways of a woman are mysterious.* But, Susanna, you slip away again and again. If you are going to eat, eat with us, at least." He shivered in the wind and steadied himself for the force of her reply.

"Listen," she said, ignoring him. It had assembled in her mind at some point in the evening, and now she felt sure of it—or that there wasn't a better alternative. "Tomorrow, when they ask us why we ask for asylum, I will speak. But I need your help. You look at the floor. Close your hands together and look at the floor with grief. All right?"

"But what will you say?"

"I will simply speak about it in terms they understand."

She felt him wanting to press, to know. She hoped his fear of provoking her would prevail instead. To distract him, she closed her hand over his, startling him. It was her first intentional touch of him in three months. She wanted to weaken his objection, but she had also missed this hand, the whirling pads of the fingertips, the jiggling bracelet, the watch shrouded in the hair of the wrist, the soft hair of the knuckles. The bristling darkness of George's body always made the softness of his skin a surprise. Yes, he was not a manual laborer, but the softness was because he scrubbed himself with a loofah each day. He was the cleanest man she had ever known. Even in this filth, he was clean and soft. He had hauled his loofah to this continent. She had groaned when he had handed it to her, for the suitcase.

Eventually, he said, "And how do you know so much about what they want?"

"In my safe walls, I watched a lot of television," she said. "In our country, you never have a film based in a courtroom. It wouldn't be interesting—the verdict is known before the trial has started. But the Americans are always making television in the courtroom. They love this argument that happens there." She laughed, not unkindly, a real laugh. "And if you are only willing to separate yourself from the exact truth, you can win any argument."

She allowed her head to fall into his collarbone, away from the wind. He moved a paver and covered her with a corner of the blanket. He lifted a piece of flatbread and, with his arm around her, chewed slowly. Soon, she inclined her head slightly upward, and he carefully placed a piece of it in her mouth, afraid to touch her too closely. When he'd let go of the food, her lips closed around it and met the pad of his finger. She held them there, and he the fingertip, trembling, for quite a long while as they rocked slowly in the rush of the wind.

* * *

Susanna woke first. Susanna never wanted to wake. Usually, George and Dina were already back from the bathrooms by the time Susanna opened her eyes. In their first weeks at the camp, it was all she could do to make it to nighttime. By first darkness, she was scrolled on the cot, dinner forgotten, her lids clamped like locks. But then this solace was by some curse drained of its power, and she developed insomnia. For hours, she lay as her husband and daughter wheezed around her, her mind visiting places she rarely wanted to visit. She counted, prayed even though she didn't know how, shook, left the tent, returned, left again, falling asleep at four, five, to be pulled awake by George and Dina's noise at seven, shattered.

She made herself go to the infirmary. She lingered by the entrance, where a stand of information brochures had been laid out for people like her—people with medical difficulties they did not wish to discuss. The dreadlocked doctor looked at her, smiled quickly, looked away. Susanna sympathized with her—the woman had to pretend she didn't see who was looking at what. The hair made the woman look like a dog.

When Susanna's eyes passed a brochure on sexual assault, her hand reached for it mechanically before quickly retracting. Surely, they kept count. Maybe there was even a camera. She read, on the cover: "Victims of sexual assault who can demonstrate a pattern of abuse or a likelihood of repeated assault may be automatically eligible for asylum." Again her hand, as if someone else's, went to the brochure, and again she withdrew it.

The insomnia brochure was as informative as it was useless. You were supposed to get up from the cot, turn on a low light in another part of the dwelling, and read until your eyelids got heavy. In another part of the dwelling? Perhaps another bedroom in their palace? And what were you to do about the husband and daughter this would awaken? There was also medicine, the brochure said—just ask. Susanna resolved to try again to fall asleep on her own, and if nothing changed in a week, she would risk a conversation with the dog-woman.

It was eating that saved her. Destroyed her. It worked only if she did it at night, if she filled herself to such discomfort that she was forced to focus on the discomfort—in her stomach, her anus, her throat, her tongue—rather than anything else. Sometimes, this weary disgust turned into sleep. Then she started doing it during the daytime. Then she did it all day.

Now, after the seaside picnic with George, she couldn't fall asleep because she was thinking about the asylum interview. Enervated, her mind went to Theo and her father on his knees. The story was strange, almost theatrical. Susanna's father could never do something so self-abasing. But hadn't he, by remaining in Arid to take care of her mother? He condemned her mother for her refusal to improve, but he wouldn't leave her at the asylum.

Then Susanna was in the back seat of her father's old Paykan as they rumbled over the low hills between Arid and the border. On three sides was another country. They had anti-psychotics her country did not. For more than a month, once a week, when the old woman was there to look after her mother, who sat wrapped in her shroud-like shawl in a scavenged wheelchair whose wheels didn't turn, her father loaded Susanna into the Paykan, an old model with wood paneling and scratched leather that smelled like milk from the pail, and they drove to the border market on the other side because he had been told a shipment would come. For one hour in each direction, they bounced silently as women and men in the radio sang about love, and dust rose all around. Susanna's body memorized the knocks and bumps of the road—they swerved here, they dipped here, here they bounced and waddled. For one month, they returned over the same sinkholes in the other direction, with more love songs but no medicine.

And then one day, her father parked at the front of the market, as he never did, and walked to the end of the line of parked cars, checking for what she didn't know. Then they returned to the front. There he found a man who inspected the Paykan and took a bumpy ride in it as they waited.

When the man returned, he gave her father a clutch of bills and drove off. With it, her father bought the entire supply of the medicine—he had to pay extra to get all of it. Then they walked the line of cars again until her father found the one he'd marked in his mind. This one was a Samand, newer but plainer inside. He looked around and told her to climb in. The owner had thought it safe to leave the keys in the ignition. When they got home, her father changed the license plate and repainted the car, and they never went to the border market again. The medicines made no difference.

Susanna looked at Dina, her hands in a prayer under her temple, thinking of her new pen pal. George whistled in sleep, blowing out his herbal air like a power plant in standby. (Here from tarragon or thyme, pilfered from the kitchen by Susanna.) She was grateful for the protecting proximity of his bulk in the night. Sometimes she awoke, and it was that night again, but when she saw George's faint outline in the next cot, she knew it was not. The camp barber George had found had done decently for Dina's hair, which no longer looked like the top of a muffin. And George, by now, would look stranger if his moustache returned. After George and Dina had found Fares, George's barber at home, closed, Dina began climbing the sink to do what Fares had used to, snipping George's moustache as she sang love songs and George tried to interfere with lines of poetry he wanted Dina to try reciting instead.

Susanna's heart lurched with feeling for her husband. She wanted to touch his hand again, the lined knuckles and the signet ring. She creaked down from her cot. There were certain positions that made it impossible not to notice that she felt numb between her legs. This part of her body burned with its defilement and felt numb, all at once. The hand on the neck, the shirt across her mouth—it all flashed before her, as usual. She sat, shaking. Before her, George's brows trembled in sleep, his eyes dashing under the lids. Sometimes, even his hand opened, as if he was debating some odds. She lay back down in her cot.

* * *

They walked toward the camp gate in their finery, feeling the eyes of their neighbors. Some watched with envy, but some placed their hands on their hearts. Susanna felt ill at ease in Mikki's clothes, which chafed her skin in the heat. George knew little enough about her wardrobe to have no questions about their provenance.

When they got near the mailbox, Dina deposited her letter to the boy Vasi, which briefly declared, in a wildly looping cursive in her non-writing hand, corrected by her mother's better English, Dina's acceptance of his invitation. When the bus arrived, the young guard held out his hand so that Susanna could take the steps up to the payment machine. Their eyes exchanged a small acknowledgment of Susanna's escape the previous night. The guard lifted Dina all the way into the bus. He shook George's hand. He said, several times, in his language, what Susanna imagined was "Good luck, good luck, good luck."

Outside the cracked window of the bus, Susanna saw what she hadn't in the darkness of the previous night. On the right, the mountains periodically dissolved, revealing cloudy valleys where sheep grazed and cement trucks climbed the roadways. Susanna was a fish on a reel that was permitted to reach a maximum length of eighteen miles, the distance to the American consulate. But she would break the reel. They could not remain where they were for much longer. She didn't have the mystical feeling that America set off in other refugees. It was merely somewhere else. But that was good enough. Behind its gilded doors, maybe something would change.

Dina jumped up and down the rubber corduroy of the aisle, eliciting looks of apology from Susanna and tolerant smiles from the natives. George allowed himself to cover Susanna's hand with his. She did not take it away. Wishing to avoid endangering this detente, he did not close his hand around hers, just left it extended as if he were feeling a stove grate for whether it remained hot to the touch.

Taking a steep switchback near the edge of the capital, the bus expressed a strangled cry and stalled. The driver cried out. Susanna and George looked at each other. They had left themselves an extra hour, fifteen minutes of which they'd lost because at one point, the driver had to work a special ramp to bring inside a woman in a wheelchair. They had broken down in the most unsafe portion of road, the creaky hulk of the bus divided from a drop by a bent guardrail. Because of the angle, the bus blocked not only its own lane but half of the oncoming. From both sides, cars tried to dash through the narrow aperture with no order.

Susanna moved to the head of the bus. The driver stepped out of his pen to block her path. He had an owl's narrow, flat nose buried in a heavy-jawed face, and the reeds of his hair sprang up like turnip leaves. He waved his arms. They were the one set of people he could not allow to disembark. Susanna pointed to a watch she didn't have to indicate their appointment. It had no effect. The din awoke the woman in the wheelchair, who moaned loudly. Susanna realized she was a refugee from another camp on the coast.

Everyone heard the crumple of metal outside. Two cars had tried to move through the opening at the same time. A large woman in sunglasses that covered most of her face stepped out from one of the cars and shouted. A terrier yelped alongside her, its nails skittering on the pavement with the force of each yelp. The other driver draped his head over his hands on the steering wheel, in weariness or defeat. The bus driver disembarked to adjudicate.

George felt a hand on his shoulder. The man was middle-aged, with the wispy moss of a younger man's beard. With his thumb, he indicated the back door. George's gaze fell across the woman in the wheelchair, who stared with desperate eyes. The bearded man nodded, and they moved toward her, working off the complicated restraints that kept the wheelchair from moving. The driver did not see them. Susanna clutched Dina's good hand. The bearded man kicked the rear door. It gave in with a wounded hiss. They were all five on the ground before the driver noticed. He ran toward them. The bearded passenger stepped in his path while George, Susanna, Dina, and the woman moved rapidly toward freedom.

* * *

When the consular agent called their names, Susanna rose, but the agent patted the air like a child's head: They should stay where they were. Susanna sat down. As the agent approached, her nostrils twitched. To those coldhearted people who said that *these people were animals*, here was inconvenient proof: Susanna, George, and Dina smelled like wet, dirty wool.

It hadn't been so long before that Susanna had been the one sitting in the cars into which beggars stared. But forty-five minutes before, as she held Dina's hand and George wheeled the woman, they were the starers. The drivers looked away. But then a honk went off down the line. It was a farm truck, a canvas cover cinched over the bed rails. In the cab were a man, a woman, and a boy, his face swollen by some malady.

The animals in the bed stomped, confused by the appearance of such different travelers. One nearly crushed Dina's foot. The driver pushed one sheep between George's legs, where it bleated belligerently. The woman in the wheelchair stared in disbelief. Dina was laughing. The bus driver's angry eyes followed them on their way.

In fact, Susanna and George had never felt animal fur under their fingers, even though Susanna had grown up in a village, something she recalled rarely considering how often she remarked on the village behavior of others. The fur was tranquillizing, like the hair of a child. When they arrived at the consulate, they failed to understand that people were staring at them because their noses had picked up an ambivalently familiar scent of home.

"I have bad news, I'm sorry," the agent now said with extra volume, as if they were deaf. The woman's hair rose high off her forehead. She wore a mauve skirt and blazer, and black flats crowned with miniature bows. Through her black stockings, Susanna could see an old scar on the knee, a strangely intimate vision, and she looked away.

"The interpreter's delayed," the agent said. She tapped her complicated watch, which looked useful underwater, or in military situations. "There was a crash on his way. I can't pull another—every terp's working right now. We have to reschedule." She pulled out her mobile.

"Madame, I can speak English," Susanna said. "We don't need the interpreter."

"Trust me, you do," the agent said. "Even if you speak. Which I appreciate, by the way, that you already possess the language of the country you're trying to reach. But he's trained. He'll represent your case more professionally. You'll be more comfortable in your language."

Susanna tried to control her expression. With this information, the agent destroyed Susanna's plan. This was her punishment for keeping away from the other people in camp, who knew people who'd gone through this. If she'd known there would have to be an interpreter, she would have told George what she was going to say. It would have upset him, but he might have agreed, been able to prepare. Now he would react with shock instead of the defeat and despair she needed. George was leaning toward her conversation with the agent, as if that would make it comprehensible. Next to him, Dina tried to make a tiny ponytail out of her hair with one hand.

"But, madame," Susanna tried, "how can I practice my English if I have to speak only my language? Also, it's not easy for us to just come back tomorrow."

"Why tomorrow?"

"For the new appointment."

"That's not how it works, unfortunately. But it won't be long. Two–three weeks."

"Two–three weeks?" Susanna exclaimed. "Madame, we cannot. I will lose my mind. How much time do you have in there for us?"

"An hour."

"So let's go inside. Let us say names, dates of birth, all this simple information. For this, you don't need interpreter, come on. And maybe he comes in time, and we finish. Please."

The agent considered her. "You're persistent," she said. "I appreciate that."

"This word I don't know," Susanna said.

"I'm also persistent. I don't think anyone in my family's ever said a nice thing about the federal government. But it's what I wanted. I believe in what government does."

"So then we have this in common, madame," Susanna said. "I mean the persistence, not our government. We want your government."

The agent succumbed to a smile. Her eyes ran to Mikki's dress, also mauve. "We have our fashion sense in common, too, don't forget. Okay, we'll do names and dates. If he comes, he'll take over. If he doesn't, we have to reschedule for the rest of it. Deal?"

The office was larger than Susanna expected—only ministers and superintendents had such large offices in her country. A small window in one of the vast white walls looked out onto a row of iron bars. There were three chairs on the supplicants' side of the desk. Susanna took courage from this, as if it meant their family had the right number for acceptance.

"It used to be a home for the mentally troubled," the agent said.

"What happened with them?" Susanna said.

"I don't know. I guess they got better."

"That is good news for me."

The agent acknowledged her effort. "Funny lady."

Susanna wondered if she was bending it too far—a person who wanted to say what she planned did not speak in jokes. But how to say it before the interpreter came?

The agent typed into a computer while Susanna anxiously watched the door. Dina stared at the bumblebee-patterned pennants that spanned the wood-paneled bookcases. "Not a lot of hockey where you are, I'm sure," the agent said, noticing Dina. Susanna stared at Dina to stop looking, so the agent could focus on her notes. "It froze four months of the year where I'm from. Everything stopped for the Red Wings. Okay, let's do dates."

Susanna turned over a paper she'd prepared with their details. It was impossible that this woman could not hear Susanna's heart stomping. Dina tried to stand on her chair. George raised his palms in loving exasperation. Susanna called Dina's name harshly. The agent looked up, not smiling this time. Dina slunk back to her seat.

George leaned forward. "Tell her we apologize. It's because we're nervous."

"Honey?" the agent said to Dina. "That has real value to me. Back on the shelf, okay?"

"Dina," Susanna hissed. "Madame, I'm sorry—can the girl wait outside?"

"The family members have to stay together," the agent said. "But I guess it's all right for a child. And I get to keep my Second Place Midwest Finals in one piece. There's a play area by the vending machines. Tammy watches the kids, she's great. What's wrong with your girl's hand? What's going on with your hand, Dina?"

"It's nothing, madame," Susanna said. "Dina, my love, play outside. There's a mat—"

Dina slid from her seat. George rose, too, but Susanna said, "Not you. She won't let you go." George remained half standing, as if he was about to defecate. Slowly, he sat back down.

Susanna led Dina to the door. When she opened it, she saw a tall man with a briefcase waving it at a man in short sleeves. "These goddamn bus drivers!" the tall one said. "I would do better with a blindfold and a crossword puzzle. I need the little boys' room, and then I'm late for a depo." Her heart sank—saying the last words, he had gestured his narrow head toward their room. Susanna released Dina and slowly closed the door, her back to George and the agent. She closed her eyes and took a long breath.

"What is it, ma'am?" the agent said. "Can you return to your seat?"

"I'm sorry," Susanna said, still facing the door. "I had—"

"Are you unwell?"

"No, no, it'll pass."

"But what is it?"

"For three months we've lived in a tent, you see. No doors."

"Not following."

"I'm sorry, Madame. It's a bad memory."

"What is it?"

Susanna hesitated.

"Ma'am?" the agent said.

"One day when I was at home . . . it was maybe six months before we left. I heard a knock on the door. It was a heavy door, just like this one. It was the Administrator at my husband's university."

"The Administrator?"

"The person who gives him the students for his classes."

"The Registrar?"

"Yes. Such a person never comes to the house when the husband is not there, you understand, not in our culture. I'm confused and worried, but I must be polite, so I invite him for tea. He is already holding a teapot for some reason, so he makes a joke that he already has the tea. And when we are sitting for tea, he informs me . . ." She trailed off.

They listened to the muffled drone of the waiting room's chatter.

"Go on," the agent said. "Please. Can you turn around?"

"Please don't make me do that."

"Okay, that's all right."

"He said—very calm—that he will come once a week, the same day and time when he knows George has a class, except for the week I am bleeding. I will wash myself before he arrives. I will greet him, we will have tea, and then I will go to another room and remove my clothing. With his yellow teeth, he is saying all this, like he is telling me something about university. And he says that if I tell George—anyone—"

"George will lose his job," the agent said.

"No, madame. We will be killed. He is dominant-sect and we are—"

"Minority-sect."

"Yes."

Behind her, Susanna felt the agent take this in. "What did you say?" the agent said.

"What could I say, madame?"

"Will you turn around to look at me?"

"It's difficult just now, madame."

George's head moved between them as at a tennis match, but the women ignored him.

"How long did it go on?" the agent said.

The tears came freely to Susanna. She worked through them, she couldn't delay. How could something be a lie and the truth at the same time, fully each? "Six months," she said. "As the day of the week became close, I became more upset. Very impatient with my daughter. On the day he would come, I prepared George his lunch and then I sat on the divan and stared at the door. I just waited for that knock."

"Your husband didn't have suspicions?"

"I said I had a woman's difficulty. He's a good man, he didn't question me. Of course he understands a woman cannot have difficulty all the time, every week. But he didn't bother me. After this—this person—left, I washed and washed, and the windows were open until George came home, because of this spice cigarette the man smokes. Even when the man leaves, it is in my nose all the time, I smell it in the divan, in the sheets." She paused. "He would not do it in the family bed. This is from respect for George, he said."

"This is why you left."

"I say it with shame, madame, but no, that's not the reason. This man, he didn't come one week. Or the following. Then one day, George came home very worried, upset. This man informed him: 'Tomorrow they will come for your family.' So we ran. If you ask George, he is very grateful to this man. For George, this warning was respect for George's work at the university. My husband believes this man saved our lives."

"Your husband doesn't know," the agent said.

"No," Susanna said.

"Why does he think you're crying right now?"

"There are lots of reasons to cry."

"You'll have to turn around, please. Please sit. I'll get you some water."

"You know," Susanna said through the wet on her face, "this man never looked at me." She was shaking. She had to be dramatic enough for the agent, but not so dramatic that George would become unduly suspicious—having her back to him helped. But it was hard to keep herself in control. "He always did it from . . ." Susanna tried to gesture behind herself. "Before he began, he covered my head with his shirt. So he wouldn't see anything but my body."

"Ma'am," the agent said stiffly. "I am so very sorry." She took her nails off the keyboard. "I need you to turn around now. Please."

Susanna did so. Her eyes were swollen and her lips trembled.

"Ma'am," the agent said, "what would you have done if the interpreter had been present from the start?"

"Then I tell you a different story, madame. I cannot tell the truth if he understands." She indicated George.

"You would rather compromise your chances of asylum than have your husband find out?"

Susanna made herself look directly at the woman's eyes, and as firmly as she could, knowing the effect it would have, said: "Yes."

They remained in silence, the agent gazing at them with an unreadable expression. Finally, she said, "Call your daughter in, please."

"Why, madame?" Susanna said.

"Just do it."

Nervously, Susanna opened the door. Dina was rocking a plastic palm tree with the full force of the hurricane in one hand as the woman named Tammy tried to persuade her to stop. Susanna had to wave, then call, then shout, but finally Dina bounded in.

"Dina, honey," the agent said. "Please sit." Dina took a chair, and stuck the good hand under a leg. The other one stuck out as if she was about to shake hands. "Tell me what happened to your hand."

"Madame, let me explain," Susanna said.

"Let her say it," the agent said.

"She doesn't speak English," Susanna said.

"I do speak English," Dina called out resentfully. Susanna's face filled with color. The agent gazed at her disapprovingly. She turned back to Dina. "Well?"

"They did it in school," Dina said. Susanna looked over uncertainly.

"At the camp?"

"No, of course not at the camp." The small note of exasperation in the "of course" startled the agent, but added to Dina's credibility. George looked at Susanna imploringly—their daughter speaking had not been explained to him; in fact, nothing had been. With her eyes, Susanna tried to indicate that this wasn't part of her plan. "At the camp, they are nice," Dina said. "Teacher Volos is always smiling. Loving to smile. She loves life, I think."

"At which school, then?" the agent said.

"School at home. It was triangles. The homework was, Go home and cut triangles from that paper made of little squares."

"Graph paper."

Susanna was staring in bafflement at her daughter.

"We don't have this math paper. I come with triangles from just regular paper. And they did this to me."

"Who they?"

"The sisters. Aya and Belem and other children also don't use the math paper, but they don't get no hurt. You know, Belem didn't do it at all, the homework."

"And they're dominant-sect," the agent said.

"Yes, of course."

"How did they do it to you?"

"Madame, please," Susanna said, but the agent held up her hand.

"They hit the"—Dina patted the bad knuckles with the good like a bazaar merchant persuading bad joints to awaken—"with a ruler. The small side of the ruler." The index finger and the thumb of the good hand came together to show it was the narrow edge of the ruler. The agent winced. "They hit and hit. Until . . . crack."

"You have to go to the infirmary," the agent said. "There's an infirmary at the camp."

"We went to the hospital at home. They said to wait. It gets better."

"There's different medicine here. You have to try again. Ma'am, you have to take her."

"Okay, of course," Susanna said. Her tears had dried, and her trembling ceased. She stared, incredulous and emptied, at her daughter.

"I will tell you another story," Dina was starting to say when the noise of the hallway burst in. It was the tall man with the briefcase. There were tiny pits in his face and a graying ring of hair around his mouth. "Wait till you hear this fiasco," he said to the agent. "It's not the first crash that gets you, it's the tenth. This country . . ." He looked around. "Why are these people here? You know you can't do anything without a terp."

The agent took the pendant of a necklace out from behind her silk blouse. It was the color of her suit. She held it for a moment, then brought it to her lips, like a little microphone. She looked at Susanna and back at the man.

"You're new," the man went on, "so you don't understand—"

"We're practicing English," the agent said. "Killing time waiting for you. Weren't we?"

"Persistent," Susanna said through the mucus in her throat.

"Then why is she crying like she just missed her flight to New York?"

"She thought you wouldn't show," the agent said. "She thought it was all over."

"I came as fast as I could," he said defensively. "I didn't even go to the bathroom." Reluctantly, he slouched out of his posture of instruction, and, switching to Susanna's language, which he spoke with the dialect of the country where Susanna's father had gone for the useless medicines, asked her and her husband to state their names for the record.

* * *

Leaving the deposition room, Susanna took George's hand. Behind them, the interpreter, whose name was Donald, was leaning over the agent, whose name was Meghan, discharging information in a steady tone. He didn't notice that Meghan wasn't listening. Meghan nodded slightly at Susanna. Susanna lifted the corners of her mouth in return.

When they were clear of the door, George turned to Susanna with pleading eyes, wishing to understand what had transpired.

"Don't worry, please," Susanna said. "You are a good man with love for his wife."

George's face loosened. "But this is what I have been hoping you'd remember," he said.

"And this young lady played a part also," Susanna said, marveling at Dina, who stared ahead coolly.

The reception was more crowded than earlier, so at first they didn't notice the commotion. A young man in a wheelchair was shouting "Dog! Dog! Cursed dog!" His finger was extended toward their side of the room. It took them time to realize that it was extended toward them—toward George. The door of their interview room opened to reveal Meghan, and behind her Donald, positioned so closely behind her that his lips nearly touched her hair. With displeasure, she bent her head away from his mouth.

Susanna looked back and forth between George and the pointing young man, who had a pink, piggish spot above his forehead where no hair grew. There was a patch over one eye, and he kept one of his arms close to his chest, as if he couldn't move it. But with the other finger, extended in indictment, Kamil, returned from the dead, was pointing at George in the reception of the temporary American consulate as the people around them stared in confusion and relish, like the windows lighting up in their apartment building as the false street sweeper killed Kamil over and over. To the watchers, the scene felt like home.

* * *

Susanna and George were led into one room—Dina was again foisted on Tammy, her eyes burning with resentment at being demoted this way—and Kamil wheeled into another. Susanna, unable to take hold of reality in the detail required, didn't dare look up when she passed Meghan, who was still standing in the doorway with Donald floating too closely behind her. Susanna knew this made her seem guilty.

After a brief conversation with another consular officer, a bearded man with a broad waist whose fingers were smudged from lunch, they were sent home and told to return for an investigation the following day. For this, the calendar had parted. Passing through the waiting room, Susanna could not spot the solitary woman in the wheelchair whom they'd helped. She decided that no such woman existed and that, earlier, in the roadway, it was Kamil they'd helped. In the back of the farm truck, the woman had pointed to her mouth with a crooked finger. But she wasn't mute—if she spoke, Kamil's voice would emerge. They had opened the door to a demon in disguise, and after their arrival at the consulate, the creature had returned to its original form. Susanna did not have the presence of mind to dismiss this mystical village rubbish as rubbish. Sometimes, the village was right.

At the bus shelter, Dina kept darting toward the roadway, and because Susanna had no voice to admonish her, she tried to take her daughter's good hand to ask her what creature that cloud resembled. Dina liked the game but not the player, and demanded that her father, who was seated with his head in his hands, play it with her instead.

As the bus approached, Susanna was overcome by the certainty that it would be operated by the same man who had driven them earlier. She did not fear his reproach; rather, she wished that she had obeyed when he had insisted they remain where they were. But the driver turned out to be someone else.

The bus was nearly empty except for two older women in flowing beach garments with nautical signage, and a young man and woman with army-colored backpacks. They had dirty fingernails and clutched hands tenderly. One of the women, Susanna saw, was discreetly running her fingers over the nails of the other. It was the bus of love. Susanna took George's forearm. Now everyone on the bus was holding each other except Dina, who fluttered between the seat poles like a moth, and the driver. But he had his wheel.

George flinched at her touch. Her poor husband thought his sin now extended forever. It had forced them to flee, and now—because the U.S. government favored the rebels over their intermittently genocidal government, Kamil's word would certainly prevail against theirs—it would force them to return. But Susanna had a surprise for George. She had never believed in all this. It was like a grotesque holiday, and now it was over. There was only the question of where to hide in their country, as they couldn't go home because Kamil's people would surely take their revenge.

She regretted allowing herself the pleasure of not contacting George's parents, whose help, and funds, would now be useful—every day, they planned to turn on their mobile, and didn't. They could go to Dostat, in the Triangle, which was under government control. It had a small technical college, and while the administration surely didn't care about poetry, there had to be a position for someone like George. She would finally call on her parents . . .

She was sufficiently lifted by these thoughts that she was able to give the camp guard the cautious smile he was hoping for. The residents in their path watched them with wary interest. As they were passing the kitchen, Theodosia stepped out, holding her yellow cleaning gloves aloft as water dripped onto the gravel. "I'm drowning without my helper," she called out good-naturedly, and Susanna forced her cheekbones to rise. "I would cross these fingers for you if I could." Susanna placed a hand on her heart, but couldn't bear to stop and speak to her.

Dina raced to the tent because maybe the boy Vasi had answered. Susanna said it was too soon. Dina kicked a stone at the neighbors' fire ring, and disappeared down the path to the water.

It was too soon and too late. Unlike asylum, deportation was instantaneous—they would leave the day after the judgment. Dina would resent her only more. Thinking of Dina scattered Susanna's resolve. No good things awaited their daughter in Dostat.

George lowered himself to his cot and fell asleep heavily. When he awoke, Susanna made him a glass of tea. George could not understand the inversion—now that the thing they had feared had finally happened, his wife was kinder. The ways of a woman were pure enigma. He slurped loudly as Susanna sat on Dina's cot and ate squares of un-yeasted cake.

"So he came back from the dead?" Susanna said through the mush in her mouth.

"He was always persistent," George said. "In class once, he raised his hand and said, 'Excuse me, sir—such-and-such poet was born in a different city, you will find.' The other students stared. I realized, with a terrible feeling, he was right. I had been giving this lecture for ten years, and for ten years, I had given the poet's birthplace correctly. Why had I named another city this time? It was like coming home and calling you by a different name all of a sudden."

George shook his head, but the memory did not make him unhappy. "The university failed to give his brother, the blind one, several benefits—walking assistance on campus, audio recordings of the lectures, that kind of thing—and do you know Kamil somehow managed to get the attention of the governor of the province? But then it went too far in the other direction—the governor's office became involved, the university became frightened, and the blind brother received the best grade even if he didn't prepare. So he stopped preparing. That time the blind students were cheating, the teacher probably knew all about it. To think, it was Kamil who solved the problem, and created a new one, and solved it again in a terrible way when he gave them away, because once Kamil filed an official complaint about the cheating, the university had no choice but to expel the brother. But that is the way things are in our country." George sipped his tea, hoping for warmth, but by now it was tepid.

"So you are saying death called Kamil and he declined to listen?" she said.

George smiled wearily. "Something like that."

* * *

As if they were dignitaries, the next morning a private car took them to the consulate. Inspecting the faces of the people who would determine their fate, Susanna had the impression that the asylum-interview system seemed organized to address allegations of deceit more readily than expressions of need. Need prompted a fatigued skepticism, one man's electrocuted testicles fading into another's smashed ribs. Accusations like Kamil's, on the other hand, seemed to bring the consular staff to a fresh edge of feeling.

When he was wheeled in, Kamil did not take his eyes from George, whereas George struggled to meet the gaze of his student. The plaintiff went first. As misfortune would have it for Susanna and George, the chief commander of Kamil's rebel group had recently met publicly with a staff member for a deputy assistant U.S. secretary, which seemed to make Kamil's claims unimpeachable for the personnel present. As Kamil spoke, the senior consular agent nodded gravely as the stenographer popped the keys of her little machine.

The plaintiff stated that he had asked the defendant for war funds and made no threat for noncompliance. In response, George turned in his commander—turned a man in for torture and death—not because George feared for his life but simply to gain extra favor with those who tortured and killed. Here, Kamil hung his head at his naivete regarding George, but George was his teacher, and he couldn't imagine . . . The raw pinkish spot on Kamil's head, which caused him to resemble a rejected leopard, pulsed and flushed.

In response to George's betrayal, Kamil lost sleep and developed heartache. He decided to address the issue directly with his former teacher, his pure intention proven by the fact that he had arrived at George's apartment building without weapons. Kamil didn't know by whom he was attacked, though the man wore a street sweeper's uniform, and everyone knew that's what undercover intelligence agents often wore. The government had thanked George for turning in Kamil's superior by providing protection in the form of the agent who maimed Kamil for life.

"It is not correct . . ." George tried, when his turn came. "Why would you wear a face wrapping . . . why would you raise your hands to the sky in prayer . . . in the middle of the night . . ."

"To disguise myself in a mixed neighborhood!" Kamil interrupted. "To pray for peace with a teacher! Look at what was done to me, dog!" He banged his chest with the mangled arm, saliva sputtering from his mouth. "Look!" He lifted the eye patch, behind which lolled a dead eye. With his good hand, he rattled the rails of his wheelchair. Then the plaintiff began to apologize for his outburst.

"He came to my office to threaten me," George said. "I am a university teacher, please understand. For many years, there was not one available spot in my classes."

Susanna sat numbly. She understood the English part of the exchange sooner than George. Once, the door of the hearing room opened to reveal Meghan, and, beyond her, Dina poking a finger into the tube of fat above Tammy's waistline. Susanna looked at Meghan, but now Meghan's gaze fell away, and the door quickly closed.

The senior consular agent, who wore glasses with circular rims, leaned toward Kamil.

"Sir, this is an uncomfortable question because . . . well, anything with women and children." He paused, sighed in a tired way, and rubbed the glasses with a kerchief. "As much as I am sure you don't wish to hurt vulnerable people—the same way *you've* been hurt, though what happened to you is far worse than a deportation order—the United States government needs to ask you, and needs you to answer truthfully. Was the spouse involved in her husband's efforts to compromise your organization?"

Susanna leaned forward. She wanted Kamil to say yes.

"No." Kamil shook his head. "I do not have this knowledge."

Too soon, Susanna and George were asked to step out. They stood in the waiting area, watching Dina play. George's heart seized violently enough for him to take a hand to his chest. His daughter was eight. Nearly nine. She was magnificently beautiful, the eyes big as thumbs, and while the hair would need many years to recapture its glory, there was always something lurid for him in its earlier length, as if such belligerently luxurious hair belonged only on older women. Now, finally, Dina looked like a child. Dina was less fearful than both George and Susanna—because they'd sheltered her well, he wanted to think, but it was something else, too, something her own. The achievement did not need to be his for him to think: He loved his daughter. He was always very fond of her, of course, but he wouldn't have put it this way three months before.

"Wait a minute," George said. "Wait a minute."

"What?" she said. "What?"

"How could I forget this? But who remembers anything now."

"What is it? Please tell me."

"The second time that Kamil came, I recorded the conversation. He threatened me. Once they hear that—God, how could I forget it."

"What?" Susanna said. "And you have the recording?"

"No," he said. "But it's there, in the drawer of my desk. If someone could go there . . ."

Her face fell. "I am sure they cleaned your office long ago . . . There is a new man in it."

"There is still value in mentioning something like that," he said. "I will go back inside. I must say all I can." She didn't have the heart to dissuade him, and watched him recede, feeling pity for his sudden hopefulness. When he emerged, he shrugged. Because he was not in possession of the recording, the information was retained without great promise to their cause.

The hired car took them back to the camp. It gave the wrong idea to the guard, who pumped two raised thumbs as they emerged from its tinted darkness. They had turned from people ordinary enough to receive the camp residents' resentful good wishes to VIPs driven by private vehicle. As they approached their tent, Dina slatted her eyes with her working hand, but the mailbox was empty. To increase her unhappiness, she was sent to the shipping container for the last two hours of school.

"You should go to the kitchen," George said. "We should act without difference."

Susanna thought unhappily of trying to explain to that tall, heavy, kind bird of a woman. She didn't think she could tell the truth. They each sat down on a cot.

"I brought this on us," George said.

"You do not have to say that anymore," Susanna said. "It has been said enough."

"I don't mean what happened with Kamil," he said.

"There's more?" she said, trying to make light of it.

He clawed his hair with his fingers. "Do you remember the old man who spoke to us at the camp? In the line for food? He said they don't want people to come anymore. So they were arresting whoever was driving the boat. As a discouragement." His eyes fell to his hands. "Yacoub didn't suddenly decide to return home."

"I'm not following."

"You didn't see it because you weren't feeling well." He explained from the beginning, staring at his sneakers. The day before, he had gone to sleep wearing them. The yellow dust of the transfer camp had never entirely gone away. The sneakers looked like a kitchen counter on which a housewife had worked carelessly with turmeric.

Susanna stared at him numbly. "What do you think happened to him?" she said.

"He said he would go east, to the Triangle. No one would know him there."

"It's where all the unwanted go," Susanna said. "Sometimes, I wish I had remained there. It is away from the world. You know, yesterday, on the bus, I thought that we should go there."

"We?"

"Or do you expect to return to your previous life?"

George didn't answer. His wife was finally showing him tenderness, and for some reason he had chosen to confess about Yacoub. His own mind was as incomprehensible to him as Susanna's. He had used to be a more practical man.

She said: "I have a confession to make also."

He understood this comment as a gesture of generosity, and nodded.

"It's about Fares, the barber," she said. "You had gone with Dina and said he was closed. Well, one day, I was walking that way, I think for the new identity cards, and I saw that he was open. But I never told you. I liked so much looking at you and Dina in front of the mirror. There was so little that you did together."

A shadow crossed his face. She inspected his eyes. He looked away.

"What is it?" she said.

"Nothing, nothing."

"You didn't tell me the truth about Fares, did you," she said. Her anger was just on the other side of some door, ready to run back into her arms. "What is this lie now?"

He looked past her. "Fares wasn't closed. When Dina and I walked in, he asked us to wait outside. He didn't kiss me on the cheek, didn't ask about Dina, only pointed outside. I was confused more than insulted—the shop was empty except for the person in his chair. But maybe there was a new regulation of some kind, one person at a time. So we waited outside. He locked the door and drew down the curtains. When that client stepped out, Fares just locked it again. He never looked at me." George opened his mouth as if to say more, but then closed it.

She shook her head and reached for his hand. He let her take it. They sat next to each other in silence, like passengers at a rail point, waiting for departure.

"Why did we apply to go to America?" she said. "We hardly know anything about it."

"Your English," he said. "And Dina's English. Look how good it is now. I am the exception. Do you remember when the American professor came to the university? I don't think he was American-born, but he had lived there a long time. He said, 'America is so free that even stupid people can make lots of money.' He said, 'Even stupid people have respect in America.' Isn't that something?"

She nodded and smiled weakly.

"I am fifty-one years old, Susanna," he said. "I am in the last third of my life."

"Are you speaking in riddles?"

"At first, it was all right," he said. "We must give up six months to a deserving matter like a civil war. It's all right, it happens from time to time. Take a year! When one year became two—all right, what's two years? Let them have it—but no more, all right? That is all we ask. But then two became three and three became four, with no end. I was a middle-aged man when it began. And now . . . I am a man in his fifties asleep in his shoes on a cot. And I feel ten years older than that. Are you listening?"

"Of course."

"Where did your mind go?"

"Dina is so excited to hear from this boy. We have to explain to her it's not possible."

"Let us wait one more day," he said. "Perhaps they will surprise us. I am a professor. I am not a schemer. He is less than half my age, but—they know this—he has killed one hundred times as many people, and with his own hands. Why should they believe him and not me?"

"It's a nice thought," she said. "But we should speak to her."

"I will speak to her tomorrow," he said.

Susanna yelped because the mobile was ringing. "What is that?" she said.

"Dina must have turned it on," he said irritably. "Why would she do that? It costs for us to receive calls." He snatched up the phone and listened. "Incorrect number," he said. "It's just a family here. Yes, goodbye." He held a button until the phone shut off.

After a while, she said, "You don't think about calling them?" She meant his parents.

"Of course, I do," he said. "Of course I do. I abandoned my mother. She's ill . . ."

"So now we are the same," she said.

He smiled contemplatively at her. She wanted to mention the thought she had had before leaving—that they had come together because they were both orphans of a kind—but for some reason, she refrained.

"The person on the phone understood our language?" she said, suddenly thinking of it.

"It was a person from another camp," he said. "They must have similar numbers for the SIMs they give to the refugees. He was wanting to speak to one of two brothers. Susanna, why don't we write Dina a letter from this boy? Let's say his family is leaving for the summer."

Susanna slid her hands under her legs. "You have so much feeling and concern," she said. "But you are always making secrets." She sighed. "What would it say?"

"*I'm sorry for the delay in writing to you.* No—he wouldn't phrase it so formally. *I am sorry that you waited for me.* No—he's a boy. He doesn't understand she was waiting for him."

"*I was very excited to play with you*," Susanna said. "*However, my father says we are leaving for the summer.*"

"*And I said to my father, But how will you work without your computer? And he said—you will not believe this—he said, I am not taking my computer.*"

"*So it will be a very short vacation*," she finished, and they laughed at the same time. It was an unfamiliar sound, and they let it ring in their ears.

"I've forgotten what it's like . . ." he started.

"It is not a good time for my body," she said, giving the automatic excuse.

He had meant he had forgotten what it was like to laugh together. But now her lie was between them. It had been with them so long it was like a houseguest who never left, burdensome but familiar.

She turned toward him. The area above his lips was perspiring—she could smell the sweat mixed with his shaving lotion, that glue, and some other quintessence of him, distant to her all these months, but molecularly recognizable, even if it was inflected by the dust and sun of this place. It was good for him here. As her body bloated and betrayed her, he acquired the skin meant for him. At home, he was a portly professor with pink fingers and an unflattering hairline on his belly. But here he was again a version of that laborer slurping his lunch on a roof. But only she saw it. He claimed to feel old and slow.

Returning from school, Dina encountered the strangest sight: her parents touching lips like teenagers. Seeing his daughter, George reluctantly separated himself from Susanna—it was the job of a child to walk in at the most infelicitous moment!—and brought Dina into the embrace, not allowing either woman to drift out of his touch.

* * *

Susanna awoke after seven. She had had a series of indeterminate dreams—one of an insistent but elusive noise in the old apartment, another of an important document that Dina had destroyed before Susanna could submit it to the authorities. At first light, she had dimly perceived George shuffling out to use the bathrooms. Dina snored slightly, *Uncle Neem's Fairy Tales* between her legs like a pillow. It was really time to get her a new book. Unfamiliarly, Susanna felt the weight of unfinished sleep. She was alert long enough to register an impression for which she hunted so often these days—*perhaps I am improving*—and closed her eyes again.

When they opened, she saw that George was already gone to breakfast. He almost never went by himself—he must have wanted time to think. His sheets were tossed about—it daunted her husband to try to be neat with his bed. Amid the billows, there was a small tent of paper, a little white roof on a disordered home. The noise Susanna made as she read stirred Dina, who watched her mother bolt from the tent, the letter falling to the floor. It was in her father's cursive.

My dear Susanna—

On my last day at the university, I stopped at the main gate to smell once more the lilac that always blooms that time of year. And suddenly, it was 14 years before, when I was your age now, and you were only 14 years older than Dina—isn't it strange, this pattern of years?—and we were standing at the gate together. We could very nearly see each other's hearts moving. We couldn't walk through the gate as teacher and student, so we did it as husband and wife . . .

I'm eager to tell you that I meant none of what is happening now, that in responding to Kamil as I did, I wanted only to help my family . . . But that is what the person in my position always says. I understand things like that now. As I understand, with special bitterness, that just as you seem to have forgiven me, I am once again betraying you with a secret. But you would never have agreed to this otherwise—be honest about that—and we owe our spectacular daughter a better life than Dostat. Please be honest about this.

I didn't make an audio recording of the second meeting with Kamil. And I didn't walk back into the consular office to discuss it. And it was not a man looking for one of two brothers on the mobile. It was so unfamiliar to have it on that I had forgotten to set it to vibrate rather than ring. The consular people agreed to accept my offer to return so you could remain. A car came early this morning—only private cars for us now!

I wish I could say that my action persuaded them to clear the slate for you. They said that protocol required them to conclude their investigation of you. It's a formality. If they are at all concerned with the truth, they will find nothing. They are concerned with the letter of the truth, not the spirit, but you are clean in any department.

I wish for but do not expect your understanding. I do beg you to allow me to hear my daughter's voice once I've found my place. It can be in a recording. And one day the war must end, mustn't it? I told Yacoub all about family reunification. It was why he agreed to take the controls. I didn't think that, one day, it would be for my sake that I'd hope I was telling the truth.

Your loving husband,
George

Barefoot, in a nightgown, Susanna dragged the still-unfamiliar heft of herself up the path, the camp residents parting in their walks from the bathrooms. Then they parted again for Dina. When Susanna reached the guard booth, she bent over, spittle falling from her mouth.

"Lady . . ." the guard said. He pointed to a car idling past the gate, and in its window, the broken face of her husband. Susanna was in one of those dreams when the body knows it must move forward, but can't. She tried, and fell, scraping the pavement. The guard rushed to help.

Dina moved past Susanna. She was shouting, *Don't leave me with this drug addict!* George smiled awkwardly—he thought Dina was making an odd joke. As the car rolled away, he reached a hand through the window. Dina kept shouting, *That night by the sea, she left us! She went only drug addicts know where!* Now George's expression changed. His fingers slackened and withdrew, and for some reason he touched his face, as if it was slick with blood whose source he couldn't decipher. The car receding, Dina's body shook with sobs, and she jumped several times in rage and helplessness. In the rear window, George watched his daughter's face vanish into an invisible point, but not before he saw his wife rake her hand roughly across it.

* * *

After her mother hit her, Dina fell. This made Dina lose critical time in her pursuit of the car. There was a sharp curve just ahead of the entrance to camp, so the cars that typically raced down the coastal road were braking when they came into view of her, running down the road in her T-shirt and sleeping shorts, and were able to stop in time. The guard ran after Dina. From the way he lofted her up, it was clear he was a father. She wailed in his arms as he cleared her from the roadway. The impatient cars poured around them. In remorse, Susanna tried to take Dina's hand. Dina yanked it away and ran to their tent. When Susanna reached it, her daughter was pulling on school clothes, the rigid hand clumsy and useless.

"How dare you say such a thing," Susanna said weakly.

Dina ran out, clutching her rucksack. Susanna followed, but Dina was already far down the path. Susanna returned to the tent, but couldn't breathe, and stepped outside again. She sat on the patchy gravel, her head in her hands. Through a hand, she saw the mother next door push her children inside so Susanna could be alone.

Susanna spent the day on her cot. Her tears blotched George's letter to the point of illegibility. She considered burning it, but she was without the strength to get up. She sobbed until she fell asleep. She awoke in the afternoon—she knew because the eucalyptus was in her nose. Dina had not returned at the appropriate hour. Clutching the mobile, Susanna stumbled to the school. Midway, she noticed that she was still wearing her nightgown, turned around, changed her clothing, started again.

In the fluorescent stillness of the classroom, the afternoon teacher was writing in a notebook. "Check that tent," he said, pointing. "We have an exam tomorrow. They study together." Susanna nodded and turned away. He cleared his throat. She turned back.

"She's a very intelligent girl," he said. "Children want to do what she says. Because when she speaks, there is no question in her voice. It's a very special quality." Susanna nodded again. She knew she needed to thank him, but the words wouldn't come. Instead, tears came.

"However . . ." the teacher started, then saw the tears and fell silent.

The sweat from Susanna's hands fell into the crevices between the buttons of the mobile. She tried to bite back her tears.

"Actually, would you mind if I went with you?" he said. "To the tent where the girls are studying?"

He stopped to the side of it, so he wouldn't be visible through the window flap, Susanna behind him. They were like parents spying on a child engaged in precocity. Through the flap, they saw Dina pacing beaten earth—this tent didn't have a concrete platform. Dina held the stiff right hand behind her back, so it wouldn't diminish her authority. On a small rug, two girls with dark skin clutched workbooks and followed Dina's commands with their eyes.

"You're not trying hard enough," they heard Dina say matter-of-factly. "You're lazy. They will definitely send you back to your village.'"

"Tell me how old they are," the man said.

"Six?" Susanna said.

"They are making themselves so small, do you see? They are actually older than her."

"Thank you," Susanna said. "I understand now." She whipped back the canvas. "Let's go," she said to Dina. As the words left her mouth, she relished her power over Dina, but then guilt caught up, and she added, "Please." Dina, her power interfered with, stared at Susanna hatefully. Stepping out, she said to the girls, "You don't need to practice. There's no point." Susanna yanked her hand roughly, Dina squealed, and the teacher looked away. Dina tried to squirm out of her grip, but Susanna wouldn't let go. If she found the strength for only one thing, she wasn't going to let go of her daughter.

"Why did you talk to them that way?" Susanna said once they were on the path back to their tent.

"They're dumb village girls. They understand only if you make them."

"Well, your mother's from a village."

"When will papa come back?"

Susanna stopped and stared at her daughter. "You are like a bird that pecks, and pecks, and pecks, until the tree is worn away."

Dina's eyes filled with tears. She forced out her hand, and ran ahead.

Susanna ran after her, got a shoulder, spun her daughter around. "You want to know?" she called. "We left because your father made a mistake. He stuck his nose in the wrong business. So we're here because of him. But now he's not. Tell me what sense that makes."

Dina mumbled something Susanna couldn't make out.

"You were all mouth with those girls, but now I can't make out a word."

"I said I don't know," Dina said, her eyes on the ground. She worked herself free once again, and walked on by herself.

* * *

George had it wrong—not only did Susanna and Dina remain under investigation, but their stipend was suspended. Susanna wondered whether he had merely wanted to be free of them. She couldn't persuade herself of it. It was she who wanted to be free of him—for three months, she did her best to elude him, and some misunderstanding God decided to deliver the wish. But it was only his body she wished to elude. She missed the awareness of his body, like a large fluttering moth, somewhere close. She kept the mobile on, but it didn't ring.

At the consulate, she was told he was flown to their capital, and there released on his own recognizance. She asked how she and her daughter were expected to get by with no stipend and no permission to leave camp. Had she saved nothing of the stipend they'd been given so far? In any case, American taxpayer funds couldn't support individuals under investigation of assistance to a terrorist regime as designated by the U.S. government. Yes, she'd saved nearly all of the stipend. It would pay for little more than several weeks of illegal residence somewhere. It wasn't a complaint she could make out loud. George had taken none of the money.

Between two sets of sliding doors, she stumbled into Meghan, holding a lunch container. She wore a cream-colored jacket over a dress printed in a botanical motif. Her heels had thick soles. Meghan told the woman next to her, who was so large that she could move forward only by shifting side to side, to go on. Meghan, Susanna, and Dina stood in the middle space between the automatic doors, which opened and closed, opened and closed, around them.

"You wanted to protect him, and look at what he had going on in secret from you," Meghan said. "Perhaps it wasn't in secret."

"If it happened, it was to protect me and our daughter," Susanna said.

"Everyone is protecting everyone," Meghan said. "And everyone gets hurt. I need to get back now. Good luck."

"Madame, please forgive. How can a woman and child live in such a situation? We are not allowed to leave camp. They have taken the stipend completely."

"You have meals," Meghan said. "They just need to research you and your daughter."

"My daughter!"

"You are free to take the next flight to your country," Meghan said coldly. "We'll pay for it, too." Meghan stepped so close that Susanna could see the ridges of her lips under her lipstick. "I *believed* you. I decided to give you a chance. What I did for you is *not* permitted. And so you will keep your mouth about it *closed*, please."

"Help us," Susanna said. A desperate woman, she added: "Help and I'll keep it closed."

"Don't you *dare*—" Meghan made herself smile because another lumbering body was coming through the doors. "Don't you *dare* threaten me. I will get you and your daughter sent back to Fucktown tomorrow. Do you understand?"

Susanna thought: *You didn't say yes to us. The interpreter insulted you.*

You were saying no to him. But of course she couldn't say that. She lowered her eyes and said, "Yes, madame."

"Now get the fuck out of my way." Because the doors had just closed, Meghan didn't see that another body was waiting for them to reopen. This penguin, having overheard Meghan's last words, wore a strained smile.

On the fourth day, the old mailman delivered the boy Vasi's reply, which consisted of two lines of driving directions and a phone number with no greeting or parting. Susanna had neglected to direct Dina to specify that Dina couldn't leave the camp, that he'd have to come here. She contemplated burning the letter, but couldn't do it. She would gather strength and write another reply. She checked the mobile—nothing. This could mean only that George had climbed the hanging rope of Dina's accusation until he got past Dina's misunderstanding to the truth of that night. Or that he had come to harm. The former possibility made her light-headed, but she would choose it over the latter. She wished for a third.

Up the path, Susanna could see Theo, large and aproned, accepting a delivery from the gas man. Susanna had not shown up for her shift in four days. She could no longer afford volunteer work. Every day, she meant to speak to Theo. She didn't know what to say.

She noticed the guard descending the path to the tents. He never came this way. He wore, as usual, a heavy jacket with many buttoned pockets. She hadn't really noticed it till now, away from his usual place. After a moment, she was startled to find him standing directly before her.

"Lady . . ." he said. He pointed over his shoulder. Susanna smiled weakly—she didn't understand. He was only twenty-five or so, but his eyes had deep creases and the skin there looked puffy and worn. He pointed behind him again and put a hand over his eye. Her skin ran. She hadn't eaten in four days, and she stumbled when she rose, but then she experienced an unfamiliar lightness as she scrambled up the path.

When she reached Kamil in his wheelchair, he said, "It's easier to reach the man who fixes watches on the eighth day of the week."

"Every curse on you," Susanna panted out. "And to come here . . ."

"I've brought you money."

"Money? For what? If you give it to me, I will scream. They won't let us leave this place, but anyone wishing to enter can enter, I see."

"I haven't entered," he said. "But I have a pass." With the good arm, he raised a lanyard.

"My husband, who misses a spider with his foot when he tries to kill it, has been deported. But you—you sit here with special passes."

"For the moment," he said, "I am in the grace of the American government. I must take advantage while I can." He smiled, his mouth moving awkwardly. The teeth were unnaturally white against the grayish caramel of his skin.

"What do you want?"

"You will not invite me to your home?"

"And what a home it is. You really know nothing."

"I said, I have brought you money. I sent him away. Now I am responsible for you."

She laughed viciously. "Perhaps we should become your family? Perhaps I can become one of your wives?"

"We don't believe those things. You don't wish to accept it, but I've done you a kindness."

They were interrupted by the return of the guard, who retreated inside his booth and gently closed the door.

"Did you return from the dead?" Susanna said.

"It must be, with God's help."

"Well?"

"You're looking at the first and last man saved from his trouble by the United Nations. And they were so criticized for agreeing to meet with the Leader. Don't say the UN kisses the feet of murderers!" He considered Susanna's blank expression. "I suppose that wasn't the kind of thing you paid attention to." The white teeth clicked as he spoke.

"I am paying attention now," she said. "Believe me, I am paying attention."

"That morning, the UN person and the Leader, may his feet feel only sores, were driving to that orphanage near where you left me, by the concrete plant. Happy, safe orphans are very good to show the UN. But a dead body by the curb is not good!" Kamil laughed, baring again the block of white teeth. His gums worked oddly over them. The laughter subsided into coughing. "Your man collapsed my lung," he said. "To breathe is like trying to stand up holding a gravestone. There's no part that works the way that it used to." With his good arm, he played with the crank that moved both wheels of the chair, listening to them pop the gravel.

"They have lead cars to sweep for problems, but I suppose they couldn't get me out of the road fast enough. They couldn't do anything except heal me because now the UN was watching. I became their orphanage. I went to the Leader's private hospital! It was good for them. And for me." His face gave up its mask of bitter triumph, and he briefly looked like the boy he must have been in George's class. "When I woke up, a nurse told me the story."

"They didn't kill you after the UN left?"

"And die twice?" He tried to laugh and gave up, like a newly legless man who still perambulates in his dreams. "There are plenty of people at the hospital who sympathize with our cause. When the wind started to shift, I was covered like a dead man and wheeled out."

"Why are you here?"

He hesitated. "Certain consultations."

"You point out collaborators," she said. "You're an executioner. You go from person to person, pointing your finger."

"They have invited me to apply for asylum," he said.

"So it looks like we helped you."

With the fingers of the destroyed arm, he reached into his mouth, took out the teeth, and twirled them in the sun. "Yes, you helped me very much."

"You took an ordinary man from his family. He was only trying to protect us. How great was his sin? An ordinary man. His daughter worshipped him."

"Not you?"

"She loves her mother, of course."

"I meant: You did not worship him?"

"I do not use your language. Nothing is as simple as you people want it to be."

"Ordinary man, you say? You don't know anything about your husband."

"But you do."

"Your husband has been reporting to government intelligence for almost a decade. Long before this instance—long before the war. They laughed at him, with his little poems. But he was useful. He kept an eye on all the minority-sect people at school. Even dominant sympathizers like us. And not only at school."

She stared at him, dumbfounded.

"Tell me," he said, "what university professor, when someone like me asks him for money, is clever enough to think: 'I can get a bigger fish from all this.' Hm?"

"That means he helped intelligence?" she said. "You, a fighter, are embarrassed he fooled you, so you make up stories."

"An ordinary professor decides to give away a rebel commander—you think he just knocks on the door of the police precinct? No, he went to his handler."

"No." She shook her head. "No. He wrote poems."

"That was how he passed messages. And they decoded his riddles. Listen." He pulled a small notebook from his vest and flipped, squinting to focus the good eye.

He sits beside the churning smelters
An acolyte bereft of elders
The man who shivers silently at night
Is talking endlessly in light.

"Translation: Look at the night watchman at the auto plant, the religious one."

"How do you know all this?"

"After what happened to me, my people questioned a government person we caught. He's famous, your husband."

"Yes, he dreamed of that . . ." Susanna said numbly. Her mind refused to work through the information. "Please leave us," she said. Her mind was collapsing, like Kamil's lung. It could not accept this information. "Leave us be. Don't torture us more."

Kamil didn't respond, but once more, the mask of the adult fell away.

"Is it guilt that brought you here?" she said. "Go away from us."

"Your husband took my body," he said quietly.

"You!" she shouted suddenly. Inside his enclosure, the guard looked up. "*You* gave up your body when you came to kill us. When you came to demand money from him. You liar. You dirt on the shoe of a man. You make the truth that you want, and then you pass blame like a housewife giving soup. Every curse on you. Damnation on your half-broken head so it breaks all the way." Now she didn't care who heard her. She took her head in her hands and sobbed.

"There is no problem with you and your daughter," Kamil reaffirmed. "I am responsible for you now."

"The help I wanted was not to have my husband taken away," she shrieked.

"There was not that option." Kamil worked the crank. "I will go now. I will leave you a mobile number. I will be here for another week or two." He pointed to a sedan on the edge of the road. The driver was asleep, his mouth open.

"They gave you a car?" she said incredulously.

"Once the Americans decide you're on the same side . . . Well, it wasn't that simple. We had a meeting with Russians. Photo, photo. That put a fire under the Americans. Sometimes, you have to knock on the American head and say, *Excuse me, I think you've forgotten to love us.*" He issued his half laugh once more, the teeth riding around his tongue.

They waited silently, Kamil staring down the path and she looming above him, studying the sedan. Finally, she said: "I'll take your help."

"I am relieved to hear it."

"Not the money. That's blood money. Instead, you will drive me somewhere."

He hesitated. "I don't think that's possible."

She skewered him with her eyes. "So you are a boy, not a man. You make a man's promises, but then you reveal you are a boy."

He shifted uncomfortably. She crouched before him so that their eyes were together. She made herself take her hand to his knee. The kneecap bucked slightly under her touch. She was hiding her revulsion and he was hiding his nervousness. Probably he had never had a woman—that's what happened with the principled ones. With her other hand, she clasped one of the wheels, as if she were holding an extended part of his body.

"I will wheel you toward the car, and then climb in myself. Understand?"

"Yes," he said hesitantly.

"Give me all the money you brought."

He hesitated again.

"Give me the money. You said you brought it for me."

"But you said—"

"Be silent."

He withdrew the envelope from his fringed leather vest. She only now noticed the strange castoffs he wore. On his head, to cover the scraped pinkish spot, was a cap with a bent bill.

Susanna took the envelope, taking care to graze Kamil's fingers. She set aside a small knot of bills, knocked on the door of the guardhouse, and laid the envelope in the guard's free hand. Kamil made a noise of protest, but she held out a finger, and he fell silent. The guard also protested, but she shook her head, closed the door, and rolled Kamil's wheelchair toward his car.

To lift Kamil into the car would have humiliated him, so she shook the driver. He did not like being woken by a woman. But then she placed the knot of reserved bills in his blazer, and he relaxed. As he hefted Kamil into place, Susanna kept her hand on Kamil's leg, to keep his mind where she wanted. The young man, paralyzed, stared ahead. To her amazement, she felt a swell of pity for him. It was possible to feel revulsion, pity, and numbness at once.

* * *

The road curved away from them as they climbed. Kamil demanded to know where they were going. She said she would know it when she saw it—she chided the driver to go slowly. This brought him angry tailgating, which shamed him. Susanna beckoned Kamil, who reluctantly withdrew another clump of bills. Also reluctantly, the driver eased.

She remembered that there was a switchback, then a view of a valley, then the crosses. Road-fatality crosses weren't removed, were they? They were forever—that was the point. Now that she was looking for road-fatality crosses, they were everywhere. Most were on the side of the road that bordered the sea. They came up on a pair on her side of the road, but she remembered three, thanks to its unpleasant echo with the number of people in her own family. She walked through the world primed to see things in threes. Was that now supposed to change?

The switchback was less steep than she remembered, and the view was of a small settlement, not a valley, but eventually, she saw the trio of crosses.

"How will you get back?" Kamil said when they were at the house with red railings.

"You will wait here," she said. "I won't be long."

He clucked, but didn't argue. She was contemptuously amused by her power.

The door opened before Susanna pressed the bell. "In a Renault like that, I thought the tax man was coming," Mikki said. She wore a white silk blouse tucked into a long charcoal skirt, and the same low heels. Her face was pale. Some kind of spattered liquid had been allowed to dry and encrust on the tile behind her. "I'm both sorry and happy to see you. Come in, I'll make coffee. How did you escape that prison?"

"I remembered the crosses," she said without answering.

"Ah," Mikki said. There was a fleeting note of reproach in her voice. They listened to a thunder of feet above them, like rocks being poured from a sack.

"Summer is a hard time," Mikki said. "My son is too old for youth camp, so his friends come and play video games. Now it's girls, too. My husband is not going to have the sex conversation with him, so I had the conversation. He looked at me very confused. Because I got it all wrong. The girls are also coming just to play video games." Mikki laughed, but again there was disapproval, or contrition, on her face. "We're here only summers. It's an old family home."

Susanna tried to rehearse again the words she had rehearsed in the car, but her mind was stuck on the old woman in the transfer camp, who came into her thoughts at will with no say from Susanna, a violation that continued long after the physical one. How could the woman have no nails? Nails were supposed to grow back. And then she understood that the woman herself must have been raped many times when she was younger. A person did not travel to the far side of oneself like that without having been subjected to serial degradation. The woman was minority-sect. In her youth, the woman must have sided with whoever the rebels were in that generation's battle against the government, and was destroyed for it. Now, she took care to be on the same side as the power. Then Susanna remembered that she was also married to a man who had apparently, not ten feet away, lived life secretly on the side of the power.

She still couldn't believe it. But she knew it was true. His confession about Yacoub was the confession of a man for whom it wasn't the first time. She saw that now. As she realized that he had given himself away when he'd told her he was thinking quickly when he decided to seek out the police after Kamil asked for money. A person thinking quickly didn't think to ask for Kamil's commander instead. Just like Kamil had said. George had been, at once, frightfully adroit in the work, and bear-footed at lying about it to Susanna once it came to the surface. She took comfort from the bear-footedness, and the opposite from the fact that he had kept lying. But she also knew that he was trying to protect her. The less she knew, the safer she was.

"Are you all right?" Mikki said. The spoon going around the coffee cup was the only sound in the kitchen. The lights were off, and in the dimness, Mikki looked like a specter.

"Very sorry, madame," Susanna said. She didn't think Kamil would drive off, but he might ring the doorbell, what with his housewifely interest in meddling.

"You've come here to tell me something," Mikki said.

Susanna stiffened, realizing it. "I forgot to bring with me your dress."

"Forget it. It's yours. Tell me."

Susanna tried to smile. Wealthy people thought they were being generous when they told you to keep the thing as if it were nothing. Instead, they were being people to whom it was nothing, underscoring their difference. It made it harder to say what she planned. Yes, at home she had washed the floor on her knees, dragged a bar of soap across tracks in George's underwear, worked at shoe dirt with her nails. But that was at home.

"I'd like to clean this house for you," she finally said. "Make food for the boys. And girls. I can make them eat outside. You pay what is fair."

Mikki cradled the coffee. Her coloring was so wan that her fingers looked translucent, like she needed warmth from the cup. "My mother brought me up to clean myself," she said. "But just yesterday—honestly—I gave up and decided to call a housekeeping service. And you came today. That's a sign. But how can you leave camp?"

"I arranged it," Susanna said vaguely.

"But how will you get here?"

"There's a bus," Susanna said, hoping it would be enough.

The car horn went off outside. "Who drove you?" Mikki said.

"Just a friend today," Susanna said.

"I would love for you to make this house clean," Mikki said slowly. "Feed the boys and the girls, and make them eat outside. That sounds like a dream."

"I want to ask something," Susanna said.

"I know, I know," Mikki said. "Don't tell Theo."

* * *

The driver was asleep again, his head so far back it looked detached. Kamil was awake—he had settled into the resentful husbandly role of impatient waiting.

"You're taking your petty revenge, I see," he said. "You do your business, I sit and wait."

"Take me back, please," she said. Command worked best. They rode in silence. At the camp, she held the car door, meaning to say something. But she couldn't think what it should be.

Descending the path to the tents, her eyes met Theo's through the kitchen windows. The tall woman raised a hesitating hand. Susanna made herself step inside. A kitchen towel over her shoulder, Theo fought with a large stock pot. The towel slipped into the water.

"Do you see?" Theo said. "I lost my dishwasher and all is chaos."

"You know, don't you," Susanna said.

Theo nodded. "I don't need to know anything you don't want to say. I know enough."

"What does that mean?" Susanna said.

"It means you can't work here anymore, even informally. And it's probably best if we don't spend too much time together. But—two things. One—come here, please, if you would."

Susanna obeyed. The tall woman moved Susanna out of sight of the window, took her by the shoulders, and waited for Susanna's assent. Susanna whimpered it and Theo's arms fell around her. Through her linen tie-front, Theo's arms were heavy but flabless, dense like the limbs of a large and powerful animal. Susanna sobbed, and Theo held her.

"I'm sorry," Susanna said. She was leaving blotches on the linen.

"You remember this when we meet on the path and I have to act formal, all right?" Theo said. "When it gets dark, can you get away from your little girl for ten minutes?"

"Even if it's an hour, she won't notice," Susanna said.

"What do you mean?"

"Sorry. It doesn't matter."

"Go past the school, past the generator shed. By the eucalyptus grove. Wait there."

Susanna nodded.

Outside, the breeze had an unfamiliar coolness. She had an evening to figure out how she would reach Mikki the following morning. She dreaded her daughter's arrival from school. The tent was both airless and, in its loneliness, vast. Susanna fingered the canvas. In just months, the idea of a fixed wall had become strange.

She tried to tidy the handful of items from which their lives now consisted, then wrote the answer to the boy Vasi. Then she sat on George's cot and held her head in her hands. She tried to imagine the weight of him next to her, breathing heavily, the belly out over the elastic of his sports slacks, one of his letters between two fingers as, slowly, his eyes closed from fatigue. The motorbikes belched outside their balcony, the ice cream melted in the freezer, the sink gurgled from the bath across the hall, Dina was asleep in her room. It was late, but not too late, to sit in the kitchen with your husband and listen to him read a poem. The tea was cold in their cups, the wafers had crumbled over the tablecloth. More than wishing George had never involved himself in the business with Kamil, she wished that she had never learned any of it. Then, she believed against reason, none of what followed would have transpired. The problem was not George's lie but what she had made from it. Her resentment of her husband had conjured Kamil, had kept him alive. But she could not persuade herself that she had brought about the conductor. She didn't know why that had happened to her.

She heard footsteps. Dina opened the entry flap. "Now you sit alone in the dark?"

"Shit," Susanna said. She had lost sense of time. "I need to go to the bathroom. Where have you been?"

Dina held the flap silently.

"There has been a letter for you," Susanna said, a bribe. It worked. In the last light, her daughter tried to hide her excitement. "What did he say?" Dina said.

"He invites you to play. But we can't leave here. I wrote him to explain." She held up the letter to Vasi. "I'm sure he'll want to come here."

Dina lost her expression and said nothing.

"Dina, I have found work."

"Work? Are we always going to live here?"

"No. It's just while they decide."

"What are they deciding?"

"They're deciding when we can leave." Again, as a payment toward Dina's compliance, she added, "And then we can see your father again."

"He's your husband, also, or did you forget already?"

"It was just a manner of speaking. Please speak more softly with me. I promise, this isn't for long. While we wait, I will make money."

Dina stared through the flap, too resentful to give her mother the reaction Susanna wanted and too fearful to express her certainty that her mother's new employment had something to do with the night in the transfer camp.

Susanna understood. "I hope you never know the pain of your daughter thinking such thoughts," she said. "You are so certain you know what happened."

"So what happened?"

"I went to get a shot—I told you the truth."

"Why did you need a shot?"

"This country has different immunization requirements."

"I didn't get a shot. Papa didn't get a shot."

"It's female health. You're too young. Everything is different for a woman."

"Immuni—immu—" Dina couldn't manage. "In the middle of the night? I'm not stupid."

"So you tell me what happened," Susanna dared. She was grateful for the dark; her lip shook. She dug her nails into the flesh of her hand.

This made Dina quail, and she looked away. "What is your job?" she said finally.

"I will translate at the consulate," Susanna said. She had rehearsed it and it emerged without duress. "I will take the bus every morning. School will be finished by the time I return. I will treat you like a grown girl, if that's what you want. Can I rely on you to be safe here?"

Dina didn't speak.

Susanna rose. "I have to go to the bathroom."

Dina said, "I have to go also."

"No," Susanna said sharply. "Please wait for me here."

Dina flopped onto her cot.

"Papa will call, Dina. I promise." Susanna felt like she had been lying, only lying, for a long time now. She wished to say something that was entirely truthful. It took searching. "He went back because he wanted us to keep going. And we couldn't keep going with him."

"Why," the soft voice said in the darkness.

"I don't know how to tell you so you'll understand. But I will keep trying to explain it. That is the truth. I swear." In the darkness, she felt Dina turn toward the wall of the tent.

"I won't be long," Susanna said quietly.

There was no answer.

When she reached the eucalyptus grove, it took her a moment to find Theo between the trees. She looked like one of the trees.

"I thought you weren't showing," Theo said.

"I'm sorry. My daughter."

"How is she taking it?"

"I don't want to lie to her. But I don't know how to say a truth she'll understand."

"I am not a parent, so I won't pretend to have a suggestion. My mum's got bladder cancer. She doesn't know it. I fly back now and then, we go to the doc, the doc plays along. She thinks she's the healthiest horse around, she just has to walk around with a catheter because she's got diabetes. We all love each other to death in the Kasper family."

"You are a kind person," Susanna said.

"Wait till you see how kind I really am. Follow me."

They stepped through the grove. For a brief moment, Susanna felt she was walking through a forest with a friend. Before she had met George, she had friends, and before the war, they would travel by bus north of the city to walk through the woods there, and grill vegetables over a fire, and listen to one boy or another strum the guitar.

The grove ran out by the fence barricading the camp from the coastal road.

"I'm putting myself in your trust here," Theo said. "But I know you're going to try to get out, so you might as well . . . Look." The big fingers reached inside the fence lattice and pulled. A section gave way. "All right?" she said. "The bus drivers won't take you, but here's the number of a taxi service. Do you need help finding work? Wait—you should call Mikki. I can call her."

"No, no," Susanna said. "If I can't find—I will—" She had decided to keep her mission to Mikki a secret because she didn't know if she could trust Theo not to report her. It was clear now she could, but having embarked on the lie, a familiar trip, she didn't know how to reverse.

"That's fine," Theo said. "Fine."

Susanna hesitated. Because she didn't tell one truth, she decided to tell another. "I didn't know what my husband . . . did. I learned by accident before we left. I wish I didn't know it."

"I believe you," Theo said. "I am your friend. I want you to have what you want."

"Other people will decide what we have," Susanna said. "When you're running, other people decide."

"Maybe so," Theo said. "But you're still allowed to know what you want. Good night, friend. Use the magic gate wisely."

She stepped out of the grove. A little while later, Susanna followed. She didn't see her daughter watching from behind a wall of the school.

Later, Dina asked if she could walk the letter to Vasi to the mailbox at the top of the path. She insisted on going alone, and because Susanna felt guilty, she agreed. Dina walked until she was out of view of the tent. Then she approached the nearest fire and, without asking permission, tossed in the letter. The father and children warming their hands watched Dina with an expression with which more and more people watched Dina—disapproving, but afraid to intervene. Between the flames, Dina appeared ghostly, immaculate, and unwise to approach.

Some things were finally clear to Dina. Even as she had refused to accept her mother's explanation for what had happened in the transfer camp, Dina was periodically warmed, as if by the hot exhaust of a passing car, by the possibility that she might be wrong. And she was. Just not in the way that she thought. That was clear now.

Passing a tent on the way to school the afternoon of their consular visit, Dina heard whimpers, then squeaking, as if a laborer was drilling a nail into an unyielding wall. Sneaking toward the tent window, she saw the mashed bodies, flailing. It was like some kind of murder. She gasped and exclaimed in disbelief, "Eat shit . . ." She'd heard about this. It was confusing because it was supposed to happen only between people who loved each other, but clearly it happened also in other situations. This, not drugs, is what happened outside their building the night that they left. And it was what her mother did the following night.

Returning from school that day, Dina saw her mother kneeling before a man in a wheelchair, her hand caressing his knee. It was then that she understood what the other situations might be. Her mother sold her body for money. Dina had misled her father. Drugs was bad, but this . . . Dina could honestly say that she missed Robert. Funny little Robert, so apparently timid that he seemed deserving only of ribbing. She missed Yacoub. Robert had felt like a pet, but Yacoub had felt like a brother. She had failed them all. None of them would ever know, but she would make it right through Vasi, somehow. After burning the letter, she went home, thanked her mother for writing, brushed her teeth, and fell asleep on her cot.

After Susanna could hear Dina's soft snore, she gently unzippered Dina's rucksack and pulled out her school notebook. She tried to reject the guilt that she felt—it was a mother's right; surely Dina had doodled something that could help Susanna understand and manage her daughter. They had done a unit on containers in English—bin, pouch, drawer. They had cut out and re-pasted different kinds of triangles—that's where her story at the consulate had come from; Susanna realized in a bitter wash that she never got to acknowledge her daughter's inventiveness, which surely unraveled any doubts the agent may have had about Susanna's story.

Susanna flipped and flipped, but there was no private thought of the kind she wanted to find. Finally, she reached that day's lesson. They had talked about the Big Dipper. Next to it, Dina had written, "God is thirsty." At the top of the page, the date was circled, and trailed stars and hearts. Below them, Dina had written, "Happy birthday, Dina!" Susanna made a terrible noise, a noise of an animal under claw, of appalled astonishment. So this, too, was possible—to forget your only daughter's birthday. Dina heard her. She was awake. But she didn't turn around.

* * *

The next morning, before her mother had finished apologizing, Dina, seeking to make use of the injustice, interrupted Susanna to say she had to get to school. Eager for reprimand, Susanna fell silent. Dina demonstratively collected her school things and left.

In the classroom, she told the younger African girl who sat by the window that today they would trade. The African girl's face filled with fright, and she rapidly collected the implements—notebook, pencil, highlighter, page flags—that she carefully positioned on her desk every morning in a geometric pattern that was immediately re-established after an item was used.

Once they'd switched, Dina watched the window instead of the board. She didn't hear what Teacher Volos was saying until she heard her name—"Today, Dina is teaching herself to spot songbirds in the window." The students laughed hesitantly. They wanted to accommodate the teacher without making an enemy of Dina.

Dina liked Teacher Volos because she never wore jeans. Today, she wore a skirt the color of coffee with milk, a silky red blouse, and a necklace with a gold pendant. Her nails were always unpainted, but Dina liked this as well, perhaps because Teacher Volos had long, straight fingers, and neat, nearly rectangular nails. The other female teacher had puffy fingers with uneven nails, which no amount of polish could help.

"I am not feeling okay," Dina said the rehearsed words.

"Would you like to step outside? Some fresh air?"

"I would like to keep trying," Dina said.

Having in this way earned credibility, Dina encountered from Teacher Volos only understanding when, having seen her mother pass toward the gate, Dina raised her hand and said she felt vomit rising and needed to go home early. The children laughed uncertainly. Now, they wanted to satisfy Dina without making her feel ridiculed. Dina had credibility also because she never asked to go home early. Generally, she tried to avoid going home for as long as she could.

In the tent, Dina went to the box of dirty laundry where Susanna kept their stipend money. Her mother's underwear was the bank. Looking for it, she felt a pair of her father's large underpants. She stopped and had to rub her eyes. Was he in their apartment again? What was he eating, the man who asked his daughter to boil water? Was he growing back his moustache? Interviewing new daughters?

She went to the dresser, pulled out George's sleep shirt—he had taken almost nothing with him—and stuck her nose in the armpit. It smelled only of laundry. She sniffed another shirt. Same thing. With a rising hysteria, she realized that Susanna had washed everything. She had erased him. Dina hated her mother. Dina had meant to take only a few bills, but now, in revenge, she took half the bundle. Then she walked to the eucalyptus grove. Passing the school, she saw with satisfaction that no one had dared to replace her by the window.

The fence cutout came apart easily, though it was twice her height and briefly she struggled not to tip over. She waited for only several minutes before she saw the checkered roof light of a taxi. She held out the banded ball of bills like a wormy apple at the vendor who had fooled her into buying. But the taxi sailed by. Then another. She stamped her feet at the weed-pocked gravel. The eucalyptus grove gnarled out above her head in a protective, concealing canopy. Too concealing. She stepped out from its shadow so that she was standing in the road, and beat the bills against the fluttering wind. One more taxi driver failed to be persuaded. Then a white Opel Corsa with two dents in the rear passenger door and an unlit taxi light slowed near her, the blinker ticking loudly as the window came down. She approached. Her heart rolling around her chest, she was reassured to discover a man dressed like a taxi driver—a short-sleeved shirt open at the neck, where gray hairs clustered, and trousers of a cheap fabric over high socks. A miniature Christ rubbed his feet from the rearview mirror. The man was surrounded by a wife's blandishments: a thermos, a water bottle whose label had peeled off long ago, a sandwich wrapped in cloth.

Dina waved the bundle at him like a grenade. He pointed at the back seat. She buckled up quickly, so the commitment was harder to reverse, and showed him the directions. "How much?"

With a finger, he indicated a spot on the bundle.

"No," she said experimentally.

"No?" he said. "Then I go and tell." He pointed toward the camp gate.

"And I say you touch here." She pointed to her crotch.

He turned off the ignition. "Out," he said, tossing his finger at the window. "Out."

She separated half the amount he wanted. "Okay, sorry. But you pick me up also. Two o'clock. Then I give the rest." She had to be back before Susanna got back from the consulate.

He cursed and roughly slid off the shoulder. By the time they reached Vasi's house, his muttering had dissipated. It was a lot of money for a taxi ride. She made him write down his phone number, then poked a finger at his slim, gold-banded watch, encased in its arm nest of hair—she had a fleeting impression of poking her father—and stuck out two fingers. Two o'clock.

He rubbed his fingers together to remind her about the rest of the money. From her throat, she scraped up that exasperated croak that she had used to hear from her father. It was the international sound of old men. She was good at it. Again, she had the momentary sense that her father was near. The driver motioned for her to get out.

Vasi's home fronted a labyrinth of neatly trimmed hedges separated by gravel paths. The garden implements had their own home, a large open shed off to the side. The silence was complete except for the pained bark of a dog somewhere nearby.

The boy who answered the door, after many rings, had the smooth skin of a waxed apple. A crescent of hair fell over his eye. He stared at her with dazed evenness. She stared at him with disappointment—his eyes, behind their screen of hair, didn't have Robert's shyness. Or Yacoub's kindness.

The howling dog was somewhere near—the metal loops clanked as it strained its chain. It sounded like the grates people installed over their shop windows when the bombs started. They raised them long enough to sell someone whatever they sold and closed them again. The day was a chorus of endlessly rising and falling metal grates.

Her mind traveled to their apartment. In the evenings, after Susanna had finished reading to Dina, Dina would delay sleep by asking for a story from George. When he appeared, he'd recite from some book, but after a page or two, he'd always say, "Oh, but this is ungrammatical, you see," and set off into a discussion of syntax, which led him to meter . . .

It was by her bedside that she had first heard those words, *Your hair is like a wood, like the strings of Father's oud*. He had explained, in a lowered voice, that it was an old poem written by a minority-sect poet. It was criticized because it was without a political message. It was concerned with beauty instead of the struggle. So the poet wrote a poem on the right subject:

I sleep with this avenging rock.
It is my wife, daughter, mother.
In the morning, I bid farewell
To them all.

But this one was criticized, too, because it didn't rhyme, and this drew attention to the poem as an object of freedom instead of political use. Dina hardly understood this, but from fairy tales, she knew that things worked in threes, so she asked, "What did the poet do then?" But her father was snoring in his chair, his chin over his chest, his moustache like a ferret.

"Hello? Girl?" Vasi was waving his arms in her face.

With mortification, she realized she was failing her plan. "I am Dina," she said hurriedly. "From the place." She wanted to avoid the word *camp*. The boy rubbed his eye and stared.

"You wrote a letter," she said, extending it to remind him.

He read the lines, and looked up again. "What's wrong your hand?"

She snuck it behind her back. "Nothing. I came to play. You invited me to play."

He groaned and stepped out of the way.

Inside, a large staircase spiraled away from the main floor. The newel posts were crowned by water nymphs that looked at each other with some kind of distress, or longing. Perhaps it was sexual. Perhaps this sexual thing was going on all the time, but behind a screen through which only certain people could see. A teardrop chandelier radiated a soft yellow light. She felt the cold of the tile through the soles of her sneakers.

"Beautiful housing," Dina said. That was the word used in camp. *Housing*. She had rehearsed in the taxi.

"We're downstairs," he said, tossing the letter onto a narrow table. It swirled to the floor.

Dina watched him vanish down the stairs, then picked up the letter. Maybe he would need it. She wandered into the kitchen, so vast it had two refrigerators. She opened one and was enfolded by a purring blue coldness. Except for the distressed dog, the silence was so complete that it rang in your ears. Where were the parents? She had prepared to seduce them. With them, she would say "camp." She would smile. She went downstairs.

There were two other boys, and two girls. Vasi and another boy punched the controls of a video-game console while the third looked on with a faintly worried expression. One girl wore a rose-colored princess costume, and the other eyed it jealously.

Dina waved hesitantly and said her name. The girls stared at her, but the boys, spread along a cream-colored sectional in poses that took up unneeded space, didn't react. She was not going to play princesses with two little girls. She sat down at the edge of the sectional and swung her legs. The princess slapped the other girl, and that one started to wail. Finally, someone won something on the screen, and the boys noticed her.

"This is Dani," Vasi said, clearing the hair from his eyes and placing it back right away. Dani had a wide face with freckled cheekbones and a dimpled chin, crowned by webs of mussed orange hair. The third boy, Timo, slight with closely cut hair the color of old wood, transferred his watchful expression to Dina. The princess was Angelika, Vasi's younger sister. Vasi didn't think Angelika's friend was worth introducing. "If you want to play with us," he said to Dina, "you have to pass a test." He winked at Dani.

"What test?" Dina said.

"Make the dog stop barking," Dani said. He laughed and high-fived Vasi.

"What?" Dina said. "How am I supposed to do that?"

"If you can't, you have to leave," Vasi said, and they both laughed again. The third one, Timo, hurriedly joined in.

Dina wondered if she could shift her affiliation to the girls. No—no playing with little girls. "Where's the dog?" she said.

"Are you—?" Dani tapped his ear to mean *deaf*. They all laughed, even the girls.

She colored. Of course she could *hear* it. Where *was* it?

"Next house," Vasi said. "It barks because they're not home. They're never home."

"Okay," Dina said quietly. But they had already turned back to their game.

* * *

After climbing through the fence, Susanna took shade under a frangipani tree. Soon, a small blue Dacia pulled to a stop. When the driver showed her the price with his fingers, she made herself laugh, as she'd practiced—she was not enough of an idiot for that number. He sped off. The next two drivers showed her the same fingers. She couldn't spend that kind of money on the taxi. She fished in her bra for her mobile. The buttons felt good against her skin, like the fingertips of a child. She willed them to light up. Why didn't George call? On the third ring, she heard Kamil's pinched, adolescent voice.

"You don't have to remain this time," she said. "I'll find my own way home."

There was a resentful silence on the other line. He had offered money, not chauffeuring.

"I'd like to tell you something as an older person," she said. "Would you like to hear it?"

"I believe I have no choice," he said glumly.

"Do you think you will win the war?"

"Of course."

"And then—"

"And then we give the country what it deserves."

"Here is my prediction, boy." She emphasized the last word. "Everything will be the same. Do you want to know why?"

"It will not be the same."

"Tell me about one place in the world where the rebels have won and it isn't the same."

He thought resentfully. "It depends on what you mean by the same."

Cars rushed past her, and she had to close one ear with a finger.

"Because you'll reach the palace, and you'll ask, *What do the people need?* Right?"

"Of course, exactly. We do it for the people."

"But then, instead of asking the people, you'll answer the question yourself. Sometimes, you'll ask the people what they think. But they will be too scared to say anything other than what you want to hear. This will go on until new rebels try to destroy you. Do you understand?"

"Let us have this problem, please, madame."

She was shouting now over the roar of cars in the road. "I am asking if you are intelligent enough to understand the connection between what I just said and what you offered—"

"Yes, yes, I understand the connection," he said irritably. "You think it should be what you want, not what I offer. I am not stupid. And what will you do in ten days when I leave?"

"Ten days is forever," she yelled.

"Why are you shouting?" he said.

"I am a woman alone on a road with fast-moving cars."

His tone switched. "Retreat from the road, please," he said. "I will be there in no time."

They rode silently while the driver tapped his fingers to the radio. From the rearview mirror hung two plush dice covered with photos of one or another semi-toothed child with a woman in a housedress. No matter how you spun it, you got family.

"You studied political science?" Kamil said.

"No, why?"

"You like to make political analysis."

"You don't need to study political science to make political analysis. You just have to live in our country. I studied engineering. For one measly year. How old are you?"

"Old enough."

"You are twenty-four or twenty-five."

"Twenty-three."

"My husband is fifty-one. I am thirty-seven. You are twenty-three. Dina is nine. It's funny, no?"

"What's funny?"

"You studied math?"

"No."

"It shows."

He threw up his hands. "Why did you stop engineering?"

"Marriage. Do you have a woman?"

"There is no time for such—"

"Of course. You know nothing, but you want to change the country."

"I know enough," he said quietly. "I know that they let your people live only in places where nothing grows. I know that your daughter would have to give old Azze at the university a roll of bills to get a good grade—speaking of math. I know how they treated your husband. You sit in your easy life and you don't know these things."

"Easy life? You are joking."

"Tell me, then. What did you say in the asylum interview? What was your complaint?"

She was silent.

"Okay, how about a joke, then, if I am such a joker."

She looked at him with incredulity.

"What institution in our country has the most teachers with university degrees?"

She kept staring at him.

"Mouf Prison!" He laughed. "You call me a boy. Actually, in a way, you're correct. The first detention center they took me was near my mother's house. Your mother is right over there, making rice, or watering the plants, or whistling the music from that opera she saw once, while here they stick a heating bulb inside her son's anus. In Mouf, at least, it's clear that you've arrived in a place beyond hope. But this, two blocks from the home where you grew up . . ."

They were silent together. They had reached the house with red railings. Up front, the driver cleaned his fingernails with a key. He kept the engine going so she wouldn't linger.

She touched Kamil's hand. He nodded, acknowledging her acknowledgment.

"By the way, your husband was the only one," he said. "The only one who didn't want a roll of bills. But otherwise, he was the same. All the correct students got the correct grades."

"He had no choice."

"What do you do at this house?" Kamil said. "Who are these people?"

"I clean." She couldn't say it to Dina, but she was eager to fling her humiliation at him.

"You gave my money to the guard so you can clean?"

"Your money is poisoned," she said.

"But my car is all right."

"*Pity the man—*"

"*Forced to calculate how much to discount his soul*," he finished for her. She smiled bitterly. "*How strange everything is*," he started, willing her to finish this time, and she did: "*. . . once you leave home*." The first line was a proverb in their country. The second was from a soap opera everyone watched.

She touched the knuckles of his working hand with her fingertips. It was a calculated gesture, but she meant it as well. He was pathetic in his fringed leather vest. He closed his eyes, opened them, and closed them again.

"You would tell me, wouldn't you, if you knew anything," she said.

He opened his eyes. "About George? You mean have we taken his intestines out with a skewer?" The boy was transformed into a man who could order a murder, a torture. "I have given no orders," he said. "But I don't control everyone. If your husband is not a dumb man, he will not go back to the city. He will disappear."

"When did he start . . . doing what you said?"

"Almost a decade."

"Did they pay him?"

"It wasn't about money. What's more valuable than money in our country?"

"Protection," she said.

He clicked his tongue approvingly. "You know, when I saw him, at the consulate, I was filled with hatred. But I also felt the usual respect for a teacher. In class in his little vest, shaking his finger, he was so self-important, so ridiculous. But I just wanted to embrace him. Anyway, I will be late for the doctor. When shall I pick you up from school?"

She turned up her mouth dutifully at his joke. "By two o'clock. I have to be back before Dina comes home from school." He gave her a mock salute, and she climbed out.

Inside, she found Mikki's family gathered in a line of greeting: a man with a fringe of unruly hair arrayed like a skirt around a bald dome held Mikki; Mikki clutched a young woman with a pale, oval face; the girl's hand was around Mikki's son's waist; he seemed to be itching against it. The boy was a copy of his father, down to the mournful eyes the color of worn sandpaper, though the father seemed to have given in to this melancholy, whereas the boy's face jumped against the suggestion. He was like a syrup boiled down from the older man, the bubbles still going off. The father was Calev, the son David. The girl, Vela, was David's girlfriend. She looked at David with a teasing look, and David rolled his eyes, some game between them. The men drifted away, but Mikki remained holding the girl. Vela rubbed Mikki's knuckles as if Mikki were a good, loving animal.

Finally, Mikki let go and walked Susanna around, showing her buckets and mops. She would pay at the end of the week. Susanna could cook what she liked. What about hamburgers for lunch, if Susanna agreed? Susanna agreed.

As Susanna mopped, she felt the new belt of weight around her middle and was out of breath quickly. Her body was larger, but other parts of her felt smaller and smaller. In the bathrooms, she found pubic hair in the grout between tiles, shirts with salt rings around the armpits, a woman's dresses with wine stains, a boy's underpants from which the stickiness hadn't been cleared before it turned into hard crust in the laundry bin. In her country, a woman would never have allowed her home to remain so disordered before a cleaning woman arrived.

She realized that she had failed to take the ground meat out to thaw and rushed downstairs. She ran kettles of boiling water over the cellophaned meat, her mind trailing to the Registrar and his chipped kettle. That life felt as if it had ended years, not months, before. She had burned through the cellophane and was watering, with scalding water, a frozen tub of beef like a plant. She groaned and heard feet padding the tile. The toes were painted in a rainbow. Vela winked, unkinked the cellophane, set the meat inside the microwave, and vanished. Susanna wondered if the Registrar used the kettle to pour boiling water on people from whom he needed information. Or he was an innocent man and her mind had grown squalid?

Thirty minutes later, Susanna pressed her ear to David's door and heard whimpers. Her obligations to Mikki fought against her terror of knocking.

She was granted a reprieve: a croak, a long exhale, and then silence, followed by laughter. She knocked quickly, before the young people had a chance to start over. She had once done things like this, too.

The door opened, David fumbling with the drawstring of his shorts while Vela rubbed a knuckle at the corner of her mouth. The young woman delivered the pleasure, and the young man received it. Susanna couldn't hold David's gaze and looked down. Vela did the work for Susanna again: "Lunch?" David set himself free and surged past Susanna.

"Will you eat with us?" Vela said.

"No, no," Susanna said. "I destroyed the kitchen. It was one hundred percent cleaner before I started."

Vela touched her forearm and slid past. Susanna gazed at David's room, stranded between the block towers of a boy and the black flags of a teenager.

Somehow, Susanna had required three frying pans, two splatter screens, two cutting boards, enough knives and forks for a wedding gift, and half a dozen towels to cook four hamburgers. There was even a spot of grease on the ceiling. Through the window, she watched the back patio, where she had set up the food in a gazebo of cross-hatching beams.

David was complaining about something to Vela. He was the complainer, and she was the fixer. Vela made a gesture—she would fix it. To Susanna's mortification, she piled the hamburgers back on a plate and moved toward a grill by the French doors that led to the sunroom off the kitchen. In the silence of the afternoon, Susanna heard the click of the burners, then smelled the broiling meat, and was filled with shame at her failure. Vela's hair looked like a cape falling down her back. She had rolled up her jeans, and the band of skin below the cuffs radiated a violent healthfulness. She was pretty because of something in her body, not her face, a heedlessness that had never known the reprimand of a violation, of a reminder from the world how else things could go. Susanna both envied and resented her for it. Susanna turned away and scrubbed, opening the water to the highest flow so it could cover the noise outside.

Susanna finished a half hour before Kamil was due. David and Vela had remained outside, napping. The plates with Mikki and Calev's meals had vanished. No one had come into the kitchen, an avoidance that felt like a prelude to termination. If she was never going to return to this home, she wanted to look at the dresses. She fought with the notion, but finally took the carpeted stairs down to the basement.

In the room of hangers, one of the fluorescent light panels buzzed like surveillance. Susanna pressed the panel up with the tips of her fingers and it fell silent. She let go and it droned again. She ran her fingers against dresses, pantsuits, and wraps, then gathered the roll of fat at her midriff and squeezed it with repugnance. Sometimes, in the large bathroom mirror at the camp, if it was late enough and no one was watching (during those late hours when Dina thought her mother had vanished, Susanna was often washing herself over and over), she would stand staring at the new protuberance around her waist, willing herself to gather it in her hand.

Susanna pulled at a white cotton dress with eyeholes, a burnt-leather belt at its waist, then saw a green maxi dress with a smocked waist and a pintucked hem. She tugged at it with an unwise force, perhaps because she felt her time disappearing, though she also felt an impatience, an anger, like the itch she got from eating tangerines. Finally, it came off. She tried to force it down over her clothes. She heard the tear before the neck was over her head. She froze. Carefully, she pulled the dress up and returned it to the hanger so that the torn part was out of view. When she turned around, she saw Vela.

"When I need to get away from David, I come here too, sometimes," Vela said.

"You need to get away from David?"

"Maybe he wants to get away from me," Vela said and laughed.

"Thank you for helping me," Susanna said.

Vela winked. Susanna understood that neither Mikki nor Calev would know about the hamburgers. Vela reached for a neckless, strapless gossamer sheath—a pencil case for a woman—with extravagance in the upper arms, where the leaves of the fabric folded into each other like petals. You could tell it was a wedding dress only because it had a detachable train.

Vela dropped her jeans, revealing high-waisted orange underwear that left most of her backside exposed. Susanna sucked in her stomach. In the dress, Vela looked like a young woman trapped in a case, or a cloud trapped in a young woman. She was breathtakingly beautiful. Feeling a dark swell, Susanna said, "It's bad luck to wear a wedding dress not at a wedding."

Vela stopped moving. "That would explain it," she said, and laughed hesitantly. Feeling contrite, Susanna stepped closer to help with the zipper, but Vela swatted at it on her own.

"Do you hear the car outside?" Vela said.

Susanna only now heard the horn. Susanna flogged herself to say something—she hadn't meant to speak unkindly. But she couldn't think of the right thing to say.

Upstairs, the family reconstituted itself to say goodbye. This was how a family lined up when the polished fingernail of an agent of the security service rang the doorbell with an invitation for coffee. The man of the family had been named by George. Immortalized by poetry. All those years that Susanna had feared the ring of the bell, her imagination was too humble to conceive that the pointing finger was on Susanna's side of the door. She was a protected woman. She wished she'd known. It would have made her nights sounder. She would've walked through her city with derision instead of apology. She was ashamed at the thought.

Mikki clutched Vela again. Vela clutched back, perhaps out of politeness, but they drew some kind of shelter from each other. Susanna watched them with longing. Only months before, her daughter snailed herself inside her mother's crossed ankles as tightly as a swirl of cinnamon inside a pastry. Now, Dina seemed like the person on the other side of a one-sided mirror.

In the line of goodbye, David was discreetly scratching his testicles. Susanna said thank you and left.

* * *

The staircase spun up to a carpeted landing that spoked off into various rooms. In the main bedroom, square skylights sat in the ceiling like teeth.

Dina stood in a rectangle of light, burning under its concentration of sun. Then she dug in the drawers of the heavy walnut armoire, which had tiny walnut feet. Vasi's mother must have been a very small woman because her underwear was no bigger than rubber bands.

Faintly, the dog barked out its strangled volley of calls. She went into the bathroom, nearly as large as the bedroom. It smelled of a woman's perfume, of almonds encrusted by sugar. Dina found the vial and sprayed it at the wrist of her rigid hand, as she had seen ladies do.

Dina felt a satisfying boredom on seeing it confirmed in the cabinets: once you looked, everyone took "vitamins." If the mother was small, Dina calculated, impressed with her own cool reason, it would take more than her typical dose to put a large dog to sleep. So she looked for large pills. But she didn't want to hurt the dog, so she searched for small pills. But what if they didn't work at all . . . On one bottle, there was a warning sign, and the pink pills nesting over each other like coins were neither tiny nor huge. That seemed right.

Downstairs, the purring blue fridge was nearly empty, so she tried the second refrigerator. The entire thing was a freezer, gleaming like a box from the future. Her fingers grew sticky with frost as she searched for food a dog would eat. She decided on a cellophaned globe of ground meat, put it in a bowl of hot water, and slid it in the microwave.

Withdrawing it, she scalded the fingers of the working hand. She cried out. Now she had done it—now both hands were useless. She felt like a defective. The dreadlocked doctor had promised she would improve, and Dina—such a trusting, stupid little girl—didn't even think to ask when. The doctor had lied. That was obvious now.

Dina tried to cool the burned fingers in the freezer, but they only stuck to the frost and the freezer was dinging. The microwaved meat was half-hard. She took a knife from a rack and tried to hack up the meat. The lump slipped off the counter and fell to the floor. She picked it up and hacked again. Smashing down the blade of the knife, she missed the meat and stabbed the counter. The tile chipped. She covered the tile crack with a towel and kept hacking. Eventually, she had a dozen shallow divots—it looked like Kar's face from school. She emptied the bottle of pills into the divots. The slick, raw meat felt cool to the touch.

Outside, she dragged a bucket from the gardener's shed to the fence. Through the slats, she could see the flickering form of her antagonist, a large white dog with a black circle around one eye. The lobes of its organs strained against the skin. Behind the dog was a small house with two large parlor windows, a much smaller house than Vasi's. In a window, Dina saw the multicolored placard displayed by people who supported the refugees.

Mounting the bucket, Dina did something she had only seen others do: She crossed herself—with the meat, as it was in the good hand. Though it was still partly frozen, its scent was enough for the dog—its eyes lolled madly toward Dina. "Come on, dog," she whispered, even though she was really ensorcelling herself, her arm, her secret shot-putting powers. As she flung the meat, she felt the weightlessness of mastery—the brick made a neat arc and plopped near the animal. The frozen parts were no issue for the jaundiced, prehistoric teeth. It was all gone in seconds. She stood, watching through the slats, praying. The dog was cleaning its haunches. But then, to her astonishment, it rubbed its head through the grass, as if to quell an itch, and fell asleep with a whimper. In place of its noise, there was an extra measure of silence. Only leaves rustled, and a lattice over an outdoor seating area dripped moisture onto a padded recliner.

When she returned downstairs, Vasi and Dani, the orange-haired one, had their hands twisted around the video-game consoles, their shoulders poky in impersonation of the movements on screen. The third, Timo, stood near the screen, clutching a pillow to his chest. The little girls battered a dollhouse in the corner. No one looked up.

"Hey," Dina said. No one replied. "Hey," she said more loudly.

Vasi squinted as if trying to remember who she was. The distraction cost him on the screen, because the other two broke out in cheers. Vasi groaned.

Trying not to show her excitement, Dina said. "The dog . . ."

They stared at her.

"The dog next door," Dina said. "It's quiet."

"What dog?" Dani said. The other two could barely keep down their laughter. Only the little girl with no name stared at her with something resembling curiosity, or pity.

"Timo, did you say something about a dog?"

"I love dogs," Timo said, hoping to make the other boys laugh. They did. His face lit up.

Dina felt hot tears. She got her tongue ready to catch them. She made a grunting noise that made the boys hesitate in their laughter, but her only aim was to warn the tears to stay back.

She walked upstairs, their laughter behind her, and called the taxi man. Twenty minutes, he said. Dina walked the labyrinth outside. She sat on the bucket, her hands on her knees, like a laborer waiting for lunch, the dog asleep on the other side of the fence. Then she took the gardener's gloves from the shed, and went back in the house.

In the bedroom upstairs, she rifled through the armoire until she had the mother's drawer of underthings. She took one, and left the gardener's gloves in its place. Returning downstairs, Dina stopped in horror. She had left dusty tracks on the flawless shaggy staircase carpet. Well, the gardener had been up, hadn't he? He wanted to leave his mark, and so did Dina. She buried the underwear amid the gardener's things, and went to the road to wait for the taxi.

* * *

That night, Susanna and Dina sat on their cots as darkness fell. Susanna asked about school, and Dina answered with the detail that discouraged suspicion: Teacher Volos was starting a cold. Dina made herself ask about the embassy. It was fine, Susanna said. There were hamburgers for lunch.

"He's going to call, I promise," Susanna said. "You read the letter. His only request was to speak with you."

"Is he gone forever?" Dina said.

"Of course not. Of course not."

"Then when?"

"I don't know."

"So it could be forever?"

"I don't know, Dina—honestly."

"You did not speak to him month after month."

"When you're older, you will—" Susanna stopped herself. Once upon a time, she had promised herself that she would never say these words to a child.

"Why did you wash his things?" Dina said. "Now he is really gone."

"I wanted them to be clean for his return."

"What return? You don't know if he will return."

Susanna didn't know how to defend herself. They stared at George's cot, which remained open. Doing the laundry, Susanna had overlooked the bedding. She moved to the cot and inhaled the vanishing scent of its former occupant. Susanna sat down on the cot. She extended a hand toward Dina. "I have to brush teeth," Dina said. Susanna lowered the hand.

By the time Dina returned, Susanna was asleep, as Dina hoped. She fell into her own cot. As Dina's eyes were closing, she wondered again where her father was now, walking or sitting, happy or sad. She sniffed the air, trying to find him. She tried to wiggle her dead fingers. She had exaggerated her pain so he'd continue to hold her. She felt nauseous with longing. Yacoub had said to take Susanna's and George's hands, she had failed to do it, and her father had left. She had had the power to fix it, an awesome power that life had allowed her to glimpse again and again—she had gotten away with destroying the old dragon's garden, she had silenced the dog—but she had failed to deploy it to reconcile her parents. The power failed as often as it succeeded—she had hurt Robert, she had lost Yacoub, her father had left her. How could you know which would happen? Riding from Vasi's, she had mouthed wretched names for him and his stupid friends, but when the taxi had delivered her back to camp, and the driver had said, "Tomorrow?" she said yes. That seemed like the opposite of power—she had been ridiculed. But she had taken revenge. She needed to see what it had wrought.

She stared at her dead hand. Her father had held her hand only once.

Sometimes, he bounced his palm over the top of her head, acknowledging a good result in school, but she felt the palm as an approaching weight rather than touch. Her mother bathed her, dressed her, held her hand all the time. He only once.

It was when he had dragged Dina to his barber, Fares. After they had stepped out, the barber locked the door. They waited in the street, even after the man who was in the barber shop left. Then a policeman was talking to her father.

In a rising voice, the policeman called George bad names because he was minority-sect. A crowd began to gather. Some people objected—the man was a university professor, he had taught someone's child. It was early enough in the war that people still objected sometimes. George winked at Dina, but she couldn't move. She was old enough to understand her silence as complicity. The policeman was striding in a circle waving his baton, declaiming about the minority-sect dog wanting his dog face groomed by the barber's blessed hands. Then he told George to kneel on the pavement.

"It's all right, my beauty, it's just a game," George said to Dina, and clutched his waist as he lowered himself. It cost him something to do it. He had never called her "my beauty." He tried to whisper to the policeman, but the man ignored him. He slapped the baton in his palm. He said, "Do we punish the dog here, or should I bring a guest to the station for coffee?"

The crowd murmured disapprovingly, and in his rage at their rejection, the policeman cracked the baton across George's kidney. George crumpled. Whatever had been motionless in Dina broke out of its egg, and she thrust herself around George's neck like a tire, raising a cry from the crowd. The war had not come to humiliating children, not yet. The baton in his armpit, the policeman clapped at Dina with revulsed amusement. The dog had learned his lesson, he announced. He waved his fingers impatiently for the dog to get up.

George's knees cracked as he rose. He had been trying to find a way to signal to the policeman that he knew men ten posts above his, but having failed to do it, he was frantically scanning the crowd for someone he could trust to take his daughter away. Instead, she had saved him. "Just a game," he said almost inaudibly, and took her hand. And held it all the way home.

* * *

The next morning, Dina's driver having been placated with another roll of bills from Susanna's underwear, Vasi didn't pretend he didn't know Dina, as she feared he would. No, it was not the time for games. Even the hair that was supposed to be over his eye had strayed around his temple. "The dog is dead," he said. "I hope you're happy." She listened. It was silent next door. Dina hadn't noticed because people were yelling somewhere behind Vasi.

"Where are the—Dani? Timo?" she said.

"My mother and father are fighting," he said. "They said no friends today."

"They're fighting because of the dog?"

"No. Something about the gardener."

The sorcery was even more powerful than she thought. She had to parcel it out with care. She also had to be more precise. Knowingly and unknowingly, she had delivered damage around the spot, getting the parents, the dog.

"Wait for me here," Dina said.

"Where are you going?"

She went into the alley that separated the homes. She knocked on the heavy door by the parlor window with the sign supporting refugees. It swung open on an older couple with red faces behind glasses in thin frames. Somehow, Dina knew they were childless. That dog was their child. Dina told the truth, mostly. There had been dogs in the transfer camp before they crossed, Dina said—she was traumatized and couldn't handle the barking.

The last thing these people had expected was that the tranquilizing medication in their dog's stomach had been put there by a refugee girl. An injured refugee girl, no less, her hand like a broom of splayed bristles. The couple clasped hands at the kitchen table and wiped their eyes. They were so busy helping the refugees, they had failed the dog. They were always trying to help—when they learned that they couldn't make children, they went to a dog shelter, and asked for the most broken dog. Then they put it in a camper van and drove across six countries to come here. But the dog was alone most of the day, never with enough attention to be let off the leash.

They hadn't counted on this conundrum—to help the refugees, they had to ignore the dog. Dina listened like a counselor. There was a long silence during which it became clear that she had done them a perverse kindness. Of course it was done by a refugee girl. She was a dark delivering angel. They offered her nuts covered in chocolate.

"The problem is finished," Dina said to Vasi when she returned.

"What did you do?" he said, his eyes wide.

"Don't worry," she said. "Let's play." It was a test. His parents had said no friends today. But he stood aside so she could pass. The power was strong.

They threw horseshoes around an iron spike, and watched a video. Cautiously, he asked if she might be interested in a video game, and she laughed and said categorically not. But she was interested in kissing. His face grew tight. He was three years older than her. "So you don't know how to do it?" she said. It was the day of truth-telling, so she said, "I don't know, either." They touched lips, not moving their mouths, to the sound of Vasi's parents shouting at each other in a language Dina did not understand.

* * *

Susanna couldn't believe that in less than twenty-four hours, Mikki's home had reverted to dirty chaos. But today, the mop moved smoothly in Susanna's hands, her zucchini fritters were airy, and lunch vanished from the plates on the patio quickly. Mikki invited Susanna to join. Susanna wasn't hungry. Since George's departure, the constant itch of her tongue had been replaced by desolation. Her tongue made words, but that's all. She felt that her anatomy was surrendering feeling, piece by piece. When she washed herself, she moved her hands over her body as quickly as possible, distracting herself with a song she sang to Dina when Dina was little.

Susanna watched them through the window—the quiet husband was talking, gesturing with greasy fingertips. Something he said made the others laugh, and he lowered his eyes, as if he didn't deserve such a reward. Mikki had her hand on Vela's cheek, and smiled at the girl almost with desperation. What was it between them? Susanna turned off the rushing water that always made her think of Theo and padded downstairs. In the dressing room, the hangers clacked each other like dominoes. Why was she down here? It was cool and dim and organized, the thick carpet untrammeled. She felt like a stowaway.

A moment later, with irritation, she heard her name. She turned around to greet that young face, the sharp nose, the knobs in the cheekbones, the eyes like gray fish in blue seawater. Even at a distance, Vela's skin vibrated with an unblemished healthfulness, like a drum.

"The stove magician is here," the girl said.

"The magician has a secret assistant," Susanna said.

"Not today," Vela said. "Today is all you." She indicated the clothes. "Your turn."

Susanna, contrite about her impoliteness the previous afternoon, resolved to ingratiate herself. "Can you choose for me?"

Vela chose a tunic without a belt—the better to conceal Susanna's unseemly weight, Susanna concluded. But she submitted. She started to pull it down over her clothing, but Vela stopped her. The tunic was silk—Vela thought Susanna would want to feel it on her skin. Susanna did not want to feel anything on her skin. But she wanted to please Vela. She looked around for a place to change. "You can do it in the corner," Vela said. "I'll turn away."

Susanna was nervous and lost her footing as she tried to remove her long skirt. Finally, she stood before Vela in the tunic over her underwear and bra, the cool air of the floor touching her legs. The sleeves reached midway between elbow and wrist, where they puffed before turning into cuffs with pearl buttons.

"Wait," Vela said. From a jewelry chest, she extracted a necklace of emerald cameos encased in intricate silver rims. The cameos grew larger as the necklace swooped down to the space between the breasts, where the last cameo was the size of a chandelier pendant. Then she pulled out a gold bracelet marked with rivets. Susanna tried to smile. Vela had made of her, in the long mirror, a beautiful woman who shared Susanna's appearance but little else. Susanna wondered if she could explain this to Vela, if the girl could understand. But then they heard David's voice from upstairs.

"What is he saying?"

"He needs a second for his video game," Vela said. "You look beautiful. I'll say goodbye before you go."

Susanna opened her mouth, and closed it.

"What is it?" Vela said.

"Do you have to go because he calls?"

Vela colored. "I'll just see quickly," she said and vanished.

Susanna rode home in silence. Inside the fence, the eucalyptus grove felt unfamiliarly dense. The sun bounced behind the canopy like a supplicant trying to catch a minister's eye.

Her daughter was not in the tent. Susanna sat down heavily on her cot, and took her head in her hands. She felt light-headed and forced down some water. The calendar said autumn was only several weeks away, but after a brief dip, the temperature had vaulted again. Susanna pulled apart the laundry to re-count how much money they had. She couldn't believe her hands. There was a quarter of what had been there two days before. The lightness gave way to nausea. She raked the laundry again. Her heart was pounding. They'd been robbed. The word had got around that the woman and daughter in Tent 45/2 now had no man's protection, but no honorable person would rob them completely. She was convulsing with sobs when Dina appeared in the doorway.

"One can't even cry properly in this life because there's no wall to lean against," Susanna said. She tried to dry her face.

"What happened?" Dina said.

"Nothing," Susanna said. Mechanically, she checked the screen of the mobile. Nothing. She needed to charge it.

"Just tell me," Dina said.

Susanna covered her face. "We've been robbed. There's almost no money left. But I'll be paid at the end of the week. The woman is very generous. So don't worry, please."

"What woman?"

Susanna caught herself. "The woman who writes the checks at the consulate. She's very generous. She will write a check early."

Dina stared through the plastic window of the tent. She felt that if she only looked at her mother, her mother would know that the money had gone to her taxis. When Susanna managed to collect herself, she went to George's cot, and began taking the bedding from it.

"What are you doing?"

"He's not coming back."

"You said he'll come back."

"He won't."

"I wanted to sleep in his bed." Dina was about to invite Susanna to sleep in it with her, but couldn't bring herself to do it.

"He doesn't have a bed anymore," Susanna said. She took the mobile out of her bra, flung it at the basket of laundry, and collected the bedding in her arms like a child. When Dina saw that Susanna was going to fold up the cot, she screamed and fell onto it in protest. Susanna pulled her away, more roughly than she meant to. Dina tumbled to the concrete and burst into tears. Through her own tears, Susanna folded up the cot's groaning panels. They both stopped crying at once. All these days, it had been sitting underneath the cot, like an animal abandoned by its owner. George had not taken his letters.

* * *

Dina watched as Susanna hid the rest of the money in the little bag in which she kept menstrual pads; maybe they wouldn't dare look there. Then her mother went outside. When Dina heard the snap of the flames, she realized Susanna was going to burn George's letters. Dina hurried off her cot, swiped what she could from the top of the bag, and was smoothing her blanket over her mattress pad when Susanna came inside to retrieve the bag.

The next morning, Dina had nothing to extend to the taxi driver—she hadn't dared reach inside the menstrual bag. "I pay when you pick up," she said, hoping to project confidence. The driver did not like that. But he had made out more than well the previous two days. He agreed. It was Dina's third day out of school. Surely, Teacher Volos would come calling soon. Dina had to fix the money problem today.

At Vasi's, Dina did not ring the doorbell, just pushed the heavy handle. Heading downstairs, she walked past a woman at the kitchen table, her fingers on her temples as a cup steamed before her. She didn't notice Dina even as Dina stared at her. Dina's powers were increasing to the point of invisibility.

Downstairs, Dina ignored Vasi and went directly to that odious pepper, the boy Dani. Vasi was wrong for her mission; when it came to cruelty, he only knew how to follow. The dog game was Dani's idea, she was certain.

"I need to speak to you in that corner," she said to Dani as Vasi's face burned with jealousy. Dani rose obediently—clearly, he had heard about her problem-solving power. Vasi, Timo, and the little girls watched. Today, the girl who wasn't Angelika was permitted a costume, though only because Angelika, who was dressed as a prince, required a frog to complete her game—the smaller girl wore mantles of pea-colored construction paper. The frog kneeled before Angelika, who smacked its head with a ruler.

"Do you have money?" Dina said.

"Maybe," Dani said a little fearfully.

"How much money would you give me if I let you touch my knee?"

"What?" he stammered. His skin was turning the color of his hair. He looked down at her pleated black skirt. Her mother had once bought it for funerals. It had very fine raised paisley patterns in red.

"Are you—?" She banged her ear to mean *deaf*, just as Dani had the previous day. "Or just embarrassed? Because you look like a radish."

"I'm not embarrassed."

"You look it. I bet you've never kissed a girl before."

"Sure I have."

"So how much would you give me to kiss me?"

"You're a little whore," he said.

She slapped him. It was hard to do because only her left hand worked. He grabbed his cheek, and to his eternal mortification, began to cry.

"Stupid girl!" he said through his tears. "You want money for touching? Go to the laborer camp by the stone factory. Go through the woods there. They'll take care of you like you need." He wiped his nose and ran off, the others staring.

Dina criticized herself because she had not thought past this possibility; she was certain Dani, that fat tomato, would want to touch her knee. She had gotten arrogant. What now? There was probably money upstairs, but she was not ready for theft. She didn't know any laborers, but the ones she walked past to school always had cigarettes in the corners of their mouths and plaster on their fingers. Some moved with a hollow-eyed stupor, some spat and shouted at the boys who brought them their tea. They didn't seem dangerous. Her father had been a laborer, apparently, and except for the episode with Fares, her father didn't circulate among people who didn't have manners. He said so all the time. Manners, manners.

She told the taxi driver to go to the stone quarry. When they got near, she said to turn toward the camp in the woods. He looked at her in the rearview mirror. His grayish white hair rose in symmetric little squiggles, as if a schoolchild were practicing tracing. "Take me there," she said, "and you will have double." He crossed himself and kept going. Her heart was sliding around, but her power had been strong the last several days, and she pleaded with it to hold out once more. Her hands were sweaty. She tried to rub them on her thighs. She pulled down her skirt.

They were on the unpaved track for a mile. The stone pines all around, though gangly and sparse, blotted out enough sun for the day to seem cloudy. Finally, they reached a wide clearing. Ahead, a group of men sat around a thin fire that licked wanly at skewered cubes of meat. The men had cards in their hands and beer by their feet. They were wearing the same stained sports pants, and the same slides, as if the items had been bought, or stolen, together. From somewhere came the faint sound of women's voices. They were singing.

One of the men rose, his eyes on the windshield. He took a seed from a pocket, split it with his teeth, and threw the shell at the tire. He leaned into the driver's window and inspected the back seat. Dina opened her door. "Stay here," she said to the driver, hoping her voice carried authority. The driver didn't answer. She felt sweat on her lip.

Dina walked to the front of the car, hiding the bad hand behind her back. The man slurped another seed. There was a long, raised scar beside his left eye and streaks of red lightning around his pupils. His face was so dark from the sun it looked blue. He stared at her with contemptuous amusement.

She raised the hem of her funeral skirt and rubbed her fingers.

He kept chewing. An eternal moment passed during which the only sound was that of the black birds wheeling between the thin foliage of the pines. Then the man indicated the trailer behind the fire. He said something to the other men in their language, and they laughed.

The trailer was gray with smoke. Two disfigured couches, the armrest doilies still in place despite cigarette holes, sat by each other like old spouses. A dirty Persian carpet covered a part of the linoleum floor. The only light came from a small table lamp whose shade had come loose, a spoke peeking out. There were several filled ashtrays, a driving map of the island, and a chipped enamel mug that had fallen over because the plastic carnation in it was too long.

Through a sooty, slatted window, Dina saw one of the men at the fire wave away the matchbox of the taxi. The taxi reversed back down the track. Her chest caved away. The man pushed the coffee table aside with his foot. One of the ashtrays spilled, and the mug with the carnation fell onto the carpet. With his chin, he indicated the couch.

She swallowed heavily, hoping to conceal the knocking of her heart, and rubbed her fingers together. He laughed, baring his stained teeth. He lit a cigarette, took a long pull, and offered it to her. She shook her head, her mind trying frantically to work out its options. The man retrieved a wallet so thick it was nearly spherical, and pulled out two bills. She wanted to cry, but if she cried, it was over. Only the opposite would do. Everyone did this, she reminded herself. This was what everyone wanted. She would succeed. She moved her head no: She wanted more. His chin pointed outside: The men in the circle would add. She moved her head no.

He grabbed her chin and flung her at the couch, exclaiming something she didn't understand. She leaned forward and made herself take his hand. The skin was rough, so unlike her father's, one patch rougher than the rest: some skin condition. She pleaded with her heart to stay in its cage. She cursed the taxi driver. With her good hand—slowly, she was becoming as fluent in the left as the right—she took the fingers and brought them to her ankle. Then she took one of the bills and put it into a pocket of the funeral skirt. Then she led his hand to a shin, and put the second bill in her pocket. She nodded at the wallet: More bills, more inches.

He laughed and clapped, acknowledging her bravado, his fingertips nearly touching her eyelashes. She felt bile in her throat, and forced it down with heavy swallows. Her body tried to shake, and she tried to steady it. He placed his hand on her knee, and with his free hand pulled out another bill. She reached for it, but he knocked away her hand and pressed the money behind the band of her funeral skirt. She felt him feeling the skin of her waist and tried not to shudder.

Her heart was leaving her chest. It was walking out the door, the part of her that could, and vanishing down the track. It turned onto the highway and flew toward the consulate, where her mother made people understandable to each other, and beyond it, past the airport and the sea, to some place where her father stood on the tarmac awaiting her with carnations, and not plastic carnations. But her father didn't have a face. It was just a smooth, erased oval.

The man's hand was on her thigh. When he moved his hands, his armpits released a scent of iron and salt. She felt dizzy. She could taste the vomit on her tongue. Now the hand was nearly to the place where the leg met the hip, the skirt folded up, an inch from her underwear. This time, when the free hand forced the money behind the band of the skirt, it stayed there. She shook her head weakly no. He brought his finger to his lips: silence. "No," she said hoarsely. He yanked her roughly toward him. The violence of the gesture ruined her effort, and she covered him with vomit. They looked at each other, shocked.

She sprang to her feet, the bills she'd earned falling around them. One of his hands closed around her ankle. She reached for the lamp to steady herself, but managed to seize only the loose spoke. It came free in her hand, the force of the motion pitching her forward until she mashed herself into the vomit and drove the spoke into his neck. His blood sprayed her face. He howled and tried to yank out the spoke. She clawed through his limbs until she was at the door. She reached back over his squirming body, took the wallet, and forced open the door. She had to beat the door against his head to clear enough of him to fit through.

The men in the circle were standing because they'd heard the noise. They saw a girl covered in vomit and blood. Dina clutched the wallet like a grenade, spittle falling from her sobbing mouth. If she ran diagonally, she would cut off the men and enter a marsh of tall reeds. If the ground was reasonably solid, she might outrun them to the gravel driving track. Above, a shawl of clouds dragged itself across the sky. At home, during the winter, for a night or two, it was sometimes chilly enough to require something warmer. It was the most exciting time of the year. Dina saw her mother, the mother she'd used to know, walking into the living room with a shawl that had used to belong to her own mother, and draping it over Dina's shoulders. Dina was so engrossed in *Uncle Neem* that she didn't bother to say thank you. The kettle was rumbling quietly on the stove, and soon there would be tea for the women as they read on the divan in preparation for the arrival of a single night's winter—and of George from the university, whereupon the silent winter female stillness would end, to return again in a year.

Dina launched forward. The men moved after her. Her first step into the marsh sank her into wet muck that covered her shoulders. She bellowed. She tried to hold the wallet aloft. Some parts of the marsh were shallower, and she dragged herself forward as the men covered the same distance down the track. She couldn't go back or to the right, and to the left the marsh stretched endlessly. But she couldn't do this for a mile, and even when she reached the main road, would anyone stop for a girl covered in blood, vomit, and mud? She moved only from desperation, from the electricity that shot up and down her legs, soiled by the cracked touch of those fingers.

She heard a mechanical strain to the right, the men's voices rising. The stone pines were thick, and her eyes were filled with mud. Finally the picture resolved—the taxicab was speeding down the gravel track toward the men. They had not expected the taxi to return, and the driver did not expect them to be moving down the track, and, frozen by momentum, these forces rushed toward each other until the driver plowed into the men, who fell away like knocked-down pins, except one who had managed to avoid the car by diving into the muck.

Dina kicked her legs and wept—there was sludge in her mouth. The man in the mud was righting himself. The taxi driver was in it, moving toward her. She reached for the driver, but the movement unsteadied her, and she fell. When her eyes got above the ink, she saw the other man lunging for her. In her shrieking, she barely heard the dull thwack of the heavy branch in the driver's hands against the man's head. He fell back in the mud.

Dina dripped bloody mud onto the seat as the taxi driver reversed nearly at the speed he used to move forward—here was decades of feel for the road. But he was shaken, too, and he popped out onto the highway with such force that a small gasoline truck had to swerve to avoid him, nearly flattening a mini-sedan. There were no horns—everyone was too astonished that every car was intact. The taxi slid between the sedan and the truck and sped away.

The taxi driver was moving toward the capital. They had gone some way before Dina realized that she was frantically opening and shutting her hands. At some point, the dead hand had returned. It had driven the spoke.

* * *

Susanna had woken up with regret for burning the letters. She was off; she was making mistakes; she didn't trust her mind. In the communal bathroom, she realized she had forgotten her toothpaste in the tent. She walked back, but the toothpaste wasn't there either. Had Dina squandered it? Susanna went back—she would ask a drop from somebody else. There, she saw that she *had* brought her toothpaste—it was right there on her washcloth. There was a woman combing her hair, or Susanna would have thrown the tube at the wall.

A helpless rage coursing through her, Susanna dropped the glass she was washing in the sink in Mikki's kitchen. It splintered. Mikki was just entering the kitchen with plates. Susanna stiffened. Mikki said, "For good luck, don't worry." But her face had a mournful expression, as if it regretted the welcome it had extended to the incompetent at the sink. But then Vela came in with the rest of the dishes, and her eyes were swollen, too. Something had happened outside. Susanna sought out Vela's eyes. Failing to find them, she said, "I will clean downstairs now." At this, Vela looked up.

Mikki said, "No one goes there. It's clean."

"I took some laundry there," Vela said, looking to see whether Mikki believed her. Mikki looked from Susanna to Vela, understood that she shouldn't question. "Yes, sometimes it's good to clean it," she said.

Susanna sat on the ottoman in the dressing room like a laborer, elbows on knees, legs out. Now Susanna understood that this was the posture of people whose backs needed a rest, who had too much around their middle for physical work. She was sweating, and had dirt under her fingernails from removing the skins of peppers she'd roasted. Mikki was right—the dressing room would have remained as clean as a hospital if Susanna's visits hadn't soiled it. She would need to vacuum and dust. She would need to stop coming here.

She heard Vela. The girl sat down on the carpet, drew up her legs, and laid her head on her knees. Susanna waited.

"We wanted to give you a rest," Vela finally said. "To call out for lunch. I took David's phone to call because mine was upstairs." She stopped, and for a moment she was still. Finally, she said: "I saw messages from a girl in our school."

"I'm sure he said she was forcing herself on him," Susanna said.

"No," Vela said. "I wish he had." She thought about it. "He's young. I'm the same age, but he's a boy. He needs time. He made a mistake. We can fix it." She looked up hopefully. "Don't you think?"

"I don't know," Susanna said. "I was young when I met my husband. Too old in my country. But still too young for me."

"But Mikki said you're married. So you fixed it."

"Are you ready to be married?"

Vela didn't answer.

"I didn't want to marry fast like every woman I knew," Susanna said. "This was one good thing about this man—" She didn't know what to call the Leader now. At home, he was the Leader, just as a cypress tree had no other name, but to call him that now was to degrade oneself further. "At first, he made some things better. He wanted women to choose more in life. And it worked for me for a while. I was in a large city. I was in university. I took a subject that men take. I had boyfriend after boyfriend. When I got tired of the boyfriend, I didn't invent an excuse like, 'Please forgive me, my mother calls me to the village.' I said the truth: 'Boyfriend, I am tired of you.' And I felt strong. And I thought, *It's me. I am strong.*"

"But you weren't?" Vela said.

"No, it was luck. I was lucky because life, by accident, gave me what I wanted. But then life gave me something else, and like an animal in the circus, you go back to the moves you were taught. And when you look up, you are a married woman with a child."

"But what did life give?"

"And the child wouldn't come, you know," Susanna said, ignoring the question. "It was like life saying, *Here is one more chance to save yourself.* But then she came."

"You didn't want the child?"

"Of course, I wanted the child," Susanna said irritably, and whispered an incantation against the other implication, for then her daughter would be prone to harm. "She is the most beautiful girl. I don't mean face—but face, too. I mean she is strong. Or maybe I imagine it because I want her to be strong, unlike me. I don't know."

"So your husband took you away from your freedom."

"He is a good man also."

"But then I don't understand."

Susanna made George's noise of exasperation. "I was studying a section on temporary bridges for military purposes when I met him," Susanna said. "I will always remember this because it's like the stories they say about the village when the volcano hits. I think there is still a girl somewhere in my city, always studying this lesson that she was studying when—poof. She will never finish."

Vela was listening raptly.

"He was a nice man, like I say," Susanna said. "He was older, a professor, with respect, money, an apartment, minority-sect like me, asking questions about me, with experience the boys didn't have. And I thought, *Why not?* When he looks at me, his eyes are always on me. He is always listening when I speak. Why not?"

"But he wasn't right."

"I don't know. All I know is that I said yes too quickly. Like Susanna was sleeping that day. Then we had a child and then the war began, and you don't know, is it the child or the man or the war, and you also don't have the time to think about it. Day after day, you think, *Tomorrow, I will think about it. Yes, from tomorrow, I will live the right life.*"

"We're lucky not to have that here," Vela said.

"Really?" Susanna said. "Your boyfriend writes to another girl, but you are still here, making excuses. What's different?"

Vela's face lost its color. She looked down, and said, for some reason, "I am just a teenager."

The words were so pathetic that Susanna missed a breath. There was something loose in her, something bent on the correction of this sweet girl and her meaningless, fortunate grief, the cloying desperation with which she and Mikki hung on to each other. "You don't see how he looks at you," Susanna said.

"What do you mean?"

"He doesn't look at you. He takes his hands from yours when you put them together."

Vela's eyes filled with tears.

"I'm sorry," Susanna said. "It isn't my place."

"No, you're right," Vela said, rising. She moved toward the stairs. "I have spent too much time in this place."

* * *

Dina whimpered in the back seat, a small demon covered in blood, vomit, and mud. The grime soaked the fabric of the seat. Dina tried to make herself small so less of her would drip off.

They stopped on the back side of a small whitewashed home with dusty terra-cotta trim. A stub of a woman in an apron stepped out, her pink eventless face filling with alarm. When the driver took his hands off the wheel, they were shaking.

Dina was wrapped in a towel while the woman scraped her clothes, and fed her melon with honey, and then black tea with little wafers with ends dipped in chocolate. The driver paced the yard, talking on the phone. Periodically, the woman appeared from some new archway to return a piece of clothing. The house had only a clothesline, but there was no time for nature, so she used a hair fan. The clothes, damp in places, smelled like Susanna's hair after she had dried it with a fan in the bathroom at home. An hour later, Dina was back in the car. The entire time neither Dina nor the woman spoke, while the driver spoke ceaselessly in the yard.

They drove toward the capital—soon there were sidewalks, buses, vendors, narrow streets. As they took a roundabout, the American consulate came into view, and Dina twitched in her seat. She asked the driver to take another circle around, but he was too impatient to get where they were going. Dina had to content herself with squinting from the backseat. Of course she couldn't see Susanna at such a distance.

They stopped at a café with a money changer in the back. The driver drew on a paper for Dina: The only changers who took such dirtied money gave back 50 percent. This one would do 75 percent. Dina gave him the wallet shaped like a ball. The driver counted: 1,753. So, she would get back 1,300. She made a splitting motion—he should take half. He shook his head, but then thought. Finally, he made an up-and-down motion with his wrist: He would have to paint the car, change the plates. When he came back, he took three hundreds, and gave her the thousand. She put it in a pocket of the funeral skirt, again clean and ready for death.

He made a swimming motion to ask her if she wanted him to take her to camp. She made a circular motion, but he didn't understand. She pointed at the taxi and drew the circle twice, and then he did—the roundabout. She wanted to go to the consulate. She wanted her mother.

At the outdoor checkpoint where a Marine reviewed identification, Dina wrote her mother's name with a newly functioning right hand. The babyish black face under the camouflage cap regarded her with green eyes of amusement. He typed the name into his laptop, and spun it around to show Dina: No one. And he couldn't let her in without an adult. Her eyes welled. By this, he was momentarily undone, but then reached into a small red cooler by his feet. And withdrew a rectangle of cake frosted with cream.

"I make it myself," he said. "I brought two, and I'm giving you mine."

She was having trouble holding her tears, which were mixing with snot.

"The other one's for a lady in Cultural," he said. "Thank me by wishing me luck."

Dina ran the sleeve of her damp shirt, the faint tang of vomit and blood still somewhere in its threads, over her nose, and took the rectangle. She stood there holding it, weeping. "She's a translator," Dina said through her tears. "Please just call them."

"A translator?" he said. "That's not possible. Look, you're refugee, right? For translating, State Department employs only Americans. Can't have refugee translate refugee. I'm sorry."

The tears dropped from Dina's eyes onto the cake. The Marine didn't know what to do. The taxi driver appeared. This time, he had waited for her, just in case. He swept up Dina and led her back to the taxi. They sat in the taxi, eating the Marine's cake in silence. At first, Dina knew that her mother was inside, and then that she wasn't.

The driver took her home. In the tent, Dina went to the bag of menstrual pads, and was about to place the thousand there when she realized that only she knew where Susanna had hidden the money, and if the robbers were returning it, they would place it in the laundry bin, so Dina worked the money into the clothes there instead. Then she lay in her cot and slept.

* * *

When Susanna came upstairs, Mikki was alone at the kitchen table. She was circling a spoon through a cold cup of tea. "You are so good," Mikki said. "The house is so clean. Listen—take tomorrow off. The check for the week is on the counter. Don't do anything more today."

"Is everything okay?" Susanna said. She didn't get an answer.

Susanna went upstairs. There was noise in David's bedroom. Susanna filled the open doorway, and was relieved to find Vela rather than David. Vela was folding shirts.

"It doesn't matter how upset I am, I have to fold it correctly," she said and laughed sadly. There was a travel bag by her feet.

"I made a mistake to speak how I spoke," Susanna said. Her tongue was woolly in her mouth. "This mouth is an enemy."

"You told the truth," Vela said.

"I saw Mikki downstairs. She's very upset. She loves you so much. I was supposed to help this house. Instead, I have destroyed. There's a poison in me."

Vela stopped folding and looked up. She had the shirt she was folding against her chest, like a children's toy. "You know the crosses when you turn onto their street?" she said.

"Yes. It's how I know where to turn."

"It's how everyone knows this place. Two of those crosses are Mikki's, and one is my family's. No one has told you. They don't speak about it."

Susanna stared from the threshold.

"Our families were very close. We played at each other's house all the time. My sister was here, playing with David's brother and sister. The nanny got a call from her daughter. The daughter said she was leaving her husband. The nanny's mind was not on the children. The children took their bikes and went to the road. The rest, you imagine."

Susanna's hand covered her mouth.

"We still have three. But they have only one. At the funeral—funerals—he and I sit together, we hold hands . . . And little by little . . . I mean, you see Mikki. For her, when David and I are together . . . for one minute, she's okay. We are like the—" She put a fingertip against the wall. She meant the spackle that fills a hole drilled in the wrong place.

"So it's good for Mikki," Vela went on. "But it's not good for David. He tries, but . . . And for me . . . Mikki is so good, you know. When she hugs me, I think my bones will—poof. She's always helping, always giving. For a year, she didn't come out of her room. When she came out, she was twenty years older. She has shoeboxes of photos, albums. She goes up there and sits for hours. She says, 'I'll just go upstairs for a little while now,' like she is going to talk to a lover. We all know what it means. It's good you are here because she tries to be better in front of a new person." Vela fingered the zipper on her bag. "I wanted Mikki to be happy. I had this power to—" She made the spackling gesture again. "But I ruined everything, didn't I."

Susanna's eyes were wet, and her voice wouldn't come forth. She extended her hand toward Vela, then drew it back, ashamed. Vela approached her, and shook Susanna's fingertips in a friendly gesture. Then she walked out with the bags.

Susanna stood at the threshold to David's room. The house had a lethal silence, only branches creaked outside. Finally, she took the stairs down. The kitchen table was empty. The check was on the counter, kept in place by the kettle because a window was open. Susanna walked out without it.

In the car, Kamil seemed hesitant, or regretful.

"What is it?" she said.

"I'm leaving next week," he said.

"Where do you go?"

"Where we all must go—home."

"Some of us have to hope that not all of us must."

"Go home? Maybe, but in your heart, it will never leave you alone."

"You misunderstand people. They're not as rigid as you. They just want to live and forget. Earn money and send their children to school."

"So they are asleep. But that doesn't mean I am rigid."

He was right. She conceded only a nod.

"I wasn't here to point out collaborators," he said. "We pay the government here. What we confiscate at home, some of it we pay to the government here for taking care of our people. For taking care of you."

She had no answer to this.

"It's not a lot, but it is a gesture. And one of us comes here now and again to shake hands. The hand that still works. And now it's my time to return and fight once again."

"How can you fight?"

"There are many ways. You know that. Now you know it in a very personal way."

"Will we ever see him again?"

"I told you, I don't know where he is. That's better for all of us." He gestured toward the house they had departed. "How will you get there now?"

"That's all right. My job in that house is finished."

"I am relieved to hear it. You are not a cleaning woman."

"Oh, yes? Who am I?"

"You'll decide," he said.

She nodded bitterly. They didn't speak for the rest of the drive. At the camp, as she was climbing out of the car, she covered his hand with hers, and said, "You have helped me."

Susanna rushed through the eucalyptus grove because she wanted to lay hands on her daughter, to assure herself she existed. She had only the one. Moving past the school, she didn't notice the schoolteacher waving her arms until the young woman was directly before her.

"I am just walking," Susanna said in preemptive defense.

"I am Teacher Volos," the woman said. Her breaths rolled out heavily. "You are Dina's mother, correct? I hope she's feeling better."

"Thank you," Susanna said mechanically. Then, not mechanically, "She's not ill."

The teacher said, "On Monday, Dina said she wasn't feeling—"

Now they stared at each other. "Dina has not been to school," Susanna said. To save her dignity, she left the question mark out.

"We haven't heard anything," the teacher said, "so I just wanted to ask if she is okay."

"Yes," Susanna said numbly. "It's a fever. A long fever."

She could see the teacher hesitating. Finally, Volos said, "Some children say they see her in the evenings in the cafeteria, and she's fine." She waited. "You are allowed to move the child out of the school. We just want to know. There is another child we can put in this classroom then. Our interest is only administrative. I promise."

"Yes, administrative," Susanna repeated. "No, she will come back to school. I promise."

Volos smiled and squeezed Susanna's hand lightly. The teacher's hand was warm and soft, and Susanna wanted to continue being held by it.

In the tent, she found her daughter asleep. She remembered that Vasi's second letter had a phone number. Susanna searched all over the tent, making less and less effort to avoid noise, though Dina seemed lost to an imperturbable sleep. The letter was nowhere—another futile endeavor. Susanna was about to fall onto her cot when she remembered the armoire. She went through Dina's pants until she felt paper in a pocket. Vasi's letter, with notations from Dina about the taxi driver's route.

When Dina awoke, Susanna told her that she would no longer work at the consulate. And the next day, she would walk Dina to school.

* * *

The next day, Susanna did not return to the home of Mikki and Calev.

Four days later, Dina received a nearly perfect grade on a history examination despite having been absent all of the previous week.

Five days later, Susanna did the laundry. Not knowing that Dina had placed banknotes there, she didn't notice when they fluttered out as she absentmindedly carried the bundle to the camp laundromat. The banknotes were discovered and kept by the camp residents Susanna was certain had taken their money the previous week.

Six days later, Susanna turned on the mobile to find seven missed calls from the same number. When Dina came home, Susanna asked her to check the number at the computer in the business center. She was relieved to discover that her daughter still responded to missions.

Susanna dared to hope that the numbers would lead back to her husband, but on the seventh day, Dina informed her that they belonged to the U.S. embassy.

The eighth and ninth day were Saturday and Sunday, and of course, no one called then.

On the tenth day, the phone rang. Susanna snatched the phone, but then, in her nervousness, pressed Off rather than Talk. She flung the phone in rage at the cursed linen bin. It rang again, and now she had to go fishing for it in the depths of the basket as it rang and rang, threatening to stop before she could seize it.

"Hello? Hello?" she screamed into the phone.

"Hello?" the voice said in English. "Susanna? Mrs.—?"

"Yes," she said disappointedly. "Yes, please."

"It's Paul Friedman at the U.S. embassy. I'm the deputy head of Consular. We've been trying to reach you. Is this a good time?"

"Yes. I'm sorry, I thought it was my—"

"Well, they're always asking you to get on the bus and come up here," Paul Friedman said. "I thought I'd just call. I'm afraid you've experienced some difficult treatment. Consular affairs, you would think it was a straight shot for all involved, the law is right there. But one person's Ninth sounds nothing like somebody else's." He chuckled faintly. "The law is a living organism," he tallied. "Unfortunately, sometimes.

"Anyway, your case reached my desk. We've made inquiries. And we've also had not one or two, but three—*three*—rather remarkable testimonials submitted on your behalf, and they even mention little Dina, they do. From a Theodosia Nest, a Mikki"—he fell silent. "These surnames are challenging for me sometimes, Mah-ta-thee-ah, something like that. And we've made our own inquiries, of course."

"You said three people. Who is—if I have permission—"

"Oh, of course, sorry. Kamil—Kamil—but again, the names."

"It's okay," she said. "It's okay."

Paul Friedman said, "It's very clear to us—well, to me; the local consulate is a different matter, but I am the case manager now—that you don't have involvement in the matters that compromised your husband. And I hasten to add that, officially, his record is clear—his deal was that he leaves without admission of guilt. I hope I didn't get your hopes up in the wrong way, there's no verdict on asylum. But you're back in the queue where you were. There's no shadow over your case." There was no answer, so he added, a little hesitantly, "I hope it's good news," and chuckled like the chef who wants his meal praised.

"I'm sorry," she said. "I just want to ask—"

"Yes, of course, I'm sorry I forgot it. The stipend starts up again. We will authorize that they retro it to the point of cutoff, okay? You and your little girl, you'll be okay. So I hope you're holding up okay? I know it's not easy."

She wept on the phone, and he was a kind enough man to stay on the line, and not speak, and not try to soothe her, and not try to discreetly excuse himself from the line. For two minutes, he listened to her cry like the women cried in her village, to cry like girls cried, as if no one was watching. She tried to make herself stop.

"We hope to have good news for you soon, we really do," Paul Friedman finally said into the crying. "I will look to it myself."

"Sir," she said, speaking through her wet throat. "Please. Can you tell me anything about my husband. I have had no word, no word."

"Oh, I wish. We keep no information like that, I'm afraid."

She thanked him. When her daughter returned from school, she embraced her and held her even though Dina was limp in her hands. Susanna didn't care.

That night, Susanna called George's parents. Her father-in-law was silent for a long time. When he finally spoke, he said: "Give the phone to my son." Instead of answering, she pressed Off. He wasn't there. Her fingers thick with nervousness, she dialed their apartment. A male voice answered. The voice was like the word once known and now stubborn in its refusal to be recognized. "Who is it?" the voice demanded. "Do you know the hour? Hello?" It was the Registrar's voice. She clicked off again.

Three weeks and an additional interview later, the phone rang as she and Dina were rising. By now, Susanna took up the phone without the old eagerness because the number had entered some rotation in a telemarketing database, and now several times a day someone called to offer her a fire alarm or vine treatment, not that she understood the offer, as it was in the native language. But it was Paul Friedman, chuckling, to say that the papers had come through. The United States was ready to receive this family, minus one.

III

Revenge

14 Years Later

They had been sleeping only an hour when Dina slipped out of bed. She'd nodded off at the young woman's leg, embracing the hard pudding of the thigh, as if spent by the lovemaking there, though really because Dina sensed that the woman wanted to caress, and sweet-talk, and for this Dina had no desire. She had waited out the woman's fingers as they circled the dark, pawing for Dina's hair below, intent on pulling her up for these endearments, but finally the fingers thickened and slowed. The first thing the young woman had told Dina to do, once they were in the bedroom, was to take down her hair. Seeing it, the woman had said, "Oh, gosh."

In the bar, the woman had worn slim blue jeans over clean hiking boots and a sweatshirt with rolled-up sleeves that said NORMAL. Her hair bounced around the dome of her head like a plume. You could see the lobes of her calves through the jeans. The thighs were thick but fatless. By comparison, in her pleated black pants and low white sneakers, Dina looked like an intern. But Dina, as always, had the largest eyes in the room, and the longest hair, which grew quickly, as if her body was working extra time to secrete its defenses.

The place was called Valence. You went there to meet another body, sometimes multiple. The expectation waited over the place. People got away with things. The first time there, Dina couldn't tell whether she liked doing, for once, something that everyone did, or it made her nauseous. She kept coming back.

Once the woman had given Dina enough time to look, she caught Dina's gaze and nodded toward the door. Dina thought about the bathrooms, much closer and built large for the purpose, but she lost her nerve and moved toward the exit. In the parking lot, the woman's tongue was cool, as if she'd been chewing on ice.

Once they made it to Dina's, the woman kicked off her boots, flung her socks at different corners of the room (Dina winced), and rocked her hips until her jeans fell away. She kicked down her thong until it was an anklet, then stopped dealing with it. She put herself behind Dina, slipped down Dina's largely ornamental bra, and said, "Lean back now, please." The woman's belly received the back of Dina's head like warm batter. She gathered a clutch of Dina's hair and rubbed herself with it. "Oh, gosh," she said. "Oh, gosh." Dina wanted to laugh.

Now, in the bedroom, after hours of being distracted by it, Dina folded the woman's clothing as she had been trained for all time at the mall seconds store in the little Western mountain city to which she and Susanna were assigned once they got to the States. Then the test strip of the thong, which Dina fought with for several minutes. Folding was not one of the thong's properties of existence. Folding the jeans, she felt the thin wallet. When the woman whispered her name, Dina managed to hear nothing beyond an "S." Nervously, Dina pulled out the wallet. It was Sara. Then Dina saw the ID behind the license, and her heart fell. *Stupid Dina.*

The Agency used the same photo technology as the Information Center where Dina worked. Sara's scrubbed, aquiline face had been flattened into an omelet with eyes; in her photo, Dina looked like a pale scarecrow. There was no way this was a regular pickup. Agency people went to pickup bars, too, but Dina couldn't persuade herself it was a coincidence. Dina's armpits were moist. She looked at the body rising and falling in sleep, Dina's pillow wedged into her belly. She didn't know what to do. She needed time to think. She'd pretend she went for a run. She laced up her sneakers and slid out the door.

At the Information Center, Dina always worked the Friday-night double. She was the junior-most analyst; no one except her wanted 4 P.M. Friday to 8 A.M. Saturday, anyway. On Friday afternoons, as the metro disgorged office people taking two steps at a time in eagerness for the weekend, Dina went the opposite way, the fetor of the traveling cars down below belonging mostly to her and the unhoused men who produced it.

Sixteen hours listening and translating in her gray box at the Information Center, twelve hours asleep at home, hours of travel between the two, and then nights at Valence—it claimed over two days. She was the only person in their city who didn't complain about the public transportation. The slower, the better for Dina. She didn't like weekends. She had large headphones. The bus drivers knew her. To her smile, they nodded and said, "Okay, miss."

One driver, Hector, was always flexing a rubber band, the four long fingers lifting it up while the thumb pulled it down. The other hand held the huge scalloped wheel of the bus. From the way he pulled at the uniform at his belly, she knew that he was anxious about his weight, and from the oxbloods that replaced his comfort shoes for only a day, she knew he was anxious about money. But why the rubber band. Exercise? Physical therapy? It bothered her that she couldn't determine. She sunk a nail into a wrist for relief.

She never cut herself, but sometimes held a nail to the soft meat of the inner arm as good feeling flooded her like warm water filling a tub. She kept one fingernail chiseled for this. The rest were perfect crescents. She stayed clear of anyone with bad fingernails—it was one of the first places she looked. If anyone asked about the long nail, Dina said she played an instrument. Only once had this led to further questioning, from a young man interested in more than the instrument. Even after she had clarified her preferences, he kept speaking as if she hadn't.

Dina ran through the park, along the canal, down Federal. She hated this time of year. She could manage the snow, but not the cold wet. When people asked where she was from, she named the little western town. Educated people, people who knew the tax code, or who Hume and Locke were, always made jokes about it. The Arctic, bears, rifles, and so on. But the winters there had been mild and crisp and astringent, like paper crunched into a ball. Seeing snow for the first time shortly after she and Susanna had settled, Dina had burst out laughing. Susanna had looked up from the hot plate, and said, "Let it snow!" Dina rolled her eyes. Susanna was always quoting the windows in town, the commercials on the radio, like a show animal. Susanna was a garbage can for the things Americans said and didn't mean. Susanna walked around the house and said things like: *Thanks of a grateful nation. Clear and present danger.*

Confronted with the reality of America, her mother's English, so impressive on the island, had deteriorated. She fumbled words at the store. To Dina's annoyance, the cashiers were patient. Everyone was infuriatingly patient. Once, already a driver, Dina made herself sit through a green light without moving. She thought—if no one honks, I'm leaving this place. The seconds ticked away, the discomfort making her skin itch. The green went to yellow, then red. No one behind her, three or four cars, touched their horn. She had to get out of there. She did. The winters where she lived now, however, were like paper being slowly soaked in water. In their Western mountain city, no one asked where Dina was from. But that was because they thought they already knew she was Native.

When Dina squealed at the snow, Susanna had stared. She was hearing Dina as an excitable little girl, and also as her own mother undergoing an attack. Sometimes, Susanna's longing for her mother and father, for the Triangle, for Arid, for the dust and the heat, for the yogurt with honey, for the rotting watermelons on the side of the road, was so forceful that she became dizzy. She waited for the day it would overcome her while driving, and she would bury their Civic in a ditch. Once Dina turned fourteen and a half, she asked Dina to drive. Dina didn't like doing it because it made her mother seem disabled. She wanted her mother to try harder.

Dina ran to the café that opened at 5 A.M., bought an urn of coffee, and walked the two blocks to the overpass, the concrete shuddering under the semis above. Underneath, it was damp and cool, water dripping from the eaves of the stone. Her mother was supposed to spend her life building things like it. Instead, now she was . . . Dina couldn't say. She didn't know.

At the encampment, the puddles shimmered with light. Someone was mewling. Dina set down the urn with a thunk. A body nearby fought with the skin of its tent and then the head emerged, checking left and right like a child taught to look before crossing the road. He had been a tenor in the opera, but something had happened, and he had slipped into madness. He serenaded her sometimes, but sometimes he chased her. During a calm moment, she had asked him why he was there—there were drier spots in the city; there was even a park with bathrooms. He pointed to the overpass and then to his hat, an Afghan *pakul*. "People throw things off bridges. In the park, they won't let nothing fall to the ground." Now, he saw the urn and bellowed something. Like survivors after an explosion, the bodies began to crawl out.

Dina could delay only so long. An Agency person meant something classified, but the sex was confusing. She couldn't figure out what was going on. Things like this weren't supposed to get by her. She wasn't familiar with love. This suited her as a person, but compromised her as an analyst, she knew. The Indian woman who had been her first supervisor had told her that any half-good analyst knew how to observe, but the mistake they all made was to think that was all. The woman was vegan and went to a steakhouse once a month.

Back in the apartment, Sara was sitting on the sheets in the jeans she wore outside. Dina winced again. Those jeans had cleaned the barstools at Valence.

"Do you know the cure for being left in the morning?" Sara said. It was worse—she was using Dina's clippers to cut her toenails, a small keratinous pile by Dina's pillow. Maybe she knew it would drive Dina mad. "I always go to *their* house," Sara said. "They have to come back. Or I get a house." She waited to see if Dina would laugh, but Dina just stared.

Sara looked around, as if just seeing the space. The bedroom was several steps down from a cubbyhole bathroom and a kitchen with a two-burner stove. The walls were dark green but in the low light of morning, they looked black. There was a steady stream of cars outside.

"Can you tell me what you want?" Dina said.

Sara smiled approvingly. Sara's affiliation was the minimum that Dina had been expected to figure out on her own.

"I don't sleep with my marks," Sara said. "That part was real. And can just go ahead and stay between us. Though please don't think you have anything over me."

Dina's sweat had dried. She could smell it from her armpits. She sat down on the wicker chair that was the only other seat in the room. "Look, would you take your jeans off the bedsheets? You were outside in those clothes."

"Of course," Sara said. She undid the zipper and pulled down the jeans until only the thong remained. She moved so carelessly that the pile of nails fell onto the floor.

"Is this blanket yak hair?" Sara said. "Itches like hell. I meant to tell you last night."

"You could put your pants back on," Dina said. She reprimanded herself—the curtness made her sound defensive, as if she'd done something wrong.

"On or off? You have to decide."

"It's horsehair."

"Horsehair!"

"Please tell me what this is about," Dina said.

Sara wrapped her arms around her knees. You could tell she was one of those people who liked being naked. She loved touching her body, seeing it, paring the nails.

"What's the penalty for perjuring yourself in your intake materials at the Information Center?" she said. "Technically omission, not perjury. But when it concerns a relationship with a head of state, the weight distribution is different."

Dina's expression hardened by a degree that was imperceptible to Sara. She looked down. "I didn't have a relationship," Dina said. "My mother had the relationship."

"Even so, not even a teensy-weensy mention on the intake? You know how that looks."

"He brought me a bag of onions. I hardly knew who he was."

"Do you know how long it took us to track all this down? Special Agent in Billings had to drive seven hours to talk to your mother."

Now the hardening was perceptible.

"He almost said where you live, too," Sara said. "Hicks on either side of the law there."

Dina wasn't sure if this was a threat to disclose her location to her mother, or merely Sara marveling that Dina had allowed her relationship with her mother to lapse to such a degree.

"Bottom line, you haven't been very forthcoming, young lady," Sara said. "Tell me about the onions."

Dina's nail was in her wrist. She didn't like to think about that time, but the moment returned to her willingly. "My mother was working," she said. "I was back from school. A man came down the path in a wheelchair. He held a bag of onions like . . . he held it by the top, by the knot, like a head. I asked him how he got in, and he said, 'Everyone knows me here.' Then he said, 'I brought you a bag of onions.' He was trying to take care of us, he said."

"So you had good terms."

Dina didn't answer. She was in the sunlit dust of the camp, with the body approaching her on the path in its benighted conveyance. Several years earlier, Dina had gone to a bathhouse for women. Amid the bodies in their infinity of arrangements, spread on slabs like unproofed dough or stork-like against the walls, someone had sprayed a eucalyptus mister at the steam-room spigot—the scent of the afternoons at the camp. To her mortification, Dina cried out and burst into tears. Before she could gather herself, the bodies around her, who a moment earlier had been lost to exhalations and scrubbing, converged on her as if they had been waiting. Dina apologized and protested, and they drifted away for her dignity, but each laid a hand of recognition on her as they let go. They didn't know the exact reason, but they knew reason enough.

Dina shook her head to dispose of the recollection. "We met once. We hardly had . . . terms."

"And your mother's relationship?"

"I don't know. You'd have to ask her."

"We did. Now we're asking you."

"I was nine. I don't know what they talked about. They never talked in front of me."

"If it's so innocent, why didn't you mention it on the intake form?"

"He wasn't head of state then."

"The intake forms clearly say government personnel at all levels. He was defense minister then, am I wrong?"

Dina didn't speak.

"He brought you the onions and—"

"He said something like, 'Your mother is a good woman. Respect her.'"

"And then?"

"And then I said, 'What about my father?' And he said, "You will meet him again, I'm certain of it.'"

"That's it."

"That's it. There was an older man wheeling him. He got wheeled up and left."

"And what about your father?"

Even as Dina knew Sara was pressing there to destabilize her, her throat filled with the pressure that always came before tears. She tried to clear it away. "What about him?" she said almost inaudibly.

"No word?"

Dina forced herself to look up. She held Sara's gaze viciously. "You must know the answer to that question."

Sara studied her. "Can I tell you a little story?" she said. She embraced a pillow instead of her knees. Dina shrugged to ask whether she had a choice.

"When I was little, my dad took me on vacation to San Juan. My mom didn't like leaving her beloved U.S. of A. She didn't really like my dad either, but they were doing the old selfless routine for the kids. My brother was off doing his fencing thing. That boy couldn't stick a sleeping cow with a hot poker, but that's another story. We stayed in this nice hotel, Conquistador something. It was crazy to me that in December it was eighty degrees. The place was like a cruise ship. I don't know what I was expecting from my dad. That first day he came down with me to the pool and read his magazine while I splashed around. I was happy. Then he said he was going for a drink at the bar. Four hours later, I went looking for him. Though I kinda knew already, you know? The way a kid knows. There was a racetrack somewhere not too far.

"He came back for dinner. They had waiters in these bow ties and jackets. They picked up those platter tops all at once, like those cymbal guys in the orchestra. Anyway, there was this lady down there every night, by herself. You gotta give it where it's earned—she was magnificent. Just one of those ladies where you're like, *you motherfucker*. What devil and what bargain. I'll confess all my sins if at your age I get to look like *that*.

"One night, she asked my father to dance. Can you believe it? My father was all sorts of things, but he wasn't that. At least not that I knew. But he obliged. They looked good. Every night we ate dinner, they did smiles and eyes at each other, and at some point, they danced.

"One afternoon, my father and I were in the room, and I announced I was going to the pool. I was such a dupe—I just wanted him to say, 'I'll come with, sport!' But of course, if I was going to the pool, he was going to the track. But I had Montezuma's revenge. I was mad. I wanted to storm out. But I'm about to shit my pants.

"So I'm in the bathroom just mortifying myself when there's a knock at the door. I seize up, because I think it's housekeeping or engineering—shit just kept breaking all the time in that place. But it's this woman. And I hear her say, 'I really shouldn't have come up, but I couldn't wait for dinner, I had to bring this up for your daughter.' It was one of those Breyer dolls. The Puerto Rico version—a dark-skinned girl, and a nice little cowboy hat to go with it. Color me shocked that they talked about me on the dance floor. But he must have mentioned I was riding a lot. She found it in the gift shop. They said various nauseating things to each other, see you at dinner, save me a dance, et cetera, and she left.

"A month later, my mother says, 'Sara, let's go out.' We're at the diner, she's got a glass of pinot grigio—you know how they pour, she's like got a Diet Coke's worth of pinot grigio—and she says, 'Now, Sara, I'm going to ask you something, and you just answer, all right. Was there ever a time in Puerto Rico when your father was alone with that woman he met?'"

Sara stopped. "What did I say, Analyst A371?"

Dina understood this examination as a punishment for her omission, but she didn't understand why she was being punished instead of dismissed. They wanted something from her.

"You said yes," she said carefully. "One time you went to the pool and came back to find them both in the room. They were dressed—she was handing your father a Breyer doll."

"I was sure I was telling the truth, though. And then what happened?"

"I don't know," Dina lied. She didn't know what was coming, and she didn't want to seem overly competent. She was relieved to feel alert enough to make that calculation.

"She kicked him out. Lady Afraid finally kicked him out. Not for what happened with San Juan Woman, but it served."

"Did any of this even happen?" Dina said.

"You'll never know. They run us through stories like this all the time. But the point is—"

"Kids think one thing happened—"

"Right. So you start thinking a little harder, please. It's important."

Dina marveled at the training that could teach you to come up with something like that on the spot. She shook her head. She decided to try an attack. "A person tells you people everything they know, but it isn't enough, you keep pressing, and eventually the person has to start making things up to satisfy you, but then you figure that out, and it's proof their motive's unclean."

"And yet, there's more to your story," Sara said.

"My mother didn't talk about it," Dina said. "I knew he was connected to my father—my father's . . . my father leaving us—in some way that made Kamil wish to look out for us. That's all I know. I kept asking my mother about it, and she kept saying it was nothing. Suddenly, my mother, my . . . friend, suddenly she was a person who never told me anything, ever. And if your people really met her, then you know I'm telling the truth."

Sara stared at Dina, evaluating this, deciding whether to proceed. Finally, she said: "Here's the deal. There has been a very substantial discovery of rhodium just the other side of his border. Mostly next door, but some in-country, too. Uncombined with palladium—pure rhodium. That field alone will hold the line on regular emissions so we can refocus on China and driverless. China was in the area on another project; they strip-mined both the land and the people. So the mining concession is ours to lose. Unless your onion man decides to make life difficult for us. We all know his feelings about America. So we need to feel him out, is he going to give us trouble."

"I'm what you have to resort to?" Dina said.

"Official channels cost a lot of money. They cost a stake in the mine. Also, someone has to go there and shake his hand while the cameras are going. That's a non-starter after what he did when he took over. Different weight distribution. Okay: there *are* no official channels."

"He will feel insulted by the approach at such a low level."

"I'd rather say intimate level. But do your job, make him feel differently."

"You can't be serious. I'm an analyst. A junior analyst."

"A good one. It means something to you."

Dina didn't argue.

"You're a daughter of the nation. You understand the language. And he knows who you are. That's a very meaningful combination. I'm being straight with you."

"And if I say no?"

"You're suspended, clearance revoked. Your mother's medical benefits, ditto—all that dope she smokes, hippie-head. You'll still get a private-sector job. We'll do our best to interfere, *mentally unstable, et cetera*, but you'll get it. But only the government can sign that prescription for your mama. Nationalizing dispensaries? Strong move by the other side of the aisle. I'm not an animal—I give credit when it's due." Sara's tone softened. "No one's asking you to go secretly. Go officially. Just to talk."

"And if something happens to me?"

"It won't. You're one of them. And one of us. That combination is strong. He knows you're not Agency. You're only the messenger."

"I should play dumb?"

"The first rule of clandestine," Sara said, "is that a lot of the time, you don't need to be clandestine."

Dina shook her head. "You really didn't have to do the seduction routine."

"I hate when people don't listen. I told you that part was real."

Dina wanted to look through a window. But there were no windows in her bedroom. "You're wrong if you think I have a connection to it," she said. "They hated people like us. That was the point of leaving."

"There's a new man in charge. Your buddy. You're a VIP now."

Dina's throat was suddenly raw with anger. "I lost my father. Half my mother, too. It's all just odds and angles to you."

"You'll be there thirty-six, maybe twenty-four hours. In and out. You're willing to have your position revoked to avoid that?"

Dina buried her face in her knees.

"This is the part where I tell you you're being ungrateful to the nation that took in your refugee self. And toward your mommy and her drug habit. I was generous to my mommy."

After a while, Dina said, "I don't really remember what it was like when we lived there. That was the peaceful part, and I don't really remember it. But I remember what it was like after we left. I wish it was the other way around."

"Peaceful? There was a war."

"Right, but it was peaceful for me. My parents did that."

"Well, this is a chance—"

"Please don't," Dina said. "Please just go."

"And your father? You aren't curious?"

Dina's jaw tightened, but she retained her composure. "I'm sure you tried to find out on your own," she said. "It was a dead end, or you would have used it to get me to go."

Sara stared at her from the bed. Her skin was so free of blemish that it looked like a mask pulled over the face. There was something avian to it, like the air near a shoreline.

"We haven't asked *the Leader Kamil*," Sara said. "Only you could do that—if you went."

"My father left us," Dina said. "He never so much as called. Why do you think I want to find him?" Dina put her head in her hands. "Leave now, please."

Sara groaned. "This is very disappointing, Dina. This was my idea. Went through the full federal database, found seventeen people, ran the hell out of the cross-search like six ways, and you were the only one who had DP camp time same island, same time as Kamil. There was a promotion for me somewhere in here."

"Well, I'm sorry," Dina said. She looked at the nail buried in her wrist. There was a small nick of blood. A horn blew in the roadway—the traffic was getting worse. Before signing the lease, Dina had checked out everything about the place, but she had somehow missed that the building was on the main artery from Coastal to the west side. It was part of the reason she stayed out for as long as she could. From 6 A.M. past midnight, it was nonstop semis and garbage and sirens. Sara was right: Dina was a good analyst. But she missed the obvious thing. Not at work—in her own life. Sometimes, she made herself stay in the apartment and listen to the noise, to force herself to remember.

"Anyway," Sara said. "Think it over." She sighed and swiveled her legs off the bed. "Don't worry about your mama. I'll keep her hooked up—I'll come up with something. Can't guarantee your end of it, but you'll land on your feet. I'll slow-roll the mentally unstable bit. They get a little carried away. It's too bad. There was something in here for you, too."

She rose and shook herself back into her jeans. She walked toward Dina and touched two fingers to Dina's head. "I did the ultimatum script because I decided there was nothing I could offer you that you wanted. I mean, look at this place. Was I right there, at least?"

Dina nodded. Sara's fingers were still on Dina's head.

"You smell," Sara said and walked out.

* * *

Through the little porthole window in her entryway, Dina watched Sara vanish down the street. Then she let the tears come. She sat on the floor and wept. Her wrist was bleeding and she had used it to wipe away snot, so that when she looked in the mirror, she moaned because she looked bloodied.

She was late for work. She paced the few paces the bedroom gave her, and tried to think, but nothing useful would come. She looked at the ledge of storage above her bed: Things filed away with organization, but never used and therefore forgotten, so that Dina constantly purchased new versions. This blind spot irritated her—it was proof of inefficiency. This only perpetuated the problem.

There was no way for Dina to make a redundant purchase of *Uncle Neem's Fairy Tales*—even the copy she owned, which now lived up on the ledge, wasn't supposed to survive. Opening the boxes she and her mother had packed using the cardboard outside Theo's kitchen, the Customs guard on the island had cut too deep and sliced open the book. Dina wailed. Susanna stared at the man hatefully—for once, mother and daughter had the same cause. When they got to the departure gate, Dina discovered a reprieve—like the pocket prayer book that stops the bullet, the cover's sacrifice had saved the several pages that Dina had swiped from her father's bag of letters before her mother burned the rest. She had tucked them inside the *Fairy Tales*.

She hadn't touched the book since, just faithfully toted it from rental to rental. She climbed the bed. Sara's scent suffused the sheets. Dina's nervousness at the prospect of touching her father's relic got in the way of her tears, and her face dried. Her heart beat loudly.

She couldn't find it at first, and felt a creeping terror that she had actually failed to tote it as faithfully as she thought. But then there was *Neem*, with its cover image of a cross-legged man by a fire watching a procession of elephants. The man looked at her like a friend who might have expected the cruelty at Customs but not these years of neglect. She turned the pages, her heart rocking around her chest, until she reached the page with the letters. The breath caught in her throat, and she covered the pages with her hand before she could read them.

She had never been able to persuade herself he was dead, and so she was telling Sara the truth: For some reason, he had left them. It was bitterly painful, but she would take it over his death. It made her want to hate him. But she didn't know how to hate her father.

She pulled out her phone. She couldn't recall the last time she had spoken to Kaylee. Sara had probably chipped the phone, so Dina would have to be careful.

"You're lucky Archer woke me up at five thirty," Kaylee said when she answered. "Otherwise you'd be waking up a mother of two for no reason. Are you all right?"

Dina apologized. In her disorientation, she had forgotten to calculate for the time difference. "You still don't turn off the ringer at night," she said.

"Can't do it. Are you all right?"

"How are the boys?"

"Well, their sweet father fell out of a tree holding a chain saw. He was trimming branches. He'll be fine; Mason's made of tree himself. But you didn't call me at six A.M. to hear about trees."

Dina waited out a pause. "How is she?"

"Your mother? I should charge for the peep show. Confusing, since I'm the peeper."

Dina was silent. Kaylee said, "I'm sorry, honey. It *is* creepy, though. Let me see."

Dina listened to Kaylee crash her way through toys. Dina missed her friend, her overcrowded house, the heat, and the noise.

She heard Kaylee drawing the blinds. "Her lights are on," Kaylee said.

"She gets up early. By the time we're driving to school, she's in the greenhouse already."

"Greenhouse?"

"I told you last time all the stuff that she grows. You pump me for info and then you forget what I tell you."

"Sorry."

"You should see the stuff she carries to market. I'm not thrilled about all the weed she smokes in there, though."

"Is there—is she alone?"

"I only see service trucks, or her little van."

"She got a van?"

"I'm telling you, she carts like a dozen bins to the market. What she leaves on our doorstep—I donate most of it. We got fennel coming out of our asses. I mean, does she miss her daughter? Have to figure she does, Dina, she's your mother." After a moment, she said, "How long's this going to go on, D?"

"If it's an imposition—"

"Oh, shut up. We've been friends for fifteen years."

They shared a long silence. It grew longer and longer. It was the nice version of what it was like to be on the phone with Susanna the last times they talked. Dina had called her mother from university now and again, but there wasn't much to say. But there was one call, shortly before the calls fell away altogether, when they'd said their goodbyes but her mother had failed to click off correctly. As Dina listened, Susanna hummed to herself—an American pop song, of course. She watered plants, clipped something, the gas burners came on, something wrapped was unwrapped—Dina waited for the hiss of whatever it was over oil, and, with a satisfying affirmation, it arrived. This way, Dina was willing to listen forever. Three years later, at the university career fair, she would walk up to the booth for the Federal Information Center, the only one she walked up to, and say that she wanted to listen. When she was a girl, her mother had told her, not without love, that a deaf person paid more heed than Dina. But now Dina wanted only to vanish and listen.

That day her mother finally realized she hadn't hung up the phone, and said, "Dina?" Dina was silent. Couldn't speak. "You forgot to turn it off, blind woman," Susanna said to herself and the line went dead.

Kaylee was yelling something to Mason. Dina longed for them so intensely. In high school, she had practically lived with Kaylee, who taught Dina how to ride in middle school in exchange for a year of mucked stalls at her dad's stables. Mrs. Warren smothered Dina in pillows and gravy. Mr. Warren, overwhelmed by so much female energy, hid out in the basement, reviewing his game freezer. Something in Dina had clicked off during this time, a pilot light that had been straining to light, and was now permitted to rest and gain strength. But then Dina destroyed it with Mason. Of course she did. Dina lost Kaylee and had to return to Susanna.

Kaylee came back to the line. "You can hear the chaos knocking. Tell me what's up. You coming to visit?"

"I just want you to tell me a story, K. Can you do that?"

"Did you have a bad hookup?"

"No. I wanted to hear my friend's voice, that's all."

"What's up with you?"

"Nothing, I promise."

"I haven't even had coffee yet. All right. Well, guess who moved in two houses down. Irene Radtke. You remember her? Irene Radtke got so drunk at the Royce party she said she was done pissing like a girl. She straddled the toilet and pissed all over their goddamn shag rug."

Dina put down the phone, Kaylee's voice wafting up like a scent, warring with Sara's. Dina felt a long, heavy swell of love for her friend. She opened *Neem* again. She'd managed to get three pages in all—three poems, if you could call them that. She read and reread them in secret from Susanna after they left the island, but she couldn't understand them, except for one line in the third poem that clearly referred to her. The one on the first page consisted of a single line:

I wish there were a skin beneath this skin.

The second had a full stanza:

If you betrayed your own,
you must look to others.
The victims don't prepare.
Only killers bother.

The third was a full poem:

It's night. Next door, our girl dreams with Neem.
We dream about the time we said we'd come here
Before it was too late.
We are near madness.
If you fill my mouth with honeyed yogurt,
At last I will fall mute.
You were right about the way they make it here.
A dream that turned out like the rest.

Dina ran her fingers over her father's fading cursive. Had he married again, and surrounded himself with replacement Dinas? Hid out and never emerged, a mountain man who guided, and siphoned off, mule trains? Had a stroke and lost his speech, like his mother? Settled at the seaside, reciting poetry as he served platters of fish to the tourists who had begun to come back to the coastal areas? Lost weight, taken up smoking, wore only shorts, went barefoot, owned a small sailboat, learned how to cook, met a woman who visited him every Sunday, written a small pamphlet of poems known only to his mattress . . .

Of course, some were about his daughter:

In the transfer of the light
it seems you are yourself in flight.

Some were about his wife:

Does a braid still ask its questions
from the scroll of your back?

And some were about nothing anyone else understood:

Now, I collect only untruths.
I gave up truth after my youth.

Freed from professional—and family—obligations, he had become a better poet. Often now, he didn't bother with rhyme, and never with political matters. Dina realized that he was the minority-sect poet he told her about as he read to her in her room, the one who tried to be useful and managed only beauty instead.

She had nothing to go on, nothing. A year or two after they'd reached America, Dina awoke one morning to the cutting memory that Susanna had told her in the camp that George had left them because he'd made a mistake—a mistake that would have damned them all had he not set them free. She hadn't thought of it since. It had just floated into her sleep and shuddered her awake. She ran across the hall, shook Susanna, demanded to know what mistake. She was eleven now, she was old enough. Susanna was not remote, as she sometimes was when her daughter approached. She took her daughter by her arms, though she did not invite Dina into her bed, as Susanna of The Before would have. "I don't know what mistake, Dina-bird," she said. Dina trembled because her mother didn't use that endearment anymore. Dina said nothing further, afraid to press, hating herself for the fear.

Like the increasingly audible horn of an approaching train, she heard a chorus of Kinch-Warrens clamoring for Kaylee in the phone. The kids got both surnames; that was Kaylee's condition. She wanted that, two washing machines, Thanksgiving at the Warrens' and Christmas at the Kinches' (or vice versa), and Mason Kinch for the rest of her life. She got all of it.

"I'm sorry," Dina said, reclaiming the phone.

"I'm not going to ask."

"I wanted to have you in the phone while I did something," Dina said.

"Will we ever see you?"

"I have to take a trip first," Dina said.

"Don't fall off the map."

"I just wanted to hear your voice."

"Don't fall off the map, Dina."

* * *

The case agent, Wecker, was surrounded by little boats with petite canvas sails. Little boats on his desk, larger boats in glass cases mounted on shelves, and a cutter hanging from the ceiling, twirling in the ventilated air. Government still heated federal property starting on October 1, as if it were three decades before. Sara, re-costumed in flats and a herringbone pantsuit that ended above the ankles, removed her jacket, leaving a sleeveless silk blouse that made Dina feel as if Sara had undressed. Wecker didn't seem to notice. He twirled a gaff-rigged schooner mounted over a stem on a square wooden platform. The sails had been designed to flutter when somebody did that.

Wecker was a former Foreign Service officer. The Agency almost never took Foreign Service people, Foreign Service being soft and official, so Wecker was at pains to prove his lack of illusion concerning Kamil. Dina would not take a chartered military flight. Dina would not even accompany a humanitarian flight out of Europe. (The hopeless Europeans, insisting on helping even after it was made clear that charity was unwanted. Investment, not charity.) Dina would take commercial after flying to Canada. Sara said what Dina was thinking: It would be seen as an insult.

"Oh, I think he'll like it," Wecker said. The schooner spun like a carousel in his fingers. "We're saving our taxpayers dollars. That's his thing. Probity. Either way, he's not getting the recognition of an official flight he gets to put in his newspaper. Not after what he did to American business and property."

"You're as rigid as he is," Sara said.

"And you're out of your league talking that way," Wecker said.

Sara didn't answer, but there was invisible laughter creasing the edge of her mouth.

On ascending to office, the leader Kamil severed relations with the United States because it had switched its support from the rebels to the government as the only force that could put an end to the war. American assets were given forty-eight hours to clear the country; he nationalized the rest. The previous leader's flight to exile had been sabotaged by a mechanic bribed by the rebels, his leisure plane thudding to an emergency landing less than two kilometers from the border. He was hoisted from a crane like Wecker's cutter, his body wrapped in a banner that said: "Vermin." He was fed, like a zoo jackal, and not allowed to die. He would be kept alive for as long as it took, Kamil (then the defense minister) said, to visit on him what he had visited on others. The new word, once the minister of defense had become the new leader, was *probity*. Then *self-sufficiency*. Then *heritage*. *Probity. Self-Sufficiency. Heritage*. The country would continue a secular course, but without corruption and without division by sect. Sects were outlawed. The country would have to forge a new means of self-reference, a new nation of new women and men (now women always went first) cured of the dark temptations of self-made division.

Sectarianism was caused by ignorance and economic duress. Therefore, education and economy. The new flag bore a desk—just like Dina's school desk, because it had been the only one manufactured in the country, by a company owned by the former leader's nephew by marriage—and a staff crowned by a single eye, a reference to a blind ruler from the Middle Ages who had economically revitalized the region after centuries of stupor by reforming the tax code and abolishing government levies, which, already onerous, had devolved into outright theft by people with power. *Probity*. The nation would purify itself. Afterward, it would emerge as the regional leader, a beacon for the benighted around the globe, a third way beholden neither to America nor the tyranny of its own past. Violators and resisters would be offered re-education, and serious objectors would be incarcerated, but no one would be marginalized or dispossessed, for as the new leader knew better than most, that was how insurgencies started.

At 9 P.M., the sash of the door to Dina's basement alcove rattled. On the other side, still in work clothes, was Sara. She was holding a mesh bag of onions.

"Wecker wants to fuck you," she said when Dina opened the door. "Not literally. He wants you to fail. He thinks we should carpet-bomb the place."

"Carpet-bomb what," Dina said. "There's hardly anything left. Seventeen years of war."

"That's Wecker. He reserves surgical solutions for his tiny little boats." She shook the onions, which banged together like billiard balls. "Can I come in?"

There was nowhere to sit except the bed—the apartment wasn't made for guests. "I don't want to sully your bed," Sara said, meaning her street clothes.

"Take the chair," Dina said, and sat cross-legged on the bed.

"You didn't say a word today," Sara said.

"I was listening."

"It helped you, actually. You were deferential. Wecker won't blow up your taxi to the airport."

"It's an odd way to thank me for risking my life."

"You patriot! Don't tell me you're going out of debt to your nation. And you are not risking your life. There's no safer place in that country than where Kamil is sitting. The back channels have spoken. Your safety is guaranteed."

Dina nodded weakly.

"Are you up to this? You look kind of pale."

"Now you're asking me if I'm up to it?"

Sara shrugged.

"If I can't persuade him," Dina said, "Wecker will get to be right, and those people will go back to dying. No pressure."

"Don't think too many steps ahead. It never works out the way that you think." Sara rose. "Shall I leave?"

Dina looked at the bag of onions, still in Sara's hand.

"For what it's worth," Sara said, flinging the bag on the bed. The loose skin rustled like leaves. "Try it."

"You don't have to leave," Dina said.

Again, Dina awoke just an hour after they'd fallen asleep. Sara contoured her from behind, her hand between Dina's thighs, radiating warmth under the horsehair blanket. Dina felt cold, ill, covered in dried sweat that had turned to sweat again under the blanket. In the bathroom, she stood under cold water, shivering. As she was leaving the apartment, a hand flopped from the bed. "Onions," Sara slurred and went back to sleep. Like her mother wanting, once upon a time, to believe she was better, Dina wanted to think that she was leaving Sara in her apartment because she was becoming accustomed to love. But also, there was little here that Sara could find out about Dina that she didn't already know. Even more, Dina wasn't sure she would ever return to this place. She was leaving the body because she was leaving herself. It was Dina's fate to be a leaver.

Outside, Dina realized she hadn't packed her father's poems. She asked the taxi driver to wait. "I ain't turning off the meter," he said. His hand made circles around the gear shift. For a moment, she thought she was watching Hector, the bus driver, work his rubber band. She tried to clear her vision. Around them, the city came to life. A deliveryman urinated into a hedge at the edge of the block. Something trilled. The garbage truck hissed and strained. Normally, on her way to the bus, she wore her headphones. Now she would need to pay attention.

Dina's mother had used to warn her not to go back inside immediately after leaving. It was too late. Sara didn't stir. Dina opened *Neem* and took out the poems. She tried to remember his thick fingers, their womanly softness. She folded the poems and put them in her wallet. She hadn't noticed it last night: Sara had folded her clothes, even the socks, in a neat square on a stool next to the bed.

Outside, the taxi driver pressed his horn. She left again, for good.

* * *

Dina has never flown the national airline of the country where she was born, never visited the capital city. She has been sent here because of somebody else's history, which drew her in for one meaningless moment—a man in a wheelchair, a bag of onions, her mother absent as always. They should have asked Susanna to go, she thinks from her seat—it would have amounted to more. She watches Toronto, wet and gray in its anticipation of winter, recede like the last weak light of a findable planet. She looks around herself. When it comes to air travel, the people of her country are poor enough to dress in their finest. At the airplane gate, surrounded for the first time in fourteen years by their faces, her eyes began to scan for her father. She pitied herself for doing it, even as her eyes wouldn't stop.

Dina realizes, her body blooming with sweat, that they did ask Susanna to go—the agent in Great Falls didn't drive seven hours only to ask her about Kamil. Susanna refused. Unlike Dina, Susanna didn't change her mind. Dina is the substitute, her reconsideration rewarded by the reappearance of Sara's heavy thighs on Dina's horsehair blanket. Dina derides herself for having felt something about Sara folding her clothes—how easily Dina is had. Dina changing her mind was worse than Dina refusing. Even if Dina has given them what they want, she has signed a warrant against her advancement at the Information Center. Like a politician, an analyst can't change her mind.

Dina's mind empties like a hydrant letting out water. Her lids are heavy with too little sleep, the engine seems to drone directly into her ears, and the ventilation socket releases only a thin stream of air. But she can't manage to drift off. Her wakeful exhaustion becomes a vertiginous feeling. The man with pale eyes and long teeth next to her stares from the corner of his eye. She has breached the hermetic tube of her life—her basement alcove, the never-varying path to the bus stop and the Information Center, a run in the wet, biting cold—in a way Susanna never would have. Having run so far from Susanna, Dina has simply replicated the closed patterns of Susanna's limited life. Until now. The male passenger stares.

Dina wrestles herself out of her seat, and waits for the privacy of the bathroom. The flight attendants wear tunics over long slacks—gray for men, black for women. The airline recruits all its personnel from the same region—they all speak in an identical accent. Dina watches, through the pulled-aside curtain of the crew area, one of the female attendants restitch loose piping in the slacks of one of the male. They are ignoring the old superstition against sewing while a person continues to wear the item. They look up at Dina and smile fearfully—or pityingly? She can't read correctly.

In the bathroom, Dina throws water on her burning face with cold fingers. She works her fingers inside her trousers, slides them between her knees, and doubles over to warm her hands. This position—a woman about to be sick? a woman about to give birth?—stirs a vague recognition, but she doesn't even try to make the connection; she has no hope of getting hold of something so ghostly. It's the way she used to sit inside her mother's embrace, her mother's ankles around her own, Susanna's arms across Dina's collarbone.

Eleven hours later, the wheels jam the ground like a scribbling stylus. The plane wobbles and the passengers applaud. Her father had flown once, to a poetry conference. When he returned, he said two things: The coffee on the airplane had been served in painted porcelain cups with gold-plated handles. And the passengers had applauded, rewarding the pilot.

"And what is it like to be up there," Susanna had asked.

"It's so ordinary," he had said, shaking his head. "You're a bullet in the sky—but you feel as if you are merely sliding along, as if the sky is moving at identical speed. *Beware, o wanderer / the road is walking, too.* Except when disturbance shakes the plane—then, suddenly, you are very aware of what you are and are not."

That is also the unsettling reality of the arrivals hall: It is impressive in a familiar, interchangeable, international way. As Dina was becoming an adult, the place she was born was moving at identical speed. First, as the new leader says in his weekly radio address, with the help of war—yes, sometimes war is useful—the country undid itself down to its rotted foundation.

But now the country is building. The engineers are busy. The new leader makes a show of declining charity, of demonstrating indifference to the opinion of the countries that once mattered—that is the way he puts it, "that once mattered"—but he has refurbished the airport first. One does not need to visit the domestic terminal to know it hasn't been touched. Striding forward, trying to keep her feet straight, Dina can see a pair of headless electricians disappeared into the crawlspace of ducts above the ceiling panels. They are addressing the same problem as the giant fans that cover the hall with a roar, the heat that is laying a film of hot sweat over her neck. The air-conditioning doesn't work. Dina has lost the lungs for what remains, gulping hot air.

The passport agent looks up from Dina's documents, and again Dina tries to decide if it's pity or fear. Passport agents don't feel fear, it has to be pity. The agent doesn't speak. The round black stamp he leaves watches her like a shutter. It was the Kingdom and now it's the Republic. The hands on the expensive watch on the agent's wrist don't move, and as she passes the Plexiglas enclosure from which he delivers his authority, she sees, slumped in a corner, a plastic bag out of which peer the tufted green plaits of carrots he must have picked from his garden in the moonlit dark before taking a bus into the city. They are his meal for the day.

The wide, empty, marbled halls are besieged by a strange silence. Men in dark clothing hold each other by the shoulders, whispering into each other's ears. Families push suitcases, but do not speak with each other, and when the mothers admonish their children, they seem to do so through a small touch on their noses or hair. It must be the roar of the fans; it suffocates speech. And yet, she can hear her flats squeak against the floor of the hall. Perhaps she can hear herself, but not others—perhaps that is the cost of trying to return. She tries to freshen her wits, but she feels embalmed. That she has dressed herself in the unfamiliar invisible gray of a diplomatic functionary only makes it harder to find her sense. She feels as if she has fit herself into Sara's work clothes while Sara was sleeping.

The Customs agent, who is nearly seven feet tall, and whose jowls hang about his mouth like a dog's, holds up the bag of onions. "And what is happening here?" he says. He has the same accent as the flight attendants.

"It's a gift," Dina says. The words, uttered in a dated, artless accent, embarrass her in her mouth.

"For whom?" the agent says.

If Dina answers truthfully, the guard will feel she's ridiculing him. If she lies, she's lying.

"It's a female remedy," Dina tries. "That's all I'll say, please."

The agent turns his mouth. There is no need for her to go on: The agent has a wife, mother, sisters. He nods in acknowledgment, but then says: "Agriculture isn't permitted."

Dina doesn't know what to say. She would not have brought such a thing, but can't help feeling that parting with it would be a failure.

"We grow onions here," he says. This is her chance to accept his largesse, to avoid making a scene. But she wants to prevail. She wants to feel capable here. If she can't hold on to a bag of onions at Customs . . . She says, trying to make her voice firm, "As you know, the body responds only to local microbes and yeasts. As with honey."

They are interrupted by an agent, attired in the same gray epauletted uniform as Dina's agent, carrying a funeral wreath. He wants to know if it qualifies as agriculture. Dina's agent nods his head wearily. From the vantage point of his head, which floats near the ceiling panels like a balloon, the other man, additionally dwarfed by the wreath, seems like a child. The second agent dumps the wreath in a rubbish bin that's too small for it, and curses softly, shaking his head. Why transport a funeral wreath on an airplane—they can make wreaths locally. In fact, it was quite the specialty for a while.

It isn't that all air-travel personnel are drawn from the same region, Dina realizes. It's that she can no longer tell the regional accents apart.

The Customs agent turns back and taps the name on her passport. "You are one of ours. The local microbes await you. Pass."

She sweeps the sweat from her eyes with her sleeve. She surrenders the onions, the mesh bag still bearing the sad, powerless sticker of the supermarket where Sara bought them. Is Sara still sleeping in her bed? Is it still yesterday there, or today? The agent does not cast the onions into the refuse bin occupied by the funeral wreath. He will bring them to his wife, and they will have a dinner of onions fried in oil and tossed with yogurt, the pan cleaned by flatbread.

Dina is awaited by a foreigner in a dark suit with a barely visible check pattern, a placard with her name in his long, pale hands. A driver in gray slouches next to him. A large group of religious personnel is exiting the terminal around her, and she's swept up in the gray and black bodies before the wave releases her at the feet of the man, who introduces himself as Dellastra, a secretary to the leader. A faint smudge of recently shaved hair circles his bald head, and beneath round glasses, a potted brown mole on his right cheek watches Dina. He apologizes. Initially, the meeting was supposed to take place after she had time at the hotel to refresh herself, but they must go to the presidential administration directly.

"I need to stop at a grocery, please," she says, still thinking about the onions.

"I'm afraid that won't be possible," he says, tapping his watch. The hands on his function properly. "The leader is always wanted in five places at once."

"It's female issues," Dina tries again.

Dellastra bends his head. "Of course," he says. "This is good—you will see how we are training up that class of labor."

When they step outside, Dina grabs Dellastra's arm and, embarrassed, quickly lets go.

"The moment of return," he says, not without feeling.

A pavement-scrubbing truck is passing slowly before them, its rotating brushes edging into the curb. It's the detergent the brushes press into the roadway as the truck goes. The same one was used in her city. The scent has been waiting all these years for her nose to reclaim it. She picks up other fragments: sun-struck stone, charcoal, diesel. More than a decade of war, which killed nearly a million people, was powerless against this scent, this proprietary blended perfume of the place she was born.

The sweeping trucks have not changed, either. That day, as she and Robert walked through the sun toward his home, they saw one, cumbersome and slow, making its way down a wide avenue. Dina had pointed to it, shrugged, and said, stupidly, still trying to cover her tracks, "Look, they're cleaning the streets. Everything is normal. I don't think we have to leave, after all." Robert hadn't turned around to look at her—perhaps, she realizes now, to save her embarrassment. "They do that when the Leader comes," he said. He didn't add that they bothered only for neighborhoods like Dina's, not his.

As the driver wheels the black car out of the airport, she sees bent, aproned women passing twined bouquets of leaves over the airport pavement. Dellastra says, "They will be the cleanest streets you've seen." But her eyes are already closing in sleep. She is not meant to return Kamil's gift from all those years ago.

* * *

In becoming a man of thirty-seven, Kamil has hardly altered—the previous features have merely deepened and hollowed, the one good eye bounding around in its socket, the teeth stained in spots like pebbles colored by weather, the pink angry-leopard spot on the forehead concealed by a flapped-over wing of combed hair. The corners of the eyes are webbed with lines, there are curls of fatigue around the mouth from all the oration it has performed, and wisps of hair climb the throat with no order. But these are his only concessions to conflict and age. And in some ways he has strengthened: The arm that used to be stranded over the chest has been coaxed into nearly complete ambulation, and the patch over the eye is no longer necessary, the dead eye having been replaced by a pliable material that simulates movement. Unopposed, Kamil can remain in charge for half a century more.

"Little Dina," he says, rolling the words around like the pit of a fruit. "A woman."

Dina sits forward in her black leather armchair, as if she's receiving an evaluation.

"Your trip was comfortable?" he says.

She nods.

"You rested on your way in from the airport," he says, "so you missed it." He is interrupted by a timid knock, more of a scratch. A young man in a gray shirt, his eyes between Kamil and the floor, moves in soundlessly with a tray of cups and a heavy iron kettle, the steam curling out of its nose. Kamil thanks him, the young man nods to the same in-between spot, and again the room is silent except for the scratch of Dellastra's pen somewhere behind Dina.

"The key to everything you missed—but you will see it—is personal development," Kamil says. "Personal responsibility. The old country is destroyed, you can see that. But that's an opportunity." He stops himself. "Am I speaking too quickly for you? Have you held on to your mother tongue?"

Again, she nods. She feels it coming back, like water running downhill.

"We are making a new country," he goes on. "In this country, individuals set goals and either meet them or don't, with the appropriate consequences. The goals depend on each individual—each person is free to set the goal he believes in. But progress toward these goals is non-negotiable." He folds his hands over the desk. "That young man who served us the tea. He does not look at the floor, because he knows that in this new country we do not abase ourselves before anyone, even the leader. But he also doesn't dare to look directly at me—he is younger than you, but it's enough years for him to be controlled by the old way of thinking. Straightening his back—that is his labor. That is his goal, if he knows what is good for him."

"Does he?" Dina says. The words have come out with unintended force and cut into Kamil's monologue like an objection. Before she can correct herself, Kamil allows himself a thin smile and says, "Sometimes, we do encourage and clarify."

Dina looks for a place for her hands. Beneath her thighs makes her feel like a schoolgirl. Folded in her lap makes her feel like the functionary she is not. The gesture concealed by the height of Kamil's desk, she digs a nail into her wrist.

"So, in celebration of our reunion," Kamil says, "I would like to begin by telling each other what goals we have met since we last saw each other."

Dina blinks heavily. The sleep in the car has left her more tired, not less. She wants coffee, not tea. In a disappointing sign, she is nervous to ask.

"The mental apparatus likes entropy," Kamil goes on. "It tends toward disorder. They say knowledge is the punishment for original sin, but I think the punishment is something else. I think it's the drive to sabotage oneself—the shameful appeal of our personal ruin. But the body is different. The body is like an animal. There is a minimum of illogic. I have a unique perspective on this." He clanks one of the wheels of his motorized chair. He must be wearing a ring. "I spent many years wishing for my body to cast off its logic. My body declined to do that. But I discovered a power in this. It brushed the dust from my mind. And that is when we began to advance, to have real success against the old regime. That is when people began to understand my leadership, to urge me to take over. Today, this"—he tapped his temple—"is as free of illogic as this"—he tapped his useless legs. "That is the gift I am trying to give to my countrymen." He leaned back and scratched both temples at once.

"You are now a representative of your government, little Dina, with analytical skills to merit employment by your Information Center. So I'd like to ask you: Where did I get this idea?"

His skin is pale, she notices. He does not travel outdoors. In his Kingdom—his Republic—his safety remains hard to guarantee.

"Should I be offended that I am not studied closely?" Kamil says. "I insist on being studied closely!" He laughs and looks at Dellastra.

"I only listen to chatter," Dina says. "Low-level."

Kamil folds his mouth. "They didn't give you a file before you left? By the way, chatter is not 'low-level.' Don't patronize me. Chatter is micro. You analyze smaller blocks. They add up to the same things."

"I'm sorry," Dina says. This is not going the way she had planned.

"You are not a bad analyst, little Dina," Kamil says. "But perhaps you're a bad daughter." He laughs. "The inspiration for all this is your mother. This is why I was looking forward to seeing you. Do you remember what you said to me when I brought you those onions? You said two things. Do you remember them?"

She shakes her head.

"Tsk," he says. "It was three things, actually. You took the onions and you said, 'I guess you want to make us cry.' It was funny. Very funny! I laughed. I was charmed. It was the first time we'd met, and honestly, I expected a simple little girl. But then this darkness came over your face, an unkindness, and you said, 'I don't know what you expect us to do with this.' I understood my simpleness—I was bringing you what, for us, could have made fifteen meals, if we weren't near a village that could feed us. Fifteen men intent on a different future for this country, an end to humiliation, could live another day thanks to the bag in my hands, and you were asking me what I expected you to do with it. You had been spoiled. The refugee is spoiled and pampered, especially by the Europeans."

"The refugee is a refugee because of those fifteen men," Dina says, speaking quietly to make up for the challenge.

Kamil seems buoyed by contest rather than deference. "Yes, I have heard this logic." They look at each other across the desk, Dina managing to keep her eyes from falling.

"The third thing you said," he says, "was, 'Leave my mother alone. I will give you money. Leave her alone.' This, too, I didn't understand at first. You thought there was romance between us. No, little Dina. That is not why your mother inspired me. And she didn't *inspire* me. She shamed me. She said that under us, the country would be the same as before. I made it my task to make sure she had predicted incorrectly. The previous regime took from the people and held what it took in its fist, and it took that fist to anyone who objected. We started with a fist, yes. But since our triumph, little by little the fist opens and everything in it—sometimes it isn't a lot, we are still forming ourselves, sometimes it's only a bag of onions—goes to the people. And if the people object, they are met by the hand, not the fist. Understand?"

Dina has lost her mettle and is staring at Kamil's desk like the service boy. She nods.

"Tell me, how is your dear mother now?"

Dina remains silent. Dellastra is scratching behind her.

Kamil leans forward in his seat. "Don't tell me there's news I don't want to hear."

"She's well," Dina says quickly. "She grows plants. Flowers."

"Plants?" he says. "Well, she is building life, just like me." He contemplates this conclusion. "Wasn't she supposed to study construction?"

"I'm not sure," Dina says.

"You're not sure?" he says. "You're not certain about many details. You do understand that the only reason you—a young woman, not even a junior figure, no figure at all—were received without offense is because of that mother you seem to know nothing about?"

Dina tries to center her eyes. Something has gone astray. How to right it? When she agrees with him, he accuses her of patronizing him. When she disagrees, he is displeased to be contradicted. There is training for this. This is why they send agents, not analysts who don't know how to get their minds straight after what is, after all, no more than one overnight flight.

"We were settled in the American West," Dina says. "Mountains and cold, though not as cold as I thought. In some parts, citizens make the law—there's no government. It's beautiful. Lonely. She liked that there was almost nothing to do. It suited her. I had to cook the meals, because she would have forgotten. Some days, she took a walk, and that's all. When she came back, there were two pale vertical lines on her face. That was where the tears had fallen and frozen. Eventually, she made friends with the neighbors, the churchwomen. Everyone loved her. With them, she had smiles and laughter and jokes. And to me, she brought the old Susanna, the Susanna in grief. That was love, she explained once. Love is when you can show the truth of what's in the heart. She said that sometimes only Jesus can handle that love. Can you believe that? Susanna as a believer? But that is what she said. I filled out my own applications for university. I only applied to schools in the East. We haven't said much to each other since."

Dellastra, whose ankles are crossed to reveal banded socks and pale shins, momentarily stops writing in his notepad. Kamil leans back in his chair, his hands steepled.

Dina goes on. "I used to notice the big things and miss the little ones.

Now it's the opposite. I used to be like my father. Now I am like my mother. Like my mother used to be. Now she's like my father. Like he used to be." They sit in silence, the invocation of her father between them like a weight. She says, "You asked how I changed. I have become less powerful. I miss things. Less when it's about someone else. I don't understand it."

Kamil's eyes throw off a different light. Her maneuver has worked—the last thing he has expected from her in this situation is such candor, and an admission of weakness.

"Perhaps you can recover that power here," Kamil says. "There are three female ministers in the government. There will be more."

"What do you want with such a junior person?" Dina says, and manages to extract from him an acknowledging smile.

"You have come to me on the wings of an unknown bird," Kamil recites.

> But what bird can be known without eyes to see?
> These days, birds can only be felt, scented, and heard.
> I know them by the changed weight of a tree.

They sit in silence. Somewhere a fan chugs. Outside, the city wilts in the heat. Dellastra coughs discreetly. The leader is needed in five places at once.

Dina releases the nail from the spot. She glances at the red welt in her wrist, just off the vein. The wound is like a smelly old sock—a bad thing made good by one's history with it.

"Little Dina," Kamil says, looking at her. "Your mission is a success. You can tell your people that they have nothing to fear on the border. There will be no more territorial games. That was the people before us. We respect sovereignty. And we have our own rhodium fields to find. That is how we progress now. We find our own fields, we do not plunder the fields of others. Your country might ask itself whether it's innocent of the same. But they were smart to send you. I wouldn't have been so straightforward with them. But you are the daughter of Susanna."

Dina doesn't reply. He says, "If it serves your purpose, we can tell them that I was fiercely opposed and you argued me out of it." He laughs. "The Swedes are building a new hospital on the airport road. The profits will go to them—we insist on that—but the care to us, an even deal. You would have seen the site on your way in from the airport. It will be the number one facility of its kind in the region. But it doesn't have an obstetrics wing. Can you imagine? A nation's fortunes are tied to its ability to protect its mothers and children, don't you think?"

"I suppose so," Dina says carefully.

"So that will be your government's contribution," he says. "It will be named—after your mother. What do you think?"

"It makes me think she is dead."

"No, no, no. You don't have any experience with this. People who are alive are very happy to have their names on these things—that is the whole point of their giving the money. They are like small children in that way. They won't stop shouting their names at anyone who will listen. Death is when they finally stop, what a mercy."

"Do you have a family?" Dina asks.

"Dellastra, do I have a family?" Kamil asks.

"The leader has many families," the secretary says. "Every family in the nation is his family. He has eleven million families." The secretary extends his hand toward the door.

Kamil nods—Dellastra is the only person permitted to remind the leader of his duties. But then Kamil recites another poem. Then, again, silence.

Kamil says, "Shame, little Dina. Your father did not teach you enough poems. It's an old poem. The author's brother is in a prison. He is not permitted visitors. But he decides to have visitors anyway. He has a great feast for them, in fact. A goat has been cooked over a fire, they crowd his cell with their plates, there is even argument between two cousins who don't get along, and we have the sound of the flute, and the drum, and what elegance in such a small space . . . It's called 'I Have Heard of a Gathering in My Brother's Palace of Waiting.'"

Again, her father is between them. She delays, hoping Kamil will add something about George, but Kamil only nods, indicating it's time for her to depart. She delays more, hoping she will find the words that she needs, but she feels emptied of speech, as if her two languages have canceled each other. Able to coax her mind toward nothing, she finally rises, fatigue spreading through her, her knees waiting an extra moment to straighten. The tea is untouched in its tray, the nose of the kettle no longer steaming.

At the door, Dina pauses again. Dellastra is at her back, adjusting his sleeves.

"What is it?" the leader says to her. "Have you decided to join us already?"

Dina turns to Kamil. Next to her, Dellastra feels like a heavy door she had to press open.

"I know," Kamil says. "You want to know about your father and don't."

"I do," she manages to say.

"Are you certain?"

She knows Susanna would keep walking, would keep not-knowing as long as she could. Susanna never tried to teach Dina how to live. Once Dina became old enough to understand this, Dina hated her mother for it. But Dina has never considered that Susanna kept silent because she herself did not know how to live. And instead of telling Dina what other people would do, Susanna said nothing.

"I'm not certain, no," Dina says. There are lead plates behind her eyes. They are slowly replacing the eyes, like a screen activated to block out the sun. "Please tell anyway."

"You already know," Kamil says.

Dina's breathing quickens and her chest scrawls around, like a heart monitor unable to make sense of the inputs. She tries to hold steady, to not need Dellastra's arm one more time.

"If I know, I know in a part of myself that's a secret," she says in a barely audible voice.

Kamil smiles slightly—she is trying to speak poetically, the way they speak in the country. That part of the old culture will survive. The language is not fully innocent of what its users purveyed, but it is no guiltier than a gun. Both have no will and infinite power. "No man caused me more pain than your father," Kamil says. "And yet, would I be here without him? I doubt it. I think about him all the time."

There is so much she wants to ask, but she doesn't want to disclose how little she knows. "What do I already know?" she says carefully.

"You know that none of us know. He is lost to us all.

It isn't for us to know
why only some trees lose their leaves in the cold.

Dina moves her mouth, looking for the right tone, the right words. "A country so firmly in your hands and his whereabouts are unknown? How can his whereabouts be unknown in a country where everything's known?"

She meant it as a compliment, but it came out impertinently—she can feel Dellastra exhale nearby. So impertinently that the only thing left for the leader is to exhibit forgiveness.

Kamil leans back. "So be it. But tell me, why would a man to whom, indeed, all is known, offer to pretend that he doesn't? Only out of mercy." They gaze at each other. The edge in Kamil's face drops away. "Dina, your father was killed several months after he returned. He was at a food-distribution point near the fighting line. We were nearly to the capital then, though that time, we would have to retreat. It would be a long time before we got that close again. In any case, it was a government shell made to look like one of ours. There is no grave, I'm sorry to say. I assume you know how people were being buried during that time."

"It happened here in the capital?" she manages to say.

"Yes. I don't know why he chose the capital. Probably because it was still regime territory. Even after all that had happened, it seems that was his side. A bitter irony, isn't it—to be killed by his own."

The last words settle over her like the faraway news of a final defense giving way. She quickly dismisses them so she can re-approach them, later, on her own terms. She nods imperceptibly, the emotion over her face meant to suggest that she is reacting only to the news of his death, that she knew her father was a government man, that she knows whatever else there is to know. It's more than she can keep hold of. She slumps against Dellastra, and, of course, he understands, takes her arm, ushers her out.

* * *

After the door closes behind them, Dellastra gently unhands Dina and invites her to follow. A solitary pimple swells through the stubble on the back of his head. He has applied rubbing alcohol to it, and masked it with foundation.

Until now, Dina's father has dangled in the middle view, neither surrendered to memory, like Yacoub, Vasi, and Robert, nor part of her days. Her mother has lived in the same middle ground, and in this sense, Dina's parents were, until now, reunited.

By demanding to know about her father, Dina has failed not only Susanna's lesson, but Kaylee's. Mason was so guileless that after he reached for Dina, and Dina—stunned to discover that she was willing to try even this to quell the despair in her chest—chose to succumb, he trudged off to tell Kaylee as if he were a bird dog with prey in its mouth. Dina spent the morning waiting her turn, but when Mason called, he said that Kaylee didn't want to know with whom he had cheated. Dina ran across the street to Kaylee's, blurted out with whom. "Mason is too simple a heart not to say something, but you?" Kaylee said. "You're three months from leaving for college. Why'd you have to tell me? Now I have to know that forever."

Dina had lost her power. She was only beginning to learn it when her family left. Like magnetic interference, that departure scrambled the frequencies, though without destroying the power—nothing could do that. But the power was warped by the journey. If she had remained on the island, perhaps it would have straightened out, like one of those brain injuries that take time to heal, but heal. Yielding to Mason was a pathetic attempt to retrieve it. In her unspeaking way, Kaylee had understood this, and wished only to be left to what little non-knowledge remained.

Until ten minutes before, her father was alive, vanished to one of the lives that Dina had kept herself company by imagining—while she ran, during the nights she made use of Valence's only use, at the Information Center as she evaluated shopkeeper chatter in a border zone. All this is no more.

She and Dellastra have been walking through alcoves and hallways, offices dispersing from their path, for what feels to Dina like hours. It had not seemed to take this long earlier. Kamil has told the truth about gender equity—male assistants with dossiers stand, reporting to women seated at computer terminals, as often as the other way around.

Dina can't make out their words. It's as if they're moving lips without making speech, as if the superiors already know what they are going to say, as if their tongues are not in their mouths. Only mechanical systems make audible noise—a fan dispersing the heat, a vibrating compressor, the drone of a light panel. From somewhere floats a woman's perfume, but then the scent turns acrid, like flavored tobacco, so odd in this sealed tube of existence.

Only once, Dellastra striding steadily ahead like a guide to hell—she imagines her hand passing through him like a specter—does someone look up from his desk. A young man, his eyes inflamed and intent on some kind of speech, but she is already past the doorway, his image burned on her lids. Dina sweats on her forehead, in her armpits, her groin. In the presidential administration, they do not waste funds on air-conditioning. Such is the self-control to which the leader is exhorting his people, and his own example is first.

Finally, Dellastra, a tea-like perfume rising from his starched collar, a ring empaneled with onyx glimmering from his lady-like fingers, points her to a suited form on a bench by a set of frosted glass doors. The driver, garbed in gray, joins them as they step out into the howling white light.

They raise their palms to cover their eyes. The driver moves toward a black sedan with darkened windows and fiddles with the lock until the door gives, the interior awaiting Dina like an open black mouth. The leader has moved the presidential administration from a palace on the outskirts of the city to its hiving heart, taxi drivers honking around them. It seems they are the only people allowed to make noise.

Dellastra wants to know if she is feeling unwell.

"It's very bright after the gloom of the building," she manages. "I don't mean gloom."

"We keep lights low," he says. "We are first to the frugality that we urge on our people. You'll rest now at the hotel. I'm sorry we had to invert our plans. But I trust you are satisfied with the outcome. You know, I encouraged him to decline the meeting in view of your professional station. But he wouldn't hear of it."

The searing light makes it impossible to see at a distance. She hears horns, shouts, laughter. Her eyes wobble, trying to adjust to the glare.

"You'll rest in the hotel," he repeats, as if he knows the future. "It has elaborate grounds—it was designed by one of your architects. The capital is safer and safer, but it would be best if you remained there until your flight tomorrow. I've set up direct access to my office for the front desk should you need anything."

She nods faintly.

"As you go off," he says, "I'll remind you that professions of sect are illegal in this country. Please do not bring up the subject."

"And if it's brought up to me?" she says uncooperatively.

"Please do not engage and inform the front desk. It keeps a poisonous subject alive."

"Engaging in the subject or informing the front desk?"

He gives her a tolerant smile.

"An expatriate is the most troublesome visitor," she manages to say.

"She keeps asking for the menu from last time," he says, perhaps more candidly than he means to.

"Is it something you've experienced?"

"Italy is not a country of change. The expatriate meets the same country he left. And that is why he may choose to depart."

"You are not from Italy, however," she says. "You are from Ethiopia."

"That isn't correct," Dellastra says.

"Then your shirt—which has a mark from Tewodros Tailor in Bole—was bought for you by somebody else."

He smiles. "Very good. Very good. Originally from Ethiopia, yes." The smile goes, and he says, "I'm sorry about your father." And then, as if to remind her, "This was a very successful visit for you." He motions toward the driver and is about to take Dina's arm when he notices that the hem of the driver's gray shirt has edged into view, above the cliff of his belt. Dellastra's mouth makes a small disapproving click, and he moves toward the man.

As Dina watches them, she wheels around, and really sees the teeming square around her for the first time. Every man is wearing gray and every woman black. The outfits aren't the same—though the men, always victims of less choice in this area, look identical—but the colors are. The driver's gray uniform, she understands, is not a government standard. As it was not a religious procession that swept her up in the airport. In the capital, the country—as far as the administration's mechanisms of enforcement extend—anyone who wants the favoring eye of the government must dress according to standard.

She tunes her ears, and the speech that filters in confirms what she already knows. People speak alike not because government personnel is drawn from the same trustworthy, ancestral region, nor because she can no longer tell accents apart. The country is being made to shed the divisions of regional speech. Everyone speaks in the round accents of the capital region—even Kamil, who grew up in her city, a long day's ride away. She cranes her head toward Dellastra, who had spoken to her in English. He is speaking to the driver as to a child, softly, patiently, chidingly. Yes, Dellastra as well.

Dina looks down at her gray pantsuit. She has mistaken the gender, but otherwise she has dressed herself in the uniform of the nation. There have been many mistakes. However, she also wishes, now, to correct a nagging inaccuracy. She forced on Kaylee what Kaylee had no desire to know, yes. But they saved it, she and Kaylee, and now they speak to each other with that tenderness available only to those who've remade something broken.

Before Dina, a taxi disgorges a pair of female employees. They wear broad heels, black pantyhose, and black dresses whose sleeves, due to fashion or a shortage of fabric, end midway between the elbow and wrist. Instinctively, Dina checks their wrists to see whether they dig nails there in moments of distress, but the wrists are clean, healthy. From the wrists swing shopping bags marked with the logo of an international clothier that continues to operate in the country. Let no one say pleasure is prohibited here—look at the women's faces.

Now that the words have been uttered, it's not hard for Dina to believe that her father served the regime. That was something she knew without knowing. But the food-distribution point . . . If Kamil had said her father was in a line for food several days after returning, she would have believed it—he hardly knew how to cook for himself, and he had just arrived in the city. But several months later still . . . The man who resented every bowl of rice placed in his hands at the refugee camp—and that was in front of Europeans and village people, who didn't matter, on another continent, where it didn't count. Among his own . . . several months . . . Perhaps she can't admit that she hardly knew a fraction of him. But she can't believe this part of the story.

Another dark thought occurs to her—did Sara know her father was dead before Dina left, and merely withheld it so Dina would go? Surely, it makes her terminally naive, but Dina can't believe this, either. In the last week, she has heard more than in years, years nearly of silence, of listening only to what her headphones gave her at work, or on the way. Her mind scans for a claim she can believe—Kamil's, Sara's, her own unease. She can't choose.

The ripped burgundy lining of the taxi's backseat slowly expands after having been compressed by the women's backsides. Irresponsibly, they have failed to swing closed the door. She can hear the soft curse of the driver, who is straining to reach the handle from his seat. The women, chattering and laughing, pass between Dina and Dellastra, who is still whispering at the driver. Dina steps forward to close the door of the taxi. But then, swept by a force not fully her own, she keeps going, the astonished eyes of the government driver over Dellastra's back the last thing she sees before she disappears inside the taxi.

* * *

"I'm late for an appointment," she said to the taxi driver, trying to speak calmly.

The driver's hand was about to shift the gear, but stopped when he heard her accent. He looked in the rearview mirror. The old gesture returned to her readily: She put her thumb and fingers together, imaginary bills between them—she would pay extra. Outside, Dellastra finished reprimanding the driver.

"Move quickly, please," Dina said.

The presidential plaza fronted a large, inactive fountain, traffic moving around it like floodwater. Dina's driver slid into the slipstream though there hardly seemed space for a man to walk through. No one walked through—the group of gray men and black women waited for the streetlight to turn; the traffic lights worked and the people were meant to obey them. Dina forced herself not to look behind her. She needed an address. "Avenue of the Conquerors," she said. There had been one in every city.

The driver clicked his teeth. "They're still clearing that neighborhood," he said. "I popped a tire last time."

"Should I hire someone else?" she said impatiently.

He shrugged, conceding. He had been testing her command, and she was relieved to discover that she had had the right retort. Impatience always worked better than pleas. Out here in the street, it was easier to make the right choices; she felt as she had before she had boarded the plane in Toronto, surrounded by people like herself to whom she might know what to say. That feeling had abandoned her in Kamil's office, as if he, rather than she, were not of this place. Her momentary satisfaction distracted her from the full weight of what she had just done.

The city moved past them. She saw what she hadn't seen on the drive from the airport. Nearly every block had a traffic officer, gesticulating stiffly, and a bent woman in a kerchief sweeping a dustless sidewalk with bound branches. The awnings of the news kiosks, which once proclaimed the name of the national newspaper, had been painted with one word: *Together*.

Her mind tried to scroll through the contingencies. Kamil's people would begin issuing bulletins. Taxi drivers were the last people to concern themselves with such things, but eventually, the information would reach here, too. What was she doing? She couldn't say other than the answer required being out of Kamil's domain. When she took the handle of the taxi, she felt power. Dina had mistaken the solitude of her basement life for control. It was only solitude.

"It's Avenue of the Builders now," the driver added.

She felt the sting of the correction. A dated accent was one thing, but this mistake pegged her as uninformed, or a sympathizer with the defeated regime.

"Where on Builders?" he went on. "There isn't much left. A maternity clinic, a hair salon, and some market stalls."

"The salon," she said.

"Are you all right?" he said, checking the rearview.

"Is something the matter?" she said, trying to sound firm.

"You keep turning around."

"It's been some time," she said, not knowing what to say, wanting to be imprecise.

"We are all castaways," he said vaguely.

They had left a broad thoroughfare, and were winnowing down smaller streets. The neighborhood had been turned inside out—the storefronts having collapsed, people sold their goods in the street using cracked pieces of stone as their tables. The same countryside that fed the passport agent who couldn't afford food at the airport was feeding the rest of the capital—tomatoes, eggplant, okra. Her chest was tight. She rubbed it with her fingers.

When they arrived, she gave him far more than it could have cost. "I have another appointment afterward," she said, feeling him out.

"How far?" he said.

"Far," she said.

He scrutinized her for a moment, then made some decision, turned off the ignition, and reached for a newspaper under the seat. It was open to the sports section. In the provinces, where the war had concluded earlier, sports leagues were starting back up. Seeing her looking, he said, "It's the only part of the newspaper where you don't know what's going to happen."

Her lips parted, but she didn't know whether to acknowledge the slight mutiny in his comment. She said nothing and stepped out. The street was hot, white with light, and silent except the distant grind of an earthmover pushing rubble. There were no people on the sidewalk. Inside the salon, several women stood, arms across their chests, waiting for business. Dina looked at them. About this she was sure, even if about little else.

When Dina returned to the sidewalk an hour later, the driver had to adjust his eyes—she had them take off so much that she looked nearly a boy. The women in the salon, accustomed to modest, inexpensive requests, had come to life and busied themselves around her head with more hands than necessary. While they washed the hair, Dina nodded off. She awoke fifteen minutes later—not wanting to disturb her, they had retreated to a little table and ate biscuits with tea as they waited—but felt as if she had slept for much longer. As they finished, she understood, as if her brief rest had added intelligence: Working for the regime—that was the "mistake" her father had made. Her mother had lied to her—she had to have known what it was. Why hadn't she told her the truth? But would Dina have understood, at eleven? But Susanna hadn't said a word since.

He rolled down his window.

"You are not very smart," she said. "You picked me up at the administration building, but you spoke negligently of the country." She nodded toward the newspaper, so he understood what she meant. She had come up with this line of approach in the hair shop, and her heart beat uncomfortably. The driver's eyes moved indeterminately.

"I had just finished a meeting with the leader," she said. "He is chaste, but not in all matters. You're wondering why a woman of importance travels in a taxi, patronizes a salon in such an unfashionable district . . . But you understand, don't you?"

"The leader doesn't allow himself pleasure while his countrymen struggle," the driver answered dutifully. "I am receiving more of a glimpse into the president's desires than a simple man like me deserves." He meant the hair. He was saying the right words, but there was ridicule beneath them.

"Do you know how to be discreet?" she said, and rubbed her fingers together again. Pretending to a share in Kamil's authority, she had briefly felt the power of power—of always being right. The pleasure of it was frightening. She named her birth city. He whistled.

"You will be well compensated," she said. She stared past the sedan's dented roof, also burgundy. This part of Builders was on a rise, and not far in the distance, the plain that marked the edge of the city shimmered like a vast burial place. But the city was the burial place, its war dead shoveled underground to fertilize the new country.

"We must leave now then," he said, making his decision. "It isn't wise to drive around there in the night."

She closed her eyes in relief. She hoped he didn't understand it was relief. She climbed into the backseat.

In open terrain, the little sedan strained forward, as if released from some net. They kicked up a vast brown aura as they went, the pebbly dust of the roadway ticking the undercarriage. The interior boiled in the afternoon heat.

"So his thing works," the driver said.

She glanced up at the rearview mirror.

"The presidential apparatus," the driver said.

Still, she didn't understand.

"You are forcing me into indelicacy. You had implied that you were familiar with . . ."

Finally, she understood.

"Yes, it works rather well," she said. "Would you like to know more?"

He shook his head. "People talk about it, that's all." He looked at her in the mirror, and said, the taunt in his voice again. "But you *know* what people talk about."

"Let's have the air-conditioning," she said.

"It's broken," he said, as he overtook a fuel tanker on a distribution run from the oil fields on the other side of the city. "I'm saving to fix it. This fare will put me over the top. But by then, you'll be gone." He clicked his teeth.

She rolled down her window. The fine dust of the roadway swirled through the car.

He looked in the mirror. "Tell me, madame, how discreet is your journey?"

"It's not your concern," she said.

"Will you speak to the men at the checkpoints?"

Her skin went cold. "And how many checkpoints are there between here and there?" she said, trying to speak calmly.

"It always changes. But for a distance like we have, a dozen, at least."

"How close is the next one?"

"There's always one just short of the pass," he said. "There's a fuel depot just ahead of it—in about ten kilometers. I need to stop. But then we'll go through the checkpoint."

"Are there no roads around the checkpoint?"

"Around this first checkpoint, yes. Around one or two more, probably. Not all of them."

The checkpoints would have word right away. How had she not considered such an elementary detail? She had been so satisfied by the ruse she had worked up in the salon. She berated herself.

"After the fuel depot, we will turn around," she said. "We will return to the city." She forced herself to explain nothing more. A kind of relief went through her.

"So soon," he said. She expected disappointment at losing the fare, but it was that skewering tone.

"You will receive the full amount," she said.

"So I will receive my air-conditioning!" he said. "A mission so private even the armed forces can't know!" Again, he was goading her.

She didn't reply. She was trying to make new calculations. Her flight was a temporary folly, easily explained. She had been so shaken by her return—Dellastra was there when she had stumbled at the airport, and again in the leader's office—that she had succumbed to a whim understood only by exiles. She went to a hair salon, of all places. A senseless destination, but innocent. She got her hair cut. Like that day before she and her parents left—the power of memory had overtaken her senses, that's all. Once they confirmed with the salon, it would be simpler for Kamil's people to make nothing of it, to board her on an airplane and have their hands clear. That still left the taxi driver, she realized unpleasantly. She had told him to drive her halfway down the country. How was she supposed to secure his silence?

"If you want to keep going, we can keep going," he said. The savor at her distress had dropped from his voice.

"I already said to turn around," she said. "You'll be paid, don't worry."

"I am saying there's something we can try to get through."

They gazed at each other through the mirror.

"Why are you helping?" she said.

He rubbed his fingers together. "People in a lurch always pay more."

"I said I'd pay the full fare regardless."

"A longer journey earns a larger gratuity, then."

"I don't believe you."

He looked back at her, the car steady in its lane though his eyes were on her.

"Because I hate them," he said. He said it without hesitation. He had seen through her performance all along and just waited.

"What have they done to you?" she said.

"This set?" he said. "Nothing yet. They are better than the last one.

You played the part well when you said I would be paid for the journey. The other lot skipped that part. I used to be a janitor in a certain facility. The warden distributed every second salary. The ones in between he kept for himself. And if you complained, it was a short walk to the cells. So the nation is bursting with joy. Allowing itself to be dressed like children. To have its vocal cords adjusted. Subsidized inter-sect marriage! And no one wishes to see the direction of all this because no one wishes to feel the old fear. What a sweet time the new leader has given us—a rest from the old fear. We will do anything for it."

She stared out the window. She felt her body moving toward catastrophe.

"Close your window, please," he said. "We don't want dust in the car."

"It's warm."

"If you want to go through the checkpoints, it can't seem like we have traveled a long way. That is what they will be looking for."

She closed the window.

"Tell me the truth now," he said.

"They said my father was dead," she said. "For a moment, I didn't believe them. That moment overlapped with the moment your taxi pulled up."

"They are more trustworthy when it comes to reporting casualties, I'm sorry to say," he said. "They have a special relish for that."

She gazed out the window. She remembered, ruefully, the dropping thing that had used to happen when she was scared as a child. Now she stuck a nail in a wrist. She never did it at work. At the Information Center, she was certain. Other analysts heard a transcript of discord about sleeping arrangements in a military outpost, whereas she understood that a part of the unit was contemplating transferring its allegiance to a different commander, the one who had made comments about problems in the country's leadership. This journey was reckless. And yet she knew she would continue it, consigning this man to her fate. Her throat felt as if the dust of the road had scraped it—it was hard to swallow, and her voice was hoarse.

At the fuel depot, the driver obtained a long journey's essentials—a large bottle of cola, a package of flatbread, a jar of pepper paste, cigarettes.

As they pulled in, he told her to lie across the floor of the rear seating. While she waited, a ball smashed into the window above. A child launched after it, bumping the door as he snatched it. His voice was inches from her on the other side of the door. She prayed he was too short to look in the window.

"You are a popular woman," the driver said when he returned. "Even the clerk knows. Stay down until we've returned to the road."

Her stomach pitched. "What did he say?"

"He is the last fuel before the first checkpoint—of course they would phone him. He knows to look for a young woman with a foreigner's accent. And long hair, presumably."

"How do you plan to deal with that part of it?"

"The accent? We will take the long way round the first checkpoint. And the second checkpoint wants to say yes because the first checkpoint has already said yes. Also, they are more rural boys—they are less certain. But none of this matters. You will not speak."

"But if they speak to me?"

"I will tell you everything. One kilometer before the second checkpoint, we will stop and I will tell you then. It's better to do it then because you won't have the time to think about it." He poured the cola into a small cup and discreetly passed it to the backseat.

"And your mother?" he said. "Is she also . . ."

"She's safe," she said.

"Let's hope you can kiss her head one more time," he said. "If the clerk is looking outside his window right now, he will see a man speaking to himself. Let's go."

A minute after rolling out, they turned off the main road, the checkpoint shimmering up ahead. They picked through a gully before they emerged into mudflats, though they saw no body of water. There had been cattle here once. Now only bones remained, cleaned by birds of prey. They passed a large bleached femur bone, like a giant's lost tooth.

Eventually, a settlement came into view. There was always a checkpoint before the pass, and always people who wished to go around it, so a trade had appeared here to offer cans of gasoline, a toilet, a snack. Everything had been abandoned. The public toilets were stippled with shrapnel. The gasoline prices belonged to another era and prompted nostalgia even though that era was more miserable. Several old domed homes baked in the heat. They had managed to withstand bombardment, whereas the more recent brick and concrete homes, always built in multiple stories to signify wealth, had collapsed.

Like all frontier posts, the small settlement had outsize significance. But in times of war, this significance turned on itself to become the measure of the settlement's unreliability—by definition, a frontier post serviced both sides. The driver guessed that even though the regime held the capital region until the final year of the war, the armed forces rather than the rebels had destroyed it. They drove past the execution wall, the old yellow brick spotted with blood.

The driver looked at Dina in the mirror. She was staring out at the dead country before her. Her expression was glazed, inscrutable. There was a sudden blur of movement to the right, a hurtling barrel with spokes. The driver swerved to avoid it, they heard the roar of an explosion, a plume of dust and debris rose to the sky, and the entrails of an animal covered their windshield.

Dina's hands were shaking.

The driver cursed. "I was worried about dust on the dashboard. Now there is a blown-up gazelle over the glass."

"Did you know it was mined?" she said hysterically.

"Yes," he said. "But the driving track is safe."

"We're off the track now," she said, wheezing into her hands. "We're off the track."

"Take a breath. Everyone's time comes when it comes."

"That is a stupid notion," she said, breathing in spurts. She felt vomit rising in her throat and wanted to open the door to retch, then decided against tempting the ground with weight. "Why do people say that? By the time you know it's your time, it's too late."

"Exactly," he said.

She felt the car reversing.

"What are you doing?" she said.

"The ground we covered when I drove off the track was not mined, or I would be talking to God. It stands to reason that it's safer to reverse back across it than to drive forward to get back on the track."

They inched backward at a diagonal. It was ten yards or so. The car covered them slowly. The paved track was slightly raised, and the small sedan had a hard time reversing back onto it. Finally, they made it. They moved forward again down the paved track, continuing without word until they'd gone through the village.

Forty-five minutes later, the driver pulled over in the thin shade of a grove of pistachio trees. The ridge they were circumventing—and somewhere beneath it, the checkpoint—loomed to their left. She was with a man who could secure himself quite a step forward in life if he gave her away at the second checkpoint. But what good was the suspicion—where could she turn in this emptiness? She was at his mercy. She opened the door and felt as if she took a hot mouthful of tea—the air scorched her throat.

Barricaded from the dust by the open trunk, he was changing license plates. Under the main compartment of a large construction toolbox, there were a dozen plates with different starting numbers correlating to the regions of the country. When he was finished, he reached into a small duffel and brought out a check shirt. "I'm sorry, it's not fresh," he said. "But that is the point. Please undress." He turned away.

She was startled to discover that she was still wearing the short-sleeved gray blouse she had worn to the interview with the leader, on the airplane, in her own apartment, Sara sleeping three feet away. She took it off. "The brassiere, too, please," he said. Looking away, he ran duct tape around her chest from behind, though it was hardly necessary. The man's shirt, too large for her by several sizes, smelled of sweat. A wind kicked up and she felt it on her ears, no longer dampened by the hair that used to be there. She ran her fingers around her scalp.

"Tuck it in, and roll down the sleeves, so they can't see your wrists," he said. He crouched. "Give me your hands." When she got down, he rubbed a heap of soil over her fingers, especially under the fingernails. Then he put a wool hat over her head.

"You do not speak," he said. "I mean you are mute. They speak to you, and you make a noise. Let me see your tongue." She stuck it out. "Okay, a good, rough tongue. You can stick it out at them. People with mental ailments are the only people permitted to ridicule the armed forces." He withdrew the cigarettes he'd bought and threw out half. He picked through the duffel until he had a small package of cotton, which he wedged into a corner of his mouth. "Let's go," he said through the gauze, moving toward the passenger seat.

She remained where she was. He turned around. "I have a toothache. You are my dumb, blessed, unfortunate son." He made a gesture that indicated he was working with what he had. She had cut off all her hair, and the size of her breasts—well, they did not inhibit his plan. "You are driving me to a village with a dentist. We are too poor—you wear your father's old shirt. That is all. Simple is best."

"That can't be," she said, a senseless protest.

"You can't drive a manual transmission?"

"That's not it."

"Then what is it? Do you have a better idea?"

She didn't. She didn't want to turn around. But she was terrified by his plan.

"You are not afraid enough," she said finally. "You are playing with death. Something has happened to you, and now you don't care whether you live."

He kicked the soil by his feet. "You are better at seeing through other people than keeping them from seeing through you."

"You take care," she said, unsure what she meant. Well, she was insisting on it. "You take care," she said again, more quietly this time, with pleading. She didn't want to plead—but she depended entirely on this man. Her skin felt inflated, dense, as if fingers were pushing it out from inside. The blast had made a sudden, brief noise—like an envelope tearing open.

She touched the back of her head. More than a foot of hair had swung there two hours before. She felt demented under the wool cap. He handed her several rags. Using the cola, they pushed the intestine off the windshield onto the ground, where it was immediately floured by dust. Mainly, they succeeded in creating a new scum on the glass, but it was the kind to raise no suspicion of having avoided the first checkpoint.

Dina took the driver's seat. Soon, they had returned to the National 11, the road that went through the earlier checkpoint. Here and there, the road tar had popped in the heat.

In an excess of obedience, she started slowing well before the second checkpoint. Ahead of them was a tall-roofed minivan with German plates. The German sense of socially disengaged adventure was intact. The plates were good enough for a quick passage, and it was Dina's turn. In the passenger seat, the driver pinched off the end of a cigarette and lit the nub in his mouth.

"What are you doing?" she said.

The young, bearded soldier at the crossing waved at them impatiently. Dina closed her eyes gratefully—he was on the passenger side. They rolled forward. The soldier motioned for the passenger to lower the window. The passenger's head rested on an old scarf, and he was moaning slightly. His eyes were closed and he ignored the command.

The knuckles rapped the window, but the passenger only moaned more loudly. It occurred to Dina that she was supposed to lean over and help her father by lowering the window.

"What is it, father?" the soldier said, ignoring the boy at the wheel. The armed forces must have been exempt from the mandate on accent harmonization.

The passenger looked up, took a long drag on his cigarette, and touched his cheek. "It's bad, son. I'll need it pulled, I'm sure. Our dentist moved to the city. I don't blame him."

"Why don't you go to the city? It's closer."

"You want me to pay their prices?" the passenger said. "Will you give me the money?"

"Hold on," the soldier said, shifting his rifle.

"What is it?"

"The one in the guardhouse used to a be a dental assistant. Maybe he can help you."

The passenger cursed. Of all the professions a former dental assistant could choose to take up . . . He lowered his head so it wasn't visible in the windshield, pulled out the cotton in his mouth and scraped fiercely at his gums with a nail.

"What are you doing?" she said from the corner of her mouth.

"My nails aren't sharp enough."

Out of sight, she extended the one sharp nail. He tried to fit his mouth over it. Up ahead, the soldier was speaking into the guardhouse. She pushed the finger into his mouth, and fished through the wetness there for the gums. She scraped so hard he cried out.

"I'm sorry!"

The soldier looked back at them from the guardhouse.

"Shut your mouth!" the driver sputtered through the blood in his mouth. "May you live only in health, goddamn you," he said. "You were a torturer once, I am sure."

The soldier was walking back. Dina's finger was between her and the driver, and before she could hide it, the soldier was next to her window. The driver was doubled over.

"What happened here?" the soldier said.

"He's an idiot and he was trying to help," the passenger said.

"What did you do to your old father?" the soldier said, looking at Dina.

"He is really an idiot," the driver said, trying to suck down the blood. "He doesn't speak. He saw the blood flow and he tried to stop it with his finger."

The soldier looked between them. Dina felt she shouldn't move her outstretched, bloody hand, for fear of drawing attention to it, but the solitary long nail was in the open for the soldier to see. The soldier nodded at the guardhouse. "He only sold dental equipment. You don't have to know anything about teeth to sell dental equipment, apparently. I tried to help you."

"It's all right," the driver said. "But let us go forward. Look at my mouth."

The soldier motioned to a young sentry, who seemed to be copying the older one's beard, to raise the crossing bar. Within a moment, they were through. Dina noticed only now, in the rearview, that the soldiers wore sandals. They receded until they were indistinguishable from the white dust of the road. The landscape flashed past in a hostile unpeopled blur. She felt more adept with the wheel. She tried to hold it carefully, with both hands, in the manner of a son wishing to spare his father the warps in the road. The passenger remained slumped on his bloody scarf, and hummed slightly. His head bounced with each rut in the road.

"They don't have boots," she said.

"They have boots," he said. "The army eats before anyone else. Boots are uncomfortable in the heat. They don't need them. No one comes to check and there is no danger. It took them a long time, but they have eliminated that problem completely."

"But there are checkpoints."

"There must always be the appearance of danger. It exercises the populace."

She felt she should have deduced this herself. She said, "When did you stop being a janitor at that place?"

"The taxi driver is the freest man in the world, don't you know?" he said, not answering.

"But where are your people?" she said.

He lifted his head briefly, as if trying to remember. "Far," he said, and lowered it.

"Why did you tell me to cover my wrists?"

"In the village, in the morning, it's cold."

She was relieved—she thought he had seen the marks she gave herself.

"It's the most womanly part of you," he said.

By the next checkpoint, the blood had dried and looked even more credible. By the fourth, Dina felt confident enough to make noise at the soldier. They could have driven around the fifth and sixth checkpoint, but they decided to make up lost daylight. Once in a while, the driver changed the license plate. There were ten checkpoints in total, and as they approached Dina's birth city, the ruse became almost easy, for anyone in a village within a half day's drive of it would head there. At one checkpoint, the soldiers didn't bother at all—the crossing bar was open and the guards were off to the side, playing cards on a folding table. There was still a hem of light on the horizon when they crossed the last one. When they were out of view of it, they exchanged places. When she became the passenger again, she saw a patch of the driver's blood on the seat between her legs.

After she told him the address, he pulled out an old driving atlas, and fit the sedan into the rushing traffic of another city. She willed the passing streets to stir something in her, but she felt nothing. Maybe it looked different in daylight.

Here, Avenue of the Conquerors had not been renamed. The country's new life was like a penumbra of light that faded with distance from the capital. As they moved down the empty open span of the city, she battered herself to recall something of the surroundings—the streetlights, which had been dimmed to save electricity; the poplars lining the median; the shuttered factories outside the city center. She rolled down the window and sniffed at the night. The capital had scents she remembered, but her birthplace did not—how could that be? Or had the scents already become ordinary, the novelty of return used up in a moment? Perhaps it was something you had to experience quickly, then depart again in order to save. Perhaps, having left home, you could not return to it directly, memories being available only at a distance, or an angle, and the closer you approached, the more they scattered.

"It's just up there," he said. Holding the atlas with one hand, he looked like a poet reciting from his book of place-names. All these were also gradually changing, and in a number of years, the process complete, the use of such an atlas would constitute, rather than mere obsolescence, an ideological provocation.

They could see the silently turning lights of the police cars well ahead. She was expected. The policemen were smoking and laughing.

The driver shut off the engine on the opposite side of the street, a hundred meters down from the building, by an electronics store that also sold cheap household items. She strained to see the yard in front of the building. In that yard, Harry Soudane had given her a necklace made of pebbles. There, she learned to draw on the pavement with chalks while her mother stood ready with a bucket of water, so neighbors didn't complain, and had sought shelter in Madame N.'s garden. It was where her family's flight had begun. Disappointingly, the yard seemed like any other. But she remembered that night—the cries, the lights in the windows, the indecipherable sounds, the stunned face of her father. Even as the yard seemed to have shrunk, even as she couldn't find the bakery across the street from which George liked to purchase elephant's ears, she saw that night somewhere behind her eyes: The faint light off Engineers; her mother's warm shoulder, scratchy with multiple coats; the catch in her mother's voice as she spoke to the driver, then pleading in it, and then the command.

They ate the flatbread with the pepper paste, sharing a new cola.

"You really think he is in there," the driver said.

"I didn't know where else to try."

"What kind of a man leaves his family?"

"I'll ask him," she said resentfully. They fell back into silence.

Dina had lied to Sara—she had never managed to become angry at George. Instead, Dina had directed her anger at the available parent. As a child in the small Craftsman where they had been installed by the church, she had waited for George to press the doorbell. When Susanna was out, Dina would step outside and test the bell. But what if he chose to use the knocker? Was it audible inside? This was impossible to test by herself. Then, Kaylee was only a girl who nodded to her from the basketball hoop in her driveway. Dina had no other friends. So when Susanna came home, Dina slipped outside, and banged the knocker. No answer. Dina went back inside and found Susanna near the washer, ghost-dancing with bedsheets.

"Didn't you hear the knocker?" Dina said.

"So?"

"Why didn't you answer?"

"You're at home. Who can it be?"

And then Dina knew that George was never coming, that in telling Dina he would return, Susanna had been lying again. She hated her mother—again. And herself—it was her father who had abandoned them, but it was only her mother she wanted to hate. Dina would try to fight through this thicket of notions, fight and flail and surrender, and then go tune the little pocket radio the church gave them and listen to the chatter and draw. She always drew on a windowsill that looked out to the street, just in case.

"Haven't you asked your mother?" the driver said.

"Ask her what?"

"Haven't you asked your mother what happened?"

"I asked. She said he would return. Then she said he wouldn't, but she was angry at me at that time, so I wasn't sure what to believe. And then she refused to talk about it at all."

"Perhaps she knows as little as you."

"If so, why tell so many lies?"

"Watch your tongue."

"That's the truth."

"The truth . . ." he said and laughed. "If she lied, it was for your good." He pulled out his mobile. "Call her now. I'll pay for it."

"We don't speak."

"How is it you don't speak with your mother?"

"She doesn't speak to me, either."

"That is her concern. Forgive her."

"She hasn't asked for forgiveness."

"A person hardly has to ask in order to be forgiven!"

"Let's leave this subject."

The driver shook his head and gave her the last piece of smeared flatbread. She chewed it resentfully. "Is there a side entrance?" he said.

"Yes," she said. "There was. On that side. I think." She pointed. The police were so lazy they had not bothered to cover that side—or the person guarding it wasn't visible.

"What floor?"

"Fourth. It's 401. Do you have an idea?"

"Building maintenance."

"What's the point?" she said. "We can't get through to the apartment." The regime had changed, but it was still guarding him. She imagined again that he was there with children. With two daughters. Twins. This Dina didn't wish to know. She wondered why it wasn't until now that she thought about this—not until she had dragged this man into her trouble, just as she had done to Kaylee all those years ago, to Yacoub. She was nearly invisible as a person, had become small and smaller, but even after forgoing other people for so long, her first touch of another brought that person into distress. Why was she cursed in this way? What had she done wrong? Why had the power turned to this?

"What does he look like?" the driver said.

"I don't know," she said. "He had a big moustache. But then he took it off. His hair was like a circle around his head. But who knows now? Listen, you don't have to do this."

The driver was looking through the windshield. The cars flowed like sap. Bright fluorescent light rolled out of the electronics store, whose speakers broadcast a song about a flood that sweeps away a man's car but then carries him to his lover.

"They always write songs about rain," he said.

She didn't answer.

"You can't go," he said. "So either I go, or we leave. What do you prefer?"

Her desire fought with her conscience.

"Listen to me," he said. "My brother was a physician, a surgeon. He applied himself, and I didn't. Even before things went really bad, he said we should leave with our families. Our parents were gone by then—thank God. He liked to worry—he was a sensitive soul. I told him he was exaggerating—these things happened every several years, and they always ended the same way, right where they started. I wasn't going to pick up my life and pay some hotel manager an inflated fee—even if my brother offered to cover it. Just keep out of the way for several weeks, I said. Take your girls on vacation.

"Because I was the more practical one, he tried to listen to me—it was not one of those relationships where because he was a medical man, and I was a bricklayer, my opinion didn't count. Quite the opposite. He was a gentle soul, I am telling you. I think he wished to protect me from the impression that I was behind in life. Yes, that is how he defined his responsibility.

"He half listened to me and half to himself. They went just across the border. They lived well—he was a skilled surgeon, he did something with hearts. As you know, hearts are the first things to go around here. He was offered work right away—unlike so many of our people, who were kept down like dogs when they became refugees. But his heart hurt. That's something, isn't it? He was naive, in a way. His heart hurt that he was free while his people suffered, that children were being sprayed by shrapnel, but he was watching the sun set from a porch with a cup of tea in his hands twelve miles from the border.

"He decided to come back and build a field clinic. It would be open to anyone, either side. He said he got the money from the UN, and the Europeans gave him some—but I think he just used his own money, to be honest. I think he used everything he had. He must have been the only man building something in this country at that time. You can imagine what it meant to get building materials then, to get someone to come and pour a foundation, and frame, and wire for electricity, and plumb it, and we are talking about medical equipment, and beds, and—" The driver shook his head.

"The builders crossed the border in the morning and left at the end of the day—he paid upfront three, four times the cost. His daughters lived without him—he was a father to this building instead. Our city didn't have so much trouble then, so he came sometimes for a meal. But he never stayed. He always drove back to the hospital. He was building in open terrain, so it wouldn't get stray fire. He slept on a cot in the open—thank

God it doesn't rain in our country. He was protecting it. It became an obsession. But I think he was happy. He had found a purpose. A man who has found a purpose—beware of that man."

The driver closed his arms over the wheel, and laid his chin on his fingers. He stared at the windshield for so long that she thought he'd fallen asleep.

"Something happened when he was there one night," she said quietly.

He smiled at her naivete. "You have been away for too long." He rubbed his face as if he wished to remove a layer of it. When she had entered the vehicle, glimpsing him in the rearview, he had seemed to be in his fifties, perhaps close to sixty, nearly a grandfather. But he was in his forties—in their country, people passed through life in misalignment with the clock.

"When it was finally ready," he said, "he invited everyone he could to come cut the ribbon—a villager or an official, everyone welcome. In the end, he got only a kindergarten. They came to learn all about medicine, about what doctors can do."

The driver tried to scrape something off the wheel. He spoke into the steering. "There was no war there. It was getting closer, but it was nowhere near. He built in the open, so there was no question of concealment. That made it a very easy run for a bomber. The government did it on purpose, because he had not taken a side. I am telling you, he was naive. But I wasn't—why didn't I stop him? In any case, he was killed, and all the children were killed. Only rubble was left. It's still there."

They sat silently. She wanted to touch him, but she didn't know where. He patted the top of her hand to free her from the feeling of having to say something. He opened the door and disappeared inside the store. He returned holding a bucket and broom. He winked at her, and jogged across Conquerors, a man holding a bucket and broom.

* * *

The three police arrayed by Apartment 401 leaned against the staircase banister, their elbows on the railing. They looked like birds.

"He's my brother-in-law," one of them was saying. "On the one hand, not blood. On the other, family. It's a contradiction."

"So charge him fifteen percent," another said.

"Ask twenty percent and blame your sister," the third said.

"My sister has to live with him," the first one said.

"So blame your wife," the third one said.

"His wife has to live with *him*," the second one said, meaning the first, and they laughed.

They fell silent because they heard singing from somewhere below. It was a melancholy song about a flood that destroys a man's car but then carries him in its muddy embrace all the way to the woman he loves. The voice was luminous and graceful, the timbre vivid, the power gentle but ready to carry. As the police couldn't know, its owner had been supposed to travel internationally to make something of it—first to an academy in the neighboring country, so it could say it had a hand in his rise, then to London. But on the assigned day, he decided not to board the bus that would take him across the border. He ignored his mother's questions and didn't explain. The people at the academy called, London called, someone even came to the house, but eventually, everyone moved on. The singer became a bricklayer, then a janitor at a prison, then a taxi driver, and now, apparently, a floor washer.

The floor washer made his way up the stairs without looking at them. He was busy with the song and with the detail of his labor, working the crevices of the stairs with a brush before mopping. Besides, his duty did not extend to care for the opinions of policemen.

"You should be on the radio, dad," the first policeman said. The washer didn't reply. He was mopping by 402. The policemen shrugged and lit a cigarette.

"You better not ash that cigarette on the floor," the washer said, turning toward 401. "Stand aside." The policemen obeyed. The guilty one ashed into a hand, waiting for the washer to move out of view. The cleaner kept dusting and scraping by 401—apparently, he intended to delay until the question of where the policeman planned to put out the cigarette became urgent.

"Just toss it out that little window," the second policeman whispered.

"Rub it against the wall over there," the third one said.

The consensus was that it had to happen farther down the landing, out of the washer's sight. Because certain men must do things in groups, the policemen moved there together.

Seeing his opening, the floor cleaner allowed the end of his broom to slip out of his hands and bang loudly against the door to 401. A moment later, it was opened by an older man in a wheelchair. The policemen yelled for him to close the door and rushed back. In the confusion, the cleaner took a photo of the man with his mobile.

Dina shook her head. It wasn't him.

"They called him Academician-something," the driver said. "But I couldn't make out the surname. You said your father taught."

"My father was a university person, yes. But that isn't him." She was disappointed and relieved.

"I'm sorry. At least he's not in a wheelchair. What now?"

"Thank you for doing it," she said.

"What are you going to do?"

"What is your name?" she said.

"Emil," he said.

"Your family was also there—at the opening of the hospital—wasn't it?"

His face loosened and he exhaled heavily without opening his mouth. His mission had stoked something in him, and his face had been caught up in it. But now that went away. He smiled awkwardly. His eyes began to fill. But he didn't allow it to go further than that. He rubbed his eyes with his knuckles. "My hands are filthy from that cleaning," he said, trying to laugh. She laughed with him. Under the cover of this laughing, the water came through his hands. She touched his shoulder with her fingers. He looked away, and didn't look back until he was certain he was finished.

She told him why she was there, all of it.

He whistled, shaking his head. "You have to get across the border. The easiest place is the Triangle. We could be there by morning. I don't have plates from there, but no one will check in the dark."

"You didn't want to drive in the night."

"East of here, it matters less. There aren't even checkpoints. Nobody goes to the Triangle. It's an hour from the border to Biro, on the other side. People from the border villages go to Biro for work, so there will be early buses. From Biro, you'll get anywhere."

"Is Biro where they have the outdoor market?"

"Your people really sent you out here with no information. The market was bombed four or five years ago. The rebels used to pick up their guns there. No more market."

"I don't think my people counted on me being anywhere near the border," she said.

She was looking past him, toward the building where she spent the first eight years of her life, once upon a time a home so thorough another was unimaginable.

There was a soft rap of gloved knuckles on Emil's window. It framed the middle part of a policeman's uniform. She cursed. "Easy," he said through his teeth. She still wore her uniform of a son. "Just do the same thing."

The driver rolled down the window.

"What's your business here?" The voice was low and calm, certain of its own authority. From her seat, Dina couldn't see his face, only the gloved hands in the window slot.

"I'm showing my son the city, sir," the driver said.

"In the dark?"

"I work all day. There is never a time."

"And what is your work?"

"I'm a bricklayer. The work is good now. We are building again."

It was likely that this policeman had served the last regime just like he was serving this one. But he was obligated to respect the new progress.

"I work all the days of the week," Emil said. "I want him to live in the city, not the village. Now, something like that is possible."

"And what is there to see around here?" the voice above the window said.

"That's just it." The driver lowered his voice. "I don't want him to know, but I've gotten lost." Emil picked up the atlas. "A man needs strong eyes to decipher one of these in the dark."

"Where are you going?"

"East of here."

"That's where I grew up. What village?"

"Boud."

"That's one village from mine. Where do you work?"

"At the brickworks, sir, like I said."

"I don't know of a brickworks there."

"Forgive me, you have been in the city for a long time, then. There are opportunities now that there weren't before. And men are taking advantage of them. It's a recent operation. If there is any doubt, look at these hands."

The policeman pushed the hands away with his glove. "It's not necessary. I am not from that village. I was only testing you. Get going. Can't you see there is a police operation just that way? It isn't smart to idle here." The policeman bent down and filled the frame of the rolled-down window. He had long creases in his face, and his eyebrows extended nearly to his temples. Seeing Dina, his eyes narrowed—they were seeing something different from what his ears had heard, but the information was stuck below his awareness.

"What's wrong with him?" the policeman said.

"God made him a listener," the driver said.

The policeman's mouth relaxed—there was now an explanation for his vague sense that something was off. "Obey your father," he said, studying Dina's face. Dina nodded.

"When the red lights come on," the police went on, speaking to Emil, "turn around right here in the avenue. You have my permission. Keep going until you see the orphanage. Turn right and don't stop until you are out of the city. You'll go through another neighborhood, but then you'll be out. Get going," he said sharply and stepped away.

Emil rolled up the window and breathed out. "He was testing me, how do you like that?" he said. "An investigator, that one. The street police is so lucky to have him. Degenerate."

Dina's heart beat miserably in her chest. He saw the expression on her face. Trying to keep a respectful distance, he moved through the glove compartment until he found the mirror. He held it up to her. In her wool hat and check shirt, her hair gone, dried sweat on her face, and a fine coat of dust from the road, she really had become someone else. "Don't worry," he said.

They did as they were told, passing the orphanage—which, unlike outdoor markets and agnostic hospitals, continued to thrive—and turned into the next neighborhood. They had passed several streets before Dina realized that it was Robert's neighborhood. The vendors outside, the din in the street instead of the quiet where Dina had lived, the way those wealthy enough to afford a storefront did not go quietly about it—running lights flashed in and around their windows. For some reason, this was recognizable as her own neighborhood wasn't.

"Stop, stop," she said.

"What is it?"

"I couldn't explain. I know we must hurry. Just for a moment. Please, it's very important."

He weaved out of traffic.

"No more than a minute," she said, stepping out.

It was the candy shop, the one to which Robert had used to press his nose. It had survived. She doubted herself, but she had to be right—it was on the corner of two streets, and its wide window reached nearly to the ground. She waited impatiently for the light to change. Finally, she ran across. She stopped at the window. There were no lights around the shop, only a single dim yellow bulb over a wide tray separated into segments: spun sugar, toffees, jelly candies, coated almonds, chocolate in blocks and individual candies. In the back, under another low bulb, sat the clerk. He was reading a newspaper. She willed him to raise his eyes. Feeling the face at the window, he did. He was young. It wasn't Robert. She felt the disappointment in her stomach. She would have given something very dear to see Robert. She wouldn't have kept him a long time—she only wanted to explain, to explain.

The young man rose—he wore an imitation jean shirt over black trousers and brown sandals with stitches. He walked toward the window, one finger holding his place in the newspaper. She told herself to move away, and disobeyed. When he was at the window, he laid down the newspaper, and cut a small square of wax paper from a hanging roll. The tongs hung from a nail by thick twine. He picked up a chocolate, laid it in the square, and with a practiced hand twisted the wax paper until it had made a little boat for the chocolate. He opened the door and offered it to her. He thought she was a street boy who didn't have money. He thought she was crying because she was hungry. "Take it, take it," he said. "Take it before my father sees." She took it. "Eat well. Eat in peace." He shut the door.

They drove through the night, the city dissolving into desert. She thought she would be rewarded for stepping into the taxi. But she had been an American for too long—reckless adventures were not always rewarded. At a fuel station on the outskirts of the city, they filled five canisters while a suspicious clerk looked on. Then they hurtled through the long black tunnel of the night. What music they got on the radio quickly tripped into static. Emil turned it off.

"You never tried to leave?" she said.

"I was coming to it," he said. "But then— And how could I go somewhere now? I will die here. The sooner, the better." He copied her: "*Take care, you take care . . .*" He dared to laugh, and Dina followed.

"You should sleep," he said. "Then we'll switch."

"My nerves aren't right," she said. After a while, she added, "When I was little, my mother put my schoolbooks under my pillow. The knowledge went into your brain in the night."

He smiled. "Mothers hold up the sky. When my brother was little, he developed a very serious affection for his pillow. He gave it a name—Bas, or Bis, something like that. When he went to a friend's house, he brought the pillow. He had many friends—it won't surprise you to learn that. There were all sorts of jokes, the pillow was his best friend, his girlfriend, and so on.

"But then it caused quite a controversy—this one woman, the mother of one of his friends, she felt it was an insult against her bedding. My brother—because he was this kind of boy—didn't take his pillow anywhere after that. That woman's reaction upset him more than it upset the woman. I remember that woman. Quite an actress, that one. She was always looking for an argument. When the war started, she went to the precinct and talked about the things the people in the street had been saying. She was killed for that."

"Maybe she was trying to protect somebody," Dina said.

"Here, you can't protect yourself without hurting somebody else. Protection is like electricity here, it's rationed. It's available only sometimes for some people."

She contemplated this in the dark window. There was only emptiness there. But it was filled with the promise of violence.

"My father served the regime," she said finally. "I don't know in what way, exactly."

"So you're dominant-sect?"

She smiled bitterly. "A man decides that the country will no longer speak of sect, and half a day is enough to become an obedient animal who feels fear when someone mentions it."

"He's not wrong to have done that," the driver said. "But they outlawed the sects and didn't rename them. So if you speak of them, you can use only the old names."

"What would you have renamed them?"

"Oh, I don't know. Those decisions aren't for me."

"I'm grateful to you."

He waved her away. "I am a ghost driving this ghost ship around. Today, fooling those soldiers, screwing those policemen, I came back to life."

She watched the roadway vanish under the headlights. The night out there was freighted with threat, but in this vessel, she could still imagine whatever she wanted. She wished the light wouldn't come. "After my mother and I got to America, I had these elaborate dreams. I was in the hold of a ship, surrounded by sleeping bodies. They were laid head to foot, there wasn't an inch of free space, and I had to make it to the other end without waking anyone. Or I was in the woods at dusk, there was a ruined castle, and this big old oak a part of which was bent to the ground. It was always just about to break off. But it didn't. And the dusk never turned into night.

"I kept waking up. We had only one bedroom, so it woke my mother. She told stories until my eyes closed. She didn't like to, but she did it. In the church, they were talking about the power of suggestion—those church ladies used to lock fingers in our kitchen and close their eyes and sing 'plenitude, plenitude, plenitude'—so she told me about a man going to sleep. He liked to punch his pillow, so it was soft for his head in the night. But as he's punching the pillow, these strange waves sweep across it. The pillow turns into a kind of framed window, but he fits through it only halfway. With the white tube of the pillow around his waist, he looks like a swan. But the swans he runs into, they can't understand him. They decide they will test him. Depending on his answer, they will accept him, or peck him to death. They ask: Is it better on land or in water? And because he's still a man, he says: On land. Some of the swans cheer because he's given the right answer. But some swans jeer. It seems the swans themselves think differently about the issue. And they didn't know it till now."

"Your mother told you this story?" he said. "She has an imagination."

"Yes. I used to wish it showed up in other parts of her life. She grew up around here somewhere. In the Triangle."

One of his hands was closed around the bottom part of the wheel, as if he were holding a hand. He still wore his wedding ring. The hands were corded, the thumbs wide and nicked, the fingertips discolored from their years in clay. It was as if he had bathed his hands in those flowers that secreted an unremovable powder. "It's the dream of a person who left," he said. "That's all I can tell you. We who remained have different dreams. Take care of your mother."

She didn't hear him. She was staring at his hand. Hector, the bus driver in America, worked puppets. The flexing hand at the wheel was the hand, and the rubber band was the puppet moving up and down in the hand. Hector practiced while driving the bus. He was a puppeteer.

* * *

They stopped twenty kilometers from the border to wash at a spigot on the edge of a village most of whose residents had left to make money elsewhere. It was hardly dawn but the sun beat their heads. At a roadside stand, a man with a dyed black moustache cooked them four hotcakes, over which he smeared sesame paste. He served it on a plastic table with hot tea. He left and returned with a small earthenware bowl of honey. He pointed behind him, and said "Zzzzzz."

They ate as only night travelers eat. The moustached man had named a more than inflated price for the hotcakes, but they would order again. The food was turning in her mouth like the wash in a machine when she remembered her father's poems—or remembered that she had forgotten it. She ran to the taxi and swept frantically through the pockets of the jacket she had been wearing over her blouse. Even here in the trunk, she had made a neat square from the clothes she had removed.

She ran to Emil. "Read this," she said.

He stopped chewing and took a corner of it with a messy finger.

"What is it?" he said.

"A poem my father wrote."

"I'm farsighted."

She took away the paper and read. "*It's night. Next door, our girl dreams with Neem.*" She stopped, her father's words too intimate in her mouth.

"*We dream about the time we said we'd come here / Before it was too late.*" She stopped again and gathered herself. "*We are near madness. / If you fill my mouth with honeyed yogurt, / At last I will fall mute. / You were right about the way they make it here. / A dream that turned out like the rest.*"

They sat silently, the vendor whistling as he snipped his moustache in front of a small spotted mirror over an outdoor sink. She wondered if Emil was illiterate. Reading her father's words made him feel both nearer and dead.

"*You were right about the way they make it here*," she repeated. "Does that mean anything to you?"

"It's an old joke," he said.

"What is the joke?"

He put down the paper and wiped his mouth. "It was a long time ago," he said. "Forty or fifty years ago. The regime decided they would turn the Triangle into the land of milk and honey. It was their Siberia—a place where they hadn't ruined everything yet. They would give the people an income—so they would stop leaving and crowding the cities, so the border wouldn't be so empty. They brought thousands of cows. Gave them to the people for free. But you can see, it's desert. What cow is going to survive in a desert? Well, they had scientists who said that if you bring enough cows, their dung will fertilize the soil, and grass will grow. They were going to turn the desert into a soccer field."

"But what's the connection?"

"It was the same thing as always. Cows didn't like it here. Bees like it here. So yogurt with honey, it's a joke. It's what they gave us, the yogurt that you couldn't make from the cows, all of which died, and what we made with our hands, the honey. The yogurt is a joke. There's no yogurt. I mean, there's yogurt. But they import it like everything else."

"What part of the Triangle?"

"Around Dostat." He called to the man and asked him.

"Yes, Dostat," the man said without looking at them. His hand shook a little around his straight razor. "East of Dostat. Those villages."

She went to the man and tried to describe her father. "The better your memory works," she said, "the more hotcakes we will buy. You won't even have to cook them."

"I don't know such a man," he said. "I'm sorry."

"What about the Tahhans?"

"The Tahhans I know," he said. "That is an unfortunate family, a cursed family. God was angry the day that he made that woman."

"Where are they?"

"They were in Arid. But that was years ago. I've been here for some years. Here, I am away from the world. It suits me. I am on the road, people stop."

"That is my mother's family."

Emil steered Dina out of the man's earshot. "You think he's with them?" he whispered. "And if the police are already there also? It's harder to be discreet in a village like that."

She didn't reply.

He looked toward the border. "You're nearly across . . ." But when he saw her determination, he fell silent. He shook his head and went up to the old man. "Where in Arid?"

"It's a small place. Ask anyone, they'll know. It's an hour or so." He pointed north.

"If anyone asks—" Dina started to say.

"I know, I know," the man said, and rubbed the money fingers together.

* * *

They drove in silence. Emil, who had been relieved at having managed to deliver Dina to safety, was forced to surrender that outcome. He slapped the wheel to an inaudible melody to cover his irritation. Dina fidgeted with her hands.

"You didn't know your mother was from Arid?" he said accusingly.

"I knew she was from the Triangle," she said.

"She didn't talk? You didn't ask?"

"I already explained," she said. "Did your children know everything—" She stopped. "I'm sorry." Without looking at her, he dismissed her indelicacy with a wave of his hand.

"Something bad happened to my mother at the transit camp," Dina said. "The one before the crossing. She said it was nothing. Her face said something else. But how could I prove it?" Perhaps her confession would soften his irritation. She was trading on her mother's misfortune.

Emil only listened.

"At home, she had been calm," Dina went on. "Even after the war started, she was calm. She braided my hair, she walked me to school, and if it wasn't a shooting day, she took me to the library. At home, she was always on the divan, watching television, one foot under her bum. She felt so young, like an older sister. My grandmother—my father's mother—liked to say things like, 'There is no love like the love of a daughter for her father.' I hated going to her house because she was always declaring these eternal truths, but I already knew they were rubbish. He was not the one that I loved."

Emil's eyes were narrow against the blistering light, but he was still listening.

"After the transit camp, she wasn't the same. She had used to talk to me like an adult. But after the camp, she spoke to me like a child, like someone in the way. She never answered my questions, not truthfully. I invented my own story about the transit camp—she had crept out in the night to do drugs. I wasn't sparing her, so it had to be the truth. And she didn't correct me, not really. She said I was wrong, but she stopped there, and never said what it was. The way a liar speaks, basically. But there's only one bad thing that can happen to a woman at night in a transit camp. I understand that now. But it didn't happen by accident. She'd been summoned to it. She went to it. I've never understood that part."

She watched the road, which wound like a discolored scar down the skin of the desert.

"I think she was relieved when my father left us," Dina continued. "One less person to account to." She wanted to sink the nail into her wrist, but she hadn't done it since entering Emil's taxi, so instead she dug at the worn upholstery that hung off the door like loose parchment. "She waited me out, and then I, too, went away. I think she's finally happy. She lives in a place where they'll help you if you need it, but otherwise, you can go two lifetimes without being bothered."

"She doesn't know you're here," Emil said.

"She would say: *You fool*," Dina said. She opened the glove compartment and wrote her mother's phone number on an old newspaper clipping. "If something happens, please call her."

"Look at the other side of that," he said.

It was in German. It showed a young woman straining against a bar with weights.

"That's my daughter," he said. "She was so strong that Europe wanted her legally. She was already gone by the time . . . it happened."

"I'm sorry that I wrote on it."

"It makes it even better."

"Do you speak with her?"

"Yes, of course. She calls me every Sunday. She wants me to come. She's on the national team, she has contacts in government."

"Why won't you join her?"

"Are you happy you left?"

"I didn't have a say. But yes?" she said. "Yes."

"It cost you both parents."

"Staying here cost you—" She stopped again. "I'm sorry," she said. "My mind is not in the right way."

He didn't respond. He was leaned forward, his head nearly in the steering wheel, trying to make out the road in the dust.

"Listen," he said. "You know how these villages are. The truck comes for the market once a week, but that's all. Especially with my plates, the word will start going around right away. We won't have much time. I'll go into the market. I'll say I'm a cousin of your mother's family, visiting from abroad. That will explain some of the oddity."

"Let me do it," she said. "My accent is more foreign."

"A woman traveling alone?"

"I can say you're my husband."

"Then why did I remain in the car? No, it's better for me to do it. I'll speak like a man from the plains. It will be foreign enough."

Twenty minutes later, a worn-out sign pocked by dents from hail or slung stones directed them off the main road down to a gravel track that descended to Arid along a limestone plateau. Slowly, the village arose out of the low grass and sand. They passed a children's playground in faded blue, yellow, and pink, the panels spotted with rust. The sidewalk ran down one side of the potholed road, past a long wall that denoted the end of the village. Everything was yellow—the mud-walled homes, the sidewalks, the air, the desert vibrating in the distance. If a person materialized, they would have to be made from the dust, too, she thought. She tried to imagine her mother as a little girl on the playground. Susanna once showed Dina a photo of herself as a child looking out from behind a chair occupied by a stone-faced woman she explained was her mother. Dina couldn't detect her mother in that child, couldn't absorb the information.

Outside the market, cardboard boxes of fruit sagged in the sun even though reed matting had been unspooled for protection. Emil rolled the sedan onto a curb and looked at her. "Once a place goes crazy," he said, "you lose by going and you lose by staying. You just have to hope that all your people do what you do. Or you will be foreigners with each other."

It was a peace offering. She stayed while he went inside.

He was back only a moment later. "They said they don't live there anymore," he said. "They said a man lives there now."

She watched him desperately, fearfully.

He said, "We're going forward, aren't we?"

They rolled forward into the village. Several uncertain arteries spoked out from the main street. They felt eyes watching from behind curtains. Where the homes made no claim on the land, saltwort and wormwood grew in thickets. Soon, they were upon the house, more splendid than the others, which were plain boxes. From a central construction with a domed ceiling, four rooms radiated in the cardinal directions.

No one answered the bell, but the door gave when they pushed. Emil called out—the sound seemed to carry endlessly through the rooms. The concrete floor was cool—they could feel it through their shoes. From the foyer, the only way in was through a narrow passageway. There was daylight at the end, but they had to touch the wall to keep their footing. Forty years before, her mother walked this hallway. It was an idea without a feeling attached.

They emerged in the domed central room. It was the eating area. To one side stood a long table, and just beyond it was the galley kitchen. In between sat a figure in a worn armchair. A man, his eyes closed, his hands gathered in his lap, the wrists circled by bracelets. The matted tendrils of a beard covered his face to the eyes, curling out like plant life.

The hands that Dina thought were clasped between his legs were stumps. Both hands were gone at the wrists. He raised them now in a kind of defense and opened his eyes.

"You are in the home of an invalid," he said. "Act with mercy." It was the unchanged sound of her father's voice. "Who's there?"

Emil looked at Dina. She had turned to stone. "We're right here, father," Emil said.

"I do not see," George said.

Dina's hand went to her mouth. Then it slipped off.

"We mean no harm, father," Emil said, checking Dina again. "Is there someone who takes care of you?"

"People come," he said vaguely. "But what is your business?"

Emil looked at Dina, but she was mute. "It's a service, father," Emil tried. "We drive to the homes—people in need and the like. Groceries, if they need. How do you eat, father? Forgive me for asking."

One of the stumps disappeared from view and they heard the sound of metal connecting with metal—the bracelets were clasps for the claws with one of which the hand now returned. "Once you learn how to use it, it's quite handy," he said.

"Is there anything we can do for you, then?"

"No, no," George said hesitantly.

"You don't have to feel shame."

"Where is it from, your service?" George said. "I've never heard of such a thing."

"It's from Dostat, father," Emil said. "It's a social service. There's money for it now, with the new regime."

"The new regime is putting the country back together," George said in a rote way. "Are you alone? I heard two sets of feet."

Emil urged Dina with his eyes. "Where is your family, father?" she said almost inaudibly.

"Oh, they're far away."

"But they exist," she said.

"I don't know, to be honest," he said. "I don't know."

Emil touched her arm. "I'm sorry, father," she eased up.

"Forgive an old man . . . ," he said.

"Say it, father," Emil said. "It's why we're here."

"It's my feet. They're hard to reach when I wash myself . . ."

There was a tin basin in a doorless alcove next to the washroom. Emil took Dina's hand and dragged her along. The water came in a slow trickle. It was like time itself passing. She looked behind her. The figure in the chair was watching it pass. Emil queried her with his eyes. What was their plan? She looked at him desperately. She was shaking.

"I couldn't get it to flow hot, father," Emil said when they returned.

"Oh, it's never hot at this time of day. Sometimes toward the evening."

They kneeled before the gnarled roots of the feet. They gave off no scent, but they had a yellow, sickly pallor, with protuberances near the joints, as if someone had slipped walnuts under the skin. When they neared, George closed his eyes so they couldn't see behind the lids.

Dina looked up from her place. "What if I straighten your beard, father? It's unruly."

"Has it gotten very unkempt?" George said. "I'm sorry for my appearance. Sometimes, I have difficulties . . . It's no excuse."

"It's nothing," she said. "Let me do it."

"There are scissors—"

"I know. I saw them by the washbasin."

Emil soaped and rinsed the feet and Dina snipped at the beard. As she worked away, George's cheeks became more visible, and she could see that he was smiling. He had the scent of a man she didn't recognize, but she was looking, unmistakably, at her father. She wanted to see behind the eyelids, but was terrified of it.

"Father, what happened to you?" she said. "Forgive me for asking."

"I can tell you're good people."

"What happened, father?" she said more insistently.

"Why do you speak in such a tremulous way?"

"Because I'm seeing you, father," she said.

George made a soft, gargling sound, and she wanted to imagine that her father was making his noise of exasperation. "They took the pointing hand," he said, "and then the seeing eye. They were going to take the speaking tongue, but they left it as a sign of mercy."

"Who did this to you?"

George was silent in the way that indicated for all people from this part of the world that it was done by the people now in power.

"Your family is so far, father, they won't come to you?" she said. She dared to look at the hands. The skin at the edge of the arms had closed into smooth globes that reflected the light coming down from a skylight in the tiled ceiling. She had to look away, but not before a tear escaped her eye. It fell onto a part of the beard that remained uncut, and George didn't notice.

"To see me like this?" he said. "No, I'd rather not. After it happened, I wasn't in my right mind for several years. The authorities had me in a center . . . When they released me . . ." The voice trailed away. "I didn't want them to see me like this. You can understand."

"Don't they worry about you?" she said, ignoring him. "Shouldn't you call?"

"With what fingers," he said, and laughed drily into the beard.

"I can dial for you," she said.

"You're a kind young woman," he said. To indulge her, he said, "You will come back another time, and we'll try to find a telephone."

As they spoke, she cut closer and closer to the skin, as close as she could without a razor. She was intent on having her father emerge. She knew she was nicking the skin with the edge of the blades, but she couldn't help herself. But instead of causing him pain, her ministrations, together with those of the foot washer below, put George to sleep. Through the dense, clumped hair in his nostrils, he wheezed out happily in their hands.

She bent down to Emil's ear. "We can't leave him here," she whispered.

"On what passport do you plan to fly him out?"

"If you get us across the border, I'll get him out. I have information my people want—so this is the cost." She hated herself for lying to him—in fact, escaping with her father would enrage Kamil and compromise the security of the rhodium project.

"You think he wants to be dragged out of here by a pair of foot washers?" Emil said. "Look at him. He will think he is being taken for other reasons."

"I will tell him who I am."

"You heard him. He's ashamed. Don't do it."

"That is the only thing that leaving this country has made any of us want—to be left alone. You would leave your mother?"

"My mother? Let me tell you something about my mother, so you understand." Emil looked up to check. George was asleep. "My mother loved flowers. She was always arranging shrubs and grasses on the table because we couldn't afford real flowers. She spoke to my father about adding to our income, but he wouldn't hear of it. In any case, the nearest flower shop was an hour away. Fifty years passed this way. My father died. After the thirty days of mourning, I told her I wanted to take her for a pastry. Instead, I drove her to the flower shop—now there was one in the next town. I'd spoken to the owner. He was skeptical, but he said he would take her on, unpaid, for a week, and then see. She was embarrassed. But she went. I called her. She said what a wonder to have her hands in flowers all day. Then the owner called. He was angry. He said, 'I agree to this foolish scheme, and she doesn't return after one day?'"

"Why are you telling me this?"

"It was too late for her!"

"Fifty years isn't fourteen."

"She hadn't had her eyes put out!"

"I'll take him out myself."

Emil gave up. “Fine,” he said. “God curse everything about this place.”

“Father,” he pulled George’s sleeve gently. George stirred. “Father, we’re finished. How about some time in the sun?”

George yawned. “It gets quite warm around this time . . .” he said. He tried to feel his beard with the stump. Dina had worked it down to a thin stubble over his skin. “Besides,” George said, trying to express his gratitude in an indirect way, “my face has lost its protection.”

Dina was standing over her father and her tears were falling on his shirt. “I am going to be sick,” she said.

“What is it?” George said.

“Nothing, it’s the heat,” she rushed to say. “It’s hotter here than Dostat. Are you from here, father? From Arid?”

Emil gave her a discouraging look.

“No,” George said. “My wife’s parents lived here. They welcomed me. But my mother-in-law was unwell. My father-in-law said, ‘What’s one more?’ He did the best that he could, but taking care of her for a lifetime . . . he was used up. He passed away. Very abruptly. And it was just the two of us then, the blind and the lame. But she died very quickly thereafter. She could not live without him. She died only a month or two after.”

“Father, wouldn’t you be more comfortable in Dostat?” she said. “We could try to find you some little apartment.”

“Oh, I know every corner of this place. I wouldn’t want to learn another.”

“But, father—”

“I am assigned to be here,” he said, his voice suddenly sharp. “All right? You must understand . . .” The edge went out of his voice, and he spoke with extra softness, to apologize for the rudeness he had allowed himself. But in that brief moment of anger, she saw another man—a man who could be cruel.

“In the sun then . . .” she said weakly, not knowing what to do.

They each took an arm of George’s. They had to walk single file through the long, narrow hallway. When they emerged into the courtyard, they saw policemen arrayed before two vehicles. Ahead of them, dustless in his city suit, stood Dellastra. Emil clicked his teeth.

"We decided to be a little more circumspect than during your stop last night," Dellastra said. "That was very clever, the floor washing. However, to abduct a citizen of the nation . . . tsk, tsk." He took out a kerchief and cleaned his glasses. "This dust is merciless," he said. "If it wasn't for you, who knows when we would have remembered this place. But the center allows the periphery to languish at its peril."

George was trying to work his arms out of Emil's and Dina's. "I'll just go inside," he was saying in a fearful voice. "I'll get out of your way."

"You're safe, father!" Dellastra called out. He gestured to the policemen, who separated George from Dina and Emil. "Thank you, young men," George muttered as they took him inside. "Courageous young men . . ."

"There's one for each of you," Dellastra said to Dina, meaning the police cars. He stood only three feet from her. She wanted to tear the skin off his face. "You'll see the leader, and then you'll go to Mouf. They'll sort you out."

"The survival of your little experiment depends on what I say to my people," she said.

"Not if you don't get to say it to them."

"Do you think they'll let a person vanish?"

"A person like you? Are you so naive that you don't know how things like this work? A civilian who ventured on her own into a country that, unfortunately, remains lawless in places . . ."

"Kamil himself was at Mouf."

"Yes, we need to rename it."

"Oh, rename it . . ." she said, and laughed.

Dellastra walked toward them. His hands were still cleaning the glasses. Finally, he put them back on. Quickly, his fingers made a perfect rectangle from the kerchief.

"You know, he was very amused by your little prank," he said. "But he was the one who said to take you to Mouf."

"For me, you will surrender a hundred million dollars?" she said. "That's what he wanted for the Swedish hospital. What if it were two hundred million? You're standing in front of the world's largest bank."

Dellastra shook his head. "Offering more money is a sign of weakness. You should know whom you're dealing with. Principle comes first here. You're wasting your time."

"What about him?" she said, meaning Emil.

"I'm afraid we won't be able to offer your friend a spot at Mouf. Mouf is very selective."

Emil's face bore no expression. He took Dina's hand. She was surprised to discover that his skin was moist with fear—it had been dry and tight every time he had touched her. Then his hand left hers and flew up so swiftly that she thought a bird had swept into their scene. It flew to Dellastra's face and smashed, sideways, with the shelf of the hand, into one of the lenses of the newly cleaned glasses. There was a crack, Dellastra cried out in a thin, shocked voice, his hands flew to the attacked eye, and blood poured through the hands. He fell to his knees in the dust, shouting in panic. The policemen's handguns were already emerging when Dellastra held up one of the bloody hands. "Not so easy for you," he warbled at Emil through the blood on his lips.

The policemen moved around Dellastra to restrain Emil, turning one of his arms out of place so harshly that Dina heard the crack from several feet away. Now Emil cried out in astonishment. When they were done with him, the arm hung off at an inappropriate angle.

* * *

Dina flies to the capital on a military airplane from the airfield at Dostat. Dellastra, who required surgery, had to decide between the immediately available but medically inferior option at Dostat and the capital's surgeons, a flight away and then another wait because it was now prohibited for government personnel to receive medical treatment out of turn. Here Dostat's relative lack of population—and its distance from the center, which made it possible to bend the new regulations with less fear—was an advantage, and Dellastra remained.

On her flight, Dina is escorted by four soldiers whose supervising officer looks away from her as if repelled by her crime against the nation. His sleeves are rolled up against the heat and the burgundy beret of his unit is unmoving on the rock of his head. When she asks for the bathroom, he brings her there roughly by the arm and stands facing her as she lowers her garments, his eyes on a glass emergency case above her head.

On the tarmac in the capital, she is passed to several policemen, who drive her to the presidential building in an unmarked vehicle, Dina wedged between two malodorous bodies while an old-style crooner wails from the radio. Outside, the scene seems unaltered from the previous day—the savage sun, the honking horns of the taxis, the wall of gray men and black women, the traffic policemen whistling into the void. She feels as if all of it has stood still and begun moving again only when she approached, that her homeland is a make-believe country.

Inside, past the doors of frosted glass and the metal detectors, she feels none of the previous morning's dizzy uncertainty, but the place vibrates with the same sense of a whisper prohibited from rising in volume. In one room, some kind of seminar is starting and the adults are on their feet, intoning the national pledge of abstinence. They hold their hands in front of their chests, the knuckles of one hand against the palm of the other and the thumbs out to the sides, in a gesture of both preemptive contrition and aspiration to triumph. In a place of no scent, again she recognizes, like a zone of insurgency in a pacified landscape, something bitter and burning and sweet. A smell from her childhood, infused with exhilaration and worry.

And then they're in the anteroom to the presidential suite, where for forty minutes they listen as a male secretary on a podium transcribes the leader's weekly radio address. The subject is exile and return. The leader urges his countrymen to extend a helping hand to those who fled and will surely soon make their way back to a restored and prospering country.

The same divisions outlawed among those who remained are illegal between them and those who left.

As she sits, distracted by the start and stop of the recording in the secretary's hands, Dina thinks about her father, Kamil, her mother. She strains to understand what it must mean that Kamil crippled her father. Kamil is crippled himself . . . The effect of two nearly sleepless nights, the heat of the desert, and her encounter with the broken man in whom she was supposed to discover her father has stopped her mind. Identifying herself would have terrorized him, but avoiding it terrorized her. She found him—and still she understands nothing.

At last, a delegation in the traditional dress of an African country, bright and obscene in the muted light of Kamil's new world, removes itself from the presidential chamber. As they file past her, the door to the long, airless hallway slapping open and closed, Dina again tries to focus her mind, to pay attention to her surroundings, her body trembling in anticipation of a faraway comprehension. But before it can arrive, the door to the presidential suite opens and Kamil's wheelchair appears in the doorway.

"First I lost you, and now Dellastra," he says. "Look at you." He pats his temples to mean the vanished hair. "You've been busy." He summons her with an impatient finger. The policemen rise with her, but Kamil holds up his hand. She enters alone.

Inside, he doesn't claim the authority of his wide desk and stops in the spot that the day before had been occupied by Dellastra. He doesn't invite her to sit.

"I wanted to look in your eyes before we sent you off," he says. "The eyes say so much."

She feels nauseous. "You lied," she says. The words are muted by the wet moss in her throat.

"I wanted to spare you," he says.

"And only you could—you'd done it to him."

"There, you're wrong. If it was us, why didn't we finish him off? Why is he living in a family home with regular delivery of meals?"

"I don't believe it."

"Frankly, it doesn't matter. Is your investigation complete?"

"What do you gain from throwing me into Mouf?"

"How quickly you've lost yesterday's shyness. Today we are dealing with a formidable technician. Or was yesterday's nervousness all a show? Was the analyst a natural agent?"

She doesn't answer.

"What do I gain by letting you go?" he says.

"An ally."

He laughs. "No, we don't count on something like that. We'll wait until we need something from the Americans, and then we'll offer you up in return. So you don't have to fear for your life, little Dina. Not in its entirety. It's true that Mouf can sometimes make you wish you were dead. Of this I have firsthand experience. We will get to prison reform, of course—"

She groans, as if tossing in sleep.

"What is it?" he says, startled.

She is nearly vibrating in place. She pursues a vague knowledge, a hand in the water trying to touch something solid. She must make her mind work.

"Sit down," he says. He presses the intercom and tells the secretary to bring water.

"It's not necessary," she says, lowering herself into a seat.

"What is it?" he says impatiently.

She gazes past his shoulder. The pieces push against each other in her mind. She holds them this way and that, trying to get them to fit.

"By putting me away," she stalls, "you satisfy your anger with me, and you show your power. But those pleasures won't last. And what about the self-control you talk about?"

"This line of argument won't work," he says, closing his eyes.

"I will make you a deal," she says. "I will give you information. It is not information you are aware of wanting, but you will be grateful to have it."

He purses his lips. "I like games," he says. "But you are going to Mouf."

"Then two pieces of information. By revealing the second, I become a traitor to my country. So you have something over me when you want it—will that be enough to make you believe you have an advocate?"

"Why don't you start speaking, and we'll see."

"First, we deal. Or are you not a man of your word?"

"It appears you don't think me a man of justice. If you did, you wouldn't ask for my word. Fine, you have it."

She feels a massive weariness in her shoulders. She is still piecing together the first part of what she wants to say. She starts with the second. "My mission is window dressing for Congress. An official mission was impossible, but they want to show that they made a final plea, using a personal contact to dissuade the dictator—sorry for the language, I'm only quoting the materials—dissuade you from attacking the rhodium mine. But that's all. They are every bit as warlike as you denounce them for being, and they had already made up their mind to conduct a surgical strike on this very room when other officers intervened and explained the publicity value of a visit. But my job is to return and confirm their views."

He takes this in. "And if you don't return—"

"They're confirmed twice over."

"And if you do return—"

"I make no guarantees, obviously. But I can explain that even though you are a fanatic, you pose a danger only to your own people. Some would prefer to hear that."

Kamil smiles at her insult. "And they don't care that the people here live under the rigid, compulsive tyranny of a fanatic," he says.

"Correct."

"Tempting," he says. "Very clever. I don't believe you."

"Like you said, it doesn't matter." She decides to push into attack. "Also, I'm not dealing for myself alone. I want the taxi driver and my father."

"What if there is no more driver?"

Something inside her unravels, but she manages to take hold of it before it goes into pieces. "Show me proof."

"You can have one but not both."

"Both."

"You are so clever, but you people always forget to make a calculation for pride. That is always the American mistake, to forget to account for pride. And then the other side is accused of intransigence. What was the other piece of information?"

She's looking out the window. It faces the parapet of a neighboring part of the building. She imagines walking its edge and seeing all of the city beneath her, which makes her think of Robert and his balcony. She wanted so badly for it to have been him in the candy shop.

"I'm going to tell you a story," she says, turning back to Kamil. "It's about a family. Their apartment is old, but it has many rooms. When you open the balcony, you can smell the bread from the bakery. Your mother will find you there with a bin of socks and slippers, and ask you to put it all in order. You're so happy that your mother has asked you for help that you're nearly shaking. And then your father comes home. The women serve him his dinner. They listen closely as he tells them the day's battles, the food getting stuck in his moustache like snow in a tree. The days flow into each other like this, one into the next. It feels like sleep.

"And then, suddenly, they must leave. Why, demands the young daughter. They won't say. The house becomes a house of secrets, of soft footfalls meant to conceal, of ghosts passing through the same space in the dark. Finally, in the night, they make their escape. By morning, they're safe at the seaside. There is blue water here, and games. There is a young man who imitates a whale in such a silly way that fourteen years later you can see him, flopping. But then, again, there is night. Your mother awakes and vanishes into the black world outside. She is returned to you an hour later—just an hour—but she is changed forever. It's the worst fairy tale you've ever heard. In one hour, you can unmake a woman. Did you know that was possible?"

Kamil doesn't speak.

"Do you know how skin smells?" she says. "Have you ever been near the same skin long enough to notice its smell? I mean when it's clean. It's like a fingerprint, I am sure. I couldn't have put words to my mother's smell, but it was indelible. I didn't know I needed to put words to it—I was unaware it could disappear. When you are that age, you know something was right only because it's gone wrong, and by then it's too late. Until then, it isn't that you were actively happy—no, you were merely absent of pain. That state is beyond good or bad. You float in a silence, like when you were inside your mother. And that survived four years of war.

"I'm speaking in riddles. I will get to my point. My mother came back to that tent having lost the scent of her skin. Immediately, her former scent was impossible to re-create, no matter how many times I had grazed in her neck. I had wanted to climb into her!"

"So your life under the previous Leader was paradise," he says.

"That's what you're taking from this?" she says. "Please. Be silent and listen.

"When she returned, she smelled like a man's smoking. But everything did—the conductor had smoked through his interview with us. The scent stayed all the way through the crossing—as if now it was on her. After we reached the island, she walked into the water—to rid herself of the scent or to drown? She wouldn't have been able to drown because my father was watching her, but is that the only reason? Did I have anything to do with why she emerged, or had I already lost out to her shame? Was she already closer to the shame than to us?"

Dina realizes that the lights in the office haven't been lit, and darkness is beginning to settle outside. Away from the window, Kamil's expression is difficult to discern. She feels with new force how far from home she has traveled.

"I slept through most of the interview with the conductor, but outside, this wretched old woman who helped him spoke to my mother. I didn't hear what she said. No one would tell me what she said—not the woman, not my mother. But you can fill in the rest. If my mother didn't visit the conductor, we wouldn't be allowed to leave. It's taken me fourteen years to put that part of it together. I've only just understood it. It's incomprehensible to a child."

Kamil is now shrouded in darkness. The tall shelves of books and binders behind him look like formations of land that, given time, he will level and cover with progress.

"Why did that man do such a thing?" she says. "It's hardest when something like that happens without a reason. Perhaps he was instructed to hurt us? But that, too, isn't what happened."

She waits. Kamil waits with her, as if only she can finish the story and deliver its verdict.

"You had told him to detain us if we had slipped through your grasp, hadn't you?" she said. "To keep us from crossing until you or one of your people arrived. And surely it was what he was meaning to do because there was pay in it. But then he saw my mother, and it started something in him. But he wouldn't have wanted you to know what he had done to her, with your abstinence and principles. So he told you that George, clever George, had eluded you again by slipping away to the other conductor. And he made up for what you would have paid him for us by getting my father to pay it instead. And you believed him. You are naive. Ultimately, you are naive. Now I understand it. It's the most frightening part of you."

She can't even see his hands. Only his eyes sparkle in the fading silver light from the window.

"Perhaps it's not as bad as all that," Kamil says. He's trying to remain composed, but there is a tremor in his voice. "Perhaps he'd gotten word I was hurt. Perhaps he thought I was dead, and invented that story only when I turned out to live."

"Does it matter?" she says. Experimentally, she raises a hand to see if she can make it out in the dark, to see how solidly she exists.

"Tell me," she says. "In this sanctuary without blemish, how could you allow someone in to smoke in his office, to fill the corridors with the scent of clove cigarettes? Only someone you've known a long time, perhaps."

"There is no smoking in this building," Kamil says.

"Then, again, he's lying to you. He's down in the boiler room, or in the cafeteria kitchen, like a ghost. The ruin of your perfect new world."

"He's the minister of sport," Kamil says.

She smiles. "It's perfect," she says.

"I will summon him," he says. "He will appear before us." Kamil's voice is tight. He is imagining retribution.

"No," she says. "Your cruelties satisfy nothing in me."

She detects the slightest flutter in the dark—does he shrug, or take his hand to his heart, or cover his face with his hands?

"My mother said that my father had to leave us because he made a mistake," she says. "He served the regime. Now he is a man of pieces, thanks to you. And you are as well—is it thanks to him? Did what he had done leave you this way? And somehow you found us on the island? And chased him all the way home, so you could give as you received?"

The answer from the darkness comes slowly. "It's foolish to think a person ever leaves home."

She isn't ready to dispute this. Eventually, she says, "I wish you could have seen my mother before."

He turns away from her and rolls toward his place behind the desk. He can navigate the room in complete darkness. It is his home.

"You can have one man," he says. "I keep one to make sure you'll do as you say."

* * *

At a café in the Toronto airport, Sara waits for Dina at the scheduled time. Sara is neither the woman at Valence looking for love nor the government functionary whose clothes Dina tried to copy. In a couronne sweater tucked into broad white trousers, a rodeo buckle on her belt, Sara looks like someone Dina would be too shy to approach. Somehow, Sara knew that, and wore effectively shabby clothing to Valence. Again, Dina feels naive.

"You had quite the journey," she says, eyeing Dina's missing hair. "You found your father."

Dina thinks for one second more, and launches forth as she planned. "Yes, Kamil was willing to reunite us. But I'm not sure why he allowed me to see the Triangle. It's clear he has military plans there. There are installations in places with virtually no population. They make them look like police stations, like roadside cafés. He's certainly not building hospitals—he's getting ready for something."

"Maybe he was trying to ingratiate himself, show you his trust," Sara says. "Maybe he thinks you have power. Perhaps you're doing his bidding and we shouldn't believe you."

"Perhaps. It's more likely that he thought it was hidden too well for my notice. In any case, you have no other intel."

Sara's eyes make an imperceptible adjustment—the power has shifted to Dina, if only because the intel is the one that Sara's superiors want. "What did you think of him?"

"He's smart. Ruthless. But there's something missing inside him."

Sara nods. "I'll take it to Wecker. He'll ejaculate all over his sailboats."

Dina rises.

"You're leaving again," Sara says.

Dina nods.

"It was nice," Sara says. "With you."

* * *

From Toronto, Dina flies to Salt Lake City, and then the one-hour transfer to her little town on an Embraer that feels like a toy in the sky. The flight attendant, a hoarse-voiced man in his sixties, gives instructions. If anyone on the airplane finds themselves at the Press Box on Broadway, they are to ask for Melissa, and they are to say her father said Melissa would give them a free pint. "Watch her squirm!" he says. The plane laughs. Dina thinks about her father, Emil, about the choice that she made.

After she lands, she stands outside the terminal inhaling the cold familiar air. It has the scent of nothing—of cleanness. She pushes clods of breath out of her lungs and imagines she's recycling out something used. The taxi driver tells her about the girls' ice hockey tournament the previous weekend, the hat trick by the daughter named Britt. The woman laughs, and never looks in the mirror, and Dina remembers that she is not required to speak, hardly even to listen. Maybe the woman is content because she has a fare to the far side of town. Maybe it is the dumb violent cheerfulness of the nation that took in Dina and her mother.

Kaylee's shades are drawn. It's better that she doesn't see Dina for now. Dina pays cash. There are places in the world where it's better to pay the taxi driver in cash. The hand wants to feel money, and the money the hand. Dina walks past the little delivery van in the driveway and rings the doorbell. What does a doorbell mean now? As she waits, again she thinks of Emil's broken body arriving at the medical facility in the Commodore Quarter off Federal. She wonders what he will think when he wakes. If he wakes.

A moment later, the door opens, and her mother's slight figure fills the doorframe. After they arrived in America, Susanna lost what weight she added on the island, and kept going. She barely stopped herself before she vanished altogether. The same person greets Dina now, a person who has forgotten to eat, with five years of new age around her eyes and her mouth. Only the hair has grown—it fills half her back. It is a darkening afternoon, and Susanna wears a nightgown, as if she is awaiting the night. She is fifty-one.

"I was lying down," Susanna says without greeting. Her eyes float over her daughter's shorn head before she turns and disappears down the hallway, its creaking wood still masked by the same fidgety rug they got from the church. As a girl, she spent hours sliding on it like ice while her mother slept.

Dina washes her hands in the old sink whose faucet still doesn't extend far enough past the porcelain and walks the hallway until she's at her mother's bedroom. But the bed there is untouched. She continues to her old bedroom, and on the twin bed there finds her mother, her palms gathered under her temple. Her eyes are open, but she doesn't look at her daughter. She has neglected to replace the cover she threw off to answer the door.

Dina searches through the closet until she has an old pair of shorts and a T-shirt with the chevron of the high school cross-country team. It's Kaylee's—a loan from when Kaylee's infant brother had covered Dina's shoulder with vomit. Soon after, Dina told her about Mason. Kaylee never asked for the shirt. Dina's heart moves at the thought of going across the street, ringing the bell, all of them shouting in excitement.

Changed, Dina climbs into bed, into the narrow space behind her mother. She fits herself into her mother's shape, the knees behind the knees, the chest behind the chest. Only the hands have no place. They hang, uncertain, like little biplanes wobbling and wondering whether the air is for them. Then Dina dares. Her mother makes no objection.

They lie like this for an unknown time, the daughter's hands moving through her mother's long hair.

Acknowledgments

I would like to thank:

The Plutzik-Goldwasser family and the Betsy Hotel in Miami Beach; Antoine Flochel, Colombe Schneck, Alexander Maksik and the Can Cab artist residency in Spain; and Rick and Maureen Vershure for the generous gift of time, space, and peace of mind to work on this novel.

Caleb Leisure for a very astute read of the manuscript at a pivotal time. Caleb is on a multi-decade hiatus as a maker of some very special wines in northern California (www.calebleisurewines.com), but eventually he'll make a detour back to his roots as a novelist.

My agent Henry Dunow, my editor Millicent Bennett, my publisher Jonathan Burnham, and the entire team at HarperCollins for believing in and supporting my work. A second, emphatic thank-you to Millicent for being such a passionate champion of this novel. I'm very lucky.

The Fishman-Oder family in Delaware and the Cole family in Seattle—you subsidize my fantasy of multi-coastal living. And to my dear mix of the two, the Fishman-Coles—Jessica, Agnes, Montgomery—in rural New Jersey.

Dina Nayeri's *The Ungrateful Refugee* and Rania Abouzeid's *No Turning Back*, which inspired the story of why Yacoub must flee and the story of Emil's brother and his hospital, respectively. Both books are indispensable, and I have the fortune to know one of the authors in person. Dina

Nayeri fled Iran at the same age I fled the Soviet Union—in her case, because her mother had decided to become a Christian, in mine because we were Jews. We passed through the same refugee camps in Italy, and the same university in the States, but met in New York only as adults, already writers. She is the author of essential books that look at the inconvenient, ideology-busting heart of the matter: *The Ungrateful Refugee*, *Who Gets Believed*, and so on. She is also the inspiration for my Dina in the novel, and therefore deserves perhaps the largest acknowledgment of all.

About the Author

BORIS FISHMAN was born in Minsk, Belarus, and emigrated to the United States in 1988. He is the author of the novels *A Replacement Life* (which won the VCU Cabell First Novelist Award and the American Library Association's Sophie Brody Medal) and *Don't Let My Baby Do Rodeo*, both *New York Times* Notable Books of the Year, and *Savage Feast*, a family memoir told through recipes. His work has appeared in the *New Yorker*, the *New York Times Magazine*, the *Washington Post*, the *Guardian*, the *Wall Street Journal*, *Travel + Leisure*, *Food & Wine*, *New York* magazine, and many other publications. He has taught at Princeton University and the University of Montana, and now teaches at the University of Austin.